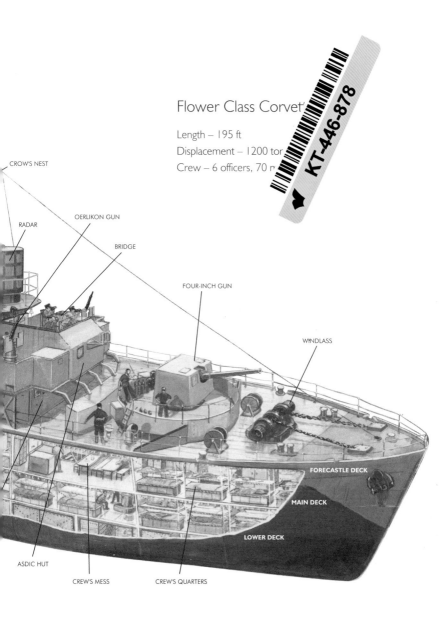

Flower Class Corvette

Length – 195 ft
Displacement – 1200 ton
Crew – 6 officers, 70 n

CROW'S NEST

RADAR

OERLIKON GUN

BRIDGE

FOUR-INCH GUN

WINDLASS

FORECASTLE DECK

MAIN DECK

LOWER DECK

ASDIC HUT

CREW'S MESS

CREW'S QUARTERS

Upon Dark Waters

Also by Robert Radcliffe

Under an English Heaven

Upon
Dark Waters

Robert Radcliffe

LITTLE, BROWN

A *Little, Brown* Book

First published in Great Britain by Little, Brown in 2003

Copyright © 2003 Standing Bear Ltd.

The moral right of the author has been asserted.

All characters in this publication other than those clearly
in the public domain are fictitious and any resemblance
to real persons, living or dead, is purely coincidental.

Endpapers courtesy of The Illustrated London News Picture Library

A CIP catalogue record for this book
is available from the British Library

ISBN 0 316 72610 9

Typeset in Perpetua by M Rules
Printed and bound in Great Britain
by Clays Ltd, St Ives plc

Little, Brown
An imprint of
Time Warner Books UK
Brettenham House
Lancaster Place
London WC2E 7EN

www.TimeWarnerBooks.co.uk

Acknowledgements

I am indebted to the following for their assistance with this project:

Señor Abelardo Viera of Uruguay's National Archive. Uruguayan broadcaster and historian María Pérez Santarcieri. Enrique Segarra of the Museo Histórico Nacional. The late Omar Medina Soca of the remarkable *Graf Spee* museum and archive. Raúl Vallarino of the Uruguayan National Library. Carlos Pereira and Arquímedes Manta, also Sr Pastorino of Montevideo's railway museum. I would also like to thank John Everard, HM Ambassador to Uruguay, and his staff for their support and hospitality, Matilde and Francisco Gallinal for having me to stay on their estancia, Captain Chris Page and Malcolm Llewellyn-Jones of the MOD's Naval Historical Branch in London for help and advice, and the indefatigable Laura Suárez for interpreting whilst in Uruguay.

Finally I would like to thank my wife, Kate, to whom this book is dedicated.

R. R. Suffolk, England

'The true gaucho is not so much a person as a state of mind. Not a nationality, yet clearly a definable identity. Not an ethnic classification, more an entire culture. He is feral, unfettered, as wild as the vast pampas that spawned him. On the day the fencing-in began, a seal was placed upon his fate. The true gaucho is now very rare.'

Dr José-Dominico Cordobihan,
Man and State, Buenos Aires, 1921

'In war, it's a good idea to be damn sure whose side you're on.'

General Willard P. Murrow,
Battle of Gettysburg, Pennsylvania, 1863

Chapter 1

My name is Stephen Tomlin. I was the midshipman on HMS *Daisy* the night she was sunk. Much of that trip, I must confess right away, and of the trips preceding and following it, are lost from my memory. Although the facts are there, scrawled into the diaries and notebooks I kept at the time, I read through them now and simply cannot recall many of the thoughts and events recorded. The reason, I suppose, is the bulk of them were unimportant, the callow scribblings of a keen but clueless eighteen-year-old. Also, in my defence, and contrary to popular belief, a great deal of the life on convoy escort duty during the war involved drudgery and routine – not to mention discomfort and deprivation. As a result, over the years, little of it has stuck in the memory.

Except those incidents of importance. Isolated moments of humanity, camaraderie, even occasional hilarity. The terrifying power of a North Atlantic gale. The dizzying thrill of one of Walter Deeds' frenzied attacks on a submerged contact. The feeling of numb helplessness watching a merchantman sink. The bunker oil and burning bodies stench of its aftermath. *Daisy*'s going, not surprisingly. As chillingly clear today as on the day it happened.

Which was New Year's Eve 1942. *Daisy* is, was, a Flower class corvette. Short, tubby, single-screwed, corvettes were based on a design for a Middlesbrough whale-catcher. A glorified fishing boat in other words. Upon the outbreak of the war the design was hastily modified for gentle coastal patrol work. Then, in classic Navy tradition, and to the abject horror of her architect, these little coastal patrollers were thrown straight into the North Atlantic, and convoy escort duty. 'But they were never designed to take that kind of punishment!' the architect protested. 'They have to take it,' replied their Lordships. And in the end more than two hundred were built, and their records speak for themselves.

Fortunately, despite the fact that, as one commentator put it 'a corvette would roll on wet grass', they turned out to be fantastically strong sea boats. Under-powered, under-armoured and underwater most of the time, at just two hundred feet and 1200 tons they were little more than cold, cramped and smelly tin boxes for the eighty or so men who lived, worked and occasionally died in them. 'Cheap-and-nasties' was another popular nickname for corvettes. Yet once you got used to them, (some folk never did and transferred out as soon as they could), you'd never want to pass your war anywhere else.

Why flowers? God knows. Although I did once make tentative enquiries, I never was able to discover whose bright idea it had been to name these little ships after flowers. Whoever it was he deserved to be stood up against a wall and shot. We on *Daisy*, like so many other corvettes, were continually the butt of jokes afloat and ashore, and, while it was mildly amusing at first, it quickly grew irksome. It certainly drove Skipper Deeds apoplectic. 'Bloody warships need names like *Spiteful*, or *Spit-in-your-eye* or *Spartacus*!' he'd curse, stamping about the bridge. He had a point. Can you imagine a German U-boat captain being terrified into an indecisive funk at the prospect of being pursued by a glorified fishing boat called *Buttercup*? I think not. So we lost the psychological advantage before we even started. Flowers. There's a famous story about HMS *Periwinkle*, one of the first corvettes off the blocks. Apparently, upon joining her first convoy the escorting destroyer signalled her:

'What are you?' the destroyer demanded.

'*Periwinkle*.' came the reply.

'Can I stick a pin in you?'

'No, I am a small blue flower, not a shellfish.'

'Then I will come over and fertilise you.' Very funny.

We were crossing the gap. That night. The 31st December 1942. The mid-Atlantic air gap. Halfway home in other words, six days out of Halifax, Nova Scotia, about a week from our base in Londonderry. We were four corvettes and one destroyer, escorting a convoy of sixty merchant ships carrying everything from tractor engine lubricant to tinned tuna. Those convoys were about all that were keeping

Britain going then, a fact that for obvious reasons was not well advertised at the time. Here's another. At the outbreak of the war, Britain depended entirely on a fleet of about three thousand mostly superannuated merchant ships for half its food, most of its industrial raw materials and *all* its oil. If Admiral Dönitz had got his way with Hitler and persuaded the mad bugger to divert his efforts into stopping those ships at the outset, it would have all been over for us inside three months. Churchill said recently that throughout the whole war, the only thing that really frightened him was the prospect of the U-boats strangling those Atlantic supply lines.

They very nearly did, but, fortunately for us, Hitler, whose grasp of the finer points of naval warfare was never his strongest suit, preferred to pour his ship-building resources into potency symbols – impressive but vulnerable monsters like *Bismarck*, *Tirpitz* and the rest – instead of amassing the large, cheap and infinitely more deadly submarine fleet that Dönitz begged him for. As a result we got a lucky breathing space, built convoy escorts as fast as we could, developed and improved our anti-submarine countermeasures and generally began to get our act together.

In a while, of course, German High Command realised the error of its ways and began getting its together too. So much so that by the beginning of '43 everything hung in the balance. By then, fighting for the convoys had evolved into a vicious, bloody, no-holds-barred business. Which side held the upper hand was a moot point. We were slowly getting better at protecting the precious merchantmen, while the

Germans were growing more adept at attacking them. And still sinking far too many – a terrifying 100,000 tons in one week alone, early that year. For a betting man – and show me a sailor who isn't – it was even money as to who would win. Incidentally, another fact. The Battle of the Atlantic, as it became known, was the only conflict of the war that began the day war was declared, and was still going on the day it ended. And another, this one grimly underscoring the savagery with which it was prosecuted. Around thirty-two thousand U-boat men met and endured what in many cases must have been an unspeakable death. That figure represents the highest percentile loss rate of any branch of the German armed services. Statistically, even an infantryman on the Russian Front stood a better chance of surviving. Curiously, over the same period, an almost identical number of Allied merchant seamen lost their lives – a figure that by chance represents the highest percentile loss rate of any branch of the Allied Services. No comfort to the widows and orphans, and probably no surprise to anyone who was there, but it puts the human cost of that theatre of the war into perspective.

So, the mid-Atlantic air gap. A lonely, three-hundred-mile-wide expanse of freezing North Atlantic, between twenty and forty degrees west, to the south-east of Greenland, way south of Iceland, and thus too far from land for even the longest range aircraft to patrol. A vast expanse of open ocean, in other words, where there was no hope at all of any protective air cover. So U-boats could gather there in safety, like wolves in a pack, choose their moments, and their targets, and attack at leisure. The Devil's Gorge, some of us called it. The Black Hole was another name. Mainly it was just The Gap. The air boys at Coastal Command had been trying to plug it for months, using specially equipped long-range Liberators. But the geography was against them. And the pitiful winter daylight. And the appalling Atlantic weather. Eventually the gap did get closed but not until later. In the meantime, convoys like ours that night faced it alone. The Germans had a name for it too. The Happy Hunting Ground.

It was the coldest night I can ever remember. So cold, crystals of hoarfrost sprouted on the wool of your duffel coat like sugar icing, and bare cheeks were nipped blue. As usual we'd been closed up for hours. Ready for action, that means. That was standard procedure then. In daytime you were safe enough because the U-boats preferred to attack by night. Under cover of darkness they could approach on the surface, get right in among the merchantmen like foxes in a chicken coop, wreak their havoc, then dive and escape. So, when operating in a danger area such as the gap, the drill was to rest up somewhat during the day, catch up on meals and sleep, pipe down and get something hot inside you at dusk, then darken ship and close up to action stations at nightfall. And then wait. In mid-winter, at those latitudes, with the ever-present prospect of a lonely five-minute death in the freezing ocean hanging over you, those nights could seem very long indeed.

I was a floater. I'd been with *Daisy* seven months by then and had grown to know her well. My job when we were

6

closed up was to help out where and when required. Sometimes aft with the two-pound pom-pom anti-aircraft gun crew, although that would generally only be in daylight. Sometimes with Sub-Lieutenant Brown on the depth charge rails at the stern, or with our other sub, Dick Woolley, on the four-inch gun for'ard. Very occasionally in the Asdic hut with Lieutenant Strang. Quite often on the bridge with the captain. I was a jack of all trades, in other words, which actually sums up something of the midshipman's traditional role. The word midshipman tends to conjure images of Nelson's navy, and smartly dressed little boys in breeches and topcoats scurrying up ratlines to swarm out along the mainyard or whatever. Many's the time a dockyard matey would say to me: 'Midshipman? Blimey, I didn't know the Navy still had 'em.' Well they do, did, particularly in '43, by which time trained junior officers were getting mighty scarce. Putting us mids to sea was yet another way of truncating a young man's training, and filling the officer void. God knows the barrel was practically empty already. As it was, we had already called up the RNR – that's the Royal Navy Reserve – and the RNVR – that's the Volunteer Reserve, or 'temporary gentlemen' as they were known. Then there were the Commonwealth boys – RAN, RNZN, RCN, that's the Royal Australian, New Zealand and Canadian navies. They were all right, mostly, but, well, pretty slapdash sometimes, and far too informal. Not like the real thing. Actually, very few of us on *Daisy* were proper RN. The first lieutenant, Strang was, I think. The coxswain, Larkin. A few of the stokers. Me, of course, although without my consent or consultation. But that's another story. Deeds, the skipper, wasn't a regular. He was ex-merchant navy, so was RNR. Villiers was RNVR.

I was on the bridge, out on the bridge wing with the starboard lookout, an HO rating called Pitt. HO stands for hostilities only, the lowest of the low. HOs were drafted in and packed aboard with practically no training at all. Most of them had never set foot on board a ship in their lives, they literally didn't know one end from the other. They had to learn everything on the job. Some picked it up quite quickly, others were absolutely hopeless. HOs were always getting their leg pulled – especially the youngsters. I remember a new HO arriving on *Daisy* one Sunday morning in 'Derry. He looked about sixteen and absolutely terrified. One of the older hands, Frank Tuker probably, spotted him and immediately set to. 'Crikey, lad, you only just made it in time! Sunday Divisions in five minutes and the captain's an absolute stickler for doing it right. Quick, go and get changed into your number one rig then go and ask the Buffer for the key to the ship's organ.' The Buffer was the chief bosun's mate. Of course there was no ship's organ, but this poor unfortunate, still humping his kit bag and gas mask and all the rest of it, was sent from pillar to post looking for the key to the damned thing. The bosun's mate didn't have it, so sent him off to ask the leading stoker. Leading stoker said he didn't have it but to try the Chief ERA. The Chief scratched his head and said he thought he'd seen it hanging on the wall of the officers' wardroom. We were all lounging about in there when the wretched boy burst in, frantic with panic and stuttering something about how the Chief said the captain would nail his balls to the deck if he didn't turn up the key to the ship's organ. Captain Deeds looked up briefly, but just sighed and shook his head and went back to his newspaper. The rest of us scoffed and sniggered like sixth formers outside the tuck shop. But Villiers – and this is the reason the incident stuck in my memory – Villiers was absolutely furious. Not with the boy, but with the way he was being humiliated. The system. 'For God's sake, what possible good can come from these ridiculous rituals!' he demanded of no one in particular. It was unusual, for I had never seen him really angry, really anything in fact, before. He rose to his feet and went to the boy.

'What's your name?' he asked, his expression changing completely in the space of about two seconds. He was smiling, not condescendingly, but in a way that just said, Look, don't take any notice, it's all right.

'Well, then, Hampton,' he went on. It was something like Hampton. 'The thing is not to worry about it now. Why don't you head on below, stow your things, then have a look around the ship. Your watch leader will show you the ropes; you'll be astonished how quickly you get the hang of it all.'

I'll never forget it. Villiers, and the incomprehension in that boy's eyes. And then the relief. Dead now, of course. Hampton. Pitt too.

The corvette's bridge then was a canvas-sided, completely open-to-the-skies affair that afforded no protection from the elements whatsoever. If it rained you got wet, although that was the least of it. There were little hinged spray windscreens on the front, like on a Jeep, but they were mostly for show and, anyway, if the weather was foul and you shipped a sea — and corvettes spent much of their time with their noses buried beneath the waves — these were completely useless and had even been known to smash. Basically there was no protection: if it was wet, so were you; if it was blowing you caught it; if it was freezing cold, then you froze. And it was cold that night, as already said. Had been for days. The cook had to collect meat from the new meat-storage locker out on deck, and put it *in* the refrigerator to thaw out. Cold, then. But not especially rough, as I recall, the wind about a four, on our quarter. *Daisy* rolled, but then she always rolled, a moderate sea heaving sluggishly about in the weak starlight like molten tar.

Daisy's station was at the rear of the convoy, sweeping back and forth in case of a stern attack, rounding up stragglers and generally trying to keep a neat formation. Not so easy in the pitch-black and with all ships darkened. And the rear of the convoy, well, tail-end Charlie, it was every crew's least favourite position. Especially our skipper's. He'd had a burr under his saddle all evening.

'Ye Gods but it's cold,' he kept saying to no one in particular, in his flat-vowelled Yorkshire voice. 'And it's too dark. Far too bloody dark.' As if it was our fault. He was on the centre portion of the bridge, the captain's normal position at action stations. I could barely see him in the gloom even though he was less than ten feet from me, but I could sense him, as could we all, pacing around as usual like a caged bear, restless and irascible.

'Shall I rustle up another round of kye, sir?' I volunteered magnanimously. Kye is Navy cocoa. It comes in these solid off-white slabs which you grind into the mug using a cheese grater. Add hot water and stir until your spoon stands up in it and that's kye, a wonderful warm lining to your ribs on a freezing night. The Navy practically runs on it. That organising it meant running below to the warmth of the galley never entered my head. But in any case Deeds wasn't having any of it.

'Not due for another half-hour, Mid,' he replied from the darkness. It was at that moment that Pitt stiffened at the rail beside me. I saw it too. A distant white flash on the starboard horizon that dulled almost immediately to a red glow.

''Ere we go,' Pitt murmured through his binoculars. 'Bang on time and a 'appy new year to us all.'

I checked my watch. Pitt was right. It was four minutes past midnight. The 1st January 1943. A new year. I felt nothing. No excitement, no sense of pages turning, no feeling that an end was nearing. Only the cold, and a dull, carefully compartmentalised compassion for the men beginning their forlorn struggle for life on the tilting deck of their ship far out at the head of the convoy.

'Shipflash, Captain!' I made the report, somewhat unnecessarily, as everyone had seen it. But procedure is procedure. 'Off the starboard bow, about five miles, looks like it's towards the head of the centre column.' Shipflash. Not ship hit by torpedo, not ship blown to smithereens, on fire and already sinking. Just shipflash. Report only what you see, Deeds had drummed into us time and again. Only what you actually see. 'But sir,' I once foolishly protested, 'surely if we know it's a torpedo hit . . .' 'And just how *do* you bloody know? Psychic are you? Could be she ran into a mine, or copped a bomb from a Dornier. Could be it's accidental, like a fire in the galley, or an explosion in the engine room. Could be some daft clod simply dropped a signal flare on deck. Until we know for sure, all we can say is that it's a flash of light on a ship, right? Got it?'

'Got it, Mid,' his voice, calm and controlled now that it was starting, came back across the bridge. 'Torpedo,' he added, perversely but predictably. Near him, other shadowy figures were training binoculars towards the stricken ship.

'God help them on a night like this,' someone said. 'It must be fifteen degrees below.'

Five minutes later, another flash. This one nearer, towards the stern of the convoy. And this time there was no need for Deeds' euphemisms. Everyone who saw it knew what it was. A brilliant yellow burst that lit the sky, briefly bathing the bridge party's faces in a sickly glow before it faded. A few seconds later the dull rumble of explosion.

'Helm starboard twenty!' Deeds bent to voice-pipes. 'Sound rattlers! Engine full ahead, that one was fired from our end of the screen.' A bell alarm rang through the ship. Moments later *Daisy* heeled to port and we all felt the increased shuddering of her plates beneath our feet as she began to accelerate across the stern of the convoy. It was beginning again. Though men were fighting for their lives barely a mile away – and we could clearly see the second victim ship silhouetted against the flicker of rising flames –

there was no denying the visceral thrill of anticipation that ran through every one of us at the prospect of going into action. Of doing something. Of hitting back. Feigning the nonchalance none of us felt, I moved nearer to the centre of the bridge, to be ready for the call. Go and man the pom-pom, Mid. Or the Lewis gun, or the searchlight. Or simply, stay close at hand, Mid, until I need you. Meanwhile, despite the fact that in theory we'd been ready for hours, the ship was stirring anew, shaking herself like a waking dog, coming to life. Exactly as she had on hundreds of occasions before.

'Bridge, engine room. Engine at two-twenty revolutions, engine room all closed up down here.'

'Bridge, wheelhouse. Coxswain at the wheel, steering zero-three-zero.'

'Bridge, Brown here. Depth charges closed up.'

'Right you are.' Deeds bent to another voice-pipe. 'Asdic. Strang! Anything?'

'Nothing.' The first officer's voice floated tinnily on to the bridge.

'What? Nothing at all?'

A pause. 'Sir, there are sixty ships out there.' Strang's voice was edgy. 'There's plenty of propeller noise, but nothing on Asdic.'

'Well, that last U-boat would have dived after he fired. He's down there now, somewhere in our sector, so keep bloody sweeping.' Deeds too was coming to life. When he was waiting, inactive, he was helpless, impotent, a prisoner. But the moment rattlers sounded, heralding the prospect of imminent action, he was transformed, energised, released.

As a result, so was the whole ship. 'Woolley!' He leaned forward over the bridge rail. Just below and ahead, muffled figures wearing white flash hoods and tin helmets were clustered around the breach of a large deck gun.

'Sir!' A face, round and pale, looked up at Deeds from among them.

'Is that four-inch peashooter of yours closed up ready, Sub?'

'Closed up and ready to fire, sir.'

'Right. We might need it. Admiralty estimates as many as six U-boats in the vicinity. Night like this they'll be attacking on the surface, so keep your bloody eyes peeled.' He stepped back, a short, stocky figure beneath the swaying canopy of stars, a heavily lined grey face, a battered uniform cap pushed back on a bald forehead. 'And that goes for the rest of you,' he added, raising his binoculars. The second ship was burning furiously now, flames clawed skywards, tinged curiously green. Iron-ore carrier that meant. So she'd sink like a stone. She was already listing hard. We could make out running figures silhouetted against the rising inferno.

'It's too bloody easy,' Deeds cursed. 'Moonless night as black as your hat, no air cover for days, sixty ships protected by four poxy little corvettes and a clapped-out destroyer. Like shooting fish in a barrel.'

As if on cue another call from a voice-pipe. 'Bridge, radio!'

'What is it?'

'Signal from *Vehement*.' *Vehement* was the destroyer in charge of the convoy.

'Read it.'

'*Vehement* to *Daisy*. Enemy penetrated convoy rear screen. Do you require assistance tracking?'

'No I do not, you bastard,' Deeds muttered, his binoculars welded to his eyes. The doomed ore carrier was going, her stern slipping under, her bow rising from the sea like a desperately pointing finger. Figures were jumping into the icy waves around it. *Vehement*'s signal was an admonishment, a ticking-off. The convoy commander, dashing back and forth way out at the head of the convoy, telling us that *Daisy* had let a U-boat slip past her and into the rear of the convoy.

'Signal no thanks, we——' Another flash lit the sky, then within seconds a fourth, both from the centre of the convoy. Deeds hesitated, his binoculars swinging from one victim to the next. It no longer mattered, it was out of his hands now, out of everyone's. '——estimate convoy screen now penetrated from all sides, will continue sweep at rear. Tomlin!'

At last. 'Sir!'

'What are you doing?'

'Nothing, sir.'

'What do you mean nothing?'

'I mean I'm on the starboard Lewis gun, sir. That and the searchlight and Aldis lamp, sir.' Nothing, in other words. Nothing really important. As usual.

'Right. Nip up top, lad. Take the glasses with you and see if you can't spot something, anything.'

I was already moving. Up top. The crow's nest – little more than an overgrown soup tin nailed to the swaying radio mast twenty feet above the deck. Lookouts hated it generally, the motion was awful, you had little protection, and if the wind was from the stern you were suffocated by engine fumes from the funnel. But I was young and agile and keen. I fair scampered across the bridge towards the companionway.

It was then that I saw Villiers.

He was stepping quietly on to the bridge from the port ladder. He was wearing his uniform jacket and sea boots, but with his heavy leather jerkin over the top, his white *pañuelo* 'kerchief thing tied about his neck as a scarf, and his curious black hat, his *boina*, like a French beret, only bigger, on his head. He must have been getting on for twenty-two, which seemed very mature and well seasoned to an eighteen-year-old like me at the time, but ridiculously young now, looking back. He glanced at me, a glimmer of friendly recognition, then looked out at the scene across the convoy. I hesitated, sensing what was coming. Deeds glanced back and saw him.

'Number Two,' he grunted in acknowledgement, before turning forward again. *Daisy* was straining spiritedly ahead now, lifting and crashing into the seas, a wide bone of a bow wave in her teeth.

'Captain,' Villiers replied noncommittally. A pause. Still I hesitated. 'Four hit, so far, is it?'

'Something like that.'

'There'll be people in the water.'

'I know that.' Deeds' back was still to him. Over to the right another flash as another torpedo hit home. 'Jesus! Just how bloody many of them are there?'

'Captain, might I . . .'

'No, confound it, Number Two, you might not! We're on a search, there is at least one submerged U-boat in our sector and I expect to be running in to attack it any minute. In fact, the moment Strang gets that blasted box of tricks of his to function.' As if to prove it he bent to the voice-pipes once more. 'Asdic! Strang? Anything?'

'Still too much clutter, sir; ships sinking, bulkheads collapsing, that sort of thing. We'll maintain sweep, get on to them as soon as they dive clear.'

'Well, keep bloody at it!'

'I could have a boat away in under two minutes, Captain.' Villiers' voice was unearthly quiet. 'Let me have four men.'

Deeds swung round suddenly. 'Sub-Lieutenant Villiers, may I remind you that, technically speaking, you are not properly a member of this crew any more. And that I am merely conveying you back to your home port to be hauled up in front of a disciplinary board, there to get your arse severely chewed, before, and quite properly in my view, it is kicked out of the Service!'

'Walter.' He was smiling. The mad so-and-so was actually smiling. A sort of guileless I-know-you-don't-really-mean-it smile. 'Walter. I have to go, we both know that. The people from that ore carrier, we'll be crossing her stern shortly, they are already in the water, and there will be many hundreds more before the night is done. Make a short turn to port, bring her about, I'll drop the port boat in the lee and have it away from *Daisy* before you know it. You'll barely have to stop.'

'Permission to accompany him, sir!' God's truth, the words were out of my mouth before I knew I'd said them.

Deeds looked from one of us to the other, his face a mask of disbelief. Then suddenly he seemed to sort of slump before us, deflate, as though overcome with weariness at it all. And age. Three solid years he'd been doing this. Three years with barely a break. It was killing him by degrees.

'It's madness, man, utter madness,' he protested doggedly. 'Quite apart from the risk bringing *Daisy* to a stop, just what do you hope to achieve? How many can you save in a fifteen-foot rowing boat?'

'We can gather them together. Get them up out of the water on to Carley floats and keep them together. They'll have a chance. If we do nothing we'll lose hundreds. Captain, you must let me try.'

The bridge, Deeds' squat bulk in the centre of it, was illuminated from behind momentarily by yet another flash, this one from the starboard edge of the convoy. Starshells and chandelier flares also sparkled in different portions of the sky, like private firework displays. 'God's teeth!' he cursed yet again. He was wearing his lifebelt, of course, and carrying his Service revolver, as he always did at action stations. It hung from a white lanyard looped around his neck, one of his many endearing little oddities. Another was the way he sometimes kept one hand inside his duffel coat, at his chest. Like Napoleon. Or so I had always assumed.

'I'll not be able to pick you up again, you do know that? Possibly for hours, at least until we've driven them off and it's safe to stop.'

'I understand. We'll stand off until you're ready, keep in touch with a signalling light.'

'Madness,' Deeds repeated, but knew he was lost. 'Michael, you are going to have to be unbelievably quick getting that bloody boat away. There are U-boats all over the place tonight.'

'I'll not hold you up more than a minute or two.'

They eyed each other. I just held my breath and waited. *Daisy* dipped into a sea, then rose, the rush and swirl of icy white ocean gurgling across her decks and into the scuppers. Almost like a father and son, I thought, watching them, and not knowing. Finally, a nod, a single nod, to us both, then he was turning forwards once more. 'Very well. Get ready. And be quick about it.'

Daisy had two ship's boats, stowed amidships, one on either side. Whalers, ship's boats were called sometimes, harking back to the days of hand-thrown harpoons when you had to row a small boat right up to your prey to be in with a chance of hitting it. And they really were small, about fifteen feet, wooden, clinker-built. Strong enough, but to the untutored eye not hugely dissimilar to the sort of thing you'd take the family out in for a jolly on the Serpentine. They hung from davits over the deck. The procedure for lowering one was to swing the davits out so the boat hung over the side of the ship, climb aboard, then lower away using ropes and pulleys, called falls, until you reached the water. Sounds simple enough, but even on a calm day on a millpond, it is surprisingly easy to cock up. At sea, in the dark, in any kind of weather, it's downright dangerous.

19

You have to stop the ship. Just for a minute or two while you lower the boat into the water and get unhooked from the falls. Otherwise the thing gets dragged about, smashing into the ship's side, or slewing sideways until it fills and overturns. It was this stopping of the ship, in an ocean full of U-boats, offering a stationary target in other words, that Walter Deeds, along with everyone else on board, was most concerned about.

But Villiers knew what he was doing. In a couple of minutes he had rounded up three more spare hands and assembled us all by the port boat. Apart from me, there was the aforementioned Frank Tuker, a notoriously surly long-service senior AB. Then there was William Harrison, a quietly spoken signalman from Wellingborough, and a spotty young HO rating on his first trip called Albert Giddings. None appeared overly pleased at the prospect of a rowing boat excursion in the middle of the Atlantic, at night, to look for dead and dying sailors, with nothing but half a dozen enemy submarines for company. Giddings in particular looked awful, white as a sheet and shaking with fear.

'I appreciate you doing this,' Villiers said simply, as if they had any choice. At least he made it sound is if they did. 'We'll be all right, you have my word on it.' I believed him. Giddings, eyes like pale saucers in the gloom, was desperately trying to. Harrison's face was expressionless, Tuker just grunted. We threw some gear, ropes, flashlights and so on, into the boat and began unfastening the falls. *Daisy* was already slowing, and turning in a half-circle to try and create an area of semi-flat sea for us to drop into. Two more hands appeared to help us launch. We clambered aboard, then waited for *Daisy* to come to a stop. It seemed an age, but it can only have been a minute or two before we were slowly bumping down her side. I remember the unusual quiet at *Daisy*'s stopped engines and the sluggish dull slap of waves against the side of her hull. 'Get on with it, for God's sake!' one of the hands urged anxiously from above. Finally, and on a more or less even keel, we hit the water with a smack and after only minimal fumbling released the shackles attaching us to the falls.

Villiers took the tiller at the stern, the rest of us shipped an oar each and, arranging ourselves side by side on the thwarts, began to pull away from *Daisy*.

Since we rowers were facing backwards, as it were, I saw the whole thing. In the most vivid slow motion.

We'd only gone about a hundred yards. Although there was an energetic frothing at her stern as the propeller bit into the water, *Daisy* was not yet properly underway, barely moving. Suddenly Villiers stood up at the stern of the whaler.

'My God. I've killed them all.' It was what he said. An instant later, a sort of throbbing vibration passed right beneath us, and an arrow-straight line of green phosphorescence shot under our boat, about three feet below the surface, racing at unbelievable speed straight towards the ship.

'*Daisy!*' It was Villiers. Not a cry of warning, or even helplessness. It was primeval. A death-cry. A cry of mourning, of loss beyond bearing. It made your spine go cold.

The torpedo struck *Daisy* amidships. Right in the fuel-oil tanks that lined her sides outboard of the forward boiler room. There was a smaller, muffled boom first, then, about half a second later, an enormous flash, a massive, concussive explosion and *Daisy* just burst apart, right into two pieces, her two halves lifting high in the middle such that they were almost completely out of the water. At the same time an eruption of flame and spray exploded upwards, sixty, seventy feet into the sky. Pieces of deck equipment, super-structure and what were unmistakably bodies, flying skywards with it. The pom-pom, all half a ton of it, just sprang from its mountings aft and flew, spinning, as though tossed, thirty yards over the stern. For'ard, the four-inch gun, its white hooded crew still clustered around it, detached itself from the madly canting deck and crashed, tumbling, forwards into the waves beyond the bow. Everything in-between, the entire mid-section of the ship in other words, seemed to vanish before our eyes.

I felt a blow to my upper body, like a two-fisted punch to the chest, as the shockwave struck us. It knocked me back-wards off the seat, so that I was sitting, legs flying, in the bottom of the dinghy. Someone, Villiers, was yelling. 'Row!' He appeared to be saying. 'For the love of Mary, row!' But we were too deafened, and too stunned to do anything, except stare in horror at our ship's destruction.

It lasted but seconds. As the first explosion subsided, she sort of settled back on to an even keel. Her two halves came almost together again, as if giant unseen hands were mirac-ulously trying to rejoin them. But then, like lovers turning away from each other, the two halves rolled on to their sides, in opposite directions, and with these awful booming noises emanating from deep in her vitals, tortured metallic shrieks and the scream of escaping steam, *Daisy* turned up her rust-streaked keel and dived for the ocean bed.

Villiers was still yelling. But there was no time. No time to understand, no time even to begin to grasp what had happened, and what it meant. Less than a minute earlier, a ship, our ship, had been sitting right in front of us. Now she was gone, erased, plummeting into the black depths. 'Row!' he was shouting, on and on. 'For God's sake all of you, row!' I saw his face close to mine, felt his hand grasping at the collar of my duffel coat, hauling me back up on to the thwart. 'Stephen, come on!' I looked at him, trying to hear, trying to understand, but still deafened, still shocked incapable. 'The depth charges, Stephen! They're all armed, they'll go off any second!' Depth charges. *Daisy*'s depth charges. Sub-Lieutenant Martin Brown's depth charges. Primed and armed and ready to go off at their preset depths.

We'd be blown to matchwood.

I hoisted myself on to the thwart, fumbling for my oar. Beside me, someone else, Harrison I think it was, began pulling on another. The other two were behind us, at the bows, I don't know if they were pulling.

Not that it made much difference. The depth charges went off.

I only remember this. An eerie ring of light, a kind of wide circular flash, like lightning, just above the surface of the water where *Daisy* had been. A violent shuddering sensation beneath my feet. A crack of thunder, then the whole sea, the whole world, erupting, pausing, then jerking upwards. Hard, jagged edges of solid water flung into the night sky, like vast stalagmites, or soaring spires, then hanging there, for what seemed like an aeon, frozen in time, before finally beginning to subside.

And then the wave. A menacing wall of solid grey that hurtled, hissing, outwards at us from the epicentre. Growing as it spread, rising to engulf us, until in moments it towered twenty feet or more over our heads. Then it was upon us, curling high above, smooth, black, noiseless. A glimpse of a foam-white crest framed by a canopy of stars, like a gaping mouth, an instant of frozen timelessness, then the stars were gone, the wall smashed down, and in an insane flailing, falling, tumbling eternity of chaos, the world came to an end.

Drowning isn't so bad after all. Not nearly so much of a mad panic as I'd always imagined. The freezing cold of the water drives the air from the lungs in a second. That's a shock. But after that you go down, it's very dark, very cold and very quiet. And very peaceful.

Well, that's that, I thought, and surrendered.

Chapter 2

Michael George José-Luis Quemada Villiers shared his birthday with a Uruguayan national hero, José Gervasio Artigas, a gamekeeper turned poacher who, through dogged guerrilla tactics a century earlier, wrested Montevideo from Argentinian control, thus establishing a tentative independence for his embryonic country.

They were also born in the same city, although thereafter all coincidental parallels ended. Michael certainly did not share Artigas' humble origins. His quest for life's meaning began at eleven-thirty on the evening of Friday 19 June 1921, in his mother Aurora's satin-curtained bedroom, in her grandmother's neo-Parisian town house off fashionable Avenida Agraciada in the wealthy Prado district of Montevideo, capital of Uruguay. As Michael materialised, sputtering and bloody, into the world, an unseasonably mild winter wind beyond the shuttered windows was shaking the last leaves from the plane trees lining the street. In the far distance, down towards the city's harbourfront heart, an appropriate clamour of merrymaking, together with the crack of fireworks, like distant rifle fire, heralded the final thirty minutes of the national holiday. It could not have been a more auspicious start to life for a young Uruguayan.

Or even a half-Uruguayan. With only token persuasion from her matriarchal grandmother Doña Madeleina, Aurora, then twenty-four, who in any case held a morbid fear of hospitals and all matters medical, had elected for a home delivery for her first-born. A sensible precaution as Montevideo's hospitals, oversubscribed and rudimentary at best, were in any case already filling with the first fever-racked victims of an emergent cholera epidemic. Beneath Doña Madeleina's hawk-eyed scrutiny therefore, Aurora stayed at home, attended throughout the delivery by the Quemada family's two private physicians, as well as her mother and father, two older brothers, sundry aunts, uncles, cousins and even family friends and acquaintances who dropped by to monitor proceedings and pay their respects to Doña Madeleina.

Aurora's labour, beginning with a dawn rupturing of her waters, lasted throughout the holiday. She bore it with mostly characteristic stoicism, only occasionally, and to Doña Madeleina's clucks of disapproval, surrendering to her pains with quavering wails of surprised agony, which grew more frequent and desperate as the long day wore on and the denouement neared.

Finally it was all over and a little while later an exhausted but triumphant Aurora, her face freshly washed and powdered, her thick auburn hair brushed to her shoulders by a maid, and wearing a bed gown bought especially from the London-Paris store on Avenida 18 de Julio was helped to a semi-reclining position and her sleeping infant son lowered into her arms.

'He has green eyes,' she said, her voice tinged with disappointment.

'Indeed,' her grandmother replied, flapping the bedclothes straight.

'And fair hair. And his skin, look, it is so pale.'

'Never mind. Quality comes from within. His colouring may be Anglo-Saxon, but you can be sure that the blood pumping through his veins is entirely Latin American. He is and always will be a Quemada. Now, sit up straight, and square your shoulders young lady. The family is waiting.'

They were admitted according to Doña Madeleina's arbitrary but unquestioned order of descending importance. Her side of the family first, naturally, beginning with her eldest son, José-Luis, Aurora's father. He entered cautiously, wrinkling his nose a little at the heavy scent of winter lilies mingled with disinfectant and bodily smells. The room was stuffy, heavily draped, dimly lamp-lit. He greeted his mother first before approaching the bed. At a table to one side the two physicians were packing up their bags.

'A little man, I hear,' he said, dutifully bending to examine the tiny bundle. Michael was his fourth grandchild. 'He has the look of a Quemada, I say.'

'Nonsense!' Doña Madeleina scoffed. 'But he is fit and strong and with proper tutelage will do well enough.'

'I mean to name him after you, Papa.' Aurora whispered.

Short of stature, fifty, bespectacled, fashionably side-whiskered, José-Luis regarded his daughter. Although a little wan of course, and uncharacteristically subdued, to his eye her radiant beauty was undimmed. Smiling weakly, her teak-brown eyes heavy with fatigue, her head sank on to the cushions at her neck. She really was changed, he concluded, a little optimistically. Marriage and motherhood had matured her, as he had predicted, into the responsible and compliant young woman he had longed for. He reached out and touched her cheek.

'Your husband will be very proud of you.'

But her husband, Keith Villiers, Michael's father, would have to wait. After José-Luis came his three brothers and two sisters – Aurora's uncles and aunts from his side of the family. Together with their spouses, they queued at the foot of the bed, and, following an orderly circuit, gave Michael a token going-over, before returning to the comfort of the Madeira decanter waiting in the downstairs withdrawing room.

Only then was Aurora's mother, Florentina, admitted. Nervously accompanied by a sister, Gertrudis.

'You've had a long day,' Florentina said to Aurora, point-edly ignoring Doña Madeleina. Her smile was thin, her round face expressionless but searching. And there was nothing perfunctory about her inspection of Michael. She examined the child closely, bending to place her face inches from his. He slept on, his mouth twisting to a grimace, waxy pink fingers balled into fists. Florentina's eyes narrowed, as though inspecting an underweight flounder at the fish stall. At last, seemingly satisfied, she straightened, nodded, planted a dutiful kiss on her daughter's forehead and turned for the door, nervous sister in tow.

Next came Aurora's two brothers, Domingo and Enriqué, and their wives and children. They were a noisy and excitable group. Dressed in evening gowns and dining suits, reeking of perfume and cigars, the brothers and their wives had been hosting a prolonged, open-house dinner downstairs for most of the evening. Domingo, an official of the Colorado Party, was red-faced, a little unsteady on his feet.

'Some of the Polo Bamba crowd dropped in,' he grinned, barely glancing at Michael. 'They all wish you well, want to know when they'll be seeing you on the dance floor again. Actually, we thought we'd head along there later. See out Artigas' birthday. And wet the baby's head, of course.' He winked blearily at Aurora. 'Willi was with them, you know? Herr Hochstetler, your German businessman friend. He specifically asked us to pass his best wishes and congratulations to you both.'

Unsurprisingly, Michael grew fretful at all the commotion, so the brothers and their families were ejected. And it was yet another full half-hour before mother and child were properly settled to Doña Madeleina's satisfaction once more. Only then, nearly two hours after Michael's birth, did she tug on the bell pull and send downstairs for his father.

Keith, slight, angular, twenty-six, knocked and entered. He was still in his stiff collar and office suit, which were a little rumpled; for, having excused himself from the family's holiday celebrations at a polite juncture earlier in the evening, he had retired to their elegant panelled library and fallen asleep in a chair. In instinctive observance of formality, before he approached the bed he turned and bowed stiffly to Doña Madeleina, seated beside the curtained window.

'May I take this opportunity to offer my congratulations to you on the safe delivery of your great-grandson,' he proffered in his best Foreign Office Spanish. Doña Madeleina inclined her head in acknowledgement, motioning him towards the bed with an imperious wave of her hand.

Aurora was asleep. There was no chair. Wide-eyed, swallowing, a little fearful suddenly, Keith knelt. Gently, he lifted his wife's free hand from the bed, placing it, like a new-born chick, between his. She stirred, licked her lips, turned her head to him. Her eyes fluttered open.

'Keith?'

'Yes, it is me, my dearest.'

'Look, Keith. Our son.'

'Yes.' His heart melted. Suddenly tears pricked his eyes, the tensions of the day, of the last months, threatening to overwhelm him. Before he could stop himself, his chest was heaving. Astonished, and oblivious to the disapproving matriarchal eyes boring into his back, he bowed his head, crushed his lips to his wife's hand, and wept.

Later, he walked. It was a chill night, but not cold. Even

30

in mid-winter, a Uruguayan frost was a rarity. He stood, his back to the Quemadas' big front door, pulling on gloves, sniffing at the air like a dog. Leafy residential Prado was deserted. Grateful for the solitude, and the cool air, he struck out. Home, he pondered, still wondering at the intensity of his emotional outpouring. He needed to go home. Try and come to terms with the enormity of it all. Not Sussex home, the one he had left eighteen months earlier, although he occasionally ached for its order, its comforting sameness, its Englishness. No – home, here, in Montevideo.

There was a surprising range of choice. He could stay right there at the big house. In the months preceding, he and Aurora had occasionally passed nights in one of its suites, and Doña Madeleina had already told him the maids were preparing a guest room for him. He'd declined politely, citing urgent legation business.

Then there was the apartment, his and Aurora's. Down in the Pocitos district of the city, near the best beaches, where all the new wealthy Montevideans were buying. It had been paid for by the Quemadas, of course, a wedding present. Although not quite, as title had yet to be transferred into their name. So it was more of a loan. He and Aurora had occupied it soon after they were married, nearly eight months ago. It was well furnished and comfortable, and pleasantly proportioned. Yet while Aurora and her socialite friends loved it for its modernity and enviable position, Keith had never quite felt that he truly belonged there. Never felt that it was his.

He kept walking, heading west until he came to Veltroni's ornate Italian amphitheatre, set on a low bluff overlooking the vast natural harbour that was the Bay of Montevideo. Recently completed, the amphitheatre was something of a folly, a rash symbol of opulence in an uncertain young country of limited wealth and widespread poverty. It faced out across the bay which curved away in both directions before him in a majestic sweep. He stared out, the coal-black waters of the near harbour beneath him, the wide muddy currents of the River Plate in the middle distance, far beyond the South Atlantic ocean, glinting in the moonlight like burnished steel.

There was also a room at the office, at the legation. More of a store cupboard with an army cot if the truth be known. Whenever business correspondence was especially heavy, or when an important diplomatic pouch was due in on the packet steamer from London, or if messages were expected over the new telegraph system, junior secretaries like Keith were required to stay overnight to deal with them. Keith didn't mind. The British legation, consisting of four pokey offices, was located in the mercantile quarter of the Ciudad Vieja, the old city, a vibrant, bustling district. During the first weeks following his arrival in Montevideo, before he was assigned his own rooms, he had spent many evening hours walking its grid-like streets, visiting its little shops and bars. Attempting to get to know the bewilderingly diverse hotchpotch of nationalities that made up its inhabitants.

His rooms. Room. Ten minutes' walk from the office. As

third secretary the legation provided him with one – although its rental was deducted from his salary. It was on the top landing of a tall stone-fronted building like those lining the less salubrious streets and alleys of Paris, or Brussels, or Madrid. The stairwell was steep, dark and narrow, the washroom was two floors down and shared, and his room was small and had mice. But, once inside and with the door closed, it was surprisingly quiet and homely. It was also light and airy, blessed with a pair of tall shuttered windows. On fine winter days he used to throw them wide, and pass his meagre leisure hours reading, or watching passers-by in the busy street below, or simply basking in the sunshine, eyes closed, like a cat. Outside the window was a tiny wrought-iron balcony. When summer nights grew sultry, the oppressive city heat lying heavy on his chest, he would rise from the sweat-soaked sheets of his bed, spread a towel on the balcony, and lie there listening to the restless city's heave and swell.

At least he used to. With a shiver, he rose from the curved stone seating of the amphitheatre, brushing dirt from the back of his topcoat. Far to his right the sweep of the lighthouse at Cerro lit the ancient fort that stood guard over the harbour's western approaches. A mile to his left the lights of the old port and its teeming immigrant quarter beckoned in exotic and anonymous welcome. Above the gentle lapping of the waves still drifted sounds of festival: music, crowds, singing, fireworks. And the smells: of sea-weed and rotting timber, cooking and wood smoke, shanty towns and street filth, as tens of thousands of unwashed souls forgot their troubles for a night to celebrate their precarious toehold on the land they now called home.

The new father picked his way carefully down the stone steps beside the amphitheatre, descended to the *rambla*, the sandy track running along the waterfront, and struck out towards them.

Keith Villiers had met Aurora Quemada barely a year earlier, at a business reception organised by the British legation at Montevideo's Uruguay Club on Plaza Matriz. He had been placed in charge of the catering – an important responsibility for an inexperienced third secretary on his first posting, in a country where food, or at least its consumption, was taken very seriously. Although there had been a British trade mission in Montevideo for decades, the legation itself had only been in autonomous existence a year or so. Originally set up as an outpost of the British Embassy in Argentina, across the River Plate in Buenos Aires, it occupied an unimpressive suite of cramped offices down near the harbour on Plaza Zabala. It was run by a dictatorial former army colonel called Rawlings.

'You can forget fruit cup and cucumber sandwiches, Villiers!' Rawlings had thundered earlier, tossing aside Keith's meticulously drawn-up menu. 'Meat, man, meat! And plenty of it. And claret. Plenty of that, too – and just mind you keep it coming, got it?'

Ostensibly, the reception, a formal evening affair, was to raise local awareness of the enhanced British diplomatic presence in Uruguay. In reality Rawlings' brief was less subtle. He and his small team were to penetrate the upper echelons of Montevidean business and political society, secure deals and shut out the competition. Quite apart from Uruguay's strategic significance geographically, Whitehall, still reeling from the debt and devastation four years' war in Europe had wrought, was well aware of the rich seam of trade opportunities in this evidently cash-rich but industrially underdeveloped region. Trouble was, so was the rest of the Western world. Making the right connections, and fast, was crucial.

'*El tiempo de las vacas gordas.*' A silken voice drifted to Keith above the swirling hubbub around him. He turned. A young woman with a small oval face and thick dark hair was standing close by, surveying the crowded room.

'I beg your pardon, Señora?' he replied, bottle in hand.

'It is Señorita. I was saying "*el tiempo de las vacas gordas*". We call this the time of the fat cows. That is what this is about, no? The imperialist powers of Europe and North America squabbling like greedy children for the food falling from Uruguay's table?' Although her English was strongly accented, her voice had an hypnotic singsong quality.

'Well, goodness me, no, I, most sincerely hope, that is, as far as we British are concerned . . .' Keith blustered.

'You are English, no?'

'English, yes.'

'Be no concerned. We in Uruguay love the English. They are always so polite. And quite honest in their dealings. My name is Aurora Quemada. What is yours?'

'Oh, ah, Villiers. Keith Villiers.'

'How long are you being in Uruguay?'

'Not long, I . . .'

'You know many people? Uruguayan people?' She pronounced 'Uruguayan' with the softest double 'o' sound at the beginning. And a silent 'g'. Oora-why-an. To Keith it sounded like music.

'Sadly no, not yet, although . . .'

'Ah, well, we must be correcting that. You are very young for important British diplomat. And very handsome.' Delicately pouting lips smiled playfully at him. Above a slender neck, she held her chin high. She was petite of stature, wearing a floor-length taffeta gown of emerald green that emphasised the narrowness of her waist, and the firm swell of her bosom.

'Oh, no. Not really,' Keith blushed. 'Not very important, that is. Not at all, in fact.' But Aurora had already decided. Suddenly she was speaking Spanish.

'Uruguay is *the* South American model of twentieth-century modernity. My father, he is over there, Señor José-Luis Quemada, is very senior in the Department of Transportation. It was he who approved the recent transaction for the British to further develop our railway system. He was also instrumental in securing approval for the Anglo meat cold-storage plant at Fray Bentos. So you see, we do love the English. Would you like to meet him?'

From that moment on, Aurora seemed to take control of his life. Bemused, unable to believe his fortune, but delighted nevertheless, he did not resist. In fact in the

36

ensuing days, everyone seemed happy, even Rawlings, impressed that his most junior, and hitherto least promising, protégé had somehow secured a seat at the top table. José-Luis also encouraged Keith's liaison with his daughter, badly misinterpreting his quiet solicitousness for influence and importance. And money.

'It could not be more perfect!' he told his wife Florentina, as they prepared for bed one night. Keith had dined with them for the first time at the big house in Prado. 'Well mannered, educated, clearly destined for high office within the British diplomatic service. Rich too, no question.'

'Good manners do not necessarily equate with wealth, dearest.'

'Tina, trust me, I do know wealth when I see it. It is just the English way. The more money they have, the more modest they are about it. Complete opposite to the Americans. Anyway, good relations with London are vitally important to the future of Uruguay. And his father is a senior official in the Foreign Office.'

'Hmm.' Florentina, brushing her hair at the dressing table, remained noncommittal. 'Aurora does seem very taken with him.'

'Yes! And you know, I do believe that his quiet way, his self-discipline, his seriousness, might be just the influence she needs, no?'

Florentina appeared not to have heard. 'But then it is not the first time she has been very taken with someone.' She glanced at her husband in the mirror. 'Is it?'

Aurora liked parties. In fact she lived for them. Night after night during that dizzy spring of 1920, Keith, bleary with lack of sleep, found himself donning his Moss Brothers dinner suit, descending from his room, and boarding a horse cab for cocktails at the house of some politician, dinner at a fancy restaurant, or front-row seats at the Teatro Solís. Followed by dancing in the Hotel Prado ballroom, or roulette in the neo-classical splendour of the Casino Carrasco. Followed by more drinking, more dancing and more eating. Or a tango show, or a dawn carriage ride along the *rambla*, or just heated, night-long intellectual discussion at Al Tupi Namba or one of the city's many other fashionable cafés.

It was fascinating, exciting, exhilarating. A magical whirlwind night-world of laughter and dancing, gay, vibrant company, and moonlit walks arm in arm with Aurora by the water's edge. Within two weeks he was completely smitten, and completely exhausted. He was also penniless. Although bills at restaurants or the drinks tab at a café would usually be picked up, magically, by one of the many rich members of the Quemada entourage, Keith still spent way beyond his meagre earnings on cab fares, tips and, when protocol and knowing looks expected it of him, the odd bottle of champagne. Rawlings was unsympathetic:

'An expense account! Good God, man, have you completely taken leave of your senses? *I* don't even have an expense account and I'm head of the blasted legation! No, lad, you know the drill. Submit valid receipts for strictly bona fide expenses, together with the triplicate forms provided, to me for approval. In due course these will be returned to Accounts back at HQ and, once verified, credited to your salary. How long? Only about six months or so. Oh, and you can forget about theatre tickets and restaurant bills; Accounts would laugh themselves silly. And for God's sake smarten yourself up, man. You look like a tramp with a hangover!'

He wrote home to his father for more money, claiming that his room rental and the cost of basic comestibles were much higher in Montevideo than anticipated. It was a blatant untruth but he didn't care. He stopped eating lunch to save a few pesos, tried going to bed for a couple of hours after work to catch up on sleep. But food was an irrelevance and sleep rarely found him. He was so nervous, so keyed up he could barely sit still, rising repeatedly from his bed to pace the floor of his room, counting the minutes until at last he could descend, like a ravenous werewolf, into the mystical night-existence that was his new world, and the woman who waited at its centre.

Far from being fit and strong, as Doña Madeleina had confidently predicted, the infant Michael turned out to be a sickly baby. Within days of his birth the family physicians were summoned back to the house in Prado for the first of many cot-side consultations. It was his chest, they informed her, one evening a few weeks later. It was weak.

'Not the cholera, then,' Doña Madeleina demanded, wincing as Michael's pneumonic squeals split the air. Lately she had begun to feel that his night-long wailing was affecting her nerves. Behind her, Aurora and Keith looked on anxiously.

'No, Señora, at least not yet, that is. Although we must be especially careful about that. In his weakened state, he would surely succumb fatally to the cholera within hours if infected.'

Wide-eyed, Aurora slipped a hand through Keith's arm. He turned to her, patting it encouragingly. Despite the worry, the trying delivery and their son's perpetual insomnia, he was amazed at how well she looked, how quickly she had recovered from the birth. Unlike Michael, she was a picture of health: clear-eyed, rested and fresh of complexion. Recently, at Doña Madeleina's suggestion, a nurse had been retained to attend to Michael through the nights, and another for the days. Aurora, always a late sleeper, had leaped at the idea, and now rose to spend a little time with him in the afternoons, which was mostly when he slept.

She had begun to resume her hectic social schedule. Once or twice she stayed overnight at the apartment in Pocitos, returning to Prado early the following evening to look in on Michael. Keith could not keep up. Tired and overworked, his body clock out of all synchrony with Aurora's, he slept at the office, or at his room, or occasionally at Pocitos. Reluctantly he was starting to acknowledge that he and his wife were spending less time together, or with their son, than would seem ideal.

Doña Madeleina dabbed distractedly at her neck with a lace handkerchief. She was still conferring with the doctors. 'Perhaps it might be best for the child's well being . . .'

she began, raising her voice against Michael's '. . . if he went to live with his parents. They have an excellent apartment in Pocitos, you know. The sea air . . .'

'I must respectfully advise most strongly against such a proposition, Señora. The south of the city is very crowded, polluted by street filth and vermin, and the atmosphere is notoriously noxious and dust-laden from all the building works and horse-drawn traffic. And the sea air in winter, well, it is cold and moist, the worst thing, really the very worst thing possible. No, here, Prado, this is significantly more healthy and sanitary.'

There was a heavy pause, Michael's cries subsiding appropriately to a wheezy whimper. Beyond the windows, the clopping of hooves as a carriage passed the gate.

'I fear the doctor may be right, Grandmama,' Aurora ventured sadly.

Doña Madeleina turned, as if noticing them for the first time. Her expression lacked warmth. 'The British always were a sickly race,' she muttered accusingly. Keith, ever the diplomat, smiled politely, as though she was joking, but said nothing.

The second doctor was clearing his throat. 'Excuse me, Señora, but am I not correct in thinking that the family has a substantial country property in the interior?'

Within a month of their meeting, Keith had fallen deeply in love with Aurora. It was as incapacitating a cocktail of sensations as it was thrilling. Hitherto, girls had featured little in his life. Bookish and shy by nature, the product of a sheltered Home Counties upbringing, boys only boarding schools, a brother but no sisters, his understanding of women and his experience in the ways of the heart were practically non-existent. Then, suddenly, Aurora, piercing him to the core, such that he felt like a fish wriggling on a stick. He hardly slept, barely ate. To Rawlings' growing exasperation, he found it impossible to concentrate at the office, lapsing into trance-like reverie, or leaping to his feet, uncontrollable with excitement, at the suggestion of an errand, or simply grinning, idiotically, and for no reason. Put simply, he didn't know whether to laugh or cry. Mostly he felt like doing both.

He existed for the time he spent with her, those delicious, spell-weaving perfumed hours of satin dresses, fleeting touches and teasing laughter. When they were together he felt he could conquer the world, that his life had purpose, that the path ahead lay clear and open. Only when they parted did the doubts gather in his head, like shower clouds in March.

There were two problems. The first was they spent so little time actually on their own together. Six hours of collective merrymaking might yield just five minutes alone with Aurora. Five minutes when his heart beat so hard he could feel it banging in his throat. Five minutes when the world stopped turning, and the only now was the gleam of her eyes, the softness of her hands and the warm touch of her lips. It was heaven on earth. But a five-minute heaven was not nearly enough.

The second problem was that Aurora attracted men. Like wasps to a picnic.

'I say, old buddy, you're looking downright peaky. Here, try this.' A brandy appeared on the wooden table before Keith. The speaker, an American, lowered himself into the vacant chair beside him. Aurora's chair. 'Anyone sitting here?'

Keith shook his head. Not for some time. He glanced towards the dance floor. Most of their party, about twenty in all, including Aurora, her two brothers, their wives and the usual cosmopolitan mix of hangers-on, were energetically disporting themselves to the raucous twanging of a Hispanic guitar band. But he'd long since had enough. He was exhausted, a little drunk. His shirt collar chafed damply at his neck, it was stiflingly hot and very late, gone three, he estimated.

'You're the Brit, right? Rawlings' boy, from the legation over at the port.'

'Indeed. Keith Villiers. How do you do.'

'Larry Dunmore.' They clasped sweaty palms. 'From Washington Consolidated. You know?'

Keith knew. Dunmore, with his deceptively boyish looks, Fifth Avenue tuxedo and black pomaded hair neatly parted in the middle, was head of a US engineering consortium, bidding hard for a river-damming contract up-country on Uruguay's Rio Negro. Aurora's brother, Enriqué, a lawyer, was closely involved with brokering the deal.

'So, how are your negotiations going?' Keith enquired dutifully. Rawlings had insisted he be kept abreast of any developments.

'It's in the bag, just about,' Dunmore grinned, mopping

perspiration from his cheeks. 'Enriqué's on side, I just got to shut out the Italian bid and we're home safe.'

'Congratulations, you must be delighted.'

'Sure. Thank God for Wilson's concessions to foreign capitalists, I say.'

'What? Oh, yes.' Keith struggled to concentrate. Woodrow Wilson, President of the United States, his recently published thoughts on global socio-economics. Required reading. What was it called? *The New Freedom*. Quite controversial. But on the dance floor the music had changed, a softer, ballad-like tune coming from the band. A dark-skinned woman in a colourful dress and flowers in her hair had got up to sing. Sweating, breathless couples were slowing in their movements, drawing closer to one another. His eyes sought Aurora. Dunmore was still quoting his President.

'". . . poorer Latin American countries granting concessions to foreign capitalists will find that those same foreigners end up dominating their domestic affairs . . ." he says, or something like that, although personally I think that's all baloney, we're only here to help.'

'Are we?'

'Sure! We build them a few bridges, they agree not to undercut our beef prices, that's fair.'

'Fair,' Keith muttered distractedly. 'Imperialism is defined as the extension of a country's power by the acquisition of dependencies.'

'Who the hell said that?'

'The English dictionary.'

'You Brits!' Dunmore roared, slapping his knee. 'You crack me up! Always have to take everything so damn seriously. Say, who's that dancing with the gorgeous Aurora?'

His name was Willi Hochstetler, a German. Always courteous, always smiling, he was a tall, Nordic-looking, life-and-soul-of-the-party type. He represented a conglomerate called, rather unimaginatively in Keith's opinion, Compania Transatlantica, which in turn represented a variety of German industrial interests in the region. Willi had recently been hurriedly moved to Montevideo from Buenos Aires. This was because the Department of Transportation, of which Aurora's father was a director, had come to the conclusion that modern inhabitants of a modern capital needed modern public transport. They should not have to rely upon inefficient, dirty and hopelessly outdated horse-drawn omnibuses to get about. What was needed was one of the latest tramway systems, like those in London, Paris and all the major cities. Following preliminary presentations by a number of possible suppliers, two groups had finally been selected to compete for this much-prized contract. One was Willi Hochstetler's Compania Transatlantica. The other, the Commercial Society of Montevideo, was British.

'Keep your bloody eye on him, lad,' Rawlings had warned. 'We foul this one up and Whitehall will have our guts.' Keith had promised to do his best, although his motives for doing so were perhaps more personal than patriotic. His eyes scanned the dance floor once more. Hochstetler's hand was resting, fingers splayed, low on Aurora's back. As Keith watched, he leaned towards her, whispering something in her ear. Then they were both laughing. Keith rose to his feet.

'Would you mind if I cut in, old boy?' he enquired a moment later.

Hochstetler's pale eyes locked on to Keith's, hesitating only fractionally before crinkling into their habitual beaming smile. 'My dear fellow! Not at all. My honour.' He clapped him on the back, bowed stiffly to Aurora, clicked his heels and left the floor.

'Do you not find,' Keith asked her after a while, 'that there isn't something vaguely comical about our Willi?' They were waltzing. Aurora was an expert dancer, fluid and graceful. Keith, in accordance with Foreign Office guidelines, knew enough to get by. She felt unbelievably exciting in his arms. Alive, vibrant. Aroused. Her palm was moist. Through the fabric of her dress he could feel the heat of her back.

'My dearest man! Why, I do believe you are a little jealous!'

'Good heavens! Me? Jealous? What an absurd idea.'

'Hmm. I think you may be. Just a little. How flattering.' Her dark-brown eyes studied his. A tiny sheen of perspiration glistened at her brow, a diffuse pink spot in the cleft of her neck. Below it, her chest rose and fell, quick with breathlessness. 'Shall we go outside?' She murmured the magic spell at last. 'I would like to be alone with you.'

Three days later, Keith, bag in hand, stepped from the legation offices into blistering sunlight, turned right on to Plaza Zabala, elbowed his way through the throngs of shipping clerks, messengers, immigrant labourers, tramps and beggars, descended to the dockside and boarded a ferry for the six-hour trip across the brown waters of the River Plate to Buenos Aires. A royal visit was imminent. The British monarch himself, George V and his queen, Mary, were due ashore for a week-long stay in the Argentine capital. To Rawlings' chagrin they would not, regrettably, have time to drop in on Montevideo, but in the meantime it was all hands to the pumps. Rawlings' superior in BA said they needed spare bodies to help out with fetching and carrying, Keith, always top of any legation list for onerous chores, had drawn the short straw.

The very night he returned, ten days later, Aurora visited him in his room.

'How is your king?' she inquired, in Spanish, after they had embraced. She seemed agitated, moving restlessly around the room, knotting and unknotting her fingers, as though undecided about something.

'I never saw him. Well, I saw him, of course, but not very close to. He appears to be well, thank you.' He hesitated. 'What about you? Can I get you something, a glass of water perhaps?' Embarrassed, he looked about his room. She had never been inside before; it looked forlorn, suddenly, squalid even. But if she noticed she gave no indication. In fact she looked close to tears.

'May I sit?' she whispered, perching on the edge of his bed.

'Of course. Aurora, dearest, what is it?'

She looked up at him. A sultry summer dusk was falling, the room's details, its bare floorboards, its simple wooden desk and chair, its curtained wardrobe, melting slowly into shadow. Outside the air lay heavy and unmoving. A mule brayed plaintively down in the street; further off the brassy blast of a horn as a steamer passed the harbour breakwater.

'Do you love me, Keith?'

'Aurora, my dearest girl. Madly! With all my heart, you must know that.'

'If you love me, would you embrace me once more?'

He went to her, knelt, clasped both her hands in his, kissing them fervently. Within seconds she was drawing him up, at the same time levering herself back on to the bed. In an instant, he realised, his heart tripping like a steamhammer, that they were lying in each other's arms on the mattress, bodies tightly entwined. She sank her fingers into the hair of his neck, pulling his head, his face, to hers. Their mouths met, her lips parted. He felt her tongue, hot and hard, flicking at his.

It was over in seconds. Suddenly she broke free, leaned forward, seized the hem of her dress and, lifting her bottom, hoisted it to her thighs. To Keith's amazement there were no garments beneath, just the shoes on her feet, little yellow satin pumps, then the silky smooth light-brown skin of her legs, and the dark triangular shadow of her pubis. As he stared, she took his hand, guiding it directly to the heat between her thighs. At the same she found the front of his trousers. Swiftly she pulled him free of his clothing, in moments was half-pulling him on top, half-squirming beneath. There were three seconds of frantic fumbling, then, with an agonised gasp, like the last shuddering sigh of the dying, he slid deeply inside her.

So, at the age of two months, Michael Villiers went to live in the countryside.

The 'substantial' country property referred to by the doctors was in fact a sprawling, slightly careworn, but beautifully situated estancia – a ranch-like farm. Its name was Estancia Sombreado, which means shady, a value added commodity in the land of the baking grass plain where few trees grew naturally. It was situated twenty miles to the south of the border town of Melo, in Uruguay's Cerro Largo department, not far from the northern frontier with Brazil. In fact the frontier, more of a region than a line, still wandered back and forth in places, as it had for centuries, as insoluble territorial disputes and internecine blood feuds rumbled on.

Estancia Sombreado was not Quemada property. Low, timber-framed, set among stands of tall Lombardy poplars, it belonged to Aurora's maternal grandfather, Florentina's father, Don Adrián Rapoza, who still lived there. Legend had it that Don Adrián, a grizzled, hard of hearing, one-legged recluse of unknown years, had been given the estancia as a reward for excessive loyalty, or in lieu of pay, by none other than General Aparicio Saravia, last of the anti-government land-owning *caudillismo*, who decades earlier had led a ragtag army of hopelessly under-equipped gauchos on a spear-waving rampage of glorious civil revolt, to the infuriation of the Uruguayan authorities, climaxing in a magnificent but disastrous lance charge against the massed cannon of the National Army.

But then again it was only hearsay, as Don Adrián never spoke of these things. Or indeed of anything much.

Journeying the two hundred and fifty miles from Montevideo to Sombreado was a significant undertaking. It began at dawn, conventionally enough at Montevideo's British-built railway terminus, a vaulted glass and steel affair reminiscent of St Pancras. Keith and Aurora, together with Aurora's parents, José-Luis and Florentina, and a carefully bundled Michael, boarded a first-class carriage built in Dagenham, arranged their considerable baggage on the Wilton carpet, and watched through the window as the engine, a Beyer-Peacock from Coventry, pulled them out into soft morning sunlight upon steel rails forged in Sheffield.

They chugged slowly north-east, at first transiting familiar territory, the Quemadas taking it in turns to point out to Keith the harbourfront, the Botanical Park, then the wealthier districts of the city: Belvedere, Prado, Cerrito, Las Acacias. In no time, however, José-Luis was shaking out his newspaper and Florentina busying herself with refreshments as the graceful avenues and leafy boulevards gave way to humbler *barrios*, with much smaller, cramped dwellings of coarse brick, wood and tin. And then in no time more, these in turn were replaced by a chaos of slums, acre upon acre of low huts, constructed, as far as a shocked Keith could see, of little but mud, straw and rubbish. Dogs scavenged at mountains of refuse. Naked, dark-skinned children ran eagerly to the trackside, hands extended. Their parents, black-haired Indians, coffee-coloured mulattos, Negro Africans, barely looked up. Squatting in the dirt, smoking clay pipes or sucking maté tea from a gourd, the men often bare to the waist, the women in simple thread-bare shifts, observed their passing without interest.

'I'd heard,' Keith said. 'In Buenos Aires, the "*villas mise-rias*". But here, I had no idea. Who are these people?'

Aurora barely glanced up. 'Poor from the interior, mestizos, immigrants without papers, criminals, beggars. I wish they'd all go away, our country is not equipped to manage them.'

'Mestizo?'

She shifted on her seat. 'People from the interior, you know, descendants of the original European settlers, who became interbred with the native Indians.'

Only slowly, as the train ground on towards the edges of the great plain, did the slums thin. 'I didn't know there were any native Indians,' Keith murmured.

The railway carried them as far as Treinta Y Tres, seventy miles south of Melo. There the line ended, abruptly, in a sheep pen. It had taken all day, and in that time the view from the carriage window had barely changed. The interior of Uruguay, it was evident to Keith, consisted of one vast grassy plain. The pampas, it was called, that much he knew. Sometimes it rolled slightly, like a gentle pale-green ocean, sometimes not, board-flat from horizon to wide horizon. Treeless, largely featureless, he'd gaze out at it, mesmerised by its tranquil beauty, watching cloud shadows sail slowly across it, like ships on a sea. Then he would return to his book. Half an hour later he'd look out again and the view was unchanged, like an illusion, as if, despite the rocking and clanging, the train had scarcely moved. There were few signs of habitation, the occasional cluster of huts at the track-side, or a clump of distant trees marking the site of a lone estancia. From time to time during the day the train slowed, a motley collection of roughly rendered houses would hove into view, and they would puff into rickety stations with names like Mariscala, Piraraja or Villa Sara.

At Treinta Y Tres they boarded the *diligencia*, an errati-cally timetabled horse-drawn coach, and set off northwards once more. By now the roads were little more than rutted dirt tracks, the motion, after the soporific rocking of the train, rough and uncomfortable. Brick-red soil dust kicked from the horses' hooves settled on them in a fine film. Aurora, slumped into a corner, sank into stupor, fanning herself feebly, her eyelids half-closed. José-Luis, too, seemed ill at ease, erect and impatient at the window. Only Florentina appeared interested, watching, a tiny half-smile on her lips as the carriage carried her closer to the land of her birth. Florentina and her grandson, that is. Michael lay on his back in his carrying basket, indifferent to the fierce rocking of the carriage. His eyes were open, his expression calm yet alert. As though waiting.

By the time they arrived, weary and dishevelled, it was well past midnight. The house was in darkness, just a single lamp burning at a side window. Evidently their party was not expected, Keith concluded, or else people went to bed very early in the country. After a minute, however, a woman appeared at the door and immediately began helping with the bags. There followed a brief shadowy interlude of hushed conversations in dark corridors smelling of wood polish, hastily eaten snacks of cold mutton and rough wine, and moonlit visits to the washroom at the back. Within half an hour everyone had retired to bed and silence descended on the house once more.

They stayed three days. During that time, Keith met Sombreado's revered incumbent, Don Adrián, just once. A brief, formal ushering into a dusty, book-lined study, followed by an even briefer and completely incomprehensible grunted conversation with a toothless ancient wearing baggy, pyjama-like trousers – known as *chiripá* – secured by a belt bearing the most lethal looking knife he'd ever seen. Then, before he knew it, an equally hasty ushered withdrawal.

Apart from the man himself, there was Florentina's sister, Gertrudis, who seemed to hover and dart everywhere, like a distracted fly, observing all but saying little. Finally there were the Luengas, a family of local retainers who took care of the house, the old man, the buildings and the general management of the estancia. They lived in a little single-storey cottage to one side of the main house. They had two children, one a teenage boy called Antonio, who, as well as assisting with general domestic chores, spent much time out with the gauchos managing the stock on the plain. Their second child was a baby daughter, Maria, just a few weeks older than Michael.

'He has a weak chest, you see, Francesca,' Aurora explained to the Luenga woman on the morning of their departure. A pink-faced Michael, trussed up in several silk-edged blankets, lay, mummy-like, in Aurora's arms. They were standing in bright sunlight outside the entrance to the Luengas' cottage. Through its low doorway Keith could see a dim, poorly furnished room with a dirt floor.

'Si, Señora,' the woman replied, her dark eyes shifting from Aurora to Keith and back. Her own baby, naked save for a thin vest, rested on her shoulder.

'And the doctors say, what with the noxious city air, and the cholera epidemic and everything, that the best thing for him would be to spend some time in the country.'

'Si, Señora.'

'So, well, that is what we propose. Would that be all right?'

'Si, Señora.'

'But you're not seriously thinking of leaving him here!' Keith sputtered, a few minutes later. Carles, the woman's husband, was loading their baggage on to a wagon.

'Of course, dearest, that was the whole point in coming. Didn't you realise?'

'No! I thought it was just for a few days, to see if the change in air had any benefit.'

'And it has! Already he breathes more freely. And his colour is so much improved, didn't you see?'

'No, well, yes, I suppose so . . . But, but for how long?'

'Not long. And we shall come to visit him often. Then, as soon as he is bigger and stronger, we will bring him home with us to Montevideo.' Aurora leaned up and kissed his cheek. 'It is the best possible arrangement, I am quite certain of that.'

The Luengas watched their departure in silence, the new arrival lying quietly in its expensive American basket at their feet. As the dust settled on the track, Carles glanced down at Michael, sniffed disdainfully and went back to the stables. Francesca waited until he was gone, then carefully lifting the baby from its cot, began freeing it from its wrapping of blankets.

Chapter 3

With neither question nor protest, as though it was fore-gone, the Luengas took him in. They called him Miguelito, little Michael, absorbed him into their family, and continued with their life as before.

They were honest, straightforward, hardworking country people. Carles Luenga, born in Melo, had been brought up to the life of the gaucho, living weeks at a time out on the pampas among the shorthorn and white-faced Herefords upon which Uruguay's fragile economy depended so utterly. He'd learned from boyhood how to be tough, independent and resourceful. How to locate himself at night by tasting the dew-laden grass, judge weather by the flight of a bird, read the circling drift of the stars. How to smell an approaching *pampero* – the short violent storm of the pampas – or spot a *cuervo* – carrion crow – at ten miles. Or track a lost calf, or the edible *mulita* armadillo, or a sheep thief. Stripped to nothing but his felt hat, he'd learned the hazardous thrill of swimming a hundred head of cattle across a river in spate. He'd learned how to wrestle a shorthorn to the ground, subsist solely upon meat and maté, win fights and tell stories, and to make his home on the desolate plains of his forefathers.

As with his forebears, Carles wore the simple garb of the gaucho: hat, hide boots, cotton blouse, poncho, *pañuelo* scarf and the *chiripá*. Secured about his waist, the broad, studded-leather belt, or *cinto*, with its *facón* – the long, sheathed blade of the plainsman – tucked in at his back. He learned the importance of the *facón*, how to take care of it, to sharpen and clean it, and to use it for everything from slitting a sheep's throat for the table, to hacking a path through razor-thorned undergrowth. From chopping wood for a campfire, to protecting himself from the brigands that still wandered the northern pampas.

He learned the legendary gaucho horsemanship. How to capture, rope and break a wiry criollo mustang. To ride it using only the thighs, knees and feet, leaving the hands free to aim a musket, or swing the *boleadores* – weighted hide balls on lengths of thong – or simply to roll a corn-husk cigarette. How to use a horse's instincts as an extension of his own. How, without even realising it, to fuse with the animal, to be not simply an unwelcome appendage on its back, but part of it, a single perfectly evolved plains creature. The horse-man.

All this he learned, and continued to learn. The pampas

lore of generations. Carles, who had begun acquiring it at the knee of his own father, was now passing it, by example, instruction and simple absorption, to his own son Antonio. Furthermore, he saw no reason, in the fullness of time, why it should not also be passed to the fair-haired, green-eyed cuckoo chick that the boss's unruly granddaughter had deposited in their midst.

But all in good time, for during the first years Michael belonged to Francesca. Right from that very first day, when she had watched his parents clatter away down the track from the house, liberated him from his stifling cocoon of blankets, and placed him to her breast, she had adopted him as her own. Having Michael was not particularly burdensome; instead of one baby to attend to, she simply had two, like twins, although as different a pair of twins no one in Cerro Largo had ever seen.

Almost from the start Michael's health problems melted away. It was as though he was born to the wide spaces, the clean air, the day-long sunshine. Soon, he and Maria were crawling among the maize stalks and bean pods of the estancia's rough vegetable patch, the soil under their fingertips, pungent grass and animal smells in their nostrils, the rasp of insects and the coarse calls of the cattle-hands in their ears. Sombreado became their universe. Their earliest memories were forged within its protective shadow, their first hesitant steps through the dappled shade and drifting blossoms of its peach orchard. In time they were venturing further, tottering down to explore its dusty pens, or the ramshackle huts and barns that encircled its perimeter. At night, oblivious to the bats dangling overhead, they slept, secure and content, side by side on a straw-filled palliasse on the floor of the Luengas' cottage.

They grew, they thrived. Life was out of doors. If the rain fell heavily, or a *pampero* sprang up, or an unseasonably cold winter wind blew in from the south, they might amuse themselves playing up on the big house's covered wooden veranda, or in one of the sheds, among the spiders' webs and roosting hens. More often, however, they would ride out passing bad weather huddling under a parked cart, or chanting tunelessly beneath the sheltering branches of a *timbó* – known, as they came to learn, as the black-man's-ear tree, because of the shape of its leaves.

As they grew, so they learned. Soon they were beginning to talk. The Luengas spoke no English. Michael, therefore, like Maria, passed from infancy into childhood with Spanish as his native tongue. And there was nothing mannered or Castilian about the dialect; this was the rough, guttural Spanish of the borderlands. To further confuse family and visitors, the two children developed their own language, a garbled short form, featuring added clicks and trills, hand gestures and grunts.

They were literally inseparable. Together from the moment they awoke, usually within an instant of each other, through the endless hours of adventure and discovery, and on until the long day waned and, arms entwined, they drifted back into slumber once more. It was a dream-like idyll, their lives, for the most part, carefree oceans of invention and play dotted with islands of incident. Once in a while, Francesca would plant them down side by side in the yard behind the cottage and, with the laundry snapping on the line above their heads, offer them meaningless instruction, drawing shapes in the dirt with a stick, or reciting little verses and songs. Sometimes Antonio would take them for a ride in the cart. Lifting them, rigid with excitement, up into the back, and trotting out through Sombreado's gates and away along the dirt track for a few miles.

And then occasionally Carles would search them out, reach down with his huge brown hands, hoist them both up on to the front of his horse and canter them out on to the plains. There to gaze out at a sea of lowing cattle, or splash along a stream bed, or ascend one of the low craggy hills punctuating the rolling flatness, to stare back along his pointing arm, speechless with wonder, at the tiny island of distant trees that was their home.

Sometimes a visitor came. There was the *organillero*. He arrived every few months, puffing up the track, bent beneath the weight of a box organ strapped to his back. With much showmanship and energetic gesticulating, he erected his box upon a trestle, opened it, and began cranking a handle. Startled parakeets squawked heavenwards from the poplars as magical music filled the air above Sombreado. Francesca would take the children by the hand and dance them in circles. The front door of the big house would open and great-aunt Gertrudis would venture shyly on to the veranda. Even Don Adrián himself would stump outside, beating time in the air with his stick. Once, Carles was at home when the *organillero* came. Face solemn, he dropped the tack he was working and strode over. Plucking the *pañuelo* from his neck, he took his wife's hand with it, and with the other stiff on his hip, began to dance with her, Michael and Maria clapping with delight.

There were others, their visits marking the seasons. Knife grinders, saddle repairers, *payador* minstrels, potion sellers, or simply tramps and beggars. These last were treated respectfully. One in particular visited biennially. He was tall and dignified of bearing, with a long beard and wispy grey hair hanging from beneath an ancient stovepipe hat. Straw was stuffed into his clothing – for insulation and comfort when sleeping at night, the children were informed. Tufts of it overflowed from his cuffs and boot-tops so that he exactly resembled a walking scarecrow. Upon arrival he would remove the stovepipe hat, clear his throat, and declare his presence with a lengthy monologue, proudly recounting in a loud, clear voice the history of his life thus far. Once again the elders of the big house would appear on the veranda, Gertrudis standing, head bowed, as though in church, Don Adrián, his eyes lifting to the distant horizon, listening intently, nodding in recognition of a past cause served, battle fought or wrong righted.

Having concluded his dissertation, which took several minutes, the man replaced his hat and, once loaded with comestibles – food, tobacco and dried yerba leaves for his maté – was courteously thanked for his call, and proceeded on his way.

Then there were the visits by the Quemadas. They came

every couple of months or so. In the antipodean winter months of June, July and August, when travelling in the interior could be difficult, it might be ten or twelve weeks between an appearance. Nobody minded. In the summer, however, stays were more frequent, and protracted, and might include several members of the clan, plus house-guests. During these periods Sombreado, normally an oasis of calm, would resound with unfamiliar city accents, and raucous parties held nightly for friends, relatives and other wealthy landowners of the district. The Luengas would be worked off their feet, Carles growing uncharacteristically subservient and withdrawn, Francesca also changing: unspeaking, tense, and impatient with the children.

These were unsettling interludes in other ways for Michael and Maria. Like it or not, Michael was expected to spend time with his parents when they came. They would arrive, strangers from another planet with their fine clothes and exotic-smelling hair. Screaming with delight, her hands clapped to her cheeks, Aurora would sweep Michael into a bosomy clinch, peppering him with kisses and whirling him in circles until he felt sick. 'Angel!' she would cry. 'My beautiful, beautiful angel!' Keith, less demonstrative, would shake his hand. But then, winking conspiratorially, gift-wrapped boxes would begin to materialise from his baggage. Within them, wondrous toys that moved when you wound them. Soldiers banging drums, a monkey swinging on a stick, a clown in a box. Then, to Francesca's tight-lipped smiles and Maria's visible dismay, Michael would be removed from them and led into the big house for tea and a sugary *bizcocho*, or lifted into the gig for an excursion into Melo, or dressed in a sailor's uniform to be paraded before friends and relations.

Michael bore it all with bemused fortitude, although as he grew older, he began resisting certain aspects of the rite. Once, when he was about four, he awoke to find himself in the alien splendour of the big house, in a real child's bed. By himself. The bed was uncomfortably hot, the room dark, silent and forbidding. Beyond its door he could hear only the resonant tocking of Sombreado's grandfather clock, like the malevolent pacing of a hungry giant. No other life, no breathing, no scurrying insects, no flutter of roosting birds, only an unearthly stillness. Noiselessly, he threw back the heavy covers, fumbling his way to the window. In seconds he was scampering across the moonlit yard to the Luengas' cottage. If they heard him creeping through the open doorway to slip beneath his blanket beside Maria, they never let on, only expressing mild surprise in the morning. And the mornings thereafter.

Then, as suddenly as they began, the visits would be over, the carriage wheels went rattling away down the track, and peace settled over Sombreado once more like a warm evening. Life quickly resumed as before. As though the visits were nothing but a fevered dream.

But the timeless contentment of the children's lives could not continue unchecked for ever. Inevitably, the question of their education arose. In typical borderland fashion, it was addressed obliquely and variously. One morning, when they were six, Carles laced each child into a pair of stout ankle boots. Hitherto almost always barefoot, they stared down at them in awe, stretching their toes against the confining unfamiliarity of the leather. He then led them, hand in hand, down to the horse paddock where so often they had watched him quell the fearsome beasts that lunged and strained, white-eyed, at the rein. This time, however, there were no rearing stallions, only an ancient brown mare known as Pingo, munching contentedly at the stubby grass, its reins held by Sombreado's equally ancient *peón*, Alberto. They were instructed to wait. A few minutes later they heard the unmistakable approach of a peg leg. It was Don Adrián, in a billowing white chemise, black *chiripá* and with his good leg encased in a knee-length riding boot of the glossiest pearl-buttoned leather. A huge, silver-sheathed *facón* was hooked into the back of his belt, in his hand he carried an ornately inlaid riding crop, or *rebenque*.

As the man, Michael was first. Propelled by Alberto on to Pingo's bare back, he was instructed by Don Adrián to place his hands upon his head, lift his chin, straighten his back and point his toes in the approved gaucho manner. Then he was told to drive the heels of his new boots into the animal's flanks. He did so and immediately fell off. Two hours later, sore and bruised from repeated falls, he was returned, manfully fighting the tears, to solid ground. He ran to the cottage and hid. But the next day training resumed. And the next. By the end of the week he was black and blue. But he was in control. His fear was gone and so was Pingo, replaced by a tough little gelding called Chiquito. With a nod from

Don Adrián, Michael grasped the animal's mane, swung smoothly up on to its back and, with only a single token buck from Chiquito, began trotting him in circles.

That evening he was summoned to the big house. Don Adrián, whom Michael had been permitted to address as 'Tata', was waiting in his study. There was a wooden stand beneath the window. On it rested a hand-tooled child's saddle of the deepest red leather. Laid upon the saddle were three items. A black felt beret, the *boina*, a scaled-down leather *cinto* and, although Michael scarcely dared believe his eyes, a short *facón* in a leather sheath.

'When he goes out to face the world, a man needs two things,' Tata said gruffly, securing the *cinto* about Michael's skinny waist. 'A hat upon his head, and a blade at his back. Never venture beyond safety without them. With them you can go anywhere.'

And so they did. From then on, he and Maria, who as a female had received less intensive tuition, but was a natural horsewoman nonetheless, rode daily. Firstly in the training ring, then in the grassy paddock below it and then, finally, through the iron cattle gate and out on to the plains beyond. They were instructed only to remain in sight of Sombreado, take care to avoid snakes and deteriorating weather, and to return well before dusk.

It was the start of a new chapter of discovery in their lives. On separate ponies when a spare could be found, more often atop Chiquito together, Maria's arms clasped tightly about Michael's waist, the months of their seventh and eighth years slipped by at the gallop, the soft purple mist of the flowering pampas grass flying beneath, the beckoning horizon stretching to infinite ahead, above, the bottomless blue.

It was all part of their education.

As was Seamus Flynn.

The main problem, Keith Villiers had begun increasingly to fret, was his son's grasp of English, or, more precisely, his lack of it. And his numeracy. Not to mention his understanding of the wider world, such as its geography and its history, particularly those of the great British Empire to which, in theory at least, Michael belonged. Hiding in the shade of an *ombú* tree counting incoming plovers was one thing. Riding out with the *troperos* to round up strays, or helping the *peón* fix a wheel on the wagon, all very well. But what did imitating the call of the *hornero* bird, or learning the analgesic properties of the *anacahuita* bush, have to do with the real world?

'It won't do,' he said one day, making a rare stand against Aurora. By now their lives ran along almost completely separate lines, rarely crossing except at odd snatched moments, or on formal occasions. His life was his work at the legation, hers was one long round of social engagements. To discuss Michael's future with her, he'd had virtually to make an appointment.

'Why not? Tata teaches him, a little,' she responded, pulling dresses from a wardrobe. They were in the perfumed disorder of her bedroom at the Pocitos apartment. 'History, I believe, so Mama tells me. And Francesca, she

66

instructs them. Carles too, natural history, estancia management, and so on.'

'But my dearest girl, I'm not talking about bird spotting, or mending a shed roof, or galloping about the place with the gauchos. I'm talking about Latin conjugation and geometry and English literature. As for your grandfather, well, with the greatest possible respect, fascinating though I'm sure his view of world history must surely be, what on earth can he know of Magna Carta, Cromwell or Elizabethan England?'

'He knows a great deal!' Her eyes blazed, then immediately faltered. 'Who is Elizabeth England?'

A fragmentary pang of longing swept over him. To Keith, Aurora's all-too-rare moments of genuinely spontaneous passion were her most endearing. And most beautiful. He retreated diplomatically.

'Forgive me, that was discourteous. It was not my intention to offend.'

'Well. That is quite all right.'

'Dearest? Am I being unreasonable?'

'No,' she conceded, sensing victory. 'Just English.'

'And you Uruguayans love the English, remember?'

A smile appeared, suddenly, like unexpected winter sunshine. She turned to him. 'Yes. We adore them.'

He reached out then, took her hands, drawing her gently to him. For a minute they stood, secured in silent embrace before the open window. Screeching seagulls wheeled overhead. Further off, motes of golden sunlight sparked off the wide waters of the Plata estuary.

'Keith,' she coaxed, at length, plucking at a button of his waistcoat, 'why don't you come out with us tonight? Everyone will be there.'

He sighed. 'Really I cannot, dearest. There's a box due in on the evening ferry from BA. We'll have to open it tonight.'

'Yes. I see. But couldn't your precious box wait?'

'I doubt the British government would approve of that. Perhaps I could join you later. If we get through it all.'

'Of course.' Intimacies over, Aurora drew back, returning her attention to her wardrobe. 'You know, I do understand your concern about Michael. But in a few months he will be able to attend the district *escuela*. Then, when he is a little older, and stronger, he can come to Montevideo, to live with us and attend private school here.'

'Yes. Of course.' Keith hesitated, then choosing his words, pressed his luck. 'But in the meantime could you not perhaps consider indulging my idiotic English insecurities, and allow that he does need some proper tuition. To be going on with. From a qualified teacher.'

'Why not,' she shrugged, closing the meeting. 'We shall hire him one.'

His name was Seamus Flynn.

He arrived at Sombreado by mule cart one baking January afternoon a few weeks later, Michael and Maria observing from a shed as he unloaded his bags and strode up the steps of the house.

'Who's that?' Maria asked, with an unspoken lift of the shoulder. They watched as the front door opened. The man plucked a bowler hat from his head, bowing deeply to Gertrudis.

'Trouble,' Michael replied.

Lessons began the next day. They breakfasted, swept the floor of the cottage, fed the chickens and milked the goat, all as normal. But then, instead of helping the gauchos, or readying the cart for a trip into Melo with Antonio, or simply saddling up Chiquito and galloping out to their grassy hide beneath the distant *ombú* tree, Francesca, in unusually grim mood, grabbed them both by the arms, wiped their faces with a cloth and propelled them towards the big house. There Gertrudis met them at the front door.

An empty bedroom had been cleared as a schoolroom, the furniture stacked against one wall. A pair of small tables stood in the centre of the floor before a blackboard on an easel. Flynn, a short, round-faced man with a broken nose and strange, mat-like red hair, was standing beside it. He wore a threadbare suit too tightly buttoned at the stomach, badly worn but fiercely polished shoes, and an unforgiving expression. He was holding a wooden ruler.

'Right we are!' he barked in an incomprehensible dialect. 'So, yous twos haythen scullywugs are here to be taught the English!'

It was the worst nightmare imaginable. The first problem was Flynn's accent, his entire language, in fact. He could speak Spanish well enough, if he so chose. When addressing Gertrudis, for example, his head respectfully inclined, his bowler hat clasped to his chest. But with the children, he used a coarse and completely unintelligible muddle of

Spanish, thick Dublin English, and something else, possibly Gaelic, all with odd Russian expletives, French bons mots and irrelevant Latin dicta thrown in for good measure. Although they tried, both children found this particularly difficult, especially Maria. Unsurprisingly, therefore, she frequently gave up, her brown eyes drifting longingly to the window and beyond. This incensed Flynn who took an early dislike to her.

The second problem was indeed his temper. This was unpredictable at best, but always at its most lethal in the mornings, when he would pace the floorboards, growling and shaking his head like a sorely baited bear. Or, worse still, slump unspeaking into his chair by the blackboard, his rheumy red eyes switching from one child to the other in undisguised contempt. It was as if he blamed them for something he had become. Or perhaps something he had failed to become.

There was no joy in his teaching, no transmitting of a sense of wonder at discovery, and no pleasure therefore to be found in learning. There were no picture books, no stories, no drawing materials, no music. Only hours each day cooped up in that dusty room with nothing but endless learning by rote, Flynn's bitter diatribes against his accursed bad fortune and the world in general, and the intimidating crack of his ruler on the table. Silently, watchfully, they learned only to hate him.

Their feelings were reciprocated in spades. In fact, the only thing Flynn appeared to despise more than his charges, his job and his accursed bad fortune, was the British. One day, to their surprise, he brought a small globe into the classroom. It was no bigger than a melon.

'Right then, look here, yous twos, this here is us, right here see, Uruguay,' He tapped his ruler on the huge, horn-like continent of South America. 'This,' he then pointed to a tiny pink dot near the top of the globe, 'is Britain, see, way up here. But, now look, this . . .' he gestured at a completely invisible dot beside it '. . . is the gerlorious Republic of Oirland that finally won its centuries-long struggle against the pro-fidious Burt-ish oppressor in the ger-lorious year of Our Lord 1922!'

Indeed any mention of England, the English, Great Britain, or the British Empire, in any context whatever, was prefaced by words such as perfidious, treacherous, deceitful, or worse.

'So you see, Moy-chael, Charles the Forst's profligate extravagances and blatant attempts to enforce episcopacy on the Scottish brethren was, in the end, that lying English pansy's final undoing. His very own people turned on him and chopped his wort-less head from his neck, may his soul rot in hell . . .'

It was one of the less tedious lessons, perhaps, but all too rare. That evening, out at the *ombú*, besides plotting to remove Flynn's own head from his neck, they played out the Irish struggle – Michael, the perfidious British oppressor, repeatedly swinging down from the branches to attack Maria, the plucky but downtrodden Irish oppressee.

Once, late one soporific afternoon, while the flies flew lazy circles through the unmoving air beneath the planked ceiling, Flynn hit Maria. It was so fast no one quite knew how or even if it had happened. He was pacing back and forth before them, as usual. His voice, as sometimes happened, had gradually subsided into a mutter, as though he was lost in thought. This, the children had learned, could go on for minutes until he regained his thread. While they were waiting, Maria moved, perhaps, or made a small sound. In a flash Flynn wheeled round and smashed the ruler down on to her table with a crack like a gunshot. Intentionally or not, it hit the backs of her fingers. She yelped, instinctively jumping to her feet. Michael, too, shocked, started to rise.

'Sit bloody down the pair of yous!' Flynn roared, his face puce with rage.

Glancing hesitantly at each other, they sat as ordered. But a line had been crossed, and the clock started. Major confrontation was inevitable.

They prayed to God for deliverance. They appealed to Carles, pleaded with Francesca, complained to Antonio. At night they commiserated with one another beneath the bed-clothes in hushed whispers. Their eyes round with anguish, they even made silent plea to Gertrudis each morning at the door of the big house. But if anything, Gertrudis, always remote to the point of inaccessibility, was even more distracted than usual.

Because something was going on. At night.

Everything came to a head one rainy autumn morning some months after Flynn's arrival. The night before, the children had been awoken by the sound of baying. Blood-chilling, unearthly, in the darkness it sounded like a wolf howling at the moon, or the crazed whinny of the criollo stallion, its leg shattered from a fall, that Carles had once had to dispatch, opening its neck with his *facón*. Startled, they made to rise, but were hushed to stillness by the squat shadow of Francesca watching from the doorway. Carles was already outside, they could hear his voice, low and urgent. And other voices, the murmuring of gauchos, the *peón* stumbling from his stable. In a few moments the howling began to subside, then stopped. But not before a final, tormented, one-word cry split the still night air in two.

'Gurr–tru–diss!'

The following morning they reported for lessons as usual. Flynn was slumped in his chair, eyes glazed. He looked unusually rumpled, even for him, as though he had been there for hours. His clothes were dishevelled and stained at the front. His hair, the strange red mat that had always looked so unnatural, was completely askew on his head. His breathing was thick and laboured. Warily, they took their places.

Nothing happened. For twenty minutes they sat in silence, waiting. If Flynn noticed them, he gave no sign, just stared wordlessly ahead through hooded lids. Michael and Maria began to look at one another. Smiles were exchanged. Then a snigger. At that Flynn stirred at last, as though from a trance.

'Laughing.' His voice was a gravelly whisper. 'So. Which one of yous wort-less haythen shites is laughing?' Then, without waiting, he hauled himself from his chair, reached out a grimy fist and yanked Maria, by the hair, to her feet.

Everything happened very quickly. Maria, her face contorted in pain, kicked out at Flynn's leg. Flynn yelped, cursed, his grip only tightening. Maria screamed. But by then Michael, leaping from his desk, was at her side, half crouching, arms spread wide. As though herding a wayward hen. Except that in one hand he held the short-bladed *cuchilla* that Tata had given him.

'Let her go.'

'Well, now!' Flynn's eyebrows raised in amusement. His wig had slipped almost to his ear. 'What have we here?' He shook his fist slightly, so that Maria's head wobbled like a puppet's.

'Let her go!'

The door crashed open. Don Adrián stumped in, an enormous flintlock musket beneath one arm.

'Release her. Now. So that I can kill you.'

Flynn froze, gaping in disbelief. 'Jaysus!' Maria's long hair slipped from his grasp, Michael grabbed her arm, pulling her away.

'Señor, I—'

'Silence! You have brought dishonour to this house and to my daughter. You have shown disrespect to me and betrayed the trust my family bestowed upon you. Three men I have killed with this *canón* for much less. You will leave now. If I ever hear of your whereabouts, anywhere, I will find you, and you will be the fourth.'

Had they but known what was to follow, Michael and Maria might have made even more of their joyous release from the tyranny of the classroom. As it was they made much of it. Flynn's name was never mentioned again, and they embraced their regained freedom like ecstatic spring lambs. Within days the familiar pattern and rhythm of life at Sombreado resumed as if the whole episode had been nothing more than a collective bad dream. But winds of change were blowing back in Montevideo as a situation developed between Michael's parents. Until it could be resolved, Keith and Aurora elected to keep it to themselves. In the meantime, and in any case preoccupied with these other matters, the issue of their son's education was shelved.

But not by Tata. An interval after Flynn's dismissal, the children, to their dismay, were once more summoned to the converted bedroom in the big house. The blackboard had gone, but the two little desks, the oppressive mustiness and the dark memories remained. Terrified that the door would open and the hated Irishman return, they waited in trepidation. But it was Tata, not Flynn, who stumped through the door. He sat himself down in Flynn's chair, poured boiling water from a jug on to the green sludge at the bottom of his maté gourd, sucked noisily through its silver *bombilla*, or straw, then, with a satisfied smack of the lips, turned his grey eyes to the ceiling and began his history of everything.

'At the beginning, the very first people did not live in Uruguay, they came from far away on the other side of the world. They lived in dark caves and spoke in grunts. They wore no clothes and hunted only with sticks and stones. There was no fire, much darkness, and life was hard. But many among them were strong and questioning, and anxious to search out our land. These were the wanderers. Soon, some began the long walk across the world to search out our land. This took them a thousand thousand years. They travelled north from the great continent called Asia, where God spawned mankind, up to the roof of the world where there is nothing but snow and ice, and down the other side to the wasteland that is the great northern provinces. The journey was long and difficult. Then they began to cross down through the land that is the continent of North America. Some of the wanderers found mountains and rivers and fertile pasture on their journey and settled at these places. These were the forefathers of the great Indian tribes of North America. But our forefathers were anxious to reach our land and so continued their journey. This took them another thousand thousand years. Eventually they reached this beautiful place. A few, unable to discontinue their wandering lives, travelled on until they reached the floor of the world, where there is nothing but snow and ice. But many, enchanted with the place they had found at last, settled here. These were our Indian forefathers. They were the very first people to live on the pampas.'

A magical quiet had descended over the room. Outside, a flurry of clucking as chickens squabbled in the yard. Spellbound, the children waited while Tata replenished his maté, prodded it with his *bombilla* and sucked anew.

'There were two tribes,' he went on, 'the Charrúa and the Guaraní. They wore only small cloths made from skin to conceal their modesty, and lived in huts made from mud and straw. The Charrúa were bold and fearless. They were hunters and warriors, travelling widely across our land. They learned to capture and ride the first wild horses of the plains, and they learned to make the first *boleadores*, and hunt the guanaco and the rhea bird. The Guaraní were less travelled and more peaceable. They were gatherers and cultivators, tilling the soil to grow maize, cassava and sweet potato.'

'You!' Suddenly he was pointing, his steel eyes boring into Michael's. 'You, Miguelito, are Charrúa! You are the grandson of my daughter, Florentina, and therefore a Rapoza. The Rapozas are descendants of the great Charrúa warriors of the olden times. Rapozas fear no man!'

Still the eyes held his. Michael hesitated. 'What about Maria?'

'Pah!' A dismissive flick of the wrist. Then, seeing the concern on their faces, he cleared his throat noisily, softening his expression. 'Well, clearly, you see, Maria is Guaraní. She is quiet and sensible and peaceable. Just like my beloved Matilde, may the Lord keep her. These are admirable qualities for a woman. And a wife.' He leaned forward, resting his arm on the knee of his peg leg, his weathered face crinkling into a mischievous smile. 'The men of the Charrúa. When they reached marrying age, they would visit the camps of the Guaraní, hiding in the long grass until they spied a beautiful girl they wished to marry. Then they would spring from the ground, seize her and carry her away to the camp of the Charrúa. After one cycle of the moon she was permitted, if she wished, to return to her Guaraní brethren unharmed. Do you know what?' He stared questioningly from one to the other. They exchanged glances, then shook their heads.

'They never did. They always chose to stay. And so they married, and their children's children became the fore-fathers of the first true gauchos.'

That evening, beneath the spreading limbs and glossy leaves of the *ombú* tree, their playing took a new turn. With Chiquito safely tethered, they stripped to their simple linen underwear. Then Michael would set off far into the long grass, while Maria scraped seed furrows into the earth, or squatted, tending an imaginary hearth. After a while she would hear rustling behind her which, despite an unaccustomed quickening of her heart, she tactfully ignored. Then, with a neanderthal roar, Michael would leap upon her. A tussle would ensue, the two of them rolling back and forth, first one on top, then the other. Eventually Maria would obligingly concede defeat, allowing Michael, still snorting breathlessly, to hoist her awkwardly on to his thighs and carry her, piggy-back, away to his waiting tribe. They were eight years old.

The end came a little while later. On the same day that Sombreado was nearly destroyed. Keith Villiers had jour-neyed up to visit his son beneath heavy, sultry skies that seemed to lower with every passing mile. He came alone. It was three months since he had last seen Michael, and the change in him was startling. No longer was this the spare body and shy bearing of a little boy. An aspiring youth, lean and taut, now stood in the airless heat before him. He was tall for his years, and still growing fast. His face, framed as ever by its straw-coloured hair, had lost its child-like roundness, was tanned and angular, with a slender nose and firm chin. His arms were brown and wiry, his legs sturdy.

'Would you like to come back with me?'

'Where?'

'To see your mother, and to see Montevideo. It is where you were born.'

He'd heard speak of it, of course. Many times. Not always in glowing terms either. But in any case it might as well be the moon. 'What is it?'

'It is a big, wonderful city, of tall buildings and wide avenues filled with carriages and omnibuses and motor cars. It has a new tram system, too, built by the British. We could ride on it, if you like.' In fact, the coveted contract, after much behind-the-scenes wrangling, had been awarded, with perverse but unarguable logic, to both the British and the German consortia. Britain's Commercial Society of Montevideo got the streets running east–west, Willi Hochstetler's Compania Transatlantica those running north–south.

Trams, tree-lined avenues wide enough to turn a coach and eight, buildings of stone and glass, five, six storeys tall – Michael tried, but it was unimaginable. Probably worth a viewing, however, he concluded, if only for the motor cars. It would be something to tell Maria. 'All right,' he agreed.

Keith patted his head. They would set out the next day, he said.

Once every five years or so, and for reasons no man could explain, the pampas was invaded by a giant thistle. Normally it grew only in isolated clumps, but in a 'thistle year' the plant went mad, springing up in every direction, spreading, hectare after hectare, as far as the eye could see. With its grey hues and fibrous, wrist-thick stalks sprouting as much as ten feet tall, it transformed the pampas from benign plain to oppressive jungle. The gauchos detested it; the leaves bore needle-sharp spines that tore at their legs as their horses cantered blindly through it. Dismounting to rescue a lost calf plunged them into a disorientating half-world of rustling leaves and jagged barbs. Livestock theft increased dramatically as opportunists took advantage of the impenetrable cover. Sheep became bloated from overgorging the mucusy stems and cows' milk tasted bitter.

There was another reason the plains people grew restive in a thistle year. By November the plants were dying, their hollow stalks lying in great dusty swathes, stick-brittle. Whether kindled spontaneously, accidentally or even in certain cases purposely, fire on the pampas was a perennial hazard. Thistle-year fires were the worst.

Keith was in the big house taking maté with Don Adrián. It was a ceremony he took little pleasure in. Making small talk with Tata was always a laboured affair. As for maté, even after nine years in-country he had failed to develop a taste for the aromatic bitterness of the yerba leaf, and he found the ritual passing of the gourd and noisesome communal sucking distasteful and unhygienic. But a British diplomat refusing an invitation to take maté was unthinkable. With an anticipatory smile pasted on to his lips, he had just accepted the gourd, this one plated in silver and about the size of an ostrich egg, and taken his first tentative draw of the hot liquid through the *bombilla* when Tata sat up straight in his chair suddenly, cocking his head, like an old dog at the cry of distant wildfowl.

'Don Adrián?' Keith enquired, after a moment. 'Señor?'

'*Maldición!*' Tata cursed, hauling himself to his feet. '*Maldición! Incendio!*'

Outside, the courtyard was deserted, the air leaden and unmoving. A cloud of starlings, screeching in alarm, flew by low overhead. With astonishing alacrity, Tata, still cursing furiously, stamped down to the paddock. The horses, restless at the danger, fretted nervously to and fro. Seizing the largest roughly by the mane, and without bothering to saddle it, he dragged himself across its back, swung upright and galloped for the gate. Keith, dumbfounded, watched him go.

'But, Señor, what can I do? Señor!'

'Here!' a shout from behind. A horse cart laden with ropes, canvas tarpaulins and bales was emerging from one of the sheds. Gertrudis, bare armed, was at the reins. 'Hurry!'

Keith ran, clambering up beside her. 'But Michael! And Maria. The children, where are they?'

Gertrudis gestured towards a mist-like cloud about a mile away, then whipped at the reins. The cart lurched forwards. 'They are there.'

In twenty minutes they were drawing near. Clouds of orange smoke twisted high into the sky, the crackling rumble of the fire's consuming progress clearly heard above the horse's hooves. The fire burned in several places at once, along a front roughly half a mile wide. Even to Keith's inexperienced city eyes, from the dense billowing curl of the smoke, the angry cackling roar and the smarting heat on his face, it was out of control. Suddenly they were engulfed in rolling waves of smoke, but, instead of turning away, Gertrudis lashed the terrified horse onward through the stifling twilight, until a wall of flame reared directly ahead, blocking their path. One arm shielding his face, Keith was sure she meant to drive straight through it, but at the last moment she wheeled to one side, turning to traverse the line of flames. Terrified, choking from smoke, he clung grimly on.

Then Gertrudis pulled the cart to a halt, jumped down and strode off into the fog. Keith followed, a handkerchief clutched to his face. Figures emerged, like ghosts, through the veil of tears blinding his eyes. Everyone was there, it seemed, about fifty in all, working in groups. The Luengas, the gauchos, other landowners, their families and their labourers, from Sombreado and neighbouring estancias. Fighting as one for their lives and their livelihoods. A smut-blackened face loomed at him from out of the smoke.

'You!' A brush stick was thrust roughly into his hand. 'Beat! Here, along this line with the others.'

'But, you don't understand, I have to find my son.'

'You will find no one in this. If we are unable to divert the fire's course towards the river, Sombreado is finished. Now, beat!'

He beat. Through the choking smoke and suffocating heat until his back ached and his arms felt like lead. After a while he threw his long-tailed jacket to the ground, continuing in his shirtsleeves and waistcoat. His throat grew so parched he could no longer swallow, his hair was singed, his lips, the skin of his face prickling from the flames. Soon he stopped thinking altogether, stopped feeling; he was beating because that was what he had always done, and there was no other reality than this choking, crackling inferno within which he had always dwelt. His beating became dogged, then furious, a cursing, violent outpouring of long pent-up frustrations. Hot tears flowed unseen and unchecked through the grime of his cheeks.

At one point he caught the thunder of approaching hooves above the burning crackle of grass. Gasping, he turned to see Gertrudis, teeth gritted, at the reins of her cart, towing bails and lengths of heavy tarpaulin through the brush to try and create a flattened break. Later, too, and scarcely able to believe his eyes, he turned again, squinting through the smoke at a scene straight from hell. Freshly slaughtered steers being dragged, their huge carcasses bouncing, by a line of galloping gauchos, Tata at their head, in a similar desperate bid. For a minute it seemed to work, the flames paused, there were feeble cheers from along the line, a moment's respite, a flicker of hope. But the relentless army of fire was only briefly slowed. Soon, replenished and regrouped, it was leaping the break and marching steadfastly onwards once more. Gradually the awful truth dawned. They were losing. Retreating, pace by pace. Sombreado was now less than a quarter of a mile behind their backs.

Suddenly it was growing dark, the sky above Keith an inky blue-grey. It scarcely seemed possible. He had no idea of time, or space, or anything. Only the scorched earth existed, that and his own rasping breaths. Then something struck him on the head. He looked down, a white stone the size of a grape lay at his feet. A moment later another. He stared at them, his fevered mind quite unable to comprehend. Suddenly the ground was covered with bouncing white pebbles. He stared on, ludicrously, still absently beating at the ground. Someone was shouting, hysterically, nearby.

'*Pampero! Pampero!*'

Then, in an instant, the *pampero* broke. A sudden draught of icy wind on his neck, a swirl of falling white pebbles, a deep concussive rumble overhead. Then the black sky opened, and rains, falling water of a ferocity quite beyond his experience or imagination, flowed to the ground as though through a rent in the heavens.

Later he stumbled through the downpour along the black mud of the fire line. The smoke was dissipating at last, here and there beaters still pounded at dying pockets of flame. After a while, he came across a group of three. They were completely unrecognisable, black from head to toe. One was short, round and stout, as he approached he saw it was a woman. The other two, one either side of her, were shorter yet, and slighter. They were still beating manfully at the dying embers at their feet. As he neared, one of them turned to him. His face, streaked with smuts, breaking into a triumphant smile.

'We did it, Papa! We all did, see? We killed the fire.'

Aurora was pregnant again. Keith explained the implications of this to Michael, over Italian *gelato* on a café terrace overlooking the *rambla* in Montevideo, about a week later. Michael shrugged, his spoon clutched tightly in his fist. His eating habits, Keith had already noted, among other things, would need attention.

'A little brother, or sister, you see. Won't that be nice?'

'Yes, Papa,' Michael agreed, wondering idly what it had to do with him. Down on the *rambla* people walked arm in arm beside the bay. The women wore long dresses and twirled parasols on their shoulders, the men had long tail coats and smoked cigars. Further along, others, much more poorly dressed, some without shoes or shirts, crowded the long breakwater, hopefully trailing fishing lines into the silty waters.

'So we'll all be a family again. The four of us together.'

'Yes, Papa.' Michael wiped his finger around the glass. Still he didn't register.

'And there's something else. Guess what? We're all going home.'

'Sombreado!' He hadn't thought about it much, except at night, a great deal had happened. But now that he did, it was with a warm glow deep inside. Sombreado, resting, squat, solid and forever beneath the shade of its sentinel-like poplars. Carles talking softly to a new stallion while he trotted it, straight-backed, around the training ring. Francesca singing as she made her delicious *dulce de leche*. Humming birds at the jacaranda tree, the smell of the pampas after rain, Tata's history lessons. Chiquito, snorting as he galloped full tilt across the oceans of grass. Playing beneath the *ombú* tree with Maria, her head cocked quizzically, like a bird's, when he spoke. How she would be amazed at all he had to tell her.

'Sombreado? No, not Sombreado, silly! I mean home. Our real home. We're all going home to England.'

Chapter 4

There was a period of nothing. Nothing at all except an empty black stillness. I don't know how long it went on for, but it seemed a fair while. Not that I was counting. Or bothered particularly.

Then, suddenly, out of nowhere, there came an excruciating pain in my head, and a terrible overwhelming fear, that rushed at me from out of the blackness like a train out of a tunnel. I remember panicking, thrashing about madly like a hooked carp. The next thing I knew was spluttering to the surface. Being hauled there, in fact, somewhat ignominiously, by the hair.

By Michael. Although I didn't realise it then. At first I was completely insensible. Shocked, concussed, half-drowned, all I could do was loll about in the lapping waves, gasping and retching. Also idly marvelling, I remember, my face turned to the heavens, at the astonishing clarity of the stars. I was not aware of the cold, not at that stage. I recall tasting blood; it seemed to be pouring from my nose. And oil, of course, the familiar acrid stench of it was everywhere. So often had I smelt it on the bodies of victims in the past. Now I was one, although oblivious to it. Oblivious to pretty much everything in fact, and it was to be quite a while longer before the full reality of the situation really began to sink in.

For the full reality of the situation was that the five of us were swimming about, in our clothes, in a freezing North Atlantic Ocean full of dead bodies and debris, in the middle of the night in January. The full reality of the situation was that, if we didn't get out of that water within ten minutes or so, we never would, and our bodies would join the hundreds, possibly thousands, of others that drifted the oceans for days, weeks or even months until our clothes rotted, the flesh was gone from our bones and our final wretched remains could sink at last from ugly view.

The first voice I became aware of was that of Albert Giddings, the young button-eyed HO who'd looked so terrified when we were preparing to launch *Daisy*'s dinghy. It took a while to register what or who it was – it was indistinct, quite a way off. And inhuman. Horrible, blood-curdling. More like the shrill cries of a dying seabird than the shouts of a full-grown man. He was clearly hysterical. He was screaming for his ship.

'*Daisy!* Where's my *Daisy*? She's got to come and find us. *Daisy!*'

Ironically it was probably Giddings' hysterics that saved us. Although we were only twenty or thirty yards apart, the chances of us locating one another or, more importantly, the remains of the whaler, in what little time was left to us, were minute. Fortunately for us, Giddings' screams, although terrifying, carried clear and loud. They were also completely unignorable.

'*Daisy*, for God's sake help us! *Daisy!* Where is she? *Daisy!*'

'Why don't you put a bloody sock in it, you idiot. She's gone!' The unmistakable tones of Able Seaman Frank Tuker, drifting from out of the darkness somewhere over to my left. Next I heard splashing behind me. Villiers swam by, kicking hard.

'Tuker! Are you there? Tuker! Head towards Giddings. You too, Stephen, come on, let's go!'

It is astonishing how quickly you can lose the will to live. Lassitude, brought on by shock and hypothermia from the extreme cold, was already setting in. Summoning the energy just to lift my arms and kick my feet a bit required the most monumental effort. I honestly felt like saying, sorry, too tired, can't be bothered. You go, I'll stay here.

But Villiers wasn't having any of that. 'Stephen, come on! Swim! They're just over here.' He grabbed me by the collar of my waterlogged duffel coat, urging me forward. In doing so he saved my life for the second time in five minutes. Reluctantly, a little resentfully, I did as he insisted.

We swam. Halfway, my hand reached out and brushed something heavy, cold and smooth. It was the bare skin of someone's back. I started in panic.

'Jesus, Michael! Look, I've found someone!'

'Where?' He stopped, trod water. As we watched, our gasps misting the air at our heads, the man rolled slowly over, so that the sheet-white face, the open mouth, the staring eyes, were looking directly at us. He was completely dead, of course, and completely naked. And something else. He was just a torso, just a top half. Everything below the waist was gone. His entrails hung in coils, trailing in the water behind him like the tentacles of a jellyfish.

'Who is it?' Villiers was aghast, but more grief-stricken than shocked.

'I don't know. One of the stokers I think.' I did know. It was Ponting. 'Do you think any of them survived?'

Villiers said nothing, just rolled over and struck out once more.

Within five minutes we were all together. Giddings, whose screaming had mercifully subsided to a whimper, was clinging to the outside of the whaler. She was right way up, but completely sunk, just two or three inches showing above the slopping waves. Harrison, the signalman, was round the opposite side, also holding on. He was barely with it, shaking with cold and very pale. Just staring. As we arrived, Tuker came splashing up, cursing roundly. Villiers called out to him to grab the gunwale too. But without waiting, Tuker hauled himself up on to the whaler's transom, at the stern. Immediately it sank from view, depositing him back into the water.

'Wait! Tuker, wait, you'll sink her!'

'Bollocks. I'm getting out of this.' He tried again, but his weight just pushed the whaler right under, also tipping it to one side so that Giddings lost his grip. Immediately he began screaming again. I, too, suddenly found my voice.

'Tuker, let go, you damned fool!'

'Who the hell are you calling a damned fool, Tomlin, you little shit!'

'I am and you are a damned fool. If you don't listen to the lieutenant we might as well all be dead.'

'The lieutenant? Christ, it's because of the poxy bloody lieutenant that we're in this bloody mess!'

'It's because of the lieutenant that we're alive.' It was Harrison, his voice little more than a shuddered whisper. 'We're the only ones who are.'

That stopped him. Giddings too. Silence descended. Now the reality of the situation was beginning to settle in all right.

'Listen,' Michael went on. God knows where he found it in him to stay so rational. 'We have, somehow, to get her baled out. That means getting someone on board to bale. Now, Giddings, you're the lightest. We'll try and hold her steady, while you get in. Giddings?'

'No, I, I can't.'

'Yes you can, and you must.'

'No, I—'

'Giddings!' Tuker exploded from the stern. 'Belay your fucking snivelling, get your arse into this boat and start baling before I come round there and drown you myself!'

It seemed an eternity, but I estimate it probably took the best part of half an hour. It was without doubt the worst half-hour of my life. Suddenly the hitherto forgotten will to live seemed to spark anew, from somewhere deep within, like the final glowing ember in a hearth. That made it worse. Giving up would have been easy, but the fact that if we could just hold on, empty the sea from the boat, and somehow get aboard, might mean life, suddenly made giving up the lesser option.

We got Giddings aboard at the third or fourth attempt. At first he just kept falling out when he was half in, as the waterlogged whaler sagged over sideways with his weight. But finally, propelled from behind by a furious Frank Tuker, he slithered in. Then, having located and untied the baler, a curved, saucepan-like thing with a wooden handle, he began the laborious task of trying to empty her out. But he was too slow. Just as we began to think he was making headway and the boat was rising infinitesimally in the water, a wave would slop aboard and she would sink to the gunwales once more. Soon things were getting desperate. I watched proceedings with growing detachment, my fingers nothing but feeling-less claws on the gunwale, all sensation below my waist gone. My mind began wandering. I found I kept thinking about Ponting, convinced that I too had somehow been cut in two. It felt like it. I had liked Ponting. We had joined *Daisy* on the same day.

'Giddings. Listen to me.' Villiers was talking. I struggled to pay attention. 'Look, I'm afraid this isn't working terribly well. So here's what we'll do.' He might have been organising a picnic in the woods. But the hollowness of his voice betrayed his fatigue, and cold. Even Tuker had fallen silent.

'Move up towards the bows, to lift the stern out of the sea a bit. The rest of us are going to turn her, so that she's stern-on to the waves, then we'll come forward as well, two on either side. When I give the word we will all try to lift her a little. Then you bale. And I want you to do it without stopping, and as fast as ever you can. Do you understand?'

It was astonishing; in minutes we had won. Giddings staggered forward as though in a drunken trance, set his legs apart, seized the baler in both hands and simply went at it like a complete madman. He didn't look up, he didn't pause for breath, he just stood there and hurled water out over the bows, arms flying, like some kind of demented machine. In no time inches of clear freeboard were showing; a few minutes more and Harrison was scrambling on board to help him. Before I knew it, hands were reaching under my arms and pulling me up too.

We finished baling, emptying her right out. We took turns, so that the exercise would restore some warmth and circulation to our deeply chilled bodies. Finally it was done; the baler fell with a clatter into the bilges, and we followed it, slumped, speechless with exhaustion, against one another. Just before I drifted off into a kind of catatonic slumber, I remember tugging at the sodden sleeve of my duffel coat for my waterproof watch, anxious, inexplicably, to know that it was still there. It was one-thirty, just an hour since *Daisy* had blown up.

I had joined her one sunny afternoon the previous May. Although based in Londonderry, she was back at Liverpool for a boiler clean. Corvette boilers needed regular cleaning; they burned the filthiest fuel oil and the water used to make steam produced corrosive deposits which ate into the boiler linings. You had to use only fresh water in the boiler, not salt. In a dire emergency you could use seawater, but you could virtually scrap the boilers afterwards. The ships did have an evaporator for making fresh water from brine. I heard a story once about a corvette that completely ran out of clean boiler water and then its evaporator broke down. The captain had no hesitation in ordering that the entire supply of drinking water go to feed the boilers, and the crew therefore would have to go short. Four days they went without a brew-up. The joys of command.

I walked from the station to the docks. Despite being on the receiving end of some of the worst bombing of the war, Liverpool was still the busiest port in the kingdom and bubbling with life. That afternoon, possibly also because it was the first genuinely summery one of the year, it was teeming. Sailors going on or coming off leave, dockyard workers changing shift, strolling khaki-clad gunners from the anti-aircraft batteries, hurrying shoppers, fagged-out factory workers, lovers-in-arms, mums pushing prams, rampaging children. Even the prostitutes were out and about, taking the air with a cheery ''Allo gorgeous!' before the evening shift got underway.

It was wonderful. I drank it in like a man in from the desert. I was seventeen and a half, straight from two joyless years in the claustrophobic confines of cadet training school at Dartmouth. With my new midshipman's uniform buttoned smartly across my chest, gas-mask case over my shoulder and leather suitcase in my hand, the sense of liberation I experienced, and of purpose, together with a deeper thrill of nervous anticipation, was hugely exciting. I felt like a newly hatching butterfly.

Which was a little odd, as I had no right to. I'd been dragooned into the Senior Service under protest. I'd never felt or demonstrated any natural affinity for things nautical, and I'd only scraped through the cadet exams and passed out from Dartmouth by the skin of my teeth. That and shameless pressure upon the powers-that-be from my father, the lieutenant commander, and my grandfather, the rear-admiral. Family tradition, you see. Like it or not, I was to be the latest in a long line of famous seagoing Tomlins. So the irony was that, despite the buoyancy of my mood that warm afternoon, I'd never wanted be a sailor.

I wanted to be a writer. Of books. Famous, critically admired ones that everyone wanted to read. I wanted to live in a shabby garret in Paris with a waitress called Yvette, writing by day and then staying up all night talking earnest claptrap with other intellectuals in cafés in Montmartre. I wanted to be Auden, Woolf and Hemingway, to win prestigious literary awards and go to the Ritz to accept them, yet all the while remain Tomlin, the famously reclusive Bohemian. I wanted the whole package, in other words, with trimmings. Very badly.

But not that day. It was being in a war that made all the difference. The prospect of suddenly putting all that meaningless training to use, of actually going into action, was powerful medicine. Plus, I reminded myself, as I strode up to the dockyard gates, good writers need to see the world, and experience things like war, and love, and life in general. Joining a ship of His Majesty's Royal Navy would mean experiencing these and more in full measure. I could write as I learned.

I showed my papers to the policeman on the gate. ('Midshipman? Crikey, I didn't know the Navy still had 'em.') He waved towards a hut. '*Daisy*, you say? There's another of your lot in there.' It was Ken Ponting.

We walked along the busy quays together, carefully bypassing mountains of dockyard detritus while searching for our new ship. Huge piles of equipment and stores lay everywhere, stacks of drums, coils of steel hawser, pressure lines, power cables and all the rest of it. It went on for miles. But despite passing a number of ships, including several grey-painted monsters whose sheer sides towered above us like blocks of flats, *Daisy* was nowhere to be seen. Eventually we slogged back to the harbourmaster's office.

'It's right there!' he insisted, jabbing a finger at a plan on the wall. 'You two clods must have walked straight past it.' Chastened, we set off once more.

'First ship?' Ponting asked. I nodded. 'You?'

'No, lad, what do you think these are?' He tapped his petty officer's insignia. 'Six years. I was on destroyers before this.'

Strictly speaking, as an officer I outranked Ponting. 'Lad' was an inappropriate form of address. But I didn't care; he meant no harm, there was none of that lower decks sneering in his manner. Secretly I was grateful he spoke to me at all.

'Oh, yes. I see. So, why corvettes?' I asked.

'Fancied a change. You?'

Fancied taking the first ship I could get, truth be known. Anything to get away from Dartmouth. But I blathered on about wanting to start my career at the coalface, working my way up through the fleet and all the rest of it. Ponting stopped me.

'Blimey! What the hell—'

We were walking towards the head of a long quay. He stopped, staring ahead. I couldn't see what he was looking at. Then I did. A mast. That was it, nothing else, just the top of a twig-like mast, sticking up at the end of the quay.

'I don't bloody believe it.' We walked forward until we reached the edge, looked down. Ponting then articulated the thoughts of both of us by hawking meatily on to the quayside.

'What the bloody hell is that scabby little tub.'

That first evening we took the scabby little tub to sea.

It was just a short hop, up the Irish Sea and round into Londonderry. *Daisy* was late, Skipper Deeds anxious to make up time. I'd barely got on board, had a quick tour and been shown to the three feet of space allocated to me in one of the sub-lieutenant's cabins when there was the shrill ringing of bells, much shouting and running of feet overhead, and a vibrating below as *Daisy*'s engine came to life. Still in my best rig, I left the cabin and ran on deck, charging to and fro like a headless chicken until I found the companionway ladder leading to the bridge.

It was another world up there. Calm, ordered, but very

busy. There were half a dozen people there, two officers, a signalman, a bridge messenger and Deeds. He was centre stage, issuing orders, bending to voice-pipes, orchestrating, exactly like a conductor, the ritual performance that was the releasing of a Navy ship from the dockside. Nobody seemed the slightest bit interested in *Daisy*'s new midshipman.

'Special sea-duty men closed up, sir.' A voice from one of the pipes.

'Very good.'

'Main engine rung on, sir.'

'Very good. Single up!'

A shouted reply from the bows. 'Single up, sir!'

'Yeoman of signals reports we are cleared to proceed, sir.' This from the officer of the watch, a round-faced sub-lieutenant called Martin Brown.

'Very good. Stand by everyone.' A pause. Deeds takes one last look around, double-checking all is set and the dock free of moving traffic. 'Right. Here we go. Starboard ten, Coxswain. Engine slow ahead, let go for'ard!'

A flurry of activity forward as the bow party recovers the mooring lines. A frothing at *Daisy*'s stern as her propeller bites filthy water, then the stern lines are released and slowly she inches her way forward, away from the quay and out towards the middle of the dock. I watch, entranced, as we turn. I am actually going to sea. *Daisy*, Albert Dock, the whole of Liverpool, is bathed suddenly in golden light as the sun sinking over Wallasey peeks from behind rose-coloured clouds.

'Leaving us already, lad?' It was Deeds. He was looking at

me, patting pockets for matches. An unlit cigarette waggled in his lips.

'What? Oh, um, sorry, sir.' I sprang awkwardly to attention, throwing my best salute. 'Midshipman Tomlin, sir. Reporting for duty. Sir!'

He lit up, regarding me with a sort of what-the-hell-have-they-sent-me-now expression. I was still wearing my number one rig and, for some absurd reason, I realised my suitcase was still clutched in my hand.

'Little bit overdressed for sea duty aren't we, Mid?' Amused glances were being exchanged around the bridge. I felt like jumping over the side.

Then, mercifully, a ghost of a twinkle appeared in his eyes. 'Go on below, son. Get yourself changed and sorted out, then come up and find us when you're ready. Oh, and there's no need to bring your suitcase with you – we'll be staying aboard for dinner.'

The remaining hours of darkness were a living hell. We passed them huddled, shuddering with cold, in the bottom of the whaler, trying to escape the wind which, although not strong, still cut through our sodden clothes like a knife. At some point it began sleeting, nothing Himalayan but enough to complete our misery. The hours crawled wretchedly by. Little happened except that we grew colder. Once in a while, one of us would stir, painfully stretching frozen limbs to raise a head above the gunwale, peering into the swirling darkness in the hope of spotting a rescue ship, or another whaler, or any other sign of life.

But there were none, nor would there be. We all knew the drill. The convoy came first and that was that. Thirty miles away or more already, and steaming steadily further from us with every passing hour, *Vehement* and the remaining three escorting corvettes would not, could not, abandon their charges to search for us. Certainly not while it was still dark and the U-boat threat remained. Our only hope, and it was a slender one, was that if they got through the night without losing too many more ships, and if, once dawn broke, *Vehement* concluded that the U-boats were gone, her commanding officer might just risk instructing a corvette to turn round, and retrace the night's course for a few hours, in the hope of finding a handful of survivors from the night's carnage. On the other hand, he might not, and no Admiralty Board of Inquiry would ever condemn him for such. His first and last responsibility was the saving of the convoy, not its victims.

The alternative? The whaler had oars, even a simple mast and sail. It was eight hundred miles to the nearest land. Longer open-boat journeys had been survived. Ernest Shackleton in the South Atlantic. William Bligh cast adrift from the *Bounty*. There were others. But Bligh was in the tropics, and Shackleton had built a canvas deck over the *James Caird*, and also had the means to prepare hot food. Water and basic survival rations were stowed on board both *Daisy*'s whalers. But long before we ever starved to death, or died of thirst, the cold would get us. Simple exposure. Two or three days at most.

Between terrifying interludes of semi-delirium, featuring

exploding ships, repeated drownings, and waking up to find half my body gone, I kept thinking about the lifeboat *Daisy* had found the winter before I joined her. The lookout spotted it late one grey afternoon. It was under sail, jogging spiritedly through the waves as though out for a jolly on the Solent. Deeds hove *Daisy* to and hailed the boat. But it just kept going, an upright figure sitting steadfastly at the helm. *Daisy*'s crew joined in the hail, leaning over the rail, cheering and waving, but all to no avail. 'Leave it,' Deeds said then, and rang for slow ahead. As she pulled away, those at the rail finally saw that the man at the lifeboat's tiller, and the others slumped in the bottom, were all long dead, little more than rag-covered skeletons. They had been out there for weeks.

'Shouldn't we at least give them a decent burial?' Villiers had asked.

'No. I'm hoping a U-boat finds them. Then they can see what this is about.'

Michael. After his superhuman efforts in gathering us all together, and then getting us safely back aboard, he just seemed to collapse inwards upon himself. Wedged into a corner at the stern, his knees hunched up, his head bowed, he hardly spoke the entire night. I was near him. At one point I woke up to find that he was humming softly to himself, or sort of keening. In Spanish. It sounded like children's songs. I believe he was grieving.

Still the hours dragged by, although time long ceased to have any meaning. Then, finally, after an eternity of nothing but creeping numbness, the bone-jarring motion of the boat, and the indolent slap of the waves on her sides, a voice.

'Lieutenant.' It was Harrison.

'Lieutenant, wake up. I think it's getting light.'

Snow-dusted heads stirred, salt-cracked eyes blinked. He was right. Dawn. Not much of one, it must be said, just the faintest perceptible notion of grey where before there had only been black. But it was enough. It meant we had survived the night. It meant, a little perversely, that, if rescue was coming, it would be coming today. It meant hope. It was the best sight imaginable. And the worst.

The view that greeted us as the greyness slowly lifted, was like a scene from Dante. The first thing that struck me was the sheer humbling size and power of the ocean, a factor you don't appreciate quite so well from up on the sturdy deck of your two-hundred-foot ship. That morning the weather was blustery, but nothing special, so the seas were relatively benign. But Atlantic rollers are huge whatever the weather; they process steadily from horizon to horizon like armies of giants on the march. In the troughs, the scale of the thing is not so pronounced, you're in a private little valley between crinkled slopes rising to about head height. Your field of vision is limited in other words, so you can fool yourself. But as each wave passes beneath, and you are lifted to its softly hissing summit, you are suddenly presented with the full uncompromising reality. You are an unnoticeable speck of nothing upon the face of something entirely limitless. Something so vast and monstrous it is powered by the planet itself.

Bobbing about in a fourteen-foot rowing boat in the middle of it teaches you the true meaning of humility. Empty, desolate, awesome. Far better pens than mine have struggled for the right adjectives. I just felt a ghastly clutching dread, certain beyond doubt that we were lost.

The second thing I noticed were the bodies. Some floating wreckage too, an empty Carley float, smashed packing cases, a section of radio mast, a mattress. Surprisingly little; mostly it was just the bodies. A lot of people had been topsides when *Daisy* blew. The four-inch gun crew, the depth-charge parties, pom-pom gun, the bridge party. Some of them may have survived the initial explosion. Those trapped down below not. They would have had no time at all, even if they were conscious, to scramble up on deck and jump clear. They went down with the ship. But when the depth charges went off, many of them, or fragments of them, like Ponting, were blown to the surface. At the same time the few remaining survivors swimming about above them would have been killed, instantly, by the shock waves and explosions.

It was simply awful. There was no chance, we all knew, that anyone could possibly be alive. Nevertheless we rigged oars just the same and began paddling, in fearful silence, to and fro among the pathetic bundles, just to be sure. Many were completely unrecognisable as human. Just floating lumps of flesh and bone wrapped in a scrap of rag. Then there were the bodies without arms or legs, or heads. Unspeaking, we prodded about among them. After a while, a macabre, muttered game of spot the shipmate got underway.

'Christ. That must be Wally Stitt. I'd recognise that belt buckle anywhere.'

'Look, over there, doesn't Kavanagh have a tattoo like that?'

'No, I don't think so. Kavanagh's tattoo is bigger than that. And it has *Daisy* written under it.'

'Oh, yes, so it does.'

'Poor bastards. At least they couldn't have known much about it.'

'Look! There. Isn't that the skipper?'

'Where?' Villiers struggled to his feet. 'Yes, it is. Pull towards him.'

He was face down, his thin grey hair waving about his head like spun silk. His arms were spread, as though he were embracing the waters. His white lanyard was still about his neck. The others had recognised him by it. As we drew alongside, Villiers reached down and fumbled at it, turning him over in the process.

'Poor old sod,' Frank Tuker said. Then added something unexpected. 'We should say something. Proper, like. For all of them.'

Some of us had hats. I'd lost my cap, but Tuker had a woolly bobble hat thing, Harrison something similar, and Michael still wore his beret, his *boina*. Without a word of command they came off.

For all of us to stand would have been madness, so, heads lowered, we stayed sitting on the thwarts. But Michael stood, his feet braced against the rocking of the little boat. Bare-headed, his fair hair blowing, he fixed his eyes on the brightening eastern horizon, and began the words we'd heard so many times before.

'Man that is born of woman hath but a short time to live and is full of misery . . .'

I went out on my first convoy two days after joining *Daisy*. Much of the early part of it, unfortunately, passed with my head in a bucket, or over the rail, or on my bunk with a damp cloth pressed to it, so I didn't see a great deal. I was so sick I wanted to die. No exaggeration. Seasickness is not just a matter of motion-induced nausea. Scientists have since worked out that it has to do with the little chalky particles that float about in your inner ear. A ship's motion, in three dimensions at once, stirs them up into a complete mess, sending a tangle of confused signals to your brain such that pretty soon it has absolutely no idea what is happening, and goes into a kind of shocked funk. Apart from puking every five minutes, you lose all sense of orientation and balance, the ability to reason, in fact the ability to function on virtually any level at all. Like I said, you just want to die.

It wasn't even as if the weather was anything special. Before leaving 'Derry I'd been warned, joshingly, by the others, about a corvette's motion at sea. But I just laughed it off as yet another leg pull, and tucked into the tinned pilchards with gusto. Once clear of Castlerock, however, and with only a moderate sea running, *Daisy* began rolling about like a pig in manure. I thought something had gone horribly wrong with her, and we'd immediately be turning back to harbour for repairs. She was overloaded perhaps, or the rudder was falling off or something. But no, the amused grins on everyone's faces betrayed the dreadful truth. This was normal. Rather better than normal as it turned out. At the end of a trip, with the fuel tanks empty, the rolling was even worse.

It was awful. But the human body is a remarkable thing. On about the fourth day, I came to on my bunk. *Daisy* still rolled, but less so. My head felt clearer; better yet, I had a bit of an appetite. I pulled myself together, got dressed and ventured forth.

The officers – there were six of us – had a wardroom to ourselves, located below decks almost directly beneath the bridge. We also had a steward, Dutton, although he was often nowhere to be found, except, magically, when the captain or first lieutenant appeared. It sounds grand but it wasn't; the wardroom was very cramped and sparsely furnished. A table for eating, another for working, a few scruffy chairs, a bookcase, a picture of the king on the wall, that was about it. As for cabins, the skipper had one to himself, as did the first lieutenant, Alan Strang. The remaining four of us shared doubles. Two of the sub-lieutenants, Dick Woolley and Martin Brown, were in one. I was put in with Villiers, who up until then had enjoyed it to himself, although he was very gracious about me cluttering up the place. Tidiness was never my strong suit. I remember, between bouts of vomiting those first few days, staring over at his bunk. There was a framed photograph on the wall, featuring a wonderfully sunlit view of a low, colonial-looking house nestling amid tall poplars. A family group stood before it. Two middle-aged adults, very poorly dressed, a strikingly beautiful dark-haired girl, and Michael, looking about eighteen. In my wretchedness, I rather clung to its simple warmth. Late one night he came in and caught me staring at it.

'How are you feeling?' he smiled, putting a hand to my brow.

'Bloody awful, sir.'

'Hold on, Stephen. You will get over it, I promise you.' Somehow, despite my misery, I believed him. I was still watching the picture. He turned, following my gaze. 'They're my family. Well, not strictly speaking, but they are the family I grew up with before I came to England with my other family.'

'Ah,' I said, more mystified than ever.

I breakfasted, in solitary splendour, upon bread, jam and leftover tea, then, donning duffel coat and cap, went up on deck to see what was happening in the war.

We might just as well have been on a Mediterranean cruise. Despite *Daisy*'s motion, the sea was actually only slight to moderate, hissing smoothly down her sides, cobalt-blue beneath cloudless skies. After the boiled cabbage, bunker oil and body odour smells below, the air up top tasted like champagne, wonderfully fresh and invigorating. The sun, dazzlingly bright, was a blissful caress on my face. Pale and pasty from my confinement, I blinked at it myopically for a bit, like a surfacing mole, before taking stock.

The first thing I saw was washing. Tons of it, hung all along the rails, draped over ventilators, pegged on to rigging wires. Shirts, overalls, socks, the lot. That didn't seem very warlike to me. Worse still, its owners didn't appear to have anything else to put on. Thin white bodies were strewn everywhere like emaciated corpses. They lay about sunbathing in their underpants, or sitting around a bucket, shirtless, peeling spuds. They sprawled on deck, snoring, or huddled together, gambling with liar dice. One group, dressed only in shorts, was busy fishing, happily flinging lines over the stern as if it was an outing to Brighton pier. Elsewhere, aft, near the smoke floats, someone had set up a little outdoor barber's shop. At sixpence a throw, his customers formed an orderly queue, lounging about the waist, smoking and reading the papers.

Perplexed, exasperated even, I wandered the sunlit decks, picking my way among my recumbent shipmates. In no time, some began taking a less than respectful interest in the newest addition to their crew.

'Hello, Mid's up and about. Feeling a bit better then are we, petal?'

'What you need is a proper fry-up, lad. Best thing for it.'

'No, no. Tot of rum and a squeeze of lemon in a cup of condensed milk, that's the ticket.'

'Does your mum know you're out and about on your own?'

'Midshipman? Blimey I didn't know the Navy still had 'em.'

And so on. After a while I escaped up to the bridge, hoping for a more gracious reception from my peers. I should have known better.

'Well, well, well, and a *very* good morning to you, Mr

Tomlin. May I say this *is* an unexpected pleasure. Really, thank you, *thank* you, for dropping by to see us.'

This was my first proper encounter with our first lieutenant, Alan Strang. He was leaning against the side of the bridge, facing aft, a cigarette between his fingers. Tall and thin with a close-set face and swept-back hair, he was in uniform trousers and open-necked shirtsleeves, his cap low on his forehead as though to keep the sun off. Beneath it, he had these deeply set eyes, sunken, very watchful.

Apart from Strang, there was a bored looking signalman and two lookouts, one on either bridge wing. They at least seemed to be gainfully employed, dutifully sweeping their binoculars from horizon to horizon. But they were the only ones on the entire ship, it seemed to me, who were. Strang flicked his cigarette butt over the side. 'Well,' he said again, suspending the sarcasm for a moment. 'There they are.'

There they were. Ships as far as the eye could see, in every direction, and of every size and description, from monstrous modern fuel tankers to ancient-looking coal-fired relics. Dozens and dozens of them. And very widely spread, the nearest no more than quarter of a mile away, the furthest a barely visible smudge on the horizon. Apart from the fact that they were all going roughly in the same direction, you would never have known that they were, in theory at least, tightly knit components of a single formation.

I suppose I was still looking baffled. An ocean full of merchantmen. Corvettes and destroyers trotting faithfully along beside them like sheepdogs. Stories, daily, in the papers at home about the terrible pasting the North Atlantic boys were taking. Yet here we were, dawdling along without a care in the world, *Daisy* more like Cleethorpes holiday camp on wash day than a ship of war, and everyone lying about in their underwear looking bored. Where was the sense of urgency, where was the threat and the danger? Where was the war?

'It's ten o'clock in the morning, fourth day out, you see, old chap,' Strang went on, reading my thoughts. He was already lighting another cigarette, a barely perceptible tremor showing in his fingers as he cupped his lighter. 'U-boats will be concentrating well to the west, mid-Atlantic, somewhere in the gap, probably. Even if there were any in our vicinity, you wouldn't see them, not on a brilliant day like this. They'd be a long way astern, shadowing the convoy.'

'Couldn't we pick them up on the Asdic?'

Strang shook his head. 'Asdic only works when they're submerged. U-boats prefer to stay on the surface during the day, using their diesel engines to charge up their batteries, ready for the night's fun and games.'

'What about radar?' The first primitive sets had begun to appear in some ships. It was all very hush-hush; I had not a clue what it was, or how it worked, but it was supposed to be magical.

Strang was rolling his eyes. 'What about it? Radar, when it deigns to work, which isn't often, is fine at spotting a big target like a bloody great tanker, or a destroyer or something. Calm day like today, a U-boat shadowing a convoy will be hull down; that means sneaking along with only a few feet of conning tower showing. Radar wouldn't have a hope in hell of picking it up.'

'What about attacks from aeroplanes?'

Strang squinted skywards. 'Too early.'

So that was that. Lessons continued over lunch. Deeds kicked off.

'Ah, Mid, back in the land of the living, I see. Feel like helping out a bit with the chores? Nothing too strenuous, of course, and only if you're really up to it.' Obviously it was national poke-fun-at-Tomlin week. We were sitting around the wardroom table, except Strang who was still on watch. Villiers was also absent. Deeds helped himself to a mountainous dollop of powdered mashed potatoes. There were some anaemic looking sausages to go with it, and the obligatory boiled cabbage.

'If you can face this, you're over the worst,' Martin Brown offered, rather more kindly.

'I was sick as a pig for a fortnight my first trip,' Dick Woolley, the other sub, added. 'Here, Stephen, isn't it? Tuck into some of this, it'll do you no end of good. By the way, you don't happen to play cricket by any chance, do you?'

'A little. At Dartmouth. Bowled a bit. Mid-order bat, that sort of thing.'

'Marvellous! Villiers will be pleased. *Daisy*'s is the best eleven in group.'

I began to feel a little better. A moment later there was a tap on the door. A rating appeared.

'Sorry sir, first lieutenant's compliments, sir, but he's

asked me to inform you that there's a Jerry spotter plane circling astern the convoy.'

'I see,' Deeds said. 'What sort is it?'

'Don't know, sir, too far to tell. Could be a Heinkel.'

Germans! This was it, surely. Action stations, all hands on deck, ring full ahead and pass the ammunition.

Deeds glanced at his watch. 'Hmm. Bang on time, as usual. Out of range?'

''Fraid so, sir. Miles.'

'Thank you, Watson, that'll be all. HP sauce, Tomlin?'

I couldn't believe it. 'But, I mean, excuse me, Captain, but isn't there anything we can do, sir?'

'About what? The sausages? I know, they're awful. But do try the sauce, lad, it does help a bit.' He glanced at Woolley and Brown, smirking into their plates.

'There's not a thing we can do, lad,' he went on, finally. 'Just keep calm and bide our time. This is the way it goes. Jerry sends out spotter planes. They fly around in circles, just out of range, reporting the convoy's position and course back to base. U-boat command passes this information to its subs so that they can get themselves into the vicinity and prepare to attack.'

'And we just have to sit here and do nothing?'

'Sit here, do nothing, but be bloody ready, Mid. It's once the attacks start that we get to hit back. And hard. It's no picnic for us, I know, but I can assure you it's no picnic for them neither.'

A few minutes later Michael walked in. Tall, tanned, fair-haired. His face was a little flushed, his shirt front spotted with blood.

'Hello everyone. Stephen! You're up and about, that's very good news. Sorry I'm late, Captain. A stoker on blue watch needed a tooth pulling.'

'How interesting. There's blood on your shirt.'

'Is there? So there is. Sorry. It was a bad one. Molar. Rotten right through. Blasted thing didn't want to come out, had to get the Chief to hold the poor man down while I grabbed at it with a pair of pliers. Bled like fury.'

'Do you mind, Number Two. I'm trying to eat.'

Number Two. That was unusual. There was a Number One, of course, that was Lieutenant Strang. Then three sub-lieutenants. But addressing one of them as Number Two, well I'd never heard of it.

'Villiers here is ship's Medical Officer,' Brown was saying. 'A damn good one, too. I say, Michael, Stephen here bowled for Dartmouth!'

'Excellent. Spin, I hope. And I'm only acting MO, by the way.' Michael corrected with a wink. 'Just until a properly qualified ship's doctor is assigned.'

'And we know what the chances of that happening this side of Christmas are,' Deeds snorted. A notebook had appeared. 'Now then, young Tomlin, we run the usual four-hour watch rota on board. I've put you on the twelve to fours, with Villiers here, if that's all right. He's a rum bugger, that's for sure, but he knows what he's doing.'

'Yes, sir, thank you, sir. And, um, what will *I* be doing? So to speak.' At last. After two interminable years of maths and maritime law and navigation and signals and more maths. Finally, sea duty. Take charge of the pom-pom, Mid.

Have a go with the four-inch. Test fire a couple of depth charges.

'Ah yes, well, you will do four things,' Deeds began counting off on stubby fingers. 'One, observe. Two, learn. Three, take absolutely no action at all without calling one of us.'

'I see. Sir. And, um, the fourth?'

'See those?' He nodded towards a mountain of charts stacked on a table. 'There's about a month's worth of correcting to be done to them. We thought it would be a kindness if we saved that for you.'

At daybreak the waiting began in earnest. Voicelessly, each of us marooned upon our own private island of hope and fear. Then, without warning, about an hour after a feeble sun had risen, only to be swallowed by banks of cloud five minutes later, Harrison broke silence.

'We've got to get out of this!' he announced, fumbling an oar into his rowlock. For a moment I thought his nerves had fallen apart, that he meant to start rowing towards Ireland or something equally insane. But he just meant that we had to get out of the immediate vicinity. Get out of that floating field of death.

He was right. There was no need to spell it out, it was understood. Tuker and I reached for our oars, Giddings, whom I suspect had little idea what was going on, following suit. Villiers took the tiller. We rowed slowly out of the debris circle. About half a mile. Although it was a relief to be away from the smashed bodies and blank, accusatory stares of our dead shipmates, it was still a dismal parting. We were finally abandoning them, and also severing our last link with our ship.

Predictably, the exercise energised us. For the first time since being thrown into the sea we felt a glimmer of body warmth far within. It probably only served to emphasise how cold we were, but at least we felt something where hitherto there had only been numbness. We broke open some rations. Ship's biscuit, a tin of corned beef and some boiled sweets, the latter, probably because of the sugar, particularly comforting. We even began to talk. Conversation, inevitably, centred on the question of rescue.

'When will they come?' Giddings kept wanting to know. He was just an HO, of course, an HO on his first trip. What a baptism. I'd seen him a few times, on lookout duty on *Daisy*'s bridge, or wielding a paintbrush down on deck. He'd tried, but was like all first trip HOs. He hadn't a clue. To him everything was either completely incomprehensible, or breathtakingly simple.

'But they will come! They have to. When will they?'

'They may not, Albert,' Harrison said quietly. It was a mind game. Not daring to admit hope, yet not wanting to give it up.

'But they have to!'

'Think about it, you twat.' Giddings seemed to bring out the worst in Frank Tuker. '*Daisy* went down in seconds, the other escorts know that. They also know hardly nobody would've 'ad time to scramble out alive, yet alone have time to swing out boats and floats and launch 'em. So they know any survivors was swimming for it, which means they know they're all long dead. So, if they do send someone to come and look, it'll be to beetle back a little way, have a five-minute nose around so's they can say they tried, then clear off quick back to the convoy. Ain't that right, Sub?'

Michael hadn't eaten. He'd taken a couple of sips of water but shaken his head at all offers of food. He blamed himself, it was as simple as that. He'd forced Deeds to stop the ship, thus killing him. Killing them all. I could only guess at the torture he was putting himself through. 'I don't know, Frank,' he said simply. 'I'm sorry.'

'Although,' he went on, after a moment. He was looking around the boat. At us. The last survivors. His chosen few. You'll be all right, he'd promised, last night as we prepared to launch. He'd given his word. Now, even with the burden of seventy deaths hanging over him, he'd do his best to keep it. By keeping our spirits up, keeping us hopeful, and therefore alive a little longer. 'Perhaps we shouldn't underestimate how respected, and liked, *Daisy* was by escort commander and the other escorts. If they possibly can, if it's safe to, I feel they'll want to try and check for survivors.'

'See?' Tuker crowed. Paradoxically, while taking sadistic pleasure in torpedoing Giddings' hopes, he too, just wanted to hear there was a chance.

There was something else the others seemed to have forgotten, although it must have been on Villiers' mind. *Daisy* wasn't the only ship sunk the previous night. Four or five were hit before we'd even launched the whaler. Several areas of the ocean were now stained with melancholy little smudges of oil and bodies, where once a ship had sailed. How could one escort possibly search them all?

I was about to add this point to the discussion when the world went completely mad. It began with a sort of far-off low-frequency rumble, like faint thunder. We looked at each other, as if to confirm we had each heard and not imagined it. Then, no more than thirty yards away, the ocean began to boil. Literally boil, right there, next to our little row boat, with seething seas, erupting gouts of steaming air and a sound like a distant roar. As though a monster was rising from the deep.

A monster *was* rising from the deep. The bows came first, a blunt nose with its curved saw-tooth net cutter, then an eighty-eight millimetre deck gun, followed by the rest of the front half, glistening black, streaming water like a breaching whale. Then the nose settled to the horizontal and the conning tower broke surface, sea gushing from its scuppers. Finally the stern appeared until, in less than a minute, the churning seas had stilled again, the rush of venting air stopped, and the U-boat lay quietly on the surface.

Right beside us. Barely a biscuit throw away.

'Jesus H. Christ,' Tuker managed to intone, the rest of us speechless.

Nothing happened. For about a minute. It just sat there, silent, menacing, rust-streaked, its slate-grey superstructure pocked here and there with dents and scratches. It was surreal. A minute earlier we'd been quite alone. Now, everything we feared and hated most, the enemy we fought but never saw, the very focal point of our entire war, was sitting quietly in the water next to us.

Then there was the squeak and clang of a hatch, and a head appeared in the top of the conning tower. Then another. Without a word, these two, bearded, clad in grubby black overalls and forage caps, descended quickly on to the foredeck and ran forward to the eighty-eight millimetre deck-gun. Another head appeared, this one holding a heavy machine gun. He slotted it into a mounting on the side of the conning tower and swung it towards us. In just a few seconds both it and the eighty-eight were trained right at us.

'Fuck me. Now what.'

'My God.' Giddings was clambering to his feet. 'My God, they're going to murder us all!'

Villiers reached out a steadying hand. 'No. It's all right, Albert. They're not. Sit down, and keep still. Nothing's going to happen.'

Another figure appeared. Also bearded, this one wore a grey leather jacket and scarf. A rumpled officer's cap sat rakishly upon his head.

'Good morning, gentlemen!' he called, in accented but clear English. 'How are you this day?'

'Been better, you bastard,' Tuker muttered. Villiers hushed him.

'Do you require medical assistance? Are any of you injured?'

'No.' Villiers called back.

'Ah, that is good. And are you adequately provisioned? Do you need food, or water, perhaps?'

'No.'

'No?' The submarine captain ducked beneath the coaming, reappearing a second later with a lit cigarette. He waved the pack. 'Anything else? Cigarettes, perhaps, chocolate?'

'We don't want anything. What do *you* want?'

'Cigs, Sub!' Tuker hissed. 'I'm gasping . . .'

'Want? Me?' The captain laughed, then addressed Michael directly. 'Are you the officer in charge of this little vessel?'

'*Ich bin. Was wollen sie?*' Michael shot back straightaway, in German.

'A German speaker. Excellent!' the captain went on, still in English, the men on the guns watching silently.

'Yes, I speak German. Now, what do you want?' Michael asked a third time.

'Herr Lieutenant . . .' he pronounced it 'Loyt-nant', '. . . but I want nothing! Everything I need is here. I am just waiting. Like you. I just want to make your wait as pleasant as possible. What is wrong with that?'

Michael hesitated. 'What do you mean, you are just waiting?'

The German was spreading his hands, as though it was obvious. Suddenly it was beginning to be. I felt the hairs pricking on my neck. 'Herr Lieutenant. Last night, someone very obligingly stopped one of your corvettes for a minute or two, presenting me with an unmoving target. It was too good to resist. Now you are here, survivors from that ship, no? Well. You and I both know there is a good chance that another ship, another corvette perhaps, or even a destroyer, will come to look for you today, yes? So. When it arrives, and it stops to pick you up, I will be ready once more. It is as simple as that.'

'No one is coming. You are wasting your time.'

'Well. We shall see.' The captain barked a command in German. Immediately the deck-gun crew began packing up, the machine-gunner dismounting his weapon. 'In the meantime, we shall be here, somewhere, keeping watch. So, if you do want anything, you need only wave.' With that, and a wave of his own, he descended from view.

Chapter 5

The newly re-formed Villiers family returned to England, descending the gangway of their packet steamer to the dock-side at Southampton early in December 1930. It was a predictably grey day, cold, raining and cheerless. Aurora, heavily pregnant, had not travelled well, passing much of the five-week passage closeted in their cabin. Wan, but relieved at least to be returned to dry land, she stood amid their baggage, Michael at her side, a bemused furrow on her brow, while Keith scurried to and fro searching for porters and a taxi to the station. Despite her best intentions, on the train journey to London her bemusement congealed to gloom. Keith made efforts to point out passing towns and villages through the veil of drizzle beyond the window, but although Michael, his face pressed to the glass, showed some interest, his mother's attention was in another hemisphere.

One hand resting on the hard mound of her belly, she sat in contemplative silence, watching boggy fields and leafless copses give way to grimy Victorian tenements peopled by blankly staring inhabitants whose skins, clothes, indeed their very lives, seemed to match the leaden colour of their sky. England, it was quickly dawning, was not to be as she had imagined.

They were met at Waterloo by Keith's parents, a nervously chatty couple in their sixties who bustled about helpfully, all the while stealing furtive glances at their exotically skinned daughter-in-law and their unknown blond-haired grandson. Apart from a brief visit to Uruguay shortly after Keith and Aurora were married, their son's family were known only to them in letters and photographs. Cyril Villiers went to lengths to welcome the nine-year-old Michael, bending to him, patting his head and feeding him sticky coils of liquorice from a paper bag. But his bluff ribbing and schoolboy anecdotes were met with blank stares, and although Michael dutifully chewed on the rich-tasting blackness, its strong flavour and rubbery texture overpowered him, and during the cab journey across town he vomited much of it on to his grandmother's shoes.

The elder Villiers had arranged rental of a flat in Marylebone for their son and his family. Not far from Regent's Park, it was a busy, slightly unkempt though pleasant enough district of modestly proportioned terraced houses with iron railings and smut-stained façades. Their rooms, which overlooked a busy high street, were on the third of four floors, and consisted of a combined sitting and dining room, a little kitchen with a two-ringed cooker, a mildew-spotted bathroom with a gas geyser, and a bedroom. Heating was a single gas fire in the living-room fireplace.

Aurora was genuinely aghast. There must be some mistake. 'But, for how long are we going to stay here?' she asked, in Spanish, within minutes of their arrival. Keith and his father were manhandling one of their trunks on to the landing.

'As long as we like, dearest. It'll be a little cramped, of course, especially when the baby arrives, but we'll manage. And who knows, another year or two and we should be able to afford something bigger.'

'But, well, I always understood, of course, that your family was not wealthy . . .' she protested with characteristic candour '. . . but surely we are not so poor either.'

If Cyril understood, he gave no sign. Keith laughed, glancing breathlessly about the landing. 'Good heavens, my dearest, whatever gives you that impression? Certainly we are not impoverished, you shall never want for life's necessities, you may be assured of that, and our children will enjoy the best education possible. But nor are we wealthy, that's equally certain. Not on a Foreign Office salary.'

The winter of 1930–31 was not especially severe by London standards. It passed in the usual fashion. Endless days of grey when the noon light seemed barely above twilight before dusk was settling once more like a damp blanket. Others, all too rare, when angular patches of blue were glimpsed above the roofs, and a wintry orange sun cast hard shadows across the street. There was sleet but not snow, then a week of blustery rain, then a cold snap when the temperature plummeted, feet skidded on icy pavements and pigeons gathered miserably on window ledges. Indoors seemed, if anything, colder. Pipes clanked as water froze in them, Michael, entranced, traced lacy fingers of frost down the windowpanes, and Aurora's laboured breaths misted the air in the kitchen. As her time drew near, Keith, together with millions of other Londoners, was forced to supplement the flat's paltry heating by opening up the fireplace in the bedroom. Coal smoke from ten thousand chimneys poured into the air above the rooftops, paused, then sank to street level once more, submerging the world in an acrid suffocating smog so thick that day became night, vehicles five yards apart collided with one another, and handkerchiefs clasped to mouths turned black.

Christmas came and went. Aurora caught a bad cold and remained in bed throughout. Keith's parents visited from Sussex; there were presents for Michael, and unusual food, and expeditions into the West End where huge shops bustled with noisy crowds and brightly decorated trees sparkled in the windows. His hand tightly clasped in his father's, Michael took it all in: the unintelligible cries of the street vendors, the honking of motor cars and omnibuses, the grey, hard-edged geography, the motor fumes, damp streets and roasting chestnut smells. He took it in, and wondered vaguely when he would be returning to Sombreado.

'When are we going home, Mama?' he asked Aurora one January afternoon. They were struggling up the staircase to their flat, arms laden with groceries. Keith was at work, settling into his new job on the South American trade desk at the rear of the Foreign Office's Whitehall headquarters. He had left instructions with Aurora to contact the old lady on the ground floor in case of emergency, arranged with his superiors for a week's leave when the new baby was born, and his mother was standing by to come the last few days before it was due. He could do no more. In the meantime Aurora had to cope on her own. Domestically inexperienced, never an accomplished cook and with her English weak, simply buying and preparing food for her family was an ordeal as baffling to her as it was arduous.

'I don't know!' she coughed chestily, in answer to Michael's question. Unable to labour the last few yards through the door into their flat, she dropped the shopping bags, and flopped on to the top stair. A throbbing pain was starting low in her back; she felt a stab of panic. Suddenly hopelessness was washing over her, like an icy wave.

'What is it, Mama?' Michael sat down beside her.

Fighting tears, she pulled him close, wrapping him tightly in her arms.

'Mama?'

'It is all right, angel.' She stifled a gasp, rocking him back and forth. 'It is just your brother, or your sister. I think they will be here soon.'

'Then will we all go home together?' His face was pressed to her bosom, he could hear the hoarse rasp of her breath, the thudding of her heart. Her constant closeness, the smell of her body, it was still new to him, yet it reminded him so of Uruguay. Strangers for years, now they were each other's only friends in this cold and hostile place. He wrapped his arms about her and pulled closer. Gradually the rocking slowed as the contraction passed.

'Home, you see, Miguel. Uruguay. You must understand, it is no more.' She stroked his hair. 'This is our home now.'

'Will we never return to Sombreado?'

'It is strange and difficult, I know. But we mustn't be afraid. We must help one another, and be fearless and strong.'

'Like our Charrúa forefathers?'

'Like them, yes,' she whispered.

'Don't ever leave me, Mama.'

'I never will,' she lied.

In fact it was barely two weeks before they were parted. One Saturday in mid-January, Keith ushered Michael into the bedroom where his mother and new brother, Donald, lay resting. Michael was wearing uncomfortably new clothes bought from an outfitters off Regent Street. A prickly flannel suit with short trousers that chafed his thighs, a jacket with a yellow emblem on the breast, stiff new lace-up shoes and a too-large cap. There were other oddments. Peculiar, string-like underwear, socks with elasticated garters that pinched the skin of his calves. A shirt, its cuffs hanging to his palms. Lastly, and painfully tight at his throat, a yellow and grey knotted tie. Michael disliked it all, except the cap.

Hands clapped to her cheeks, a look of horrified wonderment lit Aurora's face as they entered.

'But, just look at you, angel! So grown up. Surely you will be the best dressed boy at the school.'

'Yes, Mama. What school?'

Keith explained again. Aurora nodded. Michael considered.

'I don't want to. I want to stay here and be with you.'

'Well, all proper little boys must go away to school,' Keith said patiently. 'And your mother has Donald now to take care of.'

Up until then Michael had not formed strong views either way about Donald. He was small and pink and noisy and smelled rather, but that was it. At that moment however, strong views were quickly formed. Donald was the usurper. The pretender. He was the enemy. He would never be forgiven.

Holbrook House was a boys' boarding preparatory school in Hertfordshire, about an hour from Marylebone by train. Once an elegant Georgian manor, repeated change of use and generations of running feet had since pounded it into a prematurely decrepit version of its former self. Like a once-glorious but now burned-out theatre actress it could still put on a front, but beneath the flaking make-up cracks were showing. Its walls and foundations were solid enough, but everything else – roof, plumbing, electricity, as well as the manner in which it was run – badly needed updating.

Michael hated it from the start. He was placed in a class of eight- and nine-year-olds who immediately singled him out for his peculiar mannerisms and atrocious English. On the third day, after a morning spent in an airless classroom struggling to follow a single sentence, and an afternoon on a frozen football pitch having his shins kicked to bleeding, he cracked.

He was standing at his locker. A stubby ink-stained finger prodded him on the shoulder.

'Got any tuck, Froggy?'

Startled, Michael swung round. One of his class, Barlowe, a fat boy with freckles and curly hair, was standing before him, arms folded. Michael shook his head, shrugging uncomprehendingly. 'I . . . tuck? What is—'

'Tuck, you stupid Frog! Grub. Have you got any?' Barlowe, head and shoulders taller than Michael, was peering past him into the interior of Michael's locker. Others were crowding in behind.

'Frog? What is—'

'Yes, Frog. That's what you are, aren't you? A smelly French frog.'

'No, French, I, from Uruguay—'

'Here, what's that, in that little box . . .'

It was enough. As Barlowe's arm reached out, Michael's teeth sank into it. Barlowe screamed in disbelief; at the same moment Michael whipped around, reached into his locker, turned forward once more and, roaring like an enraged bull, put his head down and charged into the throng. A moment later the door opened and their astonished form teacher entered to be confronted by Michael, teeth bared and snarling, holding a goggle-eyed ring of boys at bay at the point of the gleaming steel *cuchilla* Tata had given him.

Perversely, as is the way with boys, the incident, while earning him a severe reprimand from the headmaster and the first of many letters to Keith threatening expulsion, did win him the grudging respect of his peers. The bitterest part of the episode was that his *cuchilla*, which everyone had particularly admired, was confiscated. But from then on, his classmates, without actually welcoming him into their midst – his solitary nature and sheer oddness precluded that – did at least show consideration for his space, regarding him with courteous if wary deference. Of course, he continued to be singled out for his differences and suffer periods of bullying and humiliation. But then so did they all, for that was the nature of the system. In time therefore it was the system that became the focus of his antipathy, not so much its victims.

He was the wrong species in the wrong environment. Doomed, like the Charrúa Indian prisoners Tata had taught him about. Trapped by invading Spanish conquistadors, then shipped to Europe as novelties, they quickly languished and died in captivity. English prep school boys put up with English prep schools because they were bred to it. Their fathers had endured it, and their fathers before them. And even though their fathers had hated it too, being English, it never occurred to them that they might seek to educate their sons differently or, even more unthinkable, try and change the system for the better.

But Michael was a child of the plains; he needed his freedom, he needed wide skies and open air. Above all he needed the sun. Locking him up in the claustrophobically institutionalised confines of Holbrook House was as cruel as it was ultimately senseless. Like caging a swallow.

Escape seemed the logical solution. Frequently, on free afternoons for instance, he would just climb through the fence encircling the school grounds and wander off into surrounding crop fields and orchards, sometimes for hours. Then there were his more organised bids for freedom. Four times during his first year he stole from his bed, dressed and crept down the oak staircase to the flagstoned hallway. The first time he got no further than the end of the road before he was spotted by a passing motorist. The second, during the summer term, he made off across the playing fields and hid out the night in a wood, managing to evade capture for a full twenty-four hours before a farmer caught him stealing an apple. The third time he walked all night, covering fifteen miles until, tired and lost, he came to a bus stop. He boarded the first bus to arrive and then realised he had no fare. In any case it carried him straight back the way he had come, depositing him at the school gates.

But his fourth attempt was a home run. Learning from his mistakes, he prepared more carefully, studying timetables, researching routes, working up alibis. He was returning to school, his story would go if questioned, not escaping from it. He realised he would need food and money. The school kitchens had one, matron the other, so, since the end fully justified the means, he stole bread from the larder and cash from the handbag on matron's door. Then, when all was ready, he slipped out shortly after lights out one autumn evening, took a circuitous route to a different bus stop, rode to the railway station, caught the ten-fifteen to Euston and a cab from there to the flat in Marylebone.

His welcome was not the joyous one he had so deliciously anticipated on the train. Doubling up the stairs to the flat he stopped outside, knuckles raised to knock. There was a commotion on the other side. A baby was screaming, he could clearly hear his mother's shouts above it, together with the low, urgent tones of his father. Someone must have telephoned. From the school. Warning them of his break-out. They were worried, understandably, frantic even. But they would be relieved he was safe. He raised his hand once more. Then froze.

'Of course I am unhappy!' he heard his mother scream suddenly in Spanish. 'Of course that's why I drink! I don't belong here. I don't belong with you. Or with them. This whole situation is a ridiculous sham and I detest it!'

A pause, a pleading, placatory murmur from Keith. Then Aurora's blood-chilling shriek:

'The children? For the sake of the children? Don't you see, I never wanted the children! We are only in this mess because of the children. They were both stupid mistakes!'

Later, after Michael had finally knocked, and they'd found him, ashen-faced, on the doorstep. After they'd settled Donald and telephoned the school, after they'd fed him and made up his bed in the living room, after their shock and shame had subsided a little, then, individually, they came to him. And tried to explain, and to understand.

'Your mother is very tired,' Keith sighed, burying his face in his hands. He looked pale, Michael thought. And far from being angry with him, seemed only defeated. Resigned. It was worse somehow. 'The baby is quite demanding, you see, and it has been very strange and difficult for her, leaving Uruguay and having to adjust like this. As I am sure it has been for you. Is that why you ran away again?'

Michael nodded. His father – it was the first time he had seen real anguish on his face, real emotion. The first time he had seen anything, in fact, but a scrupulously maintained mask of affirmative composure. Michael longed for him to go on, longed for him to explain more of his thoughts and feelings. But with a sad pat on Michael's chest he got up to leave.

'I have always tried only to do what is right.'

A few minutes later Aurora came in from the kitchen. She was smoking, and holding a glass. Her cheeks were flushed, she seemed a little unsteady on her feet.

'Miguel José-Luis Quemada.' She sat down beside him. 'What are we going to do with you?'

'What is wrong, Mama?'

'Wrong? Everything. Nothing. Do not concern yourself. It is not your fault.'

'What is?'

'This, everything.'

'Me. And the baby Donald . . .' Michael hesitated. '. . . Is it because of us that you and Papa are unhappy, Mama?'

'No, angel, no!' She bent to him then, burying her face in his neck. He drew her to him, inhaling deeply. It was still her, still Aurora. But the Uruguay smell was gone. Now she smelled of London, and of cigarettes and wine.

Hot wetness on his neck told him she was weeping. Awkwardly, he began to caress her hair, his eyes on the flaking ceiling plasterwork. Outside an autumn wind blew litter along the high street. Eventually she quietened, straightened, swallowed from her glass. Dabbing a handkerchief to her eye, she took his hand in hers.

'Angel,' she sniffed. 'Listen to me. No matter what takes place, you must never, ever think that any of it is your fault.'

'No, Mama.'

Her teak-brown eyes travelled his face, then fastened on to his, searching them for confirmation. 'I love you and nothing that happens will ever change that. Do you understand?'

'Yes, Mama.'

'Good. You see, your school. You run away from your school, no?'

'Yes.'

'Yes, and why? Because to you, it is like a prison.'

'Yes.'

'Yes. Well, Miguelito, prison. You see, I, too, feel . . . that is, this life . . .' But she broke off, unable to voice the unspeakable. Instead she simply stared around the room, as though seeing it for the first time. Or the last.

'Are we your prison, Mama?'

He didn't run away from Holbrook House again. There didn't seem any point. But nor did he capitulate. Instead of escaping, he rebelled. Throughout his second and third years he became increasingly troublesome. At the same time that his teachers were slowly discovering that behind this boy's combative exterior lay a powerful intelligence, his classmates were learning anew that angelic looks and blond locks were not to be mistaken for girlishness. He fought, a lot, with everyone.

As a result, he was also beaten. The headmaster at Holbrook was a hugely unimaginative retired army chaplain called Andrew Killwick. The boys, without irony, nicknamed him Killer. Killer, himself a product of Wellington and Sandhurst of the late 1800s, had no qualms at all about administering corporal punishment, usually for traditionally banal schoolboy misdemeanours such as theft or lying. Whether he questioned its effectiveness either as a punishment or a deterrent is doubtful; he regularly complained to his staff that it was always the same wretched faces and bony backsides that appeared before him as defaulters, but probably never stopped to ask himself why.

But even Killer was astonished at how ineffective the cane proved to be in Villiers' case. Term after term Michael and his latest co-combatants would be waiting at his door, their eyes blacked or noses bloodied. When explanation was demanded it was usually found that Villiers had taken disproportionately violent offence at something quite trivial the other had said or done. Teased him, mildly, about his accent, perhaps, or inferred a trifling slur on his birth country's prowess on the football field. Rarely was it anything serious enough to warrant the ferocity of the fights that ensued. If there was a pattern, it was only that Villiers almost invariably picked on boys who were older, and therefore much bigger than he. As if he was testing himself, or out to prove something. But either way analysis was for quacks and liberals, Killer quickly concluded, selecting a stouter cane from the rack. There was no logic in the boy's behaviour, so beat some into him, that was the ticket.

Despite steadily growing proficiency in the classroom, and especially on the cricket pitch, Michael's final year at Holbrook was his worst. The onset of puberty seemed only to intensify his need to challenge himself and the system that tried to contain him. There were a number of more serious incidents. A fight with some youths in the village. The mysterious, almost ritual midnight burning of a delivery of fence posts. Turning up for lessons once clad only in shorts, his face and chest painted with mud. One day he climbed to the top of a huge lime tree in the school grounds. Despite entreaties from the groundsmen, threats from the staff and the bemused cheers of his class-mates, he remained there, trance-like, for two days, finally descending on the second evening as the fire brigade was arriving.

But just when matters seemed to be becoming desperate, assistance arrived from an unexpected source.

'I wonder if he isn't deliberately trying to get himself expelled,' a member of Killwick's staff ventured innocently one day when the subject arose at lunch. His name was Francis Habershon, a nervous, slight, desperately pale young man who taught modern languages.

'Expelled?' Killwick scoffed. 'Good God man, what on earth for?'

'I'm not sure. Perhaps he feels he doesn't fit in here. Or perhaps there's something amiss at home?'

'Doesn't fit in? What utter rot! We'll damn well make him fit in, or else we're not doing our job properly.'

'Yes, headmaster.'

Killwick forked greens into his mouth, considering. Deliberately trying to get himself expelled. It was beyond comprehension. But, well, trouble at home. That was another matter entirely. Tricky. There was far too much of it these days. Yet even he was forced to concede that the stick had made no headway with Michael.

'Speak to the blasted boy, Habershon. See if you can't get to the bottom of it.'

That afternoon, after games, Habershon went in search. He found Michael, eventually, at the furthest corner of the school grounds. There were the playing fields, then a small wooded area known as the dell. The school boundary ran along the southern edge of the dell, beyond it lay open farm-land. Michael, together with half a dozen other boys, all still in their games clothes, was leaning on the wire fence separating the grounds from a lush meadow. Twenty yards away, munching contentedly, its coat gleaming in afternoon sunshine, stood a horse. Habershon swallowed, breathless with suppressed excitement. Even as he watched, Michael was ducking through the wire strands and into the meadow. At that very point, Habershon should have apprehended him for venturing out of bounds, frogmarching him straight to Killwick's office for the usual retribution. But nothing could have been further from his thoughts. He crept closer.

Evidently it was some sort of dare or bet. Habershon knew that interfering in any way with the horse, a prize hunter belonging to the local farmer, was an instant expulsion offence. Slowly, to murmurs of encouragement from the spectators on the wire, Michael closed to within a few yards of it. It snorted and shook its mane in warning, but continued eating. To Habershon's astonishment, Michael, shaking his head at the animal in return, began tearing grass from the earth, and pretending to eat it. Hesitantly, unable to resist the sound and smell of the fleshy stems, the animal began warily to approach him. Soon they were just feet apart, face to face. Habershon flattened himself against a tree to see better. A bead of sweat was trickling down one cheek, his heart racing beneath his shirt.

For a full minute the two stood, unmoving, eye to eye. Then slowly Michael's hand reached out, palm up and thick with grass. It was too good to resist. The horse stamped, stepped forward and nibbled tentatively. Another minute and Michael was right beside it, one hand caressing its neck, the other feeding it an apple pulled from his pocket. That's it, Habershon breathed. Bet won. Touch the horse, bet you can't, bet you don't dare. He waited for Michael to retreat to safety, claim his winnings. But he didn't. His hand was sliding higher on the animal's neck, fingers burying themselves tightly in its mane. Suddenly, in a single smooth movement, he gave a little jump, hoisting himself up on to its bare back. Snorting, tossing its head high, the horse immediately broke away, kicking into a gallop across the field. He would fall off now, Habershon knew. He would have to carry his beautiful bruised body back to the sick bay, there to await certain expulsion. But he didn't fall off. Effortlessly, Michael straightened on the animal's back. Soon the two creatures were cantering around the field as one; harmonised, concentrated, yet relaxed, as though they had always ridden together. It was mesmerising, beautiful beyond bearing. Habershon felt tears pricking his eyes, felt his knees weaken and the shameful hardening of his loins. Then, just when he believed he must burst, or cry out, or die, Michael turned, urging the horse directly towards him down the centre of the field, and then, still cantering, with an expression of triumph on his face, of release, of ecstasy, he threw his arms wide, like Christ on the cross, tipped his face to the sky and cried out:

'I am Rapoza of the Charrúa! Last of the gaucho *caudillos!*'

'Sit down, Villiers,' Habershon directed him curtly, later that evening. They were alone in the school library. Habershon had sent for him. 'Now then, who is Rapoza?'

Michael looked shocked. 'Sir? I . . .'

'You don't need to be alarmed. Yes, I saw what happened this afternoon. I am not going to report it, not yet, although I should. Rather, I would prefer to try and understand it. And all the other scrapes you seem to get yourself into. If you help me, then perhaps it need not go further. Understand?'

Michael regarded him warily. 'Sir.'

'Good. So, once again, who is Rapoza?'

'He, well, it is the family name of my great-grandfather,

sir. Don Adrián Rapoza of Estancia Sombreado, Cerro Largo department, Northern Republica Oriental del Uruguay.'

'Orientale, er, del . . . Uruguay, I see. Your great-grandfather. He is still alive?'

'Yes, sir. He is the father of my mother's mother.'

'And the other part, the gaucho, ah, *caudillos*, was it? What is that about?' *Caudillo*. A leader, he'd checked it in his Spanish dictionary. And gaucho, a sort of wild South American plainsman. But the dictionary was lacking. Gaucho. It was something much more than that, he sensed.

'My great-grandfather was a famous warrior, he fought beside the great Aparicio Saravia, chief among the gaucho *caudillismo*, fighting for the freedom of the borderlands.'

'Fighting against who?'

'Fighting against the profidious bureaucrats of the Colorado government in Montevideo.'

'I see.' Michael's command of English had improved immeasurably in recent months, but was there just the ghost of an Irish brogue among those strong Hispanic vowels? He was without doubt an enigma. But was he also a born liar? Or simply a gifted storyteller. The boy blinked his limpid green eyes at him. Habershon, as he had trained himself, forced his attention away from them and on to the issue at hand. 'And he taught you all this, your great-grandfather.'

'Yes, sir. He taught us the history of our country.'

'Us?' Habershon watched the eyes falter, then guessed. He already knew much more than the boy supposed. Earlier he had been through the contents of his locker. It was pitifully sparse. An unopened Bible inscribed, evidently, from his English grandfather. A small leather folder containing a photograph of each parent, his mother in particularly striking pose. A child-sized beret. A tied bundle of letters postmarked from Marylebone, the two most recent unopened. Some very dog-eared ones from Uruguay. People signing themselves Papa and Mama Luenga, apparently, very poor Spanish handwriting, Habershon had been able to decipher little of it. At the end of each, however, much-fingered paragraphs in a younger hand, signed by one Maria. Again unintelligible, but often featuring someone or thing called Chiquito, children's games and stories, and an *ombú* tree.

Michael quickly clammed up, Habershon, unable to extract more from him, drew the interview to a close. But it was the first of many. Slowly, a form of trust grew between them. It was a curious symbiosis. The misfit schoolboy and the repressed homosexual. Despite his best efforts, Habershon's feelings for the boy quickly deepened such that before long he feared they would incapacitate him altogether. At night, sweating and sleepless, he paced his attic bedroom, tormented by guilt and confusion, desperate for release, for escape, yet counting the hours until he and the boy were together once more. Each evening, alone in the little library, he sat close to Michael, questioning him, slowly drawing him out on those aspects of his life he cared to talk about, leaving aside those he didn't. His proximity was the most exquisite torture, but Habershon never surrendered to it, never so much as rested a paternal hand on his shoulder. Adopting a formal, almost brusque, yet patient questioning manner, he learned much of Michael's early life on the pampas, of his passion for the land of his birth, and how he felt more Uruguayan than English. But he learned much less of his current domestic situation. Whenever he enquired tentatively of Michael's parents, or brother, or life back in London, Michael quickly became evasive and mono-syllabic. Clearly, he began to conclude, jotting notes into a folder, and principally, despite an English father and British nationality, Michael's heart lay back in his maternal home-land. Secondly, there were difficulties going on in his parents' marriage. He also appeared to resent his younger brother, possibly for replacing him in his mother's affec-tions. Above all, he hated being shut up at Holbrook. Yet there was something else, something more fundamental that troubled Michael. Habershon struggled to label it. But to him, it was as if, at the root of everything, this boy didn't know who he was.

But talking about it was helping him. Gradually Michael's confidence grew, his attention in class became more focused, he began to join in, contribute, achieve. He became less aggressive towards his peers, or at least learned to manage his aggression better. He was still hot-tempered, quick with his fists, but the frequency of incidents declined. To help with this, Habershon began making tentative sug-gestions, distilled from the turmoil of his own troubled experiences. How to control feelings that refused to be con-trolled. How to adapt, fit in, when you felt you never could. How to come to terms with the person you were. And, most crucially, how, in the interests of self-preservation, to become someone whom instinctively you were not. With regard to the fighting, Habershon sowed seeds that were to become deeply embedded. 'It is perfectly right to want to protect that which is precious to you . . .' he said towards the end of one session '. . . but wrong to allow yourself to be provoked into fighting unnecessarily. You are highly intelligent, Michael. You must learn to use the power of your intellect to try and avoid and prevent fights, just as politicians and diplomats must use theirs to try and prevent wars.'

It had taken four years, but in just a few weeks Habershon became Michael's first true friend and ally in England. And a crucial, hitherto missing influence. Like an uncle, or older brother. Father even, to a certain extent. Then, just as Habershon was concluding that a corner had been turned, and the sessions might profitably be discontinued, Michael's fragile rehabilitation suffered a double setback.

One night, right at the end of term, Habershon was accidentally discovered by one of the other teaching staff. He was at the rear of a nearby pub, outside the gents toilet, locked in embrace with a local man. Solely to avoid any hint of a scandal, and without the slightest evidence of impropriety at school, Killwick dismissed him on the spot, furthermore insisting he leave immediately. Within the hour he was gone. The next morning, Killwick stood up at assembly and informed the school that Habershon had left. That was all, no reason was given, no explanation; he merely let it be known that staff and pupils were never to mention his name again. Unsurprisingly, Michael believed he might in some way be responsible. Indeed heads were turning as Killwick spoke. Villiers' trysts with Habershon were well known. Predictably, later in the day, Michael was summoned from his desk to the headmaster's study.

'Now, look here, boy,' Killwick began, tugging nervously at his dog collar. Unusually, he had bade Michael be seated. There was an open letter on the desk before him.

'I've had this letter from your father. We break up for the holidays in three days, as you know, but your father felt it would be best to have this explained to you, in person, as it were, before you get home. So that you are forewarned, so to speak. Have you got that?'

'Yes, sir.' Got what? Michael wondered. But something cold and hard was solidifying deep in his stomach.

'Good. Now, as you know, we have a strict no-telephoning policy here at HHS, so it falls to me to communicate this to you in person. Experience has taught me there is no easy way to break bad news; in any case I'm a firm believer in giving it to a man straight. So here it is. Your mother's gone back to South America.'

After Holbrook, he went to Westminster. Quietly and without protest. At Holbrook he'd absconded, rebelled, fought. He'd tried everything and it had brought him nothing but conflict and misery. So at Westminster, exactly as Francis Habershon had counselled, he learned to adapt. To sit tight. Go with the stream rather than struggle against it. Conserve his energy. Wait. He learned how to melt into the background, to create a persona that blended with the five hundred others around him, rather than stand out from them. He became diligent, compliant, studious, patient.

Instead of fighting the system, he ignored it, or turned it to his advantage. Westminster was still Dickensian in its outlook, steeped in the pointless, even barbaric, rituals he so detested. There was still fagging and bullying and beatings. Snobbery abounded, chauvinism too, xenophobia and a sickening kind of jingoistic ignorance. But it was also an institution that challenged the intellect, and a hotbed of political and sociological debate. In those momentous years of the mid-thirties, with Europe teetering, like a drunk on a railway line, inexorably towards catastrophe, London, and particularly Westminster, was a fascinating place for a gifted young man with an enquiring mind.

Michael remained apart; nothing would change that. Few who attended Westminster at that time, if they remembered him at all, would ever claim to have known him well. They would recall only the person he had chosen to be. Watchful, inaccessible, nondescript. Above all, like them. Overnight he became the archetypal English son of the professional classes. Mimicking with uncanny exactness his peers' plummy vowels and nasal tones, chameleon-like, he even adopted their appearance, their posture, the way they walked, ate, dressed, or cut their hair.

He applied himself academically. Languages in particular, were his strength. As well as the obligatory Greek and Latin, and perhaps driven intuitively to make sense of the upheavals shaking the world, he perfected not only his English and Spanish, but also German. He became interested in world politics, industrial globalisation and Western philosophy. He attended lectures on the rise of pacifism, debated imperialism in the Third World, argued empiricism versus rationalism. He read Confucius, Kant, Spinoza, Locke. In particular he read Marx.

Throughout his time there he developed a passion for just two English institutions – cricket and Byron, skipping an occasional afternoon's lecture to indulge both on the terraces at Lord's, *Wisden* in one pocket, *The Corsair* in the other. He also played cricket, initially for his house, later for the school, developing a lethal off-break spin-bowling technique by tossing balls, hour after hour, pitch-length into a circle marked out in the grass.

In the holidays he generally tried to arrange to stay with school friends, often to their surprise. On one such holiday, with a fellow sixteen-year-old from his house called Alastair Towning, he discovered an affinity and love for sailing, passing almost an entire summer in a small boat on an Essex estuary.

If offers for holidays were unforthcoming, however, he went home. Steady if unspectacular advancement along the corridors of Whitehall had allowed Keith to move himself and the boys to better premises, a pleasant mews cottage off Wimpole Street. There the three of them rubbed along well enough in an atmosphere of restrained cooperation. Since Aurora's departure, Keith had retreated within, growing even more introverted than before, burying himself in his work which, what with the worsening political situation, in any case kept him more and more office bound. Often he and the boys would see little of each other for days at a time.

Which suited Michael well enough. When they did talk, he and Keith discussed little of personal consequence, preferring neutral topics such as politics, school, the Test score. As for Donald, although Michael always maintained a polite manner with his little brother, even playing with him when the need arose, he never bonded. They couldn't have been more different. In appearance, Donald was a miniature Keith, right down to his slight build and smiling, placatory manner. Beyond that he was a stranger to Michael, like distant lost kin. He was even a product of a different nation, a born Londoner, a native English speaker. Finally, as if the gulf between them was not already wide enough, he was also eight years Michael's junior. Apart from the obvious absence of common ground this age difference created, his lack of years meant that Donald had not the slightest understanding of Michael's early life. Of what it had felt like to be uprooted from Sombreado and shipped to England, of the misery he had endured at Holbrook, of the torment of his mother's departure. In fact, apart from Keith, about the only thing they did have in common was a mother who had run out on them both. And Donald's memories of her were little more than fragmentary.

Yet he was so desperate to learn. All of it. Of Aurora, and Uruguay, Montevideo and the Quemadas. Of Sombreado and growing up on the estancia. Of Tata and learning to ride. Maria, the Luengas, Chiquito, life on the pampas and all the other things he'd only heard mention of so fleetingly.

Above all, he longed for the love of the older brother he knew so slightly, yet worshipped so completely.

But Michael was otherwise preoccupied. As the end of his time at Westminster drew nearer, he, along with the world, grew increasingly edgy. Trapped on the sidelines by his age, he watched, helpless with frustration, as hundreds of conscientious young Englishmen went to the aid of his republican kinsmen in Spain, struggling against Franco's fascist tyranny. Before that conflict could be resolved, the escalating German situation was monopolising the headlines. The rearming of the Rhineland, the annexation of Austria, the Sudeten crisis and the fiasco that was Chamberlain and Munich. War was coming, then it wasn't, then it was, and the newspaper pundits and the politicians across the road, and his fellow sixth-formers and the man in the street all said that, if it did, it would be worse than anything anyone could ever imagine.

Suddenly, he was eighteen. It was June 1939, he was completing his School Certificate examinations. His school career was drawing to a close. He must think of university, of a career, a future. Invited by Keith, he took the bus home on the evening of the nineteenth to celebrate his birthday and discuss these matters. Keith gave him a sherry then took him to a restaurant in Baker Street, where they ate steak, drank claret, talked of a possible career in the Diplomatic Service and the worsening political situation. The news that day was of stalling Anglo-Soviet-French economic negotiations, and rumblings of possible aggression by Germany against Poland.

'Will there be war, Father?' he asked, towards the end of the evening. It was the question on everyone's lips. But this was no mere polite enquiry. Michael knew that Keith's views, balanced and informed as always, would also be based upon Foreign Office inside knowledge.

'It hardly bears thinking about, but I believe there can be little doubt.'

'How soon?'

'Soon enough, I fear.' Keith signalled a waiter for the bill. 'Our intelligence suggests that Germany is preparing to invade Poland. Possibly within as little as two months. If she cannot be persuaded against such a course of action, and Halifax's PPS told me himself that this seems doubtful, then Chamberlain will have no option but to declare war.' He began searching pockets for his wallet, his eyes on his son. Pensive, Michael was staring at the puddle of wine circling the bottom of his glass.

'Listen,' Keith reached forward, lightly touching his hand. 'This is supposed to be a celebration, remember? Eighteen today. Many congratulations and happy returns of the day. I've a little something for you back at the house. A package from Montevideo, too.'

Michael looked up. There was a buzzing, in his head. The wine, perhaps. 'You've heard from her?'

'Of course. You know your mother never forgets your birthdays.'

Presents. Trinkets, knick-knacks and tokens. That and meaningless three-line greetings cards or pink, scented notes about the weather and the dog and grandmother Quemada's rheumatism.

Suddenly he needed to ask, needed to know. Everything.

What happened? How could she have left? Where is she now? Why do we so rarely hear from her? And more. What about when we lived in Uruguay? Why was I raised in Sombreado? Why then did we have to leave? The questions, so many, so deeply buried for so long, crowded his mind, nagging him, jostling him, until he felt his head must burst. He had to know, *needed* to know. But finding the words, summoning the courage. They'd never spoken of these matters before, never. And now the waiter was coming, fussing with the bill. Keith's jacket was on, he was starting to rise. The moment was passing, slipping from his grasp. His head was cleaved in two, he was paralysed, helpless, and yet through it all a single small voice was calling to him, beckoning him. Like an idea. No, not an idea. Like a summons. 'I remember the night you were born . . .' Keith was saying, leading him to the door, Michael practically reeling. Yet it wasn't the wine. It was the voice, the presence. It was clear, obvious. After so long. The Spanish, the Germans. Exam results, a proper career, a future, it was all irrelevant, none of it mattered. 'It was winter there, of course, but an unusually mild night as I recall. I sat with you and your mother for a little while, then went for a long walk, all around Montevideo harbour. For hours.'

'Where you took me that day we had ice-cream and you told me we were leaving Uruguay?'

'You remember that?'

'Of course.' How could he doubt it? They walked outside. There had been rain, a sharp summer shower. Everything glistened, gleamed, washed clean and clear. The cars and buses, the streets and pavements, the night air, even the stars.

Keith was standing at the kerb, head cocked, remembering. 'I ended up at some sort of street party, you know, down in the immigrant quarter. They were the poorest people, and there I was, all togged up in my best suit. But they didn't mind a bit, immediately made me welcome, fed me, gave me a glass of some lethal home-brewed cane spirit. It was very moving, probably the happiest night of my life, come to think of it. I shall never forget it. They wouldn't let me go. We sang and danced, toasting your birth, time and again. As if they knew you, as if you were already a part of them. As if you were theirs.'

'I'm going back, Donald.'

'To London? Already? But you can't!'

'No, I mean I'm going back to Uruguay.'

'What! Can I come?'

Michael laughed. 'No, old chap. You certainly cannot.'

'But, but, golly! When, Mikey? And how long for? What are you going to do? Are you coming back? Are you going to see Mother?'

'Slowly, Don, slowly.' Out in the field there was the snick of ball edged off bat, followed by a raucous shout of triumph. Another of their team was out, the second that over. Michael, next but one to bat, began padding up, a frisson of excitement immediately washing over the spectators like a warm breeze. All around, Donald's classmates waited with baited breath. Villiers senior had come down from

Westminster for the day. Better yet, Villiers junior had managed to persuade him to play for the fourth form. He was legendary, not just as a cricketer, but as Holbrook's most infamous old boy. The man who stayed up a tree for a week, until the army had to be called. The man who ran away and took the train home to London, first class. The man who wore out all of Killer's canes and yet took his beatings without so much as a murmur.

'Soon. I'm going just as soon as arrangements can be made. How long for, I can't say at this stage.'

'Are you going to see Mother?'

'Yes, but there also are other things I need to do, and people to see.' Answers. It was about getting answers.

'Sombreado?'

'Hopefully.'

'Crikey, you lucky beast! What does Dad say?'

'Well, he was pretty anti the whole idea, as you can imagine.' Silence. Nothing but an angry pacing silence, for minutes, back and forth across the carpet. Michael had never seen him so angry. It had started badly. After the restaurant, after he'd opened the usual meaningless birthday package from Aurora. How can you stand it? he'd wanted to shout. How could you let her just walk away from us like that? But instead they'd argued about the other war. Particularly about appeasement. Keith was all for it. War is a failure of reason, he kept saying. I have to believe there is a diplomatic solution to our difficulties. But don't you ever believe in confronting failure head on? Michael had argued, deliberately provoking him. Taking failure by the scruff of the neck and just sorting it out? Don't you see, Father, it is weak to keep retreating from provocation? They both knew what he meant, the accusation hanging between them like a curse. It was then that Uruguay had come up. I'm going, Michael had said. Just like that. I have to. Keith was stunned. Simply forbidding it, at first, after the angry pacing. No, Michael, no. I simply cannot allow it. Then, when he saw that wasn't going to work, he tried persuasion, then reason, even pleading. But what in God's name do you hope to achieve, Michael? What possible good can come of it? But in the end, when he knew he was lost, had come a sort of shocked acquiescence. As if he'd known this would happen, some day. As if he'd known all along there was nothing he could do to stop it.

Michael studied the game, stretching his fingers into batting gloves. 'It was a little difficult, but we talked it through. I believe he sort of accepts it now. He's given me money, and the names of a few contacts at the embassy in Montevideo.'

'Gosh. Wish I'd been there to see it.'

'Probably best that you weren't, Don.'

One condition, Keith had pleaded. Just one condition, an odd one. Go and see your brother, would you? Go to Donald, Michael. Tell him yourself. Explain it to him. It seemed somehow terribly important to him. Michael had hesitated. See Donald? What for? They were practically strangers. And as for returning to Holbrook, that was the very last thing he had planned for. Yet now that he was actually here, he realised, the place had no hold over him, no terrors. Only memories. He had nothing to fear from it.

And, strangely, it was good to see Donald. Good to be sitting here, cross-legged on the grass beside him.

'So,' Michael ventured tentatively. 'How are you getting along here?'

'Not too bad. Food's utter mush of course and our dorm captain snores all night, but summer terms are wizard, what with all the cricket and that, and lessons are pretty much a doddle.'

'Do you have friends?'

'Loads. Hawthorne's my best friend. Him and Pascoe. We've got a gang.'

'That's good.' He hesitated. Donald was plucking grass stems, trying to make a noise by blowing through them. 'What about Killer. Had a tanning from him yet?'

'Course not! We're far too clever to get caught.'

'Yes. I believe you probably are.'

Something was happening out on the pitch. One batsman had hit the ball and started running, but the other, having initially responded, was now changing his mind. Trapped like infantrymen in no-man's land, both, shouting hysterically, were now scurrying in panicked circles. Michael began to rise, brushing grass from his whites. 'That doesn't look too good. I fear I'm about to be on.'

'Mikey? Are you coming back?'

'Of course. As soon as I'm done out there.'

Chapter 6

The SS *Runswick Bay*, under the command of Captain Dennis Beecham, sailed from Tilbury for Montevideo one blustery afternoon three weeks later. Built on the Clyde in 1928 for the Marwood Steamship Company of Whitby, *Runswick Bay* was a 4000-ton coal-fired cargo steamer. In her holds she carried engineering components for the AEC and Vanguard trucks plying Uruguay's dirt roadways, medical equipment for her sparsely equipped hospitals and Scotch whisky for her hotels and bars. She also carried twelve passengers, Michael Villiers among them.

Just before departure, Captain Beecham was summoned to the harbour-master's office where an unsmiling man in civilian clothing briefed him in unusual detail about his passage. At the end of the briefing the man handed him several sealed packets stamped 'To be opened in the event of hostilities only' and a weighted canvas bag to keep them in.

'This lot stays in your cabin under lock and key at all times,' he instructed. 'And if it all goes pear-shaped and you run into trouble, make damn sure they go over the side.'

'All a bit cloak and dagger isn't it?' Beecham hefted the bag. 'Does the Admiralty think the balloon's really going up?'

The man regarded him frostily. 'Just taking proper precautions, Captain. I would take them seriously if I were you. In the meantime, make sure your radio operator stays on the ball; you'll hear soon enough if anything happens.'

Michael was receiving a not dissimilar dockside cautioning from his father.

'This really is not a good time to be embarking on a long journey, you know,' Keith fretted, surveying *Runswick Bay*'s rust-streaked sides. 'Chamberlain insists there are still grounds for optimism, and Lord knows we must all hope and pray that he is right. But if he isn't, we could be at war in a matter of weeks. Or less.'

'I understand your concern, Father, really I do. But I have to go, we both know that. And I will be careful, I promise.' Now that the moment had arrived Michael was impatient to be aboard, longing to be alone and away. Half an hour later he was. 'I hope you find what it is you're looking for,' Keith had said, as they finally parted. They had shaken hands formally. 'But you should be prepared that it may not be to your liking.'

That night, over a lamb-chop dinner in *Runswick Bay*'s cramped saloon, Michael met Captain Beecham and his fellow passengers. There were four engineers and their wives on a two-year posting to the huge Anglo-Refrigeration meat processing plant in Fray Bentos, a retired Uruguayan politician and his wife returning home after six months touring Europe, and Michael's cabin mate, a Presbyterian clergyman from Glasgow called MacNeish, bound for a ministry in Saltó. Spirits were high, the talk, earnest and animated, was of the ship, their five-week voyage and, inevitably, the prospects for war. Afterwards, Michael stood outside on deck, listening to the water hissing along the ship's sides, watching the lights of Canvey and Sheppey slide slowly astern, as the muddy waters of the Thames widened into the Channel approaches.

Shipboard life soon settled into a rhythm. Roused by a steward with tea at seven, MacNeish and he took turns shaving at their tiny wash cubicle before joining the others in the saloon for breakfast. By eight the day was theirs until lunchtime, and then theirs again until they all met at seven for sherry before dinner. Being principally a cargo ship, *Runswick Bay* had few entertainment facilities for her passengers. There was no swimming pool or cinema, no piano bar, shops or casino, no gymnasium. There was deck quoits for the energetic, a small lounge stocked with month-old magazines and dog-eared mystery novels, deck chairs for the well wrapped, the bar in the saloon, and the sea view. It was the latter that captivated Michael from the beginning. He never tired of it, passing hour after hour at the rail, inhaling the ocean's salt freshness, watching its changing moods and hues. Brown, choppy and brackish at first, as they proceeded down Channel he noted it became a little longer, and bluer. Then, rounding Ushant and heading out into the open Atlantic, it changed again, spectacularly, *Runswick Bay* lifting to the first of a legion of cobalt-blue rollers. Within hours, all sense of land, of limits and boundaries, had melted into memory, replaced by a limitless vista of wide undulations stretching as far as he could see. Awed and thrilled, it affected him deeply, touching something primordial and complex, rooted in instincts he hadn't felt in a decade. A feeling of freedom yet of purpose, of acute loneliness and yet also of belonging.

'What do you make of it all then, lad?' a voice called from above one morning. Michael, at his habitual post at the rail, was watching storm petrels scythe effortlessly between snowy foam crests. He squinted upwards. It was Captain Beecham, leaning over the bridge wing.

'I . . . well, I like it. Thank you, sir. Very much.'

Beecham surveyed the sea. 'Yes, well, she's not always so much of the lady, the Atlantic, you know. But pretty as a picture on a day like this. Would you like to come up? You've an even better view from here.'

From then on Michael passed his every possible waking moment on the bridge. Within another week or so, with *Runswick Bay* tramping steadily southwards towards the tropics, Beecham's officers and crew had stopped remarking politely upon his arrival there each morning; instead they began chiding him if he was late. He learned the watch system and which of their faces he could expect there at what times of the day and night. He met the engineering officer, a red-faced Geordie in filthy overalls who led him down a bewildering maze of ladders and passages, deep into the stifling heat of the ship's maw, there to induct him, at the shout, into the deafening mysteries of her reciprocating steam-propulsion system. He spent hours with the first and second mates who explained in turn the basics of navigation in the little chart room behind the bridge. How to plot course, speed and distance. How to estimate the ship's position by dead reckoning. How then to verify it using a heavy brass sextant and pages of mathematical tables to sight and reduce the azimuth of the midday sun, or a clutch of stars at night.

He learned, too, after a fashion, how to steer the ship, although no matter how hard he tried, his efforts at holding a steady heading seemed serpentine at best.

'For Christ's sake, man, stop chasing her about like a drunk after a tart!' the helmsman scolded late one evening. He, like most of the crew, had long forgotten that Michael was a fare-paying passenger. 'You see, Mick, lad, you got to be gentle, like. And take your time with her, like you're havin' a good scr— like, as it were, you're taking her out for a quiet stroll along the prom, not on to the dance floor for a bloody foxtrot!' Gradually, the green-glowing wake trailing astern began to straighten.

He went down to the radio room – a mysterious humming world of valves and knobs crammed into what was little more than a cubbyhole beneath the bridge. With a spare pair of headphones clamped to his ears he listened, late into the night, to the sea of clicks, chirrups and whistles filling his head, while the radio operator, his face a distant frown of concentration, inched tuning dials back and forth, or tickled out Morse messages at impossible speed to other radio operators, in other ship's cubby holes, on other patches of ocean all across the world.

Above all, whenever he could, whenever the captain seemed in the mood, he would listen, spellbound, to Dennis Beecham's bottomless fund of sea stories. Of Pacific typhoons and oceans of Sargasso weed, Arctic icebergs and coral atolls. Roaring forties and Newfoundland fogs. He even learned, simply by watching the eyes of other seamen standing nearby, which of Beecham's stories were exaggerated and which, more intriguingly, were all the weightier for omission.

'Michael,' the Captain began, one overcast morning, apropos of nothing. He was staring straight ahead through the windscreen, his eyes glued to his binoculars. 'Take it from me. You don't want to spend . . . much time at all . . . in a lifeboat.'

Michael waited, but that was it, nothing more. He opened his mouth to speak, but the third mate stopped him with a discreet shake of the head.

Sometimes one of the other male passengers might venture on to the bridge, strutting about nosily, getting in everyone's way, cracking feeble jokes and asking idiotic questions. Michael resented these intrusions; they upset his rapport with the crew who became unnaturally polite and deferential with him, even after the visitor had gone, reminding him that he too was merely a clumsy landlubber. Mercifully, once everyone had made their requisite visit to the bridge, they seldom returned.

They preferred the club-like ambience of the saloon. Particularly mealtimes, when the prospect of cooked food and absurdly cheap offshore bar prices loosened tongues and belts. Even corsets, evidently. Sometimes discussions became heated. Late one steamy night, around the time that *Runswick Bay* was crossing the equator, as the pastor MacNeish would later recall, but for Michael's calm intervention they might easily have got out of hand.

Two of the Fray Bentos engineers were falling out apparently, because of political differences, everyone assumed. That night, as usual, the moment coffee was served, the talk had gravitated to war.

'Excuse me for saying so, Davies, but you don't have the foggiest idea what you're talking about,' the older engineer of the group was saying, rather drunkenly, to his subordinate. 'Appease these blighters and we'll never hear the end of it.'

Davies, a Londoner in his twenties, glanced across the table at the older man's wife. His own sat beside him, head lowered. 'I'm just saying, what's it got to do with us, Poland and all that? We've enough problems of our own to deal with, without the Prime Minister scuttling about the place trying to settle everyone else's. He should be at home more, sorting out the mess on the railways, and that.'

'Railways, for God's sake? Don't you know there are

more important things going on at the moment than sorting out trivial domestic matters at home?'

Stung, Davies was still watching the other man's wife. 'I know that a man who ignores "trivial domestic matters", as you call them, is a fool.'

'What the hell do you mean by that?' The older man was instantly on his feet.

'Gentlemen, gentlemen, please,' MacNeish soothed. 'There are ladies present.' But one of the ladies was already weeping into a handkerchief, while the other, tight lipped, stared at her plate. The elderly Uruguayans looked on anxiously.

'I asked you a question, Davies.' The older man spoke menacingly, his face red and perspiring. In the corners of the saloon, electric fans rattled ineffectually. 'What do you mean by that? You'll answer me, now, or I'll see you outside.'

'Clive . . .' his wife ventured, resting a hand on his arm. But he shrugged it off.

'I'm waiting, Davies!'

'Did you know, in Uruguay, in the sixteenth century, Spanish invaders would read a *requerimiento* to the Indians they captured, before they slaughtered them.' Michael spoke directly to the older engineer.

'Wha—'

'Read a what?' someone else asked.

'No, I didn't know that, Michael,' MacNeish said encouragingly.

'What the hell is a *requeri* . . . whatever he said.' The

older man, still standing, was staring around the table, a confused half-smile on his lips.

'*Requerimiento*. It is a requirement,' the Uruguayan politician joined in. 'It required them to renounce whatever faith they might have of their own, and adopt the holy Catholic faith. Then and there, or face the penalties.'

'What penalties?' one of the wives asked, her head still lowered.

'Enslavement of the women and children, massacre of the men.'

'Christ,' Davies, thrown, could only join in. 'Did they go along with it?'

'They couldn't.' Michael's eyes, firm yet calm, swung between the two engineers. 'The Spaniards read the *requerimiento* to them in Latin, a language that had never been heard in South America. But according to papal decree, as long as they read it, that was all right. Then they could go ahead and kill the Indians anyway. With the blessing of God.'

Michael disarmed these dangerously angry men with his story, MacNeish wrote later, adding: as well as having a passion for his country, he is a natural peacemaker.

About a week later, straight after his breakfast, Michael was climbing the companionway steps to the bridge, as usual. Unusually, however, he found Beecham standing far out on the bridge wing, together with both his first and second officers. All ignored him. Three pairs of binoculars were being trained on to a barely visible speck on the horizon. For minutes, nobody spoke.

'Look at the size of that foretop,' one of them said eventually.

'Hmm. And the speed of the thing. It's no passenger steamer, that's for sure.'

'One of those new twelve-thousand-ton high-speed freighters, d'you think?'

'Possibly.' Another silence, Michael waited. Still the three men stared through their binoculars.

'Those aren't deck cranes. They're gun turrets, they must be.'

'You're right. Jesus, huge ones, too. Two triples, one fore, one aft.'

Another pause. 'So. It's definitely a warship, then.' The second mate hesitated. 'One of ours, do you suppose?'

Finally Beecham lowered his glasses. 'Who knows. But he's headed our way, and in a hurry.' He gnawed his lip, studying the approaching vessel, now clearly visible at about ten miles distance. The news from home, the escalating volume of radio traffic, the streams of Admiralty signals to British ships the world over – the signs had been increasingly ominous for days. 'Better be safe than sorry. Number One, chart room, please. Fix our position, as accurately as you can, and pass it down to the radio hut. Number Two, go and wake Sparks; as soon as he's got the fix, tell him to get a signal off, on six hundred metres, plain language: "*Steamship Runswick Bay, oh-seven-twenty hours, am being closed by unidentified warship.*" Tell him to add the position and keep sending until he gets an acknowledgement.' He raised his binoculars once more. 'God, look at that bow wave! He must be going twenty-five knots.'

'Can I do anything?' Michael asked quietly.

'No, thank you, Michael. Actually, wait, yes there is something.' Beecham pulled a bunch of keys from his pocket. 'My cabin, you know where it is. There's a safe in the wall above the bunk. In it you will find a canvas sack. Don't open it, just bring it here. Oh, and while you're at it, pick up my copy of *Jane's Fighting Ships* from my bookshelf; let's see if we can't identify this so-and-so.'

By the time he got back, the so-and-so was barely five miles away. Coming straight at them, head on and flat out. Michael glanced down: passengers were appearing on deck, the two engineers' wives, arm in arm, pointing with amusement at the rapidly closing intruder. Beecham fumbled with the sack, tearing open envelopes until he found a sheaf of cards, each with the black outline of a warship on it. 'Try these.' He handed them to his first officer. 'See if you can get a match. I'll try *Jane's*.' He began thumbing pages, one eye on the ship. It was beginning to slow at last, and to turn. 'God, I think he means to come alongside!'

Mesmerised, Michael stared as the monster neared. It was vast, nearly three times the length of *Runswick Bay*, its grey-painted hull low and streamlined. Above the deck an angular superstructure rose, towering high into the sky, bristling with masts and aerials. Dominating its profile, two huge armoured gun turrets, each with three finger-like barrels stretching more than twenty-five feet fore and aft.

'It's German,' Michael said, pointing. 'Look, you can see the flag now.'

Beecham straightened, training glasses on the fluttering

black and red cross of the German Imperial Navy. 'Well that's that,' he muttered. 'Any luck with those blasted cards, Number One?'

'Still looking. What length would you say she is? Five hundred feet?'

'Six, maybe a little more. Displacement a good twelve thousand tons. As for armament, those bloody great guns are eleven-inch, I'm sure of it, two turrets of three. She's also got at least eight six-inch guns, and some four-inch, plus anti-aircraft batteries, pom-poms, torpedo tubes aft . . .' He broke off; the ship was completing its turn, drawing neatly parallel with *Runswick Bay* to match both her speed and course. The gap between them was less than four-hundred yards, and closing by the minute. Suddenly they were cast into shadow as the intruder's towering silhouette blotted out the low morning sun. 'Now what . . .'

'It's a *Panzerschiff*!' the first officer reported, holding up one of the cards.

'And what the hell is that when it's at home?' Beecham raised his glasses once more. 'Jesus, how much closer is she coming?'

'It's a pocket battleship. Deutschland class.'

'Wonderful. Does it say what he wants? Hang on, there's a name plate, or something, on the tower. *Coronel*, it says. Is that a name? I've never heard of it.'

'No, it's either the *Lutzow*, *Graf Spee* or the *Scheer*. They're the only three.'

Suddenly the ship was upon them, towering above *Runswick Bay*, the sea sluicing angrily between the closing

165

hulls like a river in spate. They could hear the deep throbbing of its engines, hear klaxons and loudspeakers relaying orders in German. Sailors in white tunics and ribboned hats hurried to their stations. Figures in immaculate white uniforms were appearing on the bridge. One of them was holding a megaphone. Michael glanced down again. Below him, Davies' wife was now pointing at the ship in alarm, one hand over her mouth, the others watching in astonishment.

'Good morning, Captain!' the white-clad figure called, in English. He waved cheerily. 'It is indeed a fine day, no?'

'Yes, indeed it is, thank you!' Beecham called back. Beside him, the first officer's binoculars were still searching the ship.

'Look,' he murmured to Beecham. 'A name board, forward of the funnel. She's the *Scheer*!'

'Odd place to put it,' said Beecham, returning the German captain's wave. 'Get a signal off, right away: "*Oh-eight-hundred, Steamship Runswick Bay intercepted by German pocket battleship Scheer*."' He eyed the canvas bag lying nearby, stuffed full of secret instructions, signal codes, shipping routes. Should he throw it overboard? If it all goes pear-shaped, the man at Tilbury had said. But what on earth did that mean?

'Please do not alarm yourself, your passengers or your crew, Captain,' the figure in white was saying. Even through the megaphone his voice had a mellifluous, almost hypnotic quality. 'I am here only to offer you a friendly caution.'

'Oh, yes? And what might that be?'

'It is unfortunate, but in just a very short time now, the open ocean will no longer be a safe place for unprotected

British merchant vessels. You should proceed to your destination with all possible speed. May I enquire where you are bound?'

'Montevideo, Uruguay.'

'Ah, yes, I know it. A delightful harbour, and a charming people. I very much hope to visit it again some day. May I take this opportunity to wish you a safe conclusion to your voyage there, and reiterate, with all respect, the importance of your doing so with the utmost haste.'

'Er, yes. Yes you can. Thank you, Captain.'

Transfixed, Michael watched as a rating handed the German captain a note. Instinctively he sensed it was about *Runswick Bay*'s radio message. Then the figure in white looked up, directly at him, it seemed, gazing right into him. 'Until the next time!' he called, still smiling. Then he saluted and turned inside. A moment later the pocket battleship was sheering gracefully away into the sun.

A few days later, on a Sunday afternoon, Beecham gathered the passengers and all available crew into the packed saloon.

'I have just received a coded radio signal to all ships from the Admiralty,' he announced soberly. 'I'm sorry about this, but, as of today, it appears we are at war with Germany. God save the king.'

A week later *Runswick Bay* entered harbour in Montevideo.

That first evening and night passed in a blur. Within minutes of docking, *Runswick Bay* was boarded by port officials, immigration officers and policemen. Since the outbreak of hostilities, it transpired, details of all arriving foreign nationals were required to be recorded; furthermore, foreigners had also to report to their own embassies before they could travel freely. Only the elderly Uruguayan politician and his wife were permitted to disembark that night, and by the time the formalities were completed for the rest, it was too late to find lodgings ashore. They stayed on board.

But the sounds of the city, the strange yet familiar shouts of the dockers, the honking of the traffic, the drifting food and fumes smells, were too much for Michael. Rigid with excitement, he lay for hours, staring at the city's glow beyond the porthole. Finally, with MacNeish snoring in the bunk above, he quickly dressed, stole ashore and vanished into the Ciudad Vieja.

The next morning, he bade his shipmates farewell, paid one last visit to *Runswick Bay*'s empty bridge, then, suitcase in hand, went in search of the British Embassy.

It had moved a few blocks from the cramped offices of Keith's day. And grown, now occupying three floors in the Edificio Commerciale on Plaza Matriz. To Michael's surprise, the moment he presented his papers to the receptionist, she got to her feet, ushering him upstairs into a comfortably furnished office with a view of the harbour. A moment later, a tall, smartly suited man with grey, close-set eyes and broadly smiling mouth, strode in, hand outstretched.

'Eugen Millington-Drake,' he enthused. 'You must be Keith Villiers' boy, Michael. Welcome to Montevideo.'

'I, well, thank you, sir. Are you the ambassador?'

'British Minister. Same thing, although strictly speaking we're still a legation, not yet a fully fledged embassy, as it were. Between you and me, I'm pushing mighty hard for our promotion to the first division.' He winked, seating himself behind an elegant mahogany desk. 'Sit, Michael, sit. Tea? Tell me, how was your passage?' He pressed a button on the desk.

'Oh, er, yes please, and fine, thank you, sir.'

'Splendid. And your father, I met him once or twice, at FO shindigs here and there. How is he?'

'He's very well, thank you, sir.'

'Good, good.' His eyes slid momentarily to a dossier on his desk. 'And your mother?'

'I, well I'm not sure, to be honest, sir, I haven't had a chance, yet to . . .'

'Of course, of course! Idiotic of me. So sorry, we're all at sixes and sevens here since hostilities broke out. Half the time I haven't a clue whether it's Monday morning or Piccadilly Circus!' A secretary entered, bearing a tea tray. There were three cups on it. Michael shifted on his chair. Something was going on.

'May I ask, sir, is everything all right? At home, that is. With the war?'

'The war? At home? Oh my dear boy, good heavens yes! Do not worry yourself about family and that. Absolutely nothing's happened, nothing at all. Nor is it likely to, not for months. If at all, at least that's our reading of the situation. Probably all be over by Christmas.'

'Oh, I see. And, Uruguay. I mean, whose side is she on? Will she be able to stay neutral? What about the socialist pressures from Argentina and Brazil?'

Millington-Drake laughed. 'Good questions, Michael, well put. Tell me, have you considered a career in the diplomatic service?' A side door opened, a man in Royal Navy uniform entering quietly. 'No, for the moment, officially at least, Uruguay is adamantly neutral. General Baldomir, the President, is popular, if something of an unknown, but his Foreign Minister, Alberto Guani, is a first-rate chap. I've known him since 'fourteen, life and soul. He's definitely on side. Ah, Henry! Come in, let me introduce you to young Michael here.'

The man in the uniform stepped forward. Michael stood, awkwardly, to shake his hand. Tea with the ambassador, small-talking about the President, now a visit from the British Navy. What on earth was going on?

'Michael, this is Henry McCall, our naval attaché. He's already spoken to Beecham and his men about your exciting encounter with that German warship. Do you feel up to answering a few of his questions?'

The pocket battleship. The *Scheer*. The smiling figure in white. That's what this was about. Nothing to do with his father, or politics, or the war at home. They just wanted to know everything there was to know about the *Scheer*.

McCall, a methodical, quietly spoken man, took over. He led Michael through every minute of the encounter from the moment the ship was first sighted, to when it finally veered away. With only minimal prompting, Michael was able to recall every smallest detail.

'Could you see any aeroplanes on board?' McCall asked at one point.

'One. On a catapult-type thing just aft of the funnel.'

'Was it a biplane, you know, with two wings?'

'No, it had one wing. And floats. It was painted dark green and had a rearward pointing machine-gun.'

McCall and Millington-Drake exchanged glances, notes were jotted, then the questions resumed. Finally after nearly half an hour, they seemed satisfied.

'One last thing.' McCall was gathering his notes. 'The German captain. How well could you see him?'

He could see him now. The relaxed yet dignified posture. The open smiling face, the smooth tones. 'Quite well. He was about five foot ten, medium build, sort-of round faced.'

'I see. How old, would you say?'

'Perhaps forty-five. He was a little way off, you know.'

'Indeed. Was he rude, in his manner, at all? Aggressive?'

'No, sir. Not at all. He was very polite.'

Again the two men swapped glances. 'Langsdorff?' Millington-Drake suggested.

'Possibly.' McCall scrawled more notes.

'Was it the *Scheer*, sir?'

McCall looked up. 'Why do you ask that?'

'Well, I just wondered. All these questions, it's as though you are trying to confirm it. Or not. And Captain Beecham. He said there was something odd about the painted name panel on the ship. Also . . .'

'Yes? Go on.'

'Well, sir, with war on the point of breaking out, why did the German captain risk coming right over and showing us his ship, knowing Captain Beecham would report its name and position? When he could have simply radioed his message to us.'

That evening, Michael went in search of Aurora. The legation had kindly provided him with temporary lodgings. Nothing grand, Millington-Drake had warned him, rarely used, but adequate enough for visiting clerical staff and so on. He'd accompanied Michael downstairs, giving him directions and a little map.

'What are your plans?' he'd asked. Passers-by eddied around them, the pavements busy with shoppers and office workers. Scattered clouds dotted a pale blue sky, the air was mild and smelled of warm city streets.

'Visit relatives, sir. Here in Montevideo and also in the interior.'

'The interior? Not sure that's a very good idea right now, old thing. Better stay put here for a while. Just in case McCall wants to talk to you again, and whatnot. You don't mind, do you?'

He found the lodgings. They were on the upper landing of a tall stone-fronted building in the heart of the mercantile district, not far from the harbour. His room, at the top of a steep stairwell, was rather small and sparsely furnished, but pleasantly light with large shuttered windows. Millington-Drake said it had been little-used for some time, not since the legation had moved from its old address. In his father's day. Sniffing the musty air like a wary dog, he dropped his bag, threw wide the windows and collapsed on to an ancient iron bedstead.

When he awoke it was growing dark. He lay for a minute, blinking, savouring the sound of the city stirring to life for the evening. He padded barefoot to the window, stood on a narrow iron balcony watching people and traffic passing below. Then, with the address of the Quemada family home in his pocket, he gathered his map and, ignoring a nagging hollowness in his stomach, went to find his mother.

It was a long walk to Prado. He struck out northwards, passing only slowly out of the bustling old city with its pavement stalls and wood-fronted bars, through the brooding harbourfront district of factories and warehouses, and then at length into the first residential streets and avenues. Initially, it was exciting, a journey both of exploration and rediscovery. Uruguay, the Uruguay he remembered, was nothing like this. Montevideo was just a name, a little boy's ice-cream, long ago. And yet this was his country's heart, and so much he sensed felt familiar. The language, ringing in his ears like long-forgotten song. The faces, the clothes, the laughter. Children playing at the roadside, strolling men drinking maté, a waft of mutton cooking on an open brazier. The clopping of a horse cart threading its way between the buses and trams. Head buzzing, he drank it in, intoxicated by its redolent strangeness.

But once away from the comforting downtown bustle, and with his destination drawing inexorably nearer, the gnawing at his stomach grew sharper. It wasn't simply hunger, he knew. It was fear. After all this time the moment was rushing suddenly upon him. It was too soon, too fast. He wasn't ready, perhaps he never would be. Seven years, of hurt, and bitter longing and uncomprehending loss. What would he say? Hello, Mama, why did you go? Alone, suddenly, the streets empty and silent save for his own plodding footfall, the old questions crowded his head. Why? Why did she leave, why did she never come back, and why did she never try and explain? More to the point, why had he come? What did he expect? From her. From their reunion. From himself. It was utter madness. He should never have come.

He looked up from the map, checking the address on the paper from his pocket. Avenida Agraciada. A large house set back from the street, imposing, shrouded in trees. There was a gate, a shadowy path. He pushed the gate open and walked to the door.

'Who?' a maid asked, eyeing him curiously. 'Wait here, I'll fetch the mistress.' A minute later a rustling of skirts behind the door, a woman's murmur, the door opened wider. 'Miguel?' an elderly woman asked. 'Miguel, is it really you?'

He followed, palms sweating, as she led him into a panelled library. 'Why did you not warn us you were coming?' she chided. 'No one is here this evening. Your grandfather, your aunts and uncles, they will be furious to have missed you.' She gestured him to a leather chair.

'I'm sorry, I did send a telegram, to my mother, at this address?'

'Your mother does not reside at this address,' the woman replied briskly. As she spoke her eyes travelled across his face, his hair, his clothes. 'My goodness,' she went on, more softly. 'It really is you.'

'Yes, Señora. Are you, excuse me, but are you Doña Madeleina?'

'Me?' She looked taken aback. 'No, no, Miguel. Sadly, Doña Madeleina passed away a few years ago, at a great age. No, I am your grandmother. Your mother's mother. Florentina.'

Michael brightened. 'Of course, Florentina Rapoza. Tata's, I mean Don Adrián's daughter, sister of Gertrudis.'

'That's right,' she smiled coyly. 'So you do remember me.'

'Well, no. A little, perhaps. Please, how is your father, Don Adrián?'

'Old, Miguel. He is old, and quite poorly. His mind wanders.'

'I am sorry. I am very anxious to see him. And the Luengas, are they well?'

Her eyes faltered fractionally. 'They are well. So I believe.'

'I am glad. I want to see them too. Very much.'

'Really? Well. As you wish.'

They talked a while longer. His grandmother appeared genuinely pleased, if a little unsettled, to see him. She enquired just once after Keith, and dear little Donaldo, but then moved swiftly on to other topics. Her husband, José-Luis, had retired from the Transport Ministry, she explained. Her sons were flourishing, growing in importance, moving up through the party hierarchy. Both had large families now, her grandchildren – her *other* grandchildren – she hastily corrected, were regular visitors.

But she never mentioned Aurora. Not once. In the end Michael had to ask for himself. Florentina immediately looked down at her hands.

'We do not see very much of her in this house.'

'Oh. Where can I find her?'

'I believe she may be found at the family apartment, in Pocitos. On occasion. I will give you the address if you don't have it.'

Interview over, she led him back to the hall. Opening the front door, she hesitated. 'This, well, I know, perhaps this cannot be easy for you,' she said awkwardly, handing him the address.

'No, grandmother. Not easy. But I am very glad to have met you.'

Suddenly, standing there before him in the shadows, a hint of spring jasmine hanging in the still night air, she reached out, cupping his cheeks in her hands. 'You were so unlucky, Miguel. With your parents, and, well, your circumstances. But very beautiful. Always. It was the first thing I noticed about you. On the night you were born, right here in this house. Unlucky but beautiful.'

He walked back to his lodgings. He took a different route, wandering west until he came to a disused Italian amphitheatre on a low bluff overlooking the bay. He descended to the waterfront, following it back towards the old city. By the time he finally arrived at his room it was gone midnight.

He lay tossing on his bed, unsleeping, for hours. Finally, around dawn, he dozed, his fitful slumbers filled with dreams of rolling oceans, a man in white uniform, and his mother's perfumed embrace. When he awoke, with a start, late in the morning, she was standing at the foot of his bed.

'Hello, angel,' she smiled. 'I hope you don't mind; the *portero* let me in.'

'Mother?' He sat up, bleary with sleeplessness, his ears still ringing with the thunder of receding surf. Was he dreaming? 'Mother, is it really you? How long have you been here? How did you know where to find me?'

Still smiling, she came round to him, kissed him, a vision of scented loveliness in satin suit and gloves. Her hair was shorter than he remembered it, fashionably styled in the modern way. Her face was powdered, lips rouged. She looked like an American film star. Better, she looked real. 'Already the questions!' She laughed. 'Yes, it is me. I have been here a little while, and your grandmother told me where to find you.'

'You've spoken with her?'

'Not exactly. She sent a boy with a note.' She sat beside him on the bed, studying him, brushing gloved fingers through his fair hair, lightly tracing the line of his face and neck. 'Miguel, my God, but look what a magnificent angel you have become.'

'Mother.' Inhaling her fragrance, mesmerised by the touch of her fingers, his eyes closed.

'Yes, angel.'

'Mother, I . . .'

'This room!' She looked around. 'I never liked it. Come. Let me take you to breakfast. Then we shall talk.'

She said she had to pay a short visit to a physician nearby. It was a little distance. She walked quickly, intently, along narrowing backstreets until they came to the door. She bade Michael wait outside; when she returned five minutes later, the smile was once more upon her face.

'Now then,' she sighed, lowering sunglasses to her eyes. 'Breakfast.'

She took him to a smart hotel on Avenida 18 de Julio. The waiters seemed to know her, bowing obsequiously, leading her to a window table. She told Michael to choose whatever he wanted. For herself she ordered only coffee, champagne ('Today is a celebration, angel!') and two packets of American cigarettes. When his food arrived, she watched, smoking and smiling indulgently, while Michael ate.

'Aren't you hungry, Mother?'

'No, dearest, I have already eaten. In any case we will be having a big meal later. With Willi Hochstetler and some friends from the German legation. You remember Willi Hochstetler, of course, Miguel?'

He shook his head.

'No? Ah. Well, Willi is, he is a very dear and special friend.' She drained her glass, lit another cigarette, blowing a long plume of spoke. 'He has shown me nothing but kindness, since, well, for a very long time. Nothing but kindness, do you understand?'

'Yes, Mother.'

'Good.' She refilled her glass, then suddenly went on, without preamble. 'You see, dearest boy, I just couldn't stay in London a minute longer. If the truth be known, it was probably a mistake that your father and I married in the first place. We are so very different in character. But while we remained in Uruguay we had, well we enjoyed, a sort of arrangement. Which worked for us both.'

'What sort of arrangement?'

'Your father had his work, and interests connected with that. I had mine. They were different, but it was possible to coexist, to continue our lives harmoniously.'

'I see. Is that why I stayed in Sombreado?'

'Yes, angel. At first it was your health, the cholera epidemic and everything. Later, I knew, we both knew, that the life we led was completely unsuited to a young child.' She hesitated. 'Also, when I visited, you looked so well, so strong. It reminded me of my own childhood there. How happy life was. How uncomplicated.'

'Mother?' A shadow of alarm, of bewilderment, was clouding her eyes.

'I did so want you with me, angel! Please believe me. But, I was afraid.'

'I do believe you, Mother, don't upset yourself. Why were you afraid?'

'I was afraid I might fail you.' I want to make our family work, Aurora, Keith had said, late one night. Work like a proper family, particularly now there is a new baby coming. He had been offered a posting back to England. He wanted them to return there, all together, and make a go of it. Just like that. She'd been appalled. Terrified. But then determined. Yes, she'd said, summoning her courage. Yes.

We will go, and I will do my utmost to be the wife and mother our family deserves. 'I'm so sorry, Michael!' Her hand flew to her mouth, tears appeared on her cheeks. Across the room the waiters pretended not to look. Michael reached tentatively for her hand.

'Mother?'

'Poor boys! You poor, poor, darling boys!' she sobbed. 'I am so sorry! I tried, the very best that I could, you must believe me. All I wanted was to love you and be a mother to you both. But I failed. It was so hard. Your father, he worked all the time, I never saw him. In any case, he didn't understand the loneliness I felt, leaving my life, my friends, my country, everything, to live in that strange place where I knew no one. And then you went away to school; it became worse, more difficult. My English, it was much weaker even than yours, I depended on you, at the shops, the doctor's and things. Then you were gone and I knew no one, I was alone in that freezing apartment with Donald. Alone and afraid. I'm so sorry. I ran away. It was unforgivable!'

'Mother, hush, nothing is unforgivable.'

'No! It can never be forgiven. It is my punishment. For my sin. I've always known it!' She was growing hysterical, her eyes wide and panicky, like a frightened animal's.

Michael strove to calm her. 'Mother, don't talk like that, I do understand. It was just that you left us so suddenly, with so few words. And since then, your letters and cards, at Christmas and birthdays and so on. You said so little. You never explained.'

'I can't explain!' she sobbed. It was almost a shriek. Heads turned. It was a lamentation, he suddenly realised, an anguished mother's lament. A too long held back outpouring of grief. And guilt. Like a weak dam finally giving way. 'I can't! Don't you see? I can't bear to face the terrible things that I have done!'

At midnight, Britain's Minister to Uruguay, Eugen Millington-Drake, was in the study of his colonial-style residence on Avenida Jorge Canning, not far from the national football stadium. He was wading through the latest sheaf of messages from London, in his pyjamas, a whisky at his side, when the night telephonist knocked on his door.

'Excuse me, Señor. A young man is waiting outside to see you,' he announced, his face a study of innocence.

'At this hour?' Millington-Drake queried. 'What on earth does he want?'

'I don't know, Señor. He seems a little excited. He says it is important. He says his name is Villiers.'

Millington-Drake lowered the papers. 'Very well, Aldo, I suppose you'd better show him in.'

Michael appeared, cheeks flushed. 'I'm so sorry, your excellency, to be intruding. So late. Like this.' His suit was rumpled, he fumbled ineffectually at his tie.

'That's quite all right. Where have you sprung from at this hour?'

'A party, sir. In Pocitos.'

'You walked here from Pocitos?'

'Yes, your excellency.'

'Michael, there is no need to call me excellency.'

'Sorry, sir. You see, I believe I may be a little drunk.'

'So it would appear.' Millington-Drake poured water from a jug. 'Here, drink this. Now Michael, what is all this about?'

'Langsdorff.'

'I beg your pardon?'

'It's about Langsdorff, sir.'

Millington-Drake's eyes narrowed. 'Michael, you're really not making a great deal of sense. Start from the beginning. You were at a party. Whose party was it?'

'Herr Hochstetler's. Willi's. He's a very close friend of my mother's. He's very nice chap and has this big house near my mother's apartment in Pocitos. Anyway, there was this big party with lots of important people, German business people, and diplomats and so forth, from the German legation.'

'Go on.'

'Well sir, we had this party, as I said, and some wonderful food, and I had quite a bit to drink, as you know. I met some very friendly people; the Germans seem to like parties, sir, don't they? Anyway, then I met this very important man called Herr Langmann. Willi says he is one of the top men at the German legation, you know?'

'Yes, I do. Otto Langmann. Go on.'

'Well, they were talking to me, and then Willi asked me to tell Herr Langmann the story about the *Scheer*, sir. About the pocket battleship we talked about, remember?'

'I remember; please go on, Michael.'

'Well, sir. At the end, when I got to the part about bringing the ship right alongside and the name painted on it and the captain having a chat and waving and wishing us a safe journey, they looked at each other, and just sort of laughed.'

'Laughed? Is that all? Didn't they say anything else?'

'Langsdorff. They said Langsdorff, sir. To be precise they said: "that Langsdorff", and then they laughed. It's the same name that you and Captain McCall said, you see, sir. I remembered it. Thought it might be important. And you said if I did think of anything else to do with *Scheer*, to come and tell you right away. So, well, I did.'

'Right. And you were absolutely right to do so, Michael. Absolutely right.' Millington-Drake was scribbling a note on to a pad; he pressed a buzzer on his desk and a moment later the night telephonist entered once more. 'This is for McCall. In BA. Send it right away, please.' He tore off the note. 'Now, Michael, I want you to stay right here in Montevideo for a while, where we can reach you, do you understand?'

'Yes, but you see sir, I have to go north to—'

'Not just now, you don't. You can go north when this business is over with. It is important, I do assure you.'

'Oh.' Michael stared into his glass. He was beginning to wish he hadn't come. 'Is Langsdorff the captain of *Scheer*, sir? Is that what this is about?'

'No, Michael. It is not. Hans Langsdorff is captain of the pocket battleship *Graf Spee*. It set sail from Wilhelmshaven in Germany some time in the last ten weeks but hasn't been seen since, although there have been numerous rumours and false sightings. McCall and his chums in naval intelligence believe she has been disguising herself. He also suspects that Langsdorff may have deliberately showed her to you that day, knowing she would be misidentified as the *Scheer*. But he couldn't prove it. Up until now.'

Chapter 7

Things went rather quiet aboard *Daisy*'s whaler following the appearance of the U-boat. Hardly surprising; I suppose there's not a great deal you can say after an encounter like that. 'Who'd have thought it?' perhaps, or, 'Blimey, there's something you don't see every day.'

No, the gloom-filled silence that followed said it all.

It was a peculiar sensation, bobbing about atop the featureless landscape of that vast ocean, knowing that down there somewhere, creeping about in the deep, was a two-hundred foot tin tube, its electric motors humming cosily, its forty occupants getting on with their daily chores. Tidying away their hammocks perhaps, writing letters home, or tucking into a hot breakfast. Unreal in one way. Comforting, almost, in another, knowing you weren't alone. But then, once you weighed it all up, not very comforting at all. Horribly ominous, in fact.

'Type seven,' Albert Giddings said eventually, breaking the silence. It was the first time since we'd all assembled on *Daisy*'s boat deck the previous night that he'd shown any interest in anything.

'Type nine,' Tuker corrected, predictably.

Giddings shook his head. 'Seven.'

'Listen, Giddings, you ignorant bloody pillock, I'm telling you, that submarine was a type nine!'

'Seven.'

We were sitting more or less in a circle, in the bottom of the boat, trying to keep out of the wind. It must have been around eight in the morning, daylight was fully up, but a tatty blanket of thick scud turned everything in our world – the sea, the sky – a cheerless metallic grey. I was next to Tuker on one side, Harrison and Giddings opposite. Michael, down at the stern, was lost to us, barricaded behind a wall of brooding abstraction. Even Tuker's grousing failed to penetrate it.

'You poxy bloody HOs are all the same! Been at sea five minutes and think you know it all. Eight years, I've got. Eight years! So you might just think I'd 'ave a bit more of a clue than a snivelling little toerag like you!'

'How come you're still just an AB, then?' Giddings shot back, unwisely.

'Why, you snotty little . . . !' Tuker actually began struggling to his feet. Immediately the boat rocked alarmingly. I grabbed his arm.

'Tuker! Leave it, for God's sake, you'll have us all in.'

'But you heard him, Mid! I don't 'ave to sit here and put up with that.'

'Well, yes, actually I'm afraid you do.'

'I agree with Albert.' Will Harrison piped up. 'I think it was a type seven.'

'And what the bloody hell would you know about it? You're just a poxy bunting tosser!'

'Leading signalman, if you don't mind.'

'Oh, well, lah-de-bloody-dah.'

Silence fell. For a while.

'About that U-boat, Mid,' Harrison went on. 'Did you notice anything?'

'It was a type seven,' Giddings muttered.

'Just a moment, Albert. No, Harrison. What about it?'

'The deck gun. That eighty-eight millimetre. Those two lads manning it.'

'What about them?'

'They never loaded the bugger,' Tuker interrupted.

'That's right. It was empty. A submarine wouldn't be mooching about under water with a loaded deck gun, and they never brought any ammo with them when they ran out to it. It was empty, had to be.'

'Good point. Well spotted, Will.' Although I couldn't say exactly what use this information might be.

'Eagle-eyes,' Giddings was muttering. 'That's what he said. Eagle-eyes.'

'What? What's he talking about now?'

'The skipper. Captain Deeds. He said I was the sharpest lookout on blue watch. When I got second best score in that last ship recognition test. And then when I spotted that barrel floating in the water just after we come out of Halifax last time. He called me eagle-eyes for spotting it. Could easily have been a mine, he said. We shall have to call you eagle-eyes from now on, he said.'

'He calls all lookouts eagle-eyes, you twit. It jollys them up, keeps them on their toes.'

'No, he doesn't! Don't say that!'

'Course he does. Didn't you realise?'

'Harrison, what was that story about the U-boat and that signalman on *Fuchsia*? What's his name, do you remember? Palmer? Patten?' It was one of Michael's tricks. For breaking up arguments. I'd watched him perform it on a number of occasions. Deflect their attention with an inconsequential side issue. It rarely failed. Harrison looked at me quizzically.

'You mean Parnwell, on *Lily*? And the muzzle flashes?'

'That's the one.'

'What story?' Tuker demanded, taking the bait.

'You tell it, Will,' I prompted Harrison.

'Well, as I heard it, *Lily* was on this convoy a couple of months back that got completely scattered during a gale. When the storm finally dies down, *Lily* and all the other escorts spend nearly four days scurrying about trying to round everyone up again. One afternoon she spots a contact in the distance and heads towards it. "Send the identification codes, get his ID, and tell him to rejoin the convoy," *Lily*'s skipper instructs his signalman. So Parnwell starts bashing out the message on the Aldis lamp and soon after gets a reply from the other ship. "What's he saying?" the skipper asks. "No idea, sir," Parnwell says. "His Morse is terrible."

Couple of seconds later there's huge explosions all round and *Lily* is straddled by eighty-eight millimetre shells. Turns out the contact is a U-boat, running on the surface. Wasn't a signal lamp Parnwell was trying to read, it was muzzle flashes from its deck gun.'

'Bloody *Lily*s always were a dozy lot,' Tuker grunted. 'What happened?'

'Well, *Lily*'s bridge is completely drenched in sheets of spray from the shells and that. Everyone dives for cover. When it dies down, they raise their heads to find Parnwell, dripping wet, still standing there at the Aldis. "Shall I send him a reply, sir?" he asks, cool as a cucumber. "Absolutely, Yeoman," says his skipper, brushing himself down. "Send: message received, will respond immediately."'

I watched, breath held, while Giddings' expression went through the motions. Blank incomprehension, doubt, pained incredulity, suspicion. Then, just as I was about to despair, it broke into a toothy grin.

'Really? Mid? Really? Is that true?'

Sometimes good, sometimes bad, often indifferent, usually wet. That was life on North Atlantic convoys. By the time I joined *Daisy* that spring of '42, a pattern had long been established to the job, almost a routine, if you can ever call war routine. *Daisy* belonged to an escort group, one of several plying the Atlantic. Our group was based in Londonderry. Put simply, its job was to pick up empty outbound convoys leaving the British Isles, and escort them the three thousand miles or so across the pond until they were safely inside US waters. Then, pick up another, inbound convoy, laden to the gunwales with much-needed essentials, and escort it back across the sea to Britain. That was it. The whole rotation would take from three to six weeks depending on the weather, the speed of the convoys and how long we had to wait the other side, which could be anything from half an hour to a week. When we got back to 'Derry having safely handed our charges over, we generally, but not always, had a few days leave before it all began again.

The composition of ships in our escort group varied, sometimes considerably, but in essence it was comprised of one destroyer, *Vehement*, and four corvettes, *Daisy*, *Fuchsia*, *Lily* and *Hornbeam*. Quite often a couple of extras came along for the ride, a Free French destroyer, perhaps, or a Dutch corvette. In charge of us was the escort group commander aboard *Vehement*. His job was to deploy and utilise his escorts specifically to protect the convoys from attack by submarine. Sounds straightforward enough, but the convoy, which could number as few as thirty, or as many as a hundred merchant vessels of all descriptions and nationalities, was commanded by a convoy commodore who sailed aboard the lead merchant ship. His responsibility was to the orderly passage of the convoy overall. In theory he outranked the escort commander; inevitably therefore, early on, occasions arose when opinions conflicted. Air attack, for example. Escorts liked to keep everyone together at all times, for good reasons. But some argued that convoys under repeated attack from aircraft were better off scattering and heading for their destinations independently. Good rapport between convoy commodores and escort commanders over this and other matters, therefore, was absolutely vital. After a certain amount of chaos in the early days, procedures gradually evolved to ensure happy working relationships. Most of the time.

The ships in a convoy were arranged in columns. The columns were generally kept quite short, four or five vessels in each, to keep them manageable. Consequently there might be as many as ten, twelve, even fifteen columns, each a mile apart, spread out across the ocean. That meant the convoy 'box' might be quite short, lengthways, but very wide. We, the escorts, patrolled the four sides of the box, forming an Asdic screen around it, keeping the columns nice and straight, and chivvying up stragglers.

When it worked, it was a joy to behold. Truly, for a sailor, there are few more heart-stirring sights than an armada of a hundred ships steaming along together in perfect formation across a tranquil ocean on a mild summer evening. Then, as if that wasn't miraculous enough, at a pre-arranged signal all hundred, at exactly the same moment, make a ten-degree turn to port on to the first leg of a zigzag, followed exactly an hour later by another to starboard, to return to the original course. No fuss, no bother, absolute heaven.

But when it didn't work it was a nightmare. Ships that couldn't tell left from right. Ships that missed pre-arranged turns at night, and went steaming off into the darkness by themselves. Ships that failed to keep a proper lookout and ploughed into the stern of the ship in front. Ships that broke down a lot and were forever having to be taken in tow.

Foreign ships, usually Greek I'm sorry to say, that were completely incapable of understanding the simplest signals. Ships that no matter how many times you begged, pleaded, requested or insisted, stubbornly refused to steam straight, or in line, or at the right speed.

Old ships, that were very slow, and made a lot of smoke. They were the worst. Ancient, coal-fired relics with long, thin funnels that shambled through the waves at nine knots, puffing dense plumes of sooty smoke high into the air, cheerfully inviting every U-boat within forty miles to come and get us.

'Number fifty-three falling astern again,' would come the terse signal from *Vehement*. 'Tell him to hurry it up.' Dutifully, we'd race round to the back of the convoy where, sure enough, number 53 would be ambling along half a mile behind everyone else.

'Any chance of giving us another knot or two?' Deeds would shout over the megaphone to its equally ancient captain. 'You are rather holding up the convoy.'

'See what I can do!' the old man would reply, cheerily lifting his bowler hat. A minute or two later, dense clouds of black smoke would be belching from his funnel as he shovelled another wheelbarrow-load of peat on to the grate. Within another minute *Vehement*'s Aldis lamp would be flashing again: 'Number fifty-three making too much smoke. Tell him to do something about it or I'll torpedo him myself.'

At least it never became dull. Repetitive, occasionally, but never dull.

I began my watch-keeping duties. While the crew were divided into three eight-hour watches called red, white and blue, the officers, at least one of whom had to be on the bridge at all times, were split into six four-hour ones. Thus each of us stood two four-hour stints in every twenty-four. I was on the midnight to four in the morning, which is called the middle watch, and the noon to four in the afternoon, which is called, unsurprisingly, the afternoon watch. The only officer who didn't stand watches was the captain, who by definition was deemed never to be off watch.

I liked my watches, particularly the midnight to four which, for obvious reasons, was the least popular. But once I recovered from the shock of having to turn out of bed in the middle of the night, I found those small-hours' stints — submarines notwithstanding, of course, and in fine weather — utterly magical. It's the quietest time aboard ship; there's no activity on deck, most of the crew safely tucked up below. The ship rolls along peacefully through the night, its bridge party an isolated little cluster of humanity beneath the dome of the heavens. Rather like campers around a fire in a wilderness, it's easy to imagine there's no one else in the world. There's intimacy yet freedom, solitude yet cama-raderie. People talk quietly and more openly than they otherwise might. Also, in those latitudes, in the summer, the hours of night are short. By the time the middle watch ends, darkness is already scurrying away to the west, together with the night's U-boat threat. As dawn breaks, there's the convoy again, safe and sound, ploughing steadily onward. It's another fresh start. New hope. New life. A hearty breakfast, then slip into the bunk for forty well-earned winks, while all around you the ship stirs to the new day like a well-oiled machine. Well, it's one of the finer things about Navy life and I quickly grew to love it.

In the summer. In good weather. With no U-boats about. The other – the apocalyptic, storm-riven carnage that was to follow – I would learn about in due course.

One more advantage of those endless wee-hours watches was that I spent a lot of time with Michael Villiers. He was of course already an interesting and articulate conversationalist, and a wonderful storyteller when he was in the mood. But, more importantly, he had this intuitive gift for drawing people out. Giving them the confidence to express their thoughts and feelings without risk of censure or scorn. Sometimes he could seem distant, and there would always be a certain underlying impenetrability about him that few ever really fathomed. But I always found him to be patient, supportive, encouraging, always looking for the good in people. In time I would be proud to call him a friend, although perhaps more accurately he was, as he was to many of *Daisy*'s crew, more like a brother.

Quite apart from bridge duties where, as Deeds had instructed, I observed and learned the business of conning the ship, station keeping with the convoy, listening to the Asdic repeater for submarines, watching for signals, fetching the cocoa and all the rest of it, my off-watch hours were filled with innumerable other duties. Mostly administrative, it seemed. There was tons and tons of paperwork. Reports to be filled out, stores to be checked and accounted for, monthly returns to be signed, requests and requisitions to be made, charts to be corrected, manuals to be updated. The list was literally endless and I never got to the bottom of it. I just waded through, as best I could. I even tried to do something useful with it once or twice, early on. Show a little nous, as Deeds was fond of saying. With predictable results.

'Thought I might hang a copy of the ship's Fire Safety Manual in the crewmen's toilets, Sub,' I proposed to Villiers late one night. A murmur of amused interest circled the darkened bridge. There was Michael, me, two lookouts, a signalman and a helmsman at the wheel beneath our feet. 'You know, so the men can, sort of, study it, as it were, while they're sitting there. Then, maybe we could extend the idea, with the First Aid Manual, next week, then the Lifeboat Drill and so on. What do you say? Think it might go down well?'

'Hmm?' Michael peered into the night at an invisible flurry of foam a mile away, marking the propeller wash of the last ship in the column. Friend he might well one day be, but he was certainly not averse to an occasional leg-pull. 'Well, yes, Mid, I should imagine that would go down very well indeed. Helm port ten!'

'Port ten, sir,' came the reply from the helmsman.

It did go down well. And fast. In fact the manual was completely gone in two days and I spent the rest of the week being congratulated by one and all for providing so thoughtfully for the men's physical comfort.

When I was able to extricate myself from the mountains

of paperwork my brother officers dumped on me, there were the myriad other chores to attend to in the day-to-day running of a warship. Housekeeping, it was, in essence. Some corvette skippers ran their ships along quite informal lines. There was some logic to this. Corvettes were so small and cramped that trying to carry on as if it was a 10,000-ton cruiser with a crew of six hundred was pretty pointless. So it was not uncommon to see people loafing about corvettes wearing odd garb, covered in stubble, fag in mouth and so on, as if they were crewing some tramp steamer out of Fleetwood. Other skippers, conversely, wanted everything absolutely neat, tidy and by the book at all times. Tiddly, as we say in the Navy. Fair enough if you've got the space and the manpower. Painting the funnel, polishing the brass, scrubbing the decks, since Nelson's day these have been traditional Navy ways of stopping sailors getting bored – and bored sailors equals trouble – and also encouraging a sense of pride in their ship. But when you've spent a week being tossed about in the worst weather imaginable, with the galley awash so there's no hot food, with the wardroom looking like its been ransacked by lunatics, with three inches of water sloshing about the mess deck and not a single dry piece of clothing to be found among the entire crew. When you haven't slept more than an hour at a time in that week because the ship is carrying on like a tin can rolling down a hill and you keep getting thrown out of your bunk, which in any case is so sopping wet you don't want to get in it, then cutting the men a little slack, as the Americans say, would seem a wise course of action for a prudent skipper.

Like Walter Deeds. Incidentally, William Bligh, did you know, spent the best part of a month trying to bash poor *Bounty* around Cape Horn through the worst storms on the planet. No wonder his crew wanted to murder him. A less stubborn captain might have worked out that he was achieving nothing, and run into Punta Arenas until the weather moderated. But brilliant seaman though he undoubtedly was, Bligh lacked judgement when it came to getting the best from his men.

Unlike Deeds, who, once you got the hang of him, was superb at it. But you could only push him so far, which in some ways was worse, because it was impossible to second-guess where you stood with him. You had to learn it, like everything on *Daisy*. The four-inch gun crew knew they could hang their laundry on the bandstand rail, but woe betide them if it was still there when rattlers sounded. And you never knew when that might be. You could peel off to your vest and shorts on a hot day in the Asdic hut, but only because if you didn't you'd melt; thus Deeds knew it allowed you to do your job properly. If an officer turned up on bridge watch wearing crewmen's overalls, odd socks and an old mackintosh, because after four days of gales that was all he could find that was remotely dry, then so be it. But if he turned up on watch wearing that lot *and* was five minutes late . . .

He was very much a seaman of the old school, Deeds. His ship-handling skills were a delight to behold, and he also had this wonderful sixth sense about things. Many's the time I'd be in the chart room behind the bridge, struggling to plot our position as we closed the Irish coast for instance. Deeds would come up to the bridge, sniff the air a bit, wander into the chart room, jab a finger on the map and walk out again. Invariably he was right to within a couple of miles. Then there was another time, in fog so thick you couldn't see the cook emptying gash over the side twenty yards away. We were creeping about trying to locate the tail of the convoy using a mixture of fog-horn signals, a recalcitrant radar set and guesswork. Strang was officer of the watch and doing the best he could under difficult circumstances. Deeds was at the back of the bridge, watching, smoking, but saying nothing, anxious that his first officer be allowed to manage the situation unmolested. But suddenly he sprang forward.

'Hard a-starboard, engine full-astern, sound rattlers, brace for collision everybody!' he roared.

Alarms trilled, sirens sounded, feet rang on steel, crew scrabbled up on deck, *Daisy* shuddered, her protesting engine groaning into reverse.

Then we waited. But nothing happened. For about a minute. Nothing. We all peered anxiously into the murk, but it was exactly the same impenetrable clag as before. Crewmen began to exchange glances. The old man's got it wrong. Taken leave of his senses, thrown a wobbly. I raised an eyebrow at Strang, but he knew better.

Without warning, looming silently out of the mist like a monstrous ghost, huge and horribly close, came the ship, a 5000-ton fuel tanker. Massive, three or four times *Daisy*'s size, bearing down on us like a bus over a tricycle. Speechless, unable to do anything but stare in fascinated horror, we watched her come, watched as her profile changed, hardened. Watched, breaths held, as the similarly shocked faces of her crew slid silently by above us, not more than thirty yards away.

Sixth sense. You can't buy it, you can't even earn it. You grow it, if you're lucky, slowly, over the years. Like antlers.

But although he may have been God, that didn't mean he was infallible. His big weakness was gadgetry. Being old-school, Deeds mistrusted it, in all its forms, which was a paradox because gadgetry formed an essential part of the job he had to do. He disliked it, intensely, as though it interfered with his antlers, which in a way it did. The ship's radar had let him down in the fog so he'd relied on his own. Quite often the Asdic operator would report an echo to him that upon investigation turned out to be nothing but a shoal of fish, or a layer of warm water a hundred feet down. Equally, it would stubbornly refuse to indicate anything when Deeds was convinced there was a U-boat lurking down there. Consequently on the rare occasions the gadgetry did perform, he often refused to believe it.

There was so much of it. Invariably when we returned to Londonderry after a patrol, there would be crates of new equipment waiting to be loaded. Barely had we tied up before men in civilian suits would start swarming all over the ship bolting on boxes and tubes, strange-looking antennas and miles of wire aerials. Crewmen would be denied hard-earned leave and sent on high-security training courses to learn how to use it. Our Asdic operator went to some place in the Midlands once, where, swear to God, he spent three days stooging around in circles practising submarine hunting exercises aboard a converted London bus.

Once thus 'trained', operators were returned to the ship bearing top-secret instruction manuals with exotic code-names printed on the front, like: 'hedgehog', 'squid', 'raspberry' and 'artichoke'. 'Foxer' turned out to be a tubular apparatus you towed behind the ship. It emitted a metallic clattering noise to confuse acoustic torpedoes. 'Huff-Duff' stood for High Frequency Direction Finding. It was a movable radio antenna which, once the bugs had been ironed out, allowed us to get bearings on U-boat radio transmissions. Sometimes some of the stuff worked. Much of it was utter nonsense. All of it offended Deeds' sensibilities.

'What's all this gubbins then, Sub?' he enquired one afternoon, mid-Atlantic. He'd wandered down to the after deck where Martin Brown and I, together with half a dozen bemused ratings, were busy trying to assemble a hugely unwieldy contraption made from wire and canvas.

'Well, it's a kite, sir,' Brown replied.

'I can see it's a kite, Sub. What the hell is it for?'

'It's an anti-aircraft kite, sir, according to the boffins. Apparently, once deployed, it flies along behind the ship at heights up to a thousand feet, the idea being to confuse and interfere with attacking dive bombers.'

Deeds viewed the apparatus in silence for several seconds before turning away, head shaking. 'Brilliant,' we heard him mutter. Half an hour later Brown and I were back on the bridge.

'Well?' Deeds demanded.

'Anti-aircraft kite deployed, sir.'

'Where? I can't see it.'

'Over there, sir.' Brown pointed to a distant dot heading in the general direction of South America. 'We launched it, sir, but the wire broke. I imagine it wasn't strong enough. Sorry, sir.' We waited, uneasily, for the axe to fall, but Deeds just shrugged.

'Anti-aircraft kite deployed,' he said, turning forward. 'Good. Carry on.'

Martin Brown was a twenty-four-year-old insurance broker with fallen arches from Orpington, so the Army didn't want him. Also rejected for pilot training with the RAF because of colour blindness, in desperation Martin had applied to be a 'weekend sailor' with the RNVR. To his astonishment, he was accepted – partly because he had an uncle who'd served in the Navy in the first war, and partly because he'd once been on a sailing holiday to Brittany. Barely eight weeks later, after 'bewilderingly minimal' training on *King Alfred*, he found himself clambering aboard HMS *Daisy* as an officer. For the next six months or so, both he and the other sub-lieutenant, Dick Woolley, whose background was not dissimilar, were by their own admission, about as much use as a pair of chocolate teapots. It was Deeds who turned them into seamen. Through patience and determination, skill and sheer hard work.

I learned all this because they told me. They told me lots more besides. Gradually, as my first weeks on *Daisy* stretched into months, and my notebook and diary began to fill, I was getting to know my fellow officers. I was also, slowly, beginning to piece together the puzzle of the ship's vital human dynamic. The way these men lived and worked together, interacted, related to one another. The reason, therefore, that *Daisy* functioned so effectively.

Because she hadn't always. Not by a long chalk.

My war started, abruptly, during my third convoy, one day in July. Everything had been going so swimmingly up until then. Four crossings and not so much as a peep from the enemy. By the time we were a week or so into the fifth one, I was beginning to wonder what the fuss was about, and whether the crewmen's horror stories hadn't been slightly exaggerated for their new midshipman's benefit.

Then, out of the blue one morning, the convoy came under air attack. Everything happened very quickly, yet the transition from peace to war was almost disappointingly prosaic. One minute we were stooging along, as normal, exactly as we had been for weeks. The next, little puffs of brown smoke were appearing in the sky above the convoy. I was in the waist, near the depth-charge throwers, being shown how to do a wire splice by a leading seaman called Bostwick, when we glanced up and saw them. Little, silent, cotton ball powder puffs, they looked like.

'What's that?' I asked, mildly intrigued.

'Fuck me!' Bostwick threw down the splice and barged past for the ladder.

Seconds later rattlers went off and hell broke loose with a vengeance. *Daisy* heeled hard over as she was turned into the action, almost immediately the steady percussive banging of the pom-pom anti-aircraft gun started up aft. I went the other way, stumbling forward after Bostwick up on to the foc's'le deck, then fighting my way through the throng to try and see what was going on. Chaos was going on, it seemed to me: guns, shouts, alarms, and everyone running in all directions. But it only appeared chaotic because I was the one person on board who didn't have a clue what was happening. Everyone else, to a man, knew exactly where to go and what to do, and they were going there and doing it very fast. The pom-pom was already shooting aft, while the four-inch gun crew closed up for'ard. A lookout was scrambling up to the crow's-nest, the depth-charge crews busy clearing away, fire teams were making ready with buckets and hoses.

'Mister Tomlin, if you please!' A familiar dour shout from above. Then I remembered. The bridge, Deeds had said, quite clearly, several weeks ago. That's where I was supposed to be. If you're off watch when rattlers sounds, you drop what you're doing, leg it for the bridge and await further instructions.

I arrived just as the action was starting in earnest. Apparently, although I couldn't see them anywhere, there were two aircraft attacking the convoy – twin-engined fighter bombers. Many merchantmen carried a single gun bolted on to their foredeck, possibly a Bofors, more likely an ancient First World War surplus twelve-pounder, or a single-barrelled pom-pom. Not a great deal of use at the best of times, particularly in untrained hands, but they made a lot of noise and clouds of smoke and at least the merchant boys felt they were throwing something back at the enemy. And they were certainly throwing it, blasting explosives about the sky like it was Blackpool prom on fireworks night. We escorts were much more heavily armed, but more disciplined. As I arrived, *Daisy*'s guns had actually stopped. I clambered up in the sudden hush, bracing myself for the expected tongue lashing from Deeds. But I was totally ignored. The bridge was very busy and crowded. A yeoman of signals and two signalmen were coping with a barrage of messages being exchanged between the five escorts and the convoy commodore's ship. Strings of signal flags fluttered to the mast head and down again in rapid succession, the second signalman equally busy rattling the shutter of his Aldis lamp. Apart from them, two men were manning the twin Lewis machine-gun on one wing, two more the Oerlikon gun on the other; there were two lookouts, the bosun's mate, Sub-Lieutenant Villiers and, centre stage, Walter Deeds.

'What's the hoist from *Fuchsia*, Yeoman?'

'She's repositioning to centre column four, sir.'

'Acknowledge. Helm midships, engine one-eight-zero revolutions.'

'Midships, sir.'

'Signal from *Vehement*, sir, maintain present station, aircraft circling to south.'

'Acknowledge.'

'Bridge, wheelhouse, Coxswain at the wheel.'

'Very good, Coxswain, steer two-zero-zero, please. Humbug anyone?'

Astonishingly, a bag of sweets went round the bridge. 'Why, thanks very much, sir, thank you, sir, thank you. Don't mind if I do. Not just now thanks, sir.'

'Signal from *Hornbeam*, sir, aircraft turning inbound now.'

'Acknowledge. Where are they, Number Two, can you see them?'

Villiers and one lookout were leaning, elbow-to-elbow, far out over the port bridge wing, binoculars trained skywards. 'Can't see them, sir, but from the concentration of AA fire I'd say they were way over on the far side of the convoy, perhaps eight miles, on the port quarter.'

'Good, getting ready to make one more pass. And they'll be doing it in our direction. Asdic?'

'Asdic, sir, all quiet down here.'

'Very good, keep listening. Now where's Strang and that spare Lewis.'

'Here, sir!' Strang pushed past me on to the bridge, in shirtsleeves and tin hat, closely followed by a red-faced rating hefting a machine-gun over his shoulder.

'Ah, good, Number One. Just in time. Rig it port side and hurry up about it, they'll be here any moment. Woolley!' Deeds leaned over the front of the bridge. 'Keep that four-inch trained over the port bow, full elevation. They'll be coming in from that direction, you might get a couple of shots in.'

'Will do, sir!'

Extra machine-guns on the bridge. Now the four-inch. What was going on? The four-inch was a heavy piece of breech-loading naval artillery used for lobbing shells at enemy ships, or U-boats on the surface. Not aeroplanes. As an anti-aircraft gun it was completely useless, too slow to reload, and in any case you couldn't elevate the barrel more than about thirty degrees. It went off with a hell of a wallop, though. I looked at Deeds: he was everywhere at once now, barking orders, firing off signals, pacing about the place like the proverbial cat on hot cinders. Yet there was nothing erratic about his actions, nothing hare-brained or slapdash. He was just incredibly focused on the job at hand. Focused, and something else. Angry, I'd call it. Angry with the enemy, that is, not just me.

'Tomlin! Where the bloody hell is your tin hat?'

'Oh, well, you see, sir, sorry, but I must have left it in—'

'For God's sake!' Without ado he wrenched his own from his head and tossed it to me. Then, to my horror he began fumbling for the lanyard at his neck, tugging his Service revolver from his pocket.

'Sir, I, look, sorry, it won't happen—'

'Signal from *Vehement*, sir, two aircraft coming in now, line astern.'

'Acknowledge. Stand by everyone. Villiers take the bridge. Hold her steady, keep any incoming targets over the port bow.'

'*Lily* has commenced shooting, sir.'

'Signal from *Fuchsia*, sir, two aircraft closing, bearing two-one-zero.'

'*Hornbeam* signalling sir, aircraft coming your—'

'Yes, yes, I get the picture! All positions, here we go, shoot when ready . . .'

Suddenly they were upon us. You could trace their progress across the convoy by following the spirited but hopelessly inaccurate barrage of fire thrown up by the merchant ships' guns. Then there was a monstrous explosion in the middle of the convoy as a bomb found a target. A moment later a shout from the lookout up in the crow's-nest and two specks appeared from out of the smoke, low, racing towards us at enormous speed. At that instant *Daisy*'s guns opened fire, en masse.

It was over so quickly it was impossible to take it all in. I have snapshot sounds and images seared into memory. The sudden, deafening, road-drill rattle of machine-guns opening up all around the bridge. The steady pounding of the pom-pom aft, the heavy crump and clouds of cordite-smelling smoke from the four-inch. The Oerlikon loader, deadpan, slotting magazines into the top of the weapon while his co-gunner calmly pulled the triggers. Strang, hunched, teeth bared, over his shuddering Lewis gun. Walter Deeds, feet braced, arms fully extended, sighting, one-eyed along the barrel of his revolver. Steadily squeezing the trigger and sucking on his humbug like it was Sunday target practice at Bisley. A green cruciform silhouette whooshing overhead, very fast and very low, a black cross on either wing. Then a second. Strang hoisting the Lewis, all fifty-pounds of it, from its mounting and swinging it furiously after them, shooting from the hip.

Through it all, Michael, the only man aboard detached from the action. Arms folded, his head slightly bowed, just staring impassively out ahead of the ship.

Then it was over, the aircraft gone. Silence descended over the bridge.

'Any good?' someone asked.

'No, bugger it,' Deeds scowled, reloading his revolver. 'Too blasted fast. Next time though. What we really need you know, is one of those new quadruple fifty-calibre machine-guns. We could bolt it down on the boat deck, aft of the AA band stand. Make a note of it, Number One, we'll put in a request, soon as we get back to 'Derry. Probably get turned down but there's no harm trying, is there . . .'

Then we went below for lunch. Just like that.

That night the submarines came. It was one in the morning, so Michael and I were holding the bridge on our usual middle watch. He'd been in talkative mood, for a change, although highly wary, as if he sensed the aircraft attack earlier had merely been the prelude to something bigger. He was right in the middle of telling me all about Uruguay's borderland wars when a yellow flash lit the sky far out to starboard. Instantly he broke off, bending to a voice-pipe.

'Captain, bridge here.'

'Yes, ah, bridge.' A bleary Yorkshire voice came back up the pipe. 'What is it Number Two?'

'Shipflash, Captain, fourth ship, column eight. Starshells now, too.'

'Very well. Sound rattlers, I'll be up in a minute.'

Starshells – big phosphorous flares that hung in the air illuminating everything below – meant the ships in the vicinity knew it was a U-boat attack. The moment the first torpedo hammers home, you fire off starshells to try and catch the raider on the surface. He could stay and fight it out there, using his superior surface speed to make a dash for it. But bathed in light like that, he usually goes under, which is exactly where you want him.

This time I was in the right place, and did have my tin hat with me. The moment Deeds appeared on the bridge, however, his pyjamas poking out the bottom of his trouser legs, he sent me below.

'Asdic hut, lad, with Strang. Watch closely but don't get in the way.'

Asdic is the original First World War name for the underwater sound-ranging equipment they used to detect submarines. It stands, believe it or not, for Anti-Submarine Detection Investigation Committee. The actual apparatus became known later as 'sonar', an acronym for SOund Navigation And Ranging. It works by firing powerful pulses of sound, every few seconds, from an emitter under the ship. You can actually hear it; apparently you can even hear it inside a submarine, which must be particularly unnerving. Anyway, it makes a loud ringing noise, ping–ping–ping, one every few seconds. That pinging noise goes on all day and all night, around the clock from the moment you go out on escort duty to the moment you come back. There's a repeater on the bridge so you can even hear it going 'ping' up there. It could drive you completely mad, but in fact, after a while, it just merges into the general background tapestry of noise you live with aboard an anti-submarine warship.

The Asdic operator sits in a stuffy little cubbyhole next to the wheelhouse directly beneath the bridge. He listens to the pinging through headphones, altering the way the sound pulse is directed by turning a steering wheel on the console in front of him. What he and everyone else is waiting for is an echo. Normally there isn't one – the wave of sound just fades into the deep. But if it happens to strike something dense and heavy, like a U-boat, for example, the noise suddenly changes. You get an echo, and instead of it just going 'ping', it goes, 'ping–go!'. The time interval between the 'ping' and the 'go' tells you the range, and cranking the steering wheel to and fro gives you a bearing. When the 'ping' and the 'go' are simultaneous, you are passing right over the top of your U-boat, so you throw depth charges over the side for all you're worth and it's goodnight Vienna.

In theory. But, like all gadgetry, it has its weaknesses, breaks down a lot and can just as easily have you chasing a school of mackerel about the ocean as an enemy submarine. Getting it right is tricky and highly skilled, requiring more patience than Job. I wedged myself into a corner of the hut and settled down to watch. A minute later Strang arrived.

It was a very different Alan Strang from the furious gun-toting hero of the morning. He looked dishevelled and bleary, possibly from sleep, although the redness in his eyes told me it was more likely a lack of it. He had this tightly wound look about him, as though it had required enormous effort to bring himself down there. He acknowledged me, barely, with a nod, sat himself between the two operators and lit a cigarette.

'Right, then, let's get on with it. Full eighty-to-eighty. Commence sweep.'

Two hours, a dozen sweeps and ten cigarettes later, we were still there and none the wiser. No echoes, no U-boats, no depth-charge attacks, nothing. Yet we knew they must be out there somewhere; there were plenty of other signs that battle was being joined. Just not in our sector. Hunting subs, I was learning, was a ticklish business. Strang, I was also learning, was a nervous wreck.

Apart from the incessant smoking there were other indicators. Nail-biting for instance, yawning and hand-wringing too. He could barely sit still for a moment. Fidgeting about on his chair every few minutes. At one point during the session, a series of stifled booms came over the repeater. There was an electronic crackling sound from the loudspeaker, then a muffled metallic crash. Another ship in the convoy had taken a hit. Clear but very distant. Strang practically jumped out of his chair. But then, obviously struggling with himself, he forced his attention back on to the Asdic, lit up yet another cigarette and just got on with it. It was an impressive if disquieting display of the power of mind over matter.

Halfway into the third hour I was summoned back to the bridge. It was a relief, frankly, to be out of the claustrophobic airlessness of the hut and back in the fresh air where you could see what's what. But the sight that greeted me made me understand why Strang might prefer the darkness of the hut.

A tanker was on fire less than a mile away, lighting the night like a giant beacon. It burned furiously, one end to the other, a single, huge, hell-like inferno. Even at that distance I could feel the heat, smell the smoke. The fire illuminated the scene for miles around, madly dancing flames clawing fifty, sixty feet into the air. Other convoy ships, bathed in its glow, processed slowly past the pyre, like shocked spectators, or floats at a pageant. Mute, helpless witnesses – there was nothing anyone could do, except watch and weep, and keep well clear in case the thing blew up. A gaping rent had been blown in the tanker's side by the torpedo. Burning oil poured from it, lava-like, on to the surface of the sea, such that a half-mile wide apron of fire was spreading over the waves downwind of the victim. Acrid clouds of smoke curled from this sea of flame, some of it rolling across *Daisy*'s deck. I stared, horror-struck, mesmerised by the sheer enormity of the disaster. Impossibly, it appeared to be growing. It was. Walter Deeds was bringing *Daisy* closer.

He and Villiers were conferring at the front of the bridge. I saw Dick Woolley standing to one side, his face a flickering yellow mask of apprehension. 'What's happening, Sub?' I asked him quietly.

'Skipper's going to bring her round to the upwind side, away from the flames, try and inch her in from there.'

'Inch her in? What on earth for?'

'Survivors. We saw some a few minutes ago, running towards the foc'sle. Look, there's an area right at the bows that's free from fire. That's where they'll be.'

Survivors. People living in the midst of that. It was

impossible to imagine. I looked at Deeds, he was pointing something out to Villiers. 'What's he going to do?'

Dick forced a sickly grin. 'I think he means to bring *Daisy* alongside.'

He was, or something like that. Five minutes later I found myself standing on *Daisy*'s foredeck surrounded by piles of ropes, Villiers and three ratings. I'd like to say they were Harrison, Tuker and Giddings but they weren't, although Bostwick, the man who'd been showing me the wire splice earlier, was one. We were wearing tin hats, flash hoods and lifebelts, of course, but the first thing that happened was Bostwick gave me a pair of overalls to put on, then emptied a bucket of seawater over them. 'Stay wet, Mid,' he said, dousing himself. 'It'll be hotter than Hades in there.'

He was right. It was like sailing up to the gates of hell. Even approaching from upwind, with the clawing flames and billowing smoke drifting away from us, the heat was agonising. You felt it tingling your lips, prickling your eyes. At a hundred yards it was already excruciating, at fifty unbearable; you had to turn your face away, or at least try and cover it. I was completely insensible, rooted uselessly to the spot, one arm shielding my head and gaping like a cod. Still we crept forward.

Then Michael was beside me, just his eyes visible above a rag tied about his mouth. 'All right, Stephen?' he shouted above the roar of flames. It was insanity, the worst nightmare imaginable. I tried to nod. He pulled a scarf from his neck, soaked it, secured it about my face. 'Stay close to me, you'll do fine!'

Going alongside the tanker was not an option; even I could see that. The heat would have fried everyone on *Daisy* alive. Quite apart from that, the ship, twice *Daisy*'s size, was ablaze from almost one end to the other, so there was nowhere to get alongside. But Deeds had been right about one thing: the foc'sle, the very bows of the ship, was as yet still free from fire, and, impossibly, there were people alive up there. We could see them. Not many, just a handful, huddled together, trying to shelter from the heat.

A seaman came running to us, bent double, bearing more ropes and a large wooden box. Villiers beckoned us forward.

'Skipper's going to nose her in as close as he can. Bow to!' he shouted. We were all gasping a bit; apart from anything else, the flames were consuming all available air and it was becoming suffocatingly hard to breathe. 'Then we're going to shoot a line to them using the Schermuly pistol, rig a breeches buoy and get them off, one by one. Got that?'

What if she blows? I kept wondering. What if this fuel-laden bomb of a burning ship just explodes? There'll be nothing left of any of us. And what about U-boats? We must stand out like a dog's balls, silhouetted there against a fifty foot-high backdrop of fire. A sitting target. I thought of Strang, smoking and twitching down there in his Asdic hut. His fear was so palpable you could smell it. I thought of echoes going 'ping–go' and of what it might feel like to be hit by a torpedo. I wondered then what the hell I was doing there, began cursing my father, my grandfather, every Tomlin who ever sailed, for getting me into this mess. Then I cursed myself for not being man enough to stop them.

But then, surveying that appalling scene, I caught sight of one of the survivors, and suddenly the gravity of my situation paled by comparison. He was crouching, hunched low, right at the very bows of his ship, as far from the murderous heat as he could possibly get. He was waving to us, beckoning. Hurry, he was saying, for God's sake hurry. It was heartbreaking. He was a civilian, not a warrior, a simple, honest, merchant sailor just doing his job. He didn't deserve this. He hadn't signed up for it. He deserved to get off. Go home. We must do it. We had to.

From that moment proceedings took on a dream-like quality. I don't know how many times we tried to get a line aboard that tanker; pretty soon I lost count. It was a painfully unwieldy business. The Schermuly pistol fired a small rod attached to a thin line which snaked out after it. If it failed to make its target, it had to be hauled laboriously back aboard, hand over hand, carefully flaked into a coil so it wouldn't tangle at the next attempt, the pistol reloaded and the whole procedure tried again. Deeds did a miraculous job, under difficult conditions, holding *Daisy* steady, bows on, forty yards from the tanker. But quite apart from a stiff wind, which didn't help the way the lines flew, the seas were steep, with a five-foot beam-swell running. I found myself lying flat out over *Daisy*'s bows, Michael's *pañuelo* covering my face, the heat singeing the hairs on my arms, hauling the fallen lines back aboard for all I was worth. We kept trying, but they kept dropping short, falling to one side or ricocheting off the tanker's hull back into the sea. After a while I stopped looking at the men huddled at the bows; I couldn't bear to. But the more we failed, the more desperate I became that we should succeed. So I just lay there and hauled in, Bostwick and the others reflaked the lines, made ready and reloaded, then passed the pistol to Villiers to try again. He just stood there, steady as a rock, ignoring the furious heat, the pitiable flailings of the doomed men, and the heaving deck beneath his feet, took aim, timed his moment as best he could, and fired.

Then, after an age, Bostwick gave a shout. A line had fallen right over the survivors and been captured. Contact. Now the process of rigging the breeches buoy could begin. Firstly, the thin line was used to haul two more ropes between the two ships. One to support the weight of the rig, a second, lighter one, to pull the breeches buoy back and forth. The men on the tanker clearly didn't have any ropes, so we attached them to our end, then waved for them to start pulling. Foot by foot, the lines crept across to them. But it was agonisingly slow. The two ships pitched up and down unevenly, making it even trickier, and all the while flames were creeping steadily up the deck towards the trapped men. Twice the lines stopped moving altogether, for no apparent reason. Seconds ticked inexorably by. Then they went on again. Finally they were across and secured.

Villiers and Bostwick then rigged the breeches buoy itself. This is a simple circular lifebuoy, fitted, literally, with a pair of canvas breeches. We suspended it by pulley from the thicker of the lines between the two ships. All the tanker survivors had to do was pull it across, put a man into it, and we'd do the rest, hauling him back to safety, and repeating the process until everyone had been rescued.

But it never happened. Rigging the buoy could only have taken a couple of minutes. Then, standing in line ready to pay out and haul in, we waved like fury at the men on the other ship to pull. After a long pause, and desperately slowly, the buoy began to move, swinging out into the void between the two ships. But halfway across, it stopped. It never moved again.

'What's happening!' one of our crewmen shouted. 'Why aren't they pulling?' I, too, standing there in line, found I was shouting. Pleading. 'Pull! Please, just keep pulling!' But Bostwick and Villiers knew. I saw them exchange glances. Then Bostwick turned away altogether, throwing the line to the deck in disgust. The tanker's foc'sle was completely engulfed. Nothing, no living creature on earth, could survive that. But I couldn't let go of the line, couldn't bring myself to sever the link and believe what my eyes were telling me. 'Pull, please, pull!' A hand was tugging at my shoulder, Michael's, his voice filling my head: 'Stephen, come back now, there's nothing more we can do.' But I shook free of him. 'Pull!' I kept shouting, on and on, willing the empty breeches buoy to start moving again. 'Can't you please, just pull!'

Chapter 8

That was the end of my phoney war. It had lasted seven weeks. I was fortunate; my indoctrination into North Atlantic convoy duty, both from the point of view of weather and enemy activity, had been a relatively tranquil one. High summer was our quiet time, the brief nights and benign weather our friends against a foe preferring long hours of darkness and troubled seas. But the pendulum was swinging, autumn approaching. Its moody weather and dwindling daylight favoured him. Before we knew it, winter would be upon us, when U-boats roamed like packs of Arctic wolves, storms raged for weeks and the unforgiving waters froze the life from a man in minutes. Not only that, unknown strategic changes were afoot. A stage was being set. Upon it, and against a backdrop of the worst weather the Atlantic had known for half a century, the next act would be played.

At the beginning of 1942, Admiral Dönitz had around one hundred U-boats at his disposal – a lethally high number you might think, at least on paper. But from our perspective the situation could have been even more dire. At any one time, it turned out, as many as half these submarines were in dock on turnaround or under repair, and those that were at sea were spread over several areas of operation – not just ours. At Hitler's insistence, half a dozen stalked the waters off Norway. Several more were in the Arctic, tasked with attacking convoys destined for a beleaguered Russia. Twenty or so were stationed west of Spain and North Africa to harry Gibraltar-bound convoys. Still more had managed to slip through the Straits and were busy wreaking their havoc inside the Mediterranean. Furthermore, quite a few were being sunk, replacements were slow coming off the ways at Krupps and Blohm & Voss, and, to top it all, there were dockyard labour shortages and delays with crew recruitment and training. So, although more than two hundred merchant ships were sunk in the North Atlantic during the first three months of the year, believe it or not, it could have been worse.

It would be, but not yet, for there was then something of a hiatus. Following Pearl Harbor and Germany's declaration of war against America, Admiral Dönitz, hungry for success after a lean winter, gambled his already stretched U-boat resources by unleashing Operation Paukenschlag, or Drumroll. Drumroll was a daring plan to send submarines three thousand miles from their bases in France, right up to Uncle Sam's front doorstep. Fraught with logistical difficulties, it was nevertheless a spectacular success. America's naval chiefs, still reeling from the humiliating catastrophe thousands of miles away in the Pacific, were completely unprepared for an underwater assault on merchant shipping right on their eastern shores. U-boat captains, positioning their submarines along the coast all the way from Canada to Florida, were astonished at the ease with which they were able to approach and pick off targets. Unescorted, undarkened, helpfully back-lit against the welcoming lights of American harbourfront towns and cities, 200,000 tons were sent to the bottom in the first fortnight of Drumbeat. The crew of one submarine – U-66 – arrived off North Carolina scarcely able to believe their eyes at the numbers of waiting ships, all brightly lit and unprotected. Further up the coast, Reinhard Hardegen of U-123 closed his boat to within a few miles of New York, reporting to his incredulous crew that he could see partygoers on the roof of the Empire State Building through his binoculars. He then dived his ship and went to work, going on to become Drumbeat's top scorer. Admiral Andrews, meanwhile, the luckless American responsible for putting a stop to the carnage, was reduced to fending off the fury of the press, and watching helplessly as ships were torpedoed almost within sight of his Manhattan headquarters.

But it couldn't go on for ever. Within six months, US convoy protection measures were in place, backed by coordinated anti-submarine forces both at sea and in the air. The turkey shoot was over. Dönitz withdrew. He was unconcerned; he knew where his priorities lay, and Drumbeat's success had won him the influence needed to strike a decisive blow there. A massive U-boat construction programme was approved by German High Command. By August '42 it was in full swing, output topping a phenomenal thirty boats a month. With total strength up to nearly three hundred, and Blohm & Voss proudly handing over a brand-new submarine every Tuesday, Dönitz was soon ready. The tide is turning, he told his men, exhorting them to new heights of daring in his radio broadcasts. Nervously, the Admiralty listened in. The moment is at hand, he said. Be strong and ruthless, for a decisive phase in the Atlantic offensive is about to begin. One where no quarter will be given, and none expected.

So be it. I went home to see my family. Just for a few days, while *Daisy* was back in Liverpool having a boiler clean and yet more gadgetry fitted. It was an unreal experience, walking up the neatly tended gravel drive to the house, sleeping between clean sheets in a bed that didn't move, waking to the sounds of twittering sparrows and the gardener sweeping leaves. It was all exactly as I remembered it, as familiar as the hairs on the back of my hand. Yet nothing felt quite the same any more. Taking afternoon tea with my mother and sisters became a daily ordeal. 'Now then, Stephen, you *have* to tell us all about it!' they kept insisting, while the maid brought the sandwiches. 'What about your ship? The crew? The other officers? What's the captain like? Have you seen any action yet? Start from the beginning and omit nothing!' But I found that I omitted pretty much all.

By the fourth day I'd had enough, and then, to cap everything, Mum announced over breakfast that my father was coming home the next day and was anxious for a 'chat'. He too was a naval officer; he'd been at sea all his life and he probably would have understood. But I just couldn't face him; I wasn't ready. I ran down to the Post Office and fired off a telegram to Dick Woolley, care of the dockyard office at Liverpool. It begged him to telephone me at home that night with urgent orders to rejoin the ship.

'Home comforts and rich living too much for you, then, Mid?' he teased, the following evening, soon after I was safely back aboard. We were in *Daisy*'s deserted wardroom, tucking into a pink gin, one of several new vices I seemed to have acquired.

'Something like that,' I puffed, relaxing for the first time in four days. Smoking was another. 'Where is everyone?'

'Only white watch aboard until the crew reports back tomorrow. Skipper's been summoned to London for a situation briefing, Martin Brown's home in Orpington having a decent meal, shaking out the old man's pockets, and getting his washing done, as he puts it. Villiers is about, or was, yesterday, but then said something about going for a walk. Haven't seen him since . . .'

'Lieutenant Strang?'

Dick's eyes flicked to the door. 'In his cabin. Sleeping it off.'

A pattern had begun to emerge, and we were all component parts of it. Walter Deeds had a wife back home in Skipton. Gladys of the spidery handwriting, I called her.

Being ship's postman and mail-sorting officer, I knew they corresponded regularly. Furthermore, if her name, or that of womenfolk in general, came up in wardroom conversation, the skipper always spoke of her with the utmost respect and affection. But, should an opportunity present itself for him to pop home and see her for a day or two, invariably something would turn up to prevent it. A summons to the Admiralty, perhaps, or a lengthy meeting with the coxswain. Or a good sleep.

Martin Brown liked to go home. Convoy life drained him, he professed, flattening him like the battery on his ancient Austin. Yet when he returned from leave, loudly bemoaning its brevity on the one hand, scattering food parcels hither and thither with the other, brimming with newly charged enthusiasm, there was no concealing his relief to be back aboard. Sniffing about the place like a dog home from the fields, I don't believe he could have stayed away even if he wanted to.

Michael never went anywhere, or if he did, rarely anywhere far, or for long. I knew he had family, a father who worked in the Foreign Office in London, a younger brother at school somewhere. I also know for certain that he did visit them, when he could. But, essentially itinerant, Michael's home was *Daisy*. So generally he took his leave aboard. Reading in his cabin, organising ship's cricket practice, talking with the crew, or simply wandering off on one of his two-day walks.

Alan Strang, too, seldom ventured far. No further than his cabin, usually, where he drank himself into oblivion.

Then he spent the rest of his hard-earned leave recovering from it. He never drank at sea, never kept a little bottle of something in the bedside cupboard in his cabin, never partook of the daily rum ration with the crew, even though he was perfectly entitled to. Never touched a drop. But once safely tied up alongside, he chose to pass his leisure hours in an alcoholic stupor, surrendering to the demons that possessed him. There was no Mrs Strang. A fiancée once, Brown told me, but it hadn't worked out. If there were other family, I never heard about them.

Because we were his family. We were all our families. Even Dick Woolley's. He was aboard that weekend because he'd drawn the short straw and volunteered to stay. But if he hadn't, he too would have gone off home, only to return sooner than needed. Exactly as I had. I couldn't find the release I sought at home. I didn't feel ready or able to talk about the things I wanted to talk about with the people there. I needed to talk about them with my own people. Or not; it didn't matter, as long as we were together. Because – and this is the only way I could define it at the time – what we were doing, and the only way we could go on doing it, was a private matter.

'What was it like before Villiers joined?' I asked Woolley, towards the bottom of the second gin.

Dick stretched out his legs, ruffling fingers through dishevelled hair. 'Pretty hopeless, actually. Well, it had been all right, for a while. Martin and I gradually got to grips with the job, then passed out for full watch-keeping duties so were able to stand bridge duty unsupervised. That lessened the load on the skipper and Strang, so you'd think, what with the officer complement being up to full strength, everything should have gone swimmingly. And I suppose it did. For a while.'

'What happened?'

'Alan began to go downhill. Nerves and that. It was practically unnoticeable at first – bags under the eyes, momentary indecisiveness on the bridge, short fuse with the crew, that sort of thing. But then one night Asdic picked up a contact. Rattlers sounded, we closed up to action stations as usual, and began to run in for an attack. Alan just didn't turn up. I was on the four-inch, Martin aft with the depth-charge crews, Skipper had to carry on without a first officer on the bridge. When it was over, I was sent to look for him. He was curled up on his bunk, with his arms over his head, shaking like a leaf. Completely paralysed.'

'God. Why didn't Deeds simply get rid of him?'

'He was going to; he even put in the paperwork. But Strang begged him not to. Just said he needed time to sort himself out, find a way to get back on top again. And in fact, as long as we weren't at action stations he was absolutely fine, his usual self, a top-notch first officer.'

'Yes, but what use is the world's best Number One if he dives under his bunk every time rattlers goes.'

'Precisely. But Deeds, well, he's incredibly loyal, to all *Daisy*'s men, you know. I think, in a way, he held himself responsible for the state Alan was in. It was an awful situation for him, he could have ended Alan's entire career in one stroke. You could see he was in a stew about it. Anyway, he persevered with him for a while longer, but in the end the ship had to come first.'

'So he put in an application for a new Number One, but got Villiers instead.'

'Yup. Spare first lieutenants were rarer than hen's teeth then. So the next time we get back to 'Derry, Villiers is standing there in his beret and cricket boots on the dockside. A Wavy-Navy temporary gent, just like me and Martin.'

'Deeds?'

'Apoplectic. Stormed off the ship, firing off wires and telephone messages to everyone from the First Sea Lord down. But it was no good. The best he could hope for was to make do until a proper replacement could be found.'

'And one never was.'

'Possibly. Although I think he cancelled the request. The thing is, the group went back out on duty next day. Both crossings were busy ones, frightful weather and no shortage of enemy activity. We picked up a lot of survivors, too. But there were no foul-ups on board that I can remember. In fact everything began to come together at last. Strang got a grip, locking himself in the Asdic hut and becoming wizard at coordinating attacks. It was as though the only way he could manage his funk was to hide in there and transfer it on to the enemy. Villiers – well, he turned out to be just the right chap to have on the bridge at actions stations. You know, like a foil, to the skipper. In fact, overall, *Daisy* did well. Got credited with a one-third probable kill, together with *Lily* and *Hornbeam*. *Vehement* even sent us a "well done" signal.'

Dick broke off, swirling his glass in contemplative silence.

Up on deck the shrill piccolo call of a bosun's pipe told us Deeds was coming back aboard.

'It's like a house of cards, he once said to us, you know.'

'Who?'

'The skipper. He was talking to Martin and me, down here in the wardroom, a while after that trip. He said putting a good scratch crew together in wartime was like building a house of cards. Surprisingly strong once you got the composition right. But, if you pulled out just one card . . .'

Michael, it was growing clearer, was *Daisy*'s trump. Much later I tottered back to my cabin, slightly the worse for wear. Passing Strang's door I heard voices, and paused to listen.

'What's it about?' I heard him ask, his voice little more than a pained croak. It was Michael who answered.

'It's about this chap's adventures in Uruguay. The author, Hudson, paints a wonderfully vivid picture of the country. I think you'll enjoy it, Alan.'

'Well,' Strang grunted. 'Thanks. Maybe I'll give it a try. So, why is it called *The Purple Land*?'

'I think it's partly to do with the blood spilled there over the centuries. But also it's to do with the grass. The pampas grass. In the spring, when it flowers, the whole plain turns purple. Just for a few weeks. It's truly beautiful, Alan. You know, you can get on a horse, ride across it all day, and never see another soul.'

Three days later we ran into my first full Atlantic gale. It was an epiphany. There are no ways adequately to prepare for this experience. Old hands can spin you yarns about it, you can read about it in Conrad or Forester, you can even study it up in heavy-weather manuals or learn about it in meteorology classes, if you happened to be paying attention that day. I wasn't, so encountering it was all the more awesome.

It came on during the morning watch, an hour or so after Villiers and I had turned in. The weather had been foul enough during our spell, steep seas, heavy rain and blown spray making for a moderately uncomfortable time on the bridge. But nothing exceptional, I thought, and with the night as black as pitch and only my limited imagination to fall back on, I was spared what it must have looked like. It wasn't until two hours later, when I was literally pitched from my bunk to the floor of our cabin, which itself was running with little wavelets of oily water, that I realised things were getting bad. Villiers was nowhere to be seen. Insensible with sleeplessness, I sat there, sliding idiotically back and forth across the floor in my pyjamas, listening to the tortured boom of *Daisy*'s hull, and wondering, idly, at the extraordinary gyrations she was performing. Then, accepting that further sleep was probably out of the question, I struggled into my already wet foul-weather gear: socks and sea boots, two layers of clothes, duffel coat and oilskins, and fought my way up to the bridge.

The sight that greeted me, now that daylight was fully up, defied both comprehension and description. The ocean was completely insane, one vast, furious landscape of towering waves that rolled away to the horizon like snow-capped mountains on the rampage. In height, perhaps thirty feet, completely dwarfing *Daisy*. Between rearing crests, clouds of foam flew like smoke, streaks of spume striping the troughs with white. The air above was a shrieking maelstrom of wind and sea. Each time *Daisy* buried her nose, seething torrents of water rushed aft, totally engulfing the four-inch gun platform, to smash against the superstructure below. Within seconds I was soaked, drenched to the bone by clouds of wind-borne spray that lashed at the skin and stung the eyes. It was humbling, thrilling and terrifying all at the same time. I staggered to the front of the bridge, clutching at handholds for support. Other figures huddled there, gleaming sou'westers lashed to their heads, ducking uselessly, like puppets, at each inundation. 'All right, Mid?' someone shouted. I just clung on, and waited for the world to end.

It couldn't take long. *Daisy*'s motion was completely mad, quite beyond reason. The ship would stagger unsteadily forward for a short while, then pitch suddenly downwards in a kind of dizzy, corkscrewing death dive. Then, as though piling into a brick wall, she would lurch to a juddering halt, rolling over on to her beam ends like a shot rhinoceros, before picking herself up with a shudder and beginning the whole hideous sequence again. How she stood it without simply diving for the bottom defied all logic. Above it all, as a kind of hellish accompaniment to the motion, was the noise. A continuous series of deep concussive booms, like a heavy artillery bombardment, as the seas pounded her hull. Then the crash of it exploding across her decks. Above that the wind, a terrifying spine-chilling siren shriek, like souls in torment.

We would sink, of that there could be no doubt. Soon. Quite apart from the insane corkscrewing, from time to time *Daisy* would make a kind of diving lurch, dropping forwards and sideways, as though tripping over a cliff. Before our eyes the bows would fall into a trough, but then not lift again, just plough straight into the next wave, completely vanishing into the sea which rolled back across the deck in a solid wall of green, until only the upper superstructure was visible. This is it, I concluded, time and again, my eyes riveted to the scene. We were going down. Seconds would pass. An eternity. But then, impossibly, *Daisy* would stagger slowly upright, shake herself like a bedraggled dog and struggle gamely forward once more. A few minutes later it would all begin again. But it couldn't go on. No things man-made could possibly withstand it.

But they were. All around us. Gradually, as the notion of life beyond the next five minutes coalesced into a possibility, I became aware of them. Despite the spray-filled air reducing visibility to a mile or two at best, ships, lots of them, could be seen all around, bashing into the teeth of the storm. You'd glimpse a bit of funnel, then nothing, then a bit of funnel again. Then you'd see someone's bows, rearing madly skywards like a broaching whale, or a fantail, a bared propeller thrashing at air for a second, before vanishing from sight behind the next monstrous roller. Astonishingly, the convoy was still on, still together, still going.

Albeit in the wrong direction, Deeds explained, between passing walls of spray. He was absolutely in his element, lurching from chart room to wheelhouse, to wireless room to Asdic hut, down to the engine room and back for a chin-wag with the Chief and his boys.

'Few o' the ships were making heavy weather of it!' he shouted, a sodden cigarette wiggling between his lips, his face gleaming with spray. 'Commodore signalled that the formation was starting to break up, so *Vehement* decided it'd be best to stick together, turn nor'east, and steam into it for a bit. More comfortable like this!'

I wondered briefly what 'less comfortable' might feel like, but thought better of asking. 'How long will it go on for, do you think, sir?'

Deeds grinned. 'Who's to know, Mid. Could be a wee while yet!'

Five days. For five solid days and nights we plugged into that gale. I stayed on the bridge for much of it, transfixed by the spectacle beyond *Daisy*'s bows. In any case there was little else to do. Food, such as it was, consisted of soggy lumps of bread with bits of corned beef stuck to it. The galley was completely unusable, trying to prepare hot meals in it as pointless as it was dangerous, so Deeds had it closed down and endless rounds of sandwiches circulated. In any case going below was a miserable business, like clambering through a flooded scrapyard. Inches of filthy bilge water sloshed across mess decks and up walls, everything stank of oil, vomit and flooded toilets. As soon as you put something down – a glove, a biscuit, a mug of cold tea – it leapt up and threw itself on the floor. Just standing upright was a major effort; in no time you were bruised bloody from collisions with furniture, bulkheads, pipes. Sleep was out of the question, even with storm sheets rigged to stop you falling out. For once the crew were better off, a hammock undoubtedly the safest place to be. But what with the perpetual running water on the lower deck, the leaks pouring on to them from overhead, the crazy motion of the ship, the incessant pounding of the hull, how they actually rested, and fed themselves, *and* went to work, I'll never know.

If all that wasn't bad enough, we were going in the wrong direction. Steaming steadily east on a convoy supposed to be going to Nova Scotia. 'Much more of this . . .' as Michael put it, poring over the charts early on the sixth morning '. . . and we'll be able to pop into Greenock to refuel.'

Then, at about noon that day, Deeds came up and did his sniffing the wind bit. 'Won't be long now, lads,' he announced, rubbing his hands. I peered about. Everything appeared exactly as before, exactly as it had, for what had seemed a lifetime. Wild, murderous seas, and a wind that howled like a banshee. What on earth had changed? But, sure enough, not thirty minutes later:

'Bridge, radio.' A tired voice from the wireless room tube.

'Go ahead, radio.'

'Signal from *Vehement*, sir.'

'Read it, lad.'

'Make ready resume westbound heading at one-three-double-oh hours. Report your storm damage.'

'Right-oh. Acknowledge, please, Yeoman,' Deeds chuckled. 'Oh, and add: "What storm?"'

A few minutes later: 'Signals coming in from *Vehement*,

sir, and also *Fuchsia*. One from *Hornbeam*, too, sir, relayed via *Lily*.'

'Go ahead, Yeoman.' Deeds was grinning like a Cheshire cat.

'*Daisy*, repeat *Daisy*. Give me your answer do. I'm half crazy all for the love of you . . .'

Half an hour later we were heading for America once more.

That night the U-boats returned. Like sharks homing on a school of whales. The weather was still bad, still blowing old boots, *Daisy* pitching and rolling like a seaside switchback, her decks awash with foaming black ocean. But it was a greatly scaled down unpleasantness by comparison with the nightmare of the previous five days.

It was about eleven p.m. Due back on watch at midnight, I was head down in my bunk, trying to bank an hour or two's sleep before returning to duty. All around me the ship was slowly putting herself back in order. Wet clothing hung like bunting over engine room steam pipes, smashed crockery was swept into corners, gashed shins and bruised heads dressed and bandaged. Up-spirits and cooks-to-the-galley was piped at six; soon delicious cooking smells were percolating *Daisy*'s decks, mingling with the odour of drying laundry and Senior Service cigarettes. In no time the combination of hot food, their precious tot of Navy rum and a shipshape mess deck transformed the men from a cluster of bedraggled zombies to a happy band of brothers. As I slept, the sound of whistling, laughter and ribaldry began to penetrate the clogged corridors of my mind. Settling deeper in the rocking cradle of my bunk, I had never felt so secure in my life.

Then rattlers went off. By now the routine was automatic. I sat up without even waking. Stamping feet rang overhead, loudspeakers blared, engine-room telegraphs clanged. Bleary with insomnia, I swung my feet to the deck and began to dress. Earlier that evening I'd peeled off sodden sea socks for the first time in a week, to find the skin beneath puckered white and reeking of ammonia. Chemical reaction to do with saltwater and natural wool, somebody explained. How interesting. I pulled them on again, gathered the rest of my gear and ran for the door.

'*Lily*'s picked up a contact over on the starboard side of the convoy,' Deeds was saying to Villiers as I arrived. 'Thinks it might be coming our way.'

'Very good, sir. Useful if we could drive it off before it can get a shot in.'

'Useful if we could blow it to kingdom come, Number Two. Bridge, engine room! One-nine-zero revolutions please, Chief, and stand by to uncork the lot if we do pick something up.'

'Engine room, one-nine-oh revs, second boiler coming on line now, sir.'

'Good. Bridge, depth charges!'

'Brown here, depth charge rails all closed up and ready, sir.'

'Thank you, Sub. Bridge, helm.'

'Wheelhouse here, sir, Coxswain now at the wheel.'

'Thank you, Coxswain, come starboard on to new heading two-eight-oh.'

'Starboard two-eight-oh, sir.'

'Bridge, Asdic here, I think we may have something. Green two-oh!'

It was Strang. Poor, skin-sweating, hands-trembling Strang, down there in the suffocating airlessness of his demon-filled hut. He'd done it again. Screwed down the lid on his terror, reached out into the depths with his nicotine-stained fingertips, and touched something.

'Put it on the repeater, Number One.'

Suddenly, there it was. After months of nothing. A 'ping'. Just like the millions of others before it. Followed by a long, long pause. Then, when all hope seemed lost, a ghostly hint of an echo. Just the merest suggestion, faint and distant. But an '-oh' nonetheless. Like an afterthought.

'That's it! Helm starboard ten. Engine room full ahead, everything you've got now. Wireless, signal to *Vehement*, contact bearing three-zero-zero degrees, am engaging. Asdic, don't lose that echo, Number One, range and bearing as soon as you can . . .'

Just then the first torpedo hammered home. Not from our submarine, from another, far out on the port side of the convoy. The now familiar flash of light, the distant rumbling boom, the flurry of bursting starshells and flares. A minute later another went off, then a third. Battle was joined.

It continued all night. There were lulls, of course, intervals of melancholic quiet, when you stood woodenly at your post, gulping a mug of kye, and allowed your salt-stung eyes to wander the desecration and take stock. Ships, once proud ships, now broken in two, turning up their ends with a shrug and just sliding without fuss from view. Others, fighting on against the rising waves, but losing, sinking lower and lower until, as though suddenly accepting the futility of it all, they rolled over, venting air like a blowing whale, and plunged for the deep. Still more, empty, drifting, nothing but abandoned flaming hulks, charred destitutes that refused to go, refused to spare us the obscenity of their lingering. Like dying vagrants on the street. And all around you the sea stank with oil, the bodies bobbed, and the carpets of wreckage drifted, like the flooded aftermath of an earthquake.

Then you went back to work. All night we pursued our contact, lost it, reacquired it, lost it again. We ran in and dropped our depth charges, our deadly dustbins of Torpex. Turned, listened, and ran in again. Time after time the sea astern of *Daisy* jumped and reared with explosion, the ship ringing with the concussion of each pattern as though struck by some furious hammer-wielding giant. Nothing could survive that onslaught, we thought, surely nothing. Then all would go quiet. Had we hit her? Was she at that very moment spiralling into the abyss, little more than a mess of twisted steel? We waited, circled, swept back and forth. But no air bubbles boiled to the surface, no wreckage, no oil, no bodies. Not good enough, Deeds would curse, ordering another sweep. Not bloody good enough. Minutes later another echo. The same? Or another. It made no difference. We found it, lost it, found it again. Harrying it, hounding it, nagging at it like a terrier after a fox.

Then, some time around dawn, it vanished from the scope for ever, slipping away into the deep to lick its wounds and regroup. With our supply of depth charges all but spent, we too gave up and secured from action stations, breaking off the hunt.

Only to commence another. The victims. As dawn came up, more and more were starting to appear, drifting, spread-eagled among the debris, or suspended, heads lolling, in their lifebelts. Or sprawled lifelessly across a Carley float. The bitter harvest of the night's toil. We began to gather them in.

Most were already dead. In no time *Daisy*'s rails were lined with dismal, blanket-covered bundles that moved macabrely from side to side as she rolled. At least they were recovered, fished from the waves, tar-black and slippery with oil, using boat hooks and lines. Retrieving the living was far harder. The seas were still much too high to launch a whaler, so scrambling nets were rigged over the sides. If they wanted to live, survivors were required to swim to a net, and with *Daisy* rolling cruelly from side to side, cling on to it and climb up. A fit man, strong and eager, would have found it perilously difficult. For these survivors, many of them injured, their lungs choked with sea and oil, weak to the point of exhaustion and numb with cold, it was practically hopeless. A few stalwarts made it. But many didn't, shrugged from the madly swinging nets by the ship's motion, their bodies crashing sickeningly against *Daisy*'s side before dropping limply to the sea. Some were too weak even to try, just holding the nets and calling forlornly to us from the greasy waves. There was little any of us could do, except lean over and shout encouragement. After a while they would fall quiet, let go and drift away. At one point a gunner from blue watch, cursing with frustration, tied a line around his chest, threw his leg over *Daisy*'s rail and began to climb down a net to help some poor unfortunate stuck halfway. Strang, who was supervising matters, stopped him, ordering him back up. He only just made it, dragged back on board by his mates, his shins and knuckles skinned to the bone.

Sickened, I went below to help Villiers with the injured.

There were about twenty. They were sitting or lying on bunks he'd taken over on the crewmen's mess deck, temporarily converting it into a sick bay. On one side, the ship's medical orderly cleaned oil from a Lascar seaman with his arm in a sling. Another helper bandaged someone's head. The whole place reeked of fuel and antiseptic.

'Hello, Sub,' I said.

Michael looked up. 'Hello, Stephen,' he smiled, wiping that fair hair back from his brow with a wrist. He was in blood-spattered uniform shirt, the sleeves rolled to the elbows. A small silver medallion swung from a chain at his neck. In one hand he held forceps, in the other needle and silk, poised ready to close the gaping wound on the leg of the man lying before him. 'This is Mr Foster, Stephen,' he went on, as though introducing us at the pub. Then he began to stitch.

Immediately the man gasped. Middle-aged, his body darkly matted with oil-stained hair, he clutched at his head with his arms. 'Jesus!' he hissed. Then, 'Go on, son, don't stop, keep going . . .'

I watched as Michael worked. He had this amazing calmness about him, a kind of serenity, as if down here at least he was at peace with what he was, and what he was doing. And those eyes. The deepest green, like emeralds. Full of compassion and concern. Yet ruthlessly penetrating. You couldn't help but feel self-conscious when he trained them on you. As if he knew exactly what you were feeling, no matter how hard you pretended otherwise.

He knew exactly what *I* was feeling. 'So. What's up, Mid?' he prompted, stitching carefully.

'Oh, nothing. Well, it's Strang. He just bawled a rating out for trying to help someone up the scrambling nets. I thought it a bit hard.'

'I see,' he murmured. 'I wonder, could you just hold this while I tie it off?'

A minute or two more and the stitches were done. The orderly came over to bandage the leg, while Michael tidied up. Foster smiled weakly.

'Thanks, doc. Hardly felt a thing.'

'Well done, sir. And thank you.'

He turned away to a basin. 'I used to tell them I'm only an acting MO,' he went on, washing his hands, 'but it only seemed to worry them, so I stopped.'

'Ah. Well, I suppose it might.'

'*Lily* lost a man like that, did you know?'

'I beg your pardon?'

'Last January it was, I think. He went down a scrambling net to try and help someone. Seas were awful, he lost his footing and fell off. The *Lily*s tried for ages to get him back, but in the end the cold got him, he just gave up, and so they left him. Had to. But *Lily*'s captain blamed the first officer, for letting the man try.'

'No. No, I didn't know that.'

'How could you, Stephen? It doesn't matter now. But, for what it's worth, I believe Alan Strang would be the first down that net if it wasn't forbidden. Now then, feel like helping out a bit?'

'What?' I looked around. 'Well, yes, of course. But what can I do?'

'You can do a great deal. These chaps, you see. Many of them just need cleaning up, and a bit of encouragement, you know?' He pointed to a youth lying on a bunk on the far side of the room. He was propped up on one elbow, staring around in confusion, covered in fuel oil but otherwise intact, evidently. 'He says his name's Taylor, he's from Devon. Thinks he might be the only survivor from that grain carrier that went up earlier. Could you talk to him?'

'Talk?'

'Yes, Stephen, talk.' The eyes were trained on me now, all right. 'I'm afraid he's swallowed a lot of fuel.'

Ned, his name was, I quickly learned. Ned Taylor from Truro. And he was the one doing the talking, not me. At least to begin with. Ten to the dozen. Last in a long line of seagoing Truro Taylors, he was, he explained. Signed on a year ago, at sixteen, like his dad. Been on convoys ever since. Born to the sea, he was. Just like me. He'd soon discovered that, too. It seemed to delight him. Sailors both, he kept saying. Same age and dead proud, he said, to both be following the family tradition.

'It's in our blood, see, Stephen. Yours and mine. A right pair of jolly Jack Tars we are, wouldn't you say?'

'Absolutely, Ned.'

We used benzene to clean oil off victims. Or surgical spirit. It stung them like hell, especially when you were trying to clean a wound. Ned had oil everywhere. In his eyes, his ears, mouth. Even his nostrils were black with it. I worked at it as best I could, swabbing carefully with wads of lint. He seemed very restless, gabbling madly for a bit, then breaking off to stare around the mess deck, as though searching for someone. I thought it must be nerves. Or shock.

'How're long we going to be 'ere, Stephen,' he kept asking in his West Country burr. ''Ow long?'

'Not too long, now, Ned,' I found myself beginning to say, after a while.

A little later he started coughing. Hard and dry at first. Then the oil began to come. Thick and black, dribbling down his chin like treacle. The smell was awful. I dabbed and mopped uselessly. Soon the spasms grew worse, quickly exhausting him. Between bouts he became quieter.

'Right pair we are, Stephen,' he coughed. His skin was changing, paling to a deathly grey. 'Right pair. Tell us about your mum and dad, Stephen. Tell us about where you grew up and that.'

'No, well, Ned, I'm sure you'd be bored to tears . . .'

'Tell us, Stephen!' His hand clutched at my arm. He jerked, convulsed, doubling up and over on to his side. More oil came up, a glistening brown rivulet hanging from the corner of his mouth, this time darkly stained with blood.

I knew then that he was going to die. I knew then that Michael had asked me to go to him, knowing he would die. They just need a bit of encouragement, Stephen, he'd said. Talk to him. Talk to him so he doesn't have to die on his own.

But I couldn't, I didn't know how. I just wanted to run away, get back on deck and forget about Ned. Forget about everything. I thought then of the conversation I'd heard outside Strang's door. Villiers calmly chatting about his childhood on the pampas while the first officer battled his terror like a fever. It was a gift. Michael had it. I didn't. I had nothing. Nothing but funk and fear.

'Well, Ned . . .' I floundered. Oil-stained fingernails still gripped the flesh of my arm. He had close-cropped ginger hair, freckles showing beneath the film of oil, ears that stuck out a bit. My age. Almost exactly. His eyes, brown, round, were still staring up at me. 'I, well, I do remember my first experience of the sea. And that it was almost enough to put me off for life, I can tell you—'

'Go on!' he pleaded hoarsely.

'Yes, well, you see my father had this little motor boat, down on the south coast at Littlehampton. I must have been six or seven, he took me out on it one day, for a fishing trip.'

'What 'appened?'

The weather turned, that's what happened. One minute

rocking about happily, trailing my arm through the glassy water, idly watching petrels dive for tiddlers, the next the sky is as black as your hat and furious blasts of cold wind are whipping the sea to a frenzy. What's happening, I ask him, terrified. Line squall, he laughs. It's nothing. But I'm frightened, I want to go back to shore. No, you can't go back, he scolds, angry at my fear, it's too dangerous. You have to ride it out, like a real mariner. But I'm not a real mariner, I am six, and scared senseless. I flee below, cowering on the madly rocking floor of the little cuddy, with its fish-bait smells and sea spray lashing at the porthole. He keeps calling for me to come up, to come and face it, show I'm not afraid. But I am afraid, and can only lie there and look up at him, framed in the companionway. Standing there, tall and fearless in the pouring rain, his hair blowing in the wind, his eyes clouded with disappointment.

I broke off to mop more bloody mucus from Ned's chin. Gradually the spasm passed, and he lay back again.

'So you see, Ned, not a very promising start to a naval career.'

His breathing was becoming laboured. 'Didn't put us off though, did it, Stephen?' he whispered. 'Didn't stop us following in the family tradition.'

'No. No, I suppose it didn't.' It was only then that I realised I'd never once spoken of it before. To anyone.

'Right pair of jolly Jack Tars, we are.'

'Yes, Ned. A right pair.'

We buried him, beneath pewter skies, at sunset that afternoon. There were eleven dead in all. Deeds did the honours, blue watch and a handful of officers ranged in a bare-headed semicircle on the foredeck before him. Behind, the weighted canvas bundles waited at the rail. As he read the words that were to become so familiar in the coming months, a watery sun split the western overcast, spilling shafts of orange over the gently rolling horizon. A lone shearwater, its huge wings twitching in the currents, effortlessly combed the valleys and hills of its ocean home a thousand miles from shore. '. . . Cut down like a flower, he fleeth as it were a shadow, and never continueth in one stay . . .' Deeds read. Then, with the clouds closing once more, *Daisy* was brought briefly to all stop, and the bundles tipped quietly from view.

I wept and I didn't care who saw that I wept. Nobody took any notice, caps were returned to heads, people sniffed and spat and stared at the clouds, then went back to work. I stayed there at the windlass, feeling *Daisy* lift to the seas as her propeller bit the water once more, listening to the renewed splash of her bow wave.

'You did very well, Stephen. Last night. With that boy,' Villiers said.

'No. Thank you, Sub, but actually I did very badly.'

'Nothing could have saved him, you know. All anyone could do was stay with him, and try to make him as comfortable as possible. You did that. And bravely.'

'No I didn't! He was ten times braver about it than me.'

'It's not a competition, Stephen.' He smiled. Standing there, his hands in the pockets of his leather jerkin, one foot resting on *Daisy*'s rusting anchor chain. 'You did what had to be done, and did it well. Really. I'm proud of you.'

It was the first time anyone had ever said that to me. Coming from him, somehow, meant even more. More than I could manage. I felt my throat tightening again. But before I could make a complete idiot of myself, he clapped a hand to my shoulder and began steering me aft.

'Showing your feelings is fine, too. My great-grandfather always used to say that a man without emotion was like a horse without a head. Never was quite sure what he meant by that. Did I ever tell you about him? Tata he was called, although his real name was Don Adrián Rapoza . . .'

Twenty minutes later rattlers sounded.

'I remember that day,' Frank Tuker said, almost to himself, after a very long pause. We were steadily losing interest, the lapses in conversation lengthening with every passing hour. Nobody noticed, nobody cared, which was even worse – the unmistakable beginning of an inevitable end.

'You do?' Harrison replied, after a bit.

'Yes, I do. I was on blue watch burial detail.' Another pause, then Tuker rambled on. 'Strange when you think about it. There was so many times we was stood up there on that foredeck burying those poor buggers. One day seemed just like another. But I do remember that one. Can't imagine why.'

I wondered dully if it was because he'd had to witness the unedifying spectacle of *Daisy*'s midshipman blubbing like a schoolgirl. But then realised I didn't care. So many times in the following weeks I would see sailor shed tears for brother sailor; there was nothing remarkable in it. I never cried again though. Somehow, Ned had got it out of my system.

We were becoming dangerously cold. I fumbled for my watch; it was shortly before noon, although you'd never know it from the sky. Dull, slate-grey, a cheerless drizzle fell from it again, compounding our misery, chilling our bones and shrinking the horizon to a blur. We'd shipped some water, a few inches now slopped about the whaler's bilges. We were sitting in it, yet ought to be baling it out. We ought to be thinking about thawing frozen limbs, about eating and drinking something. We ought to be thinking about what we were going to do to stay alive. But it was all becoming too much of an effort. And Michael. He was still lost to us. And without him to galvanise us, what the hell was the point?

'How do you do it?' Giddings asked hoarsely. His teeth were chattering, his whole body shuddering with cold. 'I mean, I've watched it, and that, seen it done a couple of times. But I never been on actual burial detail. With a real body. What do you have to do?'

Tuker considered. 'Well, see, you have to tidy him up, his wounds and that, best you can. Then you plug his oro-fices with tallow so he don't leak nor get no worms up him and that. Then you dress him in some decent fig, if there's any spare. Then you plain-stitch him into a square of canvas seven foot by four. If there's no canvas you use a blanket. At the feet end you put the weighted bag. Pig iron's best but you can use anything so long as it's heavy; box of coach bolts, lead ballast, anything. In the old days they used cannonballs. When he's all stitched in the canvas, you secure him with a double line all round, so he's in snug and nothing

246

flapping about, then you bring him up on deck. You lay 'im on a length of grating, or a piece of board or something. We used a trestle table from the petty officers' mess. Then, when the skipper says "We therefore commit 'is body to the deep . . ." you up-end the trestle, and in he goes. Then you go below, have a tot, and share out his personal effects. That's the sailor's way, see.'

I was only half listening. On the pretext of stretching cramped limbs, I had moved myself slowly down to the stern.

'All right, Sub?' I enquired, lowering myself to the boards beside Michael. His head was on his knees. If he heard, he gave no sign.

Giddings looked perplexed. 'Why the petty officers' mess?'

'What? What are you on about now?'

'Michael,' I nudged him. 'That day. Do you remember it, too? Do you remember what you said to me?'

'Yes.' His voice was barely a whisper.

'The petty officers' mess. It's all the way aft. I mean, why go to the bother of hauling one of their tables all the way from the stern of the ship, when the crew's mess deck is right there under the foc'sle?'

'Michael, you said it was all right to show your feelings, remember?'

'Well it's obvious, ain't it! We don't want some filthy old stoker laid out for hours stiff as a bloody board on one of our tables, do we? I mean, we've got to eat off that, for God's sake!'

'I wonder if he'd follow us,' Harrison said suddenly, peering to seaward.

'Who, for the love of heaven?'

'The U-boat. I mean, look at the visibility, it's down to less than half a mile.'

'So . . . ?'

'Michael. I understand what you must be feeling, but we have to start doing something. Making some kind of plan. Anything. We can't do this without you.'

'I know. I'm sorry.'

'I mean, if we were to paddle off, into the murk a bit, he'd have to follow us. If he didn't, he'd lose us in no time. We'd be able to sneak away.'

'Michael, he's right. Listen to him!'

'Yes, but 'ow's he going to do that?'

'He'd have to use his periscope,' Villiers said, raising his head. His hand gripped my arm, pushing himself stiffly up on to the thwart. 'He'd have to use his periscope and follow us. He'd have to give away his position.'

Chapter 9

Holbrook House School
Holbrook
Herts

Dear Mikey

Well I hope you had a nice voyage to Uruguay you lucky beast. Dad said your ship looked smashing. Summer hols were grand we went to stay with Granny and Grandad for a bit but Grandad got cronic arthuritis then I went to stay at Hawthornes place in Amersham for a week. We made a camp in his garden and cooked our own grub and everything then war got declared and I had to come home. The sirens went on the first day and Dad and me had to go down the shelter and so on but nothing happened, they said it was just a drill so we came up again.

Next day hols were over so here I am again back at bad old HHS but the good news is Killer is retiring!! We all said he never would *until they carried him out but he made this speech at assembly and said after thirty happiest years of his life he was drawing stumps and retiring to his sister in Wales. We all cheered like mad old killer thought it was because we loved him so much and started sniffing and dabbling his eye and that, but really its because we couldn't believe are good fortune. Mr Ashfield is going to be temprary head while they audition for a new one.*

War is deadly dull. At first it was exciting we had to have air-raid drill and practise what to do in case of gas attack also they're turning the boiler room into a shelter and we have to practise muster points and trooping down there all hours of the day and night and so on. I'm dorm fire officer which means I have to make sure the fire bucket is full of water at bed time in case of incenduries. Pascoe is blackout officer and has to do curtains and so on. But absolutely nothings happened so far not one bomb or anything so frankly we're a bit brassed off with it. Mr Ashfield said it will probabaly all be over by Christmas.

Will you be home then? Whats happening in Uruguay. Is the war there? What are you doing. Have you seen Mama yet. When is she coming home? What about Sombreado. Dad said you might have a job workign at the embassy. I think about you a lot please write me a letter.

Yours faithfully Donald A. Villiers.

Michael contemplated the page. Behind him, wings clapping, a pigeon settled unnoticed on the balcony. A zephyr plucked at the threadbare curtain of his window, a ship's horn blaring dolefully in the distance beyond it. To his recollection, it was the first letter he had ever received from his brother. His reply, he realised, would be another first. He stared at it a while longer: the painstakingly joined hand-writing, the ink smudges and crossings out, the longing beneath the trivia. Then, folding it carefully into its envelope, he returned it to a drawer.

He rose from the little table, padded to the window, the pigeon eyeing him askance. He should get ready. The light was fading, the thin walls of his room melting into shadow. Through them he heard a familiar woman's laugh, a man's grunted reply. Bottles clinked, springs squeaked. Outside, Montevideo stirred reluctantly from heavy afternoon torpor. To the south, flickering thunderclouds retreated across the chocolate-brown waters of the Plate towards Buenos Aires, leaving a sultry haze draped over the city like a blanket. The air smelled close and humid, of cooking smoke and wet concrete. Below, horse carts and motor cars clogged the narrow alleys, street sellers pushed barrows, hawkers, whores and traders jostled along muddy gutters, all heading east towards Centro, the rich people, and another night's hustle and bustle.

He would reply. Definitely, and soon. But what to write, what to say? Donald's question was highly apposite. What *was* he doing? It was a month since he had stepped ashore from *Runswick Bay*. During that time, it could be argued, he had achieved much. Immersing himself in the city, redis-covering his native tongue, moving into lodgings, even taking on employment. Thoroughly habituating himself, in fact. Yet in his heart he sensed he was accomplishing noth-ing; far from feeling liberated he felt imprisoned, and uneasiness gnawed at his stomach like hunger.

True, he had renewed acquaintance with his mother. Yet it was just that, an acquaintance, like the casual coming together of old friends. The so-longed-for reunion ultimately anticlimactic. He was starting to wonder where, if anywhere, their new relationship was leading. The truth was he had learned just about all there was to know about Aurora. His conclusion was that she seemed well, and happy enough, if a little emotionally unstable, lived an interesting and comfortable life to the full, and showed absolutely no inclination at all to return to her family in England.

Which didn't bother him as much as he felt it should.

They met regularly. Afternoons were best for visits, he'd quickly discovered; Aurora was not a morning person. This was because she led an extremely hectic social existence centred almost entirely around Willi Hochstetler, with whom, Michael had been forced to acknowledge, she was involved. She saw little of her own parents and family in Prado, who disapproved of her, and was rarely to be found in the family apartment in Pocitos. Michael arrived there once or twice in the first week, only to be greeted by blank-faced maids who redirected him to the Hochstetler residence. There he would find her, propped upon a satin-cushioned chaise longue, or sipping early evening cocktails on the veranda, or preparing for one of the endless string of social functions connected with Willi's business friends and contacts at the German legation. She always appeared delighted to see him, greeting him warmly, hugging and kissing him. But more like a favourite pet, he began to feel, than a long-lost son. She drank rather a lot, he observed, although didn't say so, and he also noted a predisposition for debilitating moods of despair and self-chastisement. For these she made regular visits to her physician in the Ciudad Vieja. The visits were not a subject for discussion, but they appeared efficacious, for afterwards the moods were gone.

That was it. As for Willi, although he felt in some nagging way it was a betrayal, Michael found it hard to dislike him. Not only was he unfailingly attentive to his mother, he was also especially warm with Michael. He was a big, jovial man who laughed a lot, went to lengths to make Michael feel included, introduced him to his associates, expressed genuine interest in his opinions and aspirations, was solicitous and generous. He frequently took Michael out to cafés and restaurants, or shopping down Avenida 18 de Julio, or to a show at the Teatro Solís.

Once or twice he drove Michael and his mother along the seaside *rambla* to Carrasco in his open-topped Mercedes. There they would sit side-by-side on the huge hotel's beach-front terrace, drinking ice-cold German beer imported by one of Willi's associates. Aurora, watching them indulgently from behind sunglasses, would sip on a gin sling, half listening as Willi held forth on his views of the world.

'How I detest politics, Michael!' he would say, tapping the little Nazi pin he wore in the lapel of his expensive American suit. 'I am a pure businessman, and pure business transcends politics.' Whether he really believed it was hard to say. If he did, he was deluding himself, Michael knew. He wore the pin because not to do so would at the very least alienate him from the German expatriate elite, with disastrous consequences for his business interests. Michael's own grasp of the situation was already sound enough to appreciate the importance of their region to the world – and to an embattled Europe in particular. As war spread, Atlantic South America, especially stoically neutral Uruguay, sandwiched between the wavering giants Brazil and Argentina, assumed increasing strategic significance. The Spanish and Portuguese had known it for centuries, Britain and Germany had soon come to recognise it. Even the United States, fearful of an escalation of hostilities, was latching on. That very month, in return for technical and industrial inducements, the USA was seeking Uruguay's approval to set up a naval air station north of Punta del Este.

'You see, Michael, my dream is for a truly unencumbered global marketplace,' Willi expounded grandly. 'With fair, open and unlimited competition between nations living in harmony with one another.'

Michael sipped his beer. 'Karl Marx said that all the destructive phenomena which unlimited competition gives rise to in one country are reproduced in more gigantic proportions on the world market.'

Willi looked aghast. 'My God, Michael, but are you a Marxist?'

'I, well, I'm not sure. But, like Marx, I believe it is just as wrong for one class in a country to enrich itself at the expense of another, as it is for one nation to enrich itself at the expense of another nation.'

'No, no, Michael, but we can all become enriched, that is exactly my point! We must all be friends and help one another, especially those less fortunate than ourselves. That way we are all partakers of the world's bounty. First, however, it is, sadly, essential that the strong take control, in order that this process can begin . . .'

It was only in this almost endearingly muddled fashion, Michael realised, that Willi could reconcile his dream of a utopian world marketplace, with the obdurate dogma emanating from his own country's political leaders. Basically Willi was an inept fascist. He genuinely believed there was no need for animosity between the British and German communities in Uruguay. Soon the troubles would be over, he kept promising, as though to convince himself, and then life could go on as before.

'And you will stay, Michael! Here in Montevideo, with your mother and me,' he repeatedly urged, enticing Michael with more beer and lavish offers of employment. 'This is your home now, you see. This is where you should remain.'

But Michael had yet to define home. As for a job, he already had one.

As did the woman in the room next door. The moaning and sighing through the wall was growing louder, the now-familiar rhythmic squeaking of her bed springs accelerating. Michael stepped out on to his balcony, trying to distance himself from the coming finale. But her window, too, was open, as he knew it would be. Eyes closed, inhaling deeply the moist night air, repelled yet all the while shamefully conscious of his own fascinated arousal, he shut his mind to the noises, while his ears strained to listen.

Michael worked as a trainee shipping clerk for Atlantic

Mercantile Limited, a London-based import/export business with offices in Montevideo's tallest building, the recently completed Palacio Salvo, a baroque, twenty-six-storey erection which rose, phallus-like, from the east side of Plaza Independancia.

But then again he didn't. For, one floor above Atlantic Mercantile, situated well away from the British legation's new premises on Avenida Jorge Canning, the consulate maintained a small satellite office known as the British Shipping Advisory Department. It was for the processing of trade applications and licences. Ostensibly.

At eight each morning Michael reported to Atlantic Mercantile. He ran errands. He collected and delivered paperwork from the offices of shipping companies down at the docks. He was shown how to fill out bills of lading, how to collect, sort and circulate the mail, how to do the filing. It wasn't taxing, not a great deal was expected of him. As long as someone knew where he was, he could come and go almost as he pleased. The other staff were friendly enough, if a little remote. Nobody took very much notice of him. So he believed.

Every two or three days, however, a message would come down asking Michael to pop 'upstairs' for a few minutes. There, seated in a low-slung chair in a plush suite commanding all-round views of the city, harbour and estuary, Michael would be debriefed on his contacts with the Germans.

Mainly it was the manager there, a grey-faced man introduced to Michael as 'Mr Martin', who asked the questions. Sometimes it was Captain McCall, the naval intelligence officer he had met on his first day in Montevideo. Occasionally it was Britain's Minister to Uruguay himself, Eugen Millington-Drake. Michael preferred the last; the others, although polite, were brutally uncompromising in their thoroughness, dismissive of information they believed of no consequence and intolerant of inaccuracy.

'You say Herr Langmann was at this reception yesterday, Michael. The head of the German legation. Is that right?'

'Yes, sir.'

'What time did he arrive?'

'I, I'm not sure, sir. Eleven, perhaps, or twelve.'

'Which? Eleven or twelve.'

'Nearer to twelve, I would say.'

'I see. Was he accompanied?'

'Yes, sir. Frau Langmann was with him, and one of his daughters. Also a party official on a visit from Buenos Aires.'

'His name?'

'Neiling, sir, I think it was.'

'Are you quite sure?'

'Yes, sir. It was Neiling. Heinrich Neiling.'

'What was the purpose of his presence there?'

'I, well, I don't know, sir. Willi, that is Herr Hochstetler, introduced him to some of his business associates. He also spent quite a long time talking with the legation information officer, Dalldorf, and also . . .'

'Yes?'

'Well, my mother. She spent time with him, made sure he had plenty to eat and drink, introduced him to some of the other wives, and so on.'

'I see. What did he drink?'

'Champagne, sir, mostly, I believe. Then hock.'

So it would go on. Millington-Drake, on the other hand, seemed less interested in the drinking habits of the Germans, and more concerned with Michael himself.

'You seem a little downhearted, old chap,' he'd observed, only that morning after a particularly gruelling session with Mr Martin. 'Anything we can do? Feeling well? Rooms all right? Got enough pocket money, all that flummery?'

'Yes, sir. Everything's fine, with the room, and so on. Thank you.'

'So why the long face?'

Michael had said nothing, but Millington-Drake, sensing trouble, had persisted. In his personable way, he was just as skilled at extracting information as the others. 'Listen, tell you what, we'll go to dinner. Tonight. My treat. That new *candombe* club off Avenida Soriano. We'll eat *parillada*, listen to some terrific music, and then you can tell me all about it. What do you say?' It was then, almost as an afterthought, that Millington-Drake had given him Donald's letter, addressed to Michael, care of the British Consulate.

Donald. Michael thought of him now, tucked up asleep in his dormitory, his fire bucket by his side. Dreaming of fame at cricket, and word of a brother on the other side of the world. A brother he worshipped but barely knew, who had gone to find their mother and then promised to come back. What are you doing? His letter had asked, simply. What are you doing?

Next door, the woman and her client had finished; low

voices now drifted from her open window. Then her door banged shut, completing the transaction. Silence grew up through the wall; Michael sensed her solitude, as an extension of his own. Suddenly, a loud click, an electric crackling hiss, followed by the tinny scratch of needle on gramophone record. A band started up. Dance music. Tango. Then a voice rose from it, haunting, heartrending, the legendary Carlos Gardel, singing the gaucho verses of loss and suffering that bled from the heart of Latin America. Through her window, a shadow began circling her room. She was in there, dancing with herself. He longed to go to her, to hold her, just dance with her and not feel so alone. But then a car horn sounded. He looked down. A cab was pulling up, Millington-Drake waving from a window. He knew then he had to go.

His bed untouched, he left early the following morning, carefully descending the stairs of his lodgings, slipping through the front door and out, unnoticed, into misty dawn light. He took only what he needed, stuffing food and a few clothes into a small sack, but leaving most of his belongings behind. He needed to travel light, principally, but he also wanted his room to appear occupied, as though he'd just popped out for an hour or two. In case anyone came looking for him.

His next priority was money, cash. He had practically none, just enough for a tram fare across town. But it was still too early for the trams, so he began to walk, passing swiftly from the old city, east through Centro and out along the wide, mile-long Bulevar España towards Pocitos. There the sophisticated night-time cafés appeared squalid and forsaken in the dawn light, the pavements outside littered with the wreckage of last night's carousing. At one place, rats swarmed over discarded kitchen scraps, inches from a sleeping tramp, his bottle cradled safely in his arm. Michael ignored all, together with a nagging muzziness in his head, and strode on, a chill spring breeze bowling paper along the deserted road before him, like tumbleweed in a ghost town.

It took him an hour and a half to walk to Willi's. By the time he arrived it was gone seven. Drawing near, he stopped, flattening himself breathlessly against the mottled bark of a plane tree. The Mercedes was already gone, he noted with satisfaction. Willi was proud of his reputation as an early riser, liked always to be first at his office, no matter how late he'd stayed up the previous night. 'Let sleeping dogs lie, Michael,' he would caution, cheerfully mixing his proverbs, 'and there will be no early worm.'

The maid, Hortensia, opened the front door. 'Señor Miguel, what a surprise! And so early. But, I am afraid your mother has not yet arisen.'

'I need to see her,' he said, pushing past into the hallway.

'But Señor Miguel, that is impossible! Please, you cannot go up . . .'

He took the carpeted stairs two at a time. Aurora's bedroom was on the first floor, at the end of a long panelled corridor overlooking the garden. With Hortensia fussing along ten paces behind, he found the door, knocked, pushed and entered.

She was sprawled, face-down, on the bed, amid a tangle

of rucked silk sheets, scattered cushions, clothes, papers and magazines. A three-quarters empty wine bottle stood on a bedside table, next to an overflowing ashtray and several bottles of pills. Clothes littered the floor around the bed; still more – lingerie, dresses, shoes – spilled from open drawers and a gaping wardrobe. The room, semidark behind shuttered windows, smelled foetid and airless, heavy with perfume and stale cigarettes.

'Mother?' Hortensia appeared behind him, but he gestured for her to withdraw. 'Mother, it is me, Michael.'

Aurora didn't move. She was dressed in her underwear, ivory satin camisole and dark silk stockings. Coin-sized bruises discoloured the paler skin of her thighs above the stocking tops. Michael went to her, shaking her shoulder. 'Mother, wake up, it's Michael!'

'Mi-gel.' The voice was a somnolent slur.

'Yes, Mother, me. Wake up, please, I need some money.'

Still the face lay buried in the sheets. In desperation he slid an arm beneath her and lifted, hoisting her on to her back. Aurora groaned, head lolling. Thick tresses of unkempt hair fell across her face. Her cheek was smudged with make-up, a silvery saliva track drying on her chin.

'Mother!'

The drugged eyes fluttered, stirred, then closed again. 'Go,' she croaked.

'But Mother, please, you must help me!' His eyes travelled the room. A lady's pocketbook stood on an escritoire near the window. Amid the detritus on the floor, a sequinned evening purse. 'Mother?'

'Mi-gel . . .' the voice gathered itself '. . . for pity's sake. GO!'

The railway station lay all the way back across town, on the north shore of the harbour. This time he did take the trams. Time was pressing. The city was coming to life, especially the busy harbour quarter where the shipping offices began early. His non-appearance at Atlantic Mercantile would soon be noticed. Reported upstairs. If not already.

'Destination?' the ticket clerk at the station demanded.

'I, well, I'm not completely sure. It is in Cerro Largo district . . .'

The clerk rolled his eyes. 'A great deal is in Cerro Largo district, young man, it is a sizable department.'

'Yes. Well, Treinta Y Tres, perhaps. No, no, north of there, Arbolito.'

'Arbolito? There is no railway anywhere near Arbolito. You would have to go to Melo and then catch a bus or something. That is if they have buses in Melo.' The clerk smirked with typical city dweller's disdain for the interior of his country.

Michael surveyed the arched steel concourse. His head hurt now, a low throbbing pain at the back of his neck. His throat felt parched, too. It was hard to concentrate. The station was becoming increasingly crowded with office workers spilling to the platforms from incoming commuter trains. Someone, surely, would recognise him soon. He must act, must be decisive. 'You absolutely cannot leave now,' Millington-Drake had emphasised, repeatedly, in the restaurant the night before. 'I understand you are unhappy,

I appreciate you have this need to see your relatives in the interior, and I know you feel uncomfortable about the work you do for us. But you must understand, you are in a unique position, and what you do is vitally important. You have a duty to see it through.'

'But a duty to who?' he'd pleaded.

Millington-Drake had looked genuinely surprised. 'Why, to your country, of course, Michael. You have a clear duty to your country.'

But Uruguay was his country, he felt it more strongly than ever. He bought a ticket to Melo, whereupon the clerk cheerfully told him there were problems on the line north of Santa Clara de Olimar and that he might find himself on foot from there. 'Only a hundred kilometros or so. Wild country, of course; be sure to watch out for gaucho bandits!'

At last he was on the train, slumping into a window seat in a shabby third-class carriage full of farmers, immigrant labourers and families returning to the interior. Head reeling, his body gripped with aches, watching them he nevertheless sensed the primitive stirrings of deeply buried recollection. These were people he recognised. People of the countryside. People he'd grown up with. As the carriage filled, he began to see the darker skins and flatter faces of the Indian and mestizo races among the rough hands and lined faces of European farming stock. The older women wore simpler clothes, plain blouses and long black skirts. Men clumped aboard wearing long boots, ponchos, baggy *chiripá* trousers. Rounded felt hats appeared above the seat backs. In a seat diagonally opposite, an old man slept, arms folded, his *boina* pulled low over his forehead, his maté gourd crooked in his arm. Beside him an elderly mestizo woman played with her granddaughter, a little girl, her chubby brown face framed with glossy curls, watchful eyes the colour of mahogany.

With a lurch the train pulled out. Within minutes the release of tension and rhythmic rocking lulled him into an exhausted trance. For a while he was aware of little, the background music of murmuring voices, a baby's soft gurgles, a vague green blur beyond the glass. Soon, however, he lapsed into full sleep, where his fevered mind unleashed a nightmare kaleidoscope of fantasy and illusion. His mother's body sprawled lifelessly across a bed. Faceless men pursuing him through a maze of empty streets. A woman's thighs straddling his to the music of Gardel. An ocean, at night, ablaze with fire.

He dozed, awoke, slept again. At some point he opened his sack, and forced his shivering body to eat. Much later he was jerked to full wakefulness by the piercing screech of brakes on steel. He opened his eyes, wiping condensation from the glass. Outside the light was dull, unbroken low cloud sailed a rolling sea of horizonless green. The train had stopped. It was raining again.

Ten minutes later, shouts from outside, slamming doors and the grumbled gathering of baggage by his fellow passengers signified the end of forward progress by rail. Shortly he found himself, a little dazed, sparks of incandescence dancing before his eyes, standing beside the track in a boggy field of cud-chewing cattle. People were pointing. He followed their gaze. A hundred yards ahead, the railway line descended smoothly from view, vanishing into what appeared to be a wide, grass-fringed lake. There, surreally, it continued, underwater, marked by the regularly spaced telegraph poles beside it, until it reappeared again on the far side.

'Well, that's that,' somebody said.

'*Maldito escándalo!* Now what are we supposed to do?'

'I suppose it has been a very wet spring.'

Michael thought he must still be hallucinating.

They gathered their bags and boxes together and set forth, like an army of homeless tinkers, across the rain-soaked field. Through a gate beyond it lay a muddy track. Beyond that, endless plains. Someone said buses would come soon. 'Why?' Another shrugged. 'Because they might.'

Gradually, with characteristic absence of fuss, they began to organise themselves. Many decided to trek to Tupambaé, the last station they'd passed, twenty kilometres back along the track. Others doggedly elected to await the promised buses. Still more set out north in the hope of finding another train further up the line. Someone else knew of an estancia not far away, where lodgings and further transportation might be arranged.

'And what about you, *muchacho*?' a voice enquired.

'I'm sorry?' Michael started. He'd been staring up at the cloud-draped sky. It was the mestizo woman with the baby. She'd fastened a little hooded poncho about its head to keep off the rain.

'I was asking where you are trying to get to.'

'Oh. To my great-grandfather's estancia, Señora. Not far from Arbolito.'

'Arbolito?' She turned about, head cocked, brown eyes searching the drifting veils of rain. Like a deer. Then she simply pointed. 'East. It is a long walk, many hours. There are no roads, but some tracks for a while and then you can follow the stream of Parao which rises thereabouts. If you become lost, continue for a few hours more; eventually you will reach the main *ruta* passing through Arbolito to Melo.'

'Well, thank you, Señora. Thank you very much. And, what about you?'

'We will wait on the train. Until something happens.'

By nightfall he was lost, drenched and delirious. The old woman had been right; after a few hours the tracks that wound deeper and deeper into the undulating plain petered out. He was left stumbling through thickly tussocked grass, knee-deep in muddy waterholes in some places, pocked with hidden rocks and boulders in others. He fell repeatedly, his clothes soon mud-plastered and torn, his palms and knees bloodied. The rain was incessant, a relentless drumming on his head, reducing the ground to sucking bog and the visibility at times to just a few hundred metres. Instead of finding one stream to follow, he found dozens, the plain a crisscross of creeks sided by sparse woods of crooked, spiky trees. So he navigated by rote, by whim and by instinct, keeping the greater darkness always ahead while there was yet light, thereafter placing his trust in God and luck.

And also in the spirit-like presence that seemed to be accompanying him. It materialised some time in the night, an unbidden travelling companion sidling up from far behind. He didn't question its appearance. Nor did his fevered mind attempt to rationalise the manifestation, or define its form or gender. It was just there. One minute he was quite alone, the next he had company.

For a while they proceeded together in silence. Soon though, since the presence seemed to be waiting for something, Michael began to talk to it. At length.

He spoke, without rancour or passion, of things he had never spoken of before. Of the progress of his life thus far, and its direction, or rather lack of it. Of the disconnection he felt with the people who dwelt in it. Of his feelings of isolation, and rudderlessness. Of his sense of failure.

It sounds a mess, the presence teased.

Indeed, Michael agreed. It was difficult, he complained, not to feel aggrieved at the apparent failure of his mission to Uruguay. His need to return to the country of his birth had been so intense. Yet now that he was here, everything seemed alien, secretive. He felt no connection with any of it.

What did you expect? Answers to everything?

Not necessarily. But, something.

His feet had lost sensation, the night now bitterly cold. Shuddering, chilled to the core, in his subconscious he knew he was both ill and dangerously under-protected. Yet somehow the presence forced him to keep moving. He plodded doggedly on.

He could sense the primal urges of his warrior forefathers, he confessed, a little sheepishly. Always had, since childhood. And those of their own Indian ancestors. And theirs, all the way back through time to the first great wandering travellers of the beginning. It was his comfort, he said, it gave him strength. Yet the difficulty was, although he felt them, he felt no part of them. No sense of belonging to them. It was a dispossession. As if he carried a photograph of someone else's loved ones in his pocket. They smiled out at him, which was nice. But they weren't his.

Yes, they are. If you sense them, they are in you.

But I don't know what I sense. I spend my days working with the British, and my nights socialising with the Germans, two enemy nations locked in war. Passing backwards and forwards between them as though through a door.

Yet you feel you neither belong with them nor to them. Either of them.

No.

Then you don't. You are, as are we all, only that which you feel.

Perhaps, Michael conceded. It was an interesting proposition.

He came to a river. Only twenty metres wide, but black and ominous, thick with fast-moving floodwater. He wanted to skirt it, but the presence said they must cross. Muttering resentfully, he slithered down the bank and out into the stream, gasping aloud as the icy torrents clawed at his legs. Halfway across, and with the water up to his chest, he stumbled and lost his footing. In a moment he was under and there was nothing but blackness and thunder and a tumbling muddy chaos. He thrashed, sputtering to the surface, gasped air, went under again. Eventually, he managed to regain his feet. Half-swimming, half-wading, he laboured towards the far shore, hauled himself up and slumped, retching, on to the bank.

That's it. He panted. No further. Finish.

Nonsense, the presence scolded. Get up. Let's go.

From then on the journey became little more than a stumbling dream. Despite repeated exhortations, gradually the presence began to slip ahead of Michael, in the same way as it had crept up from behind. Towards dawn he realised it was gone, vanished from the mists of his awareness exactly as it had appeared. He didn't mind; the rain had stopped. The ground was firmer now, too, the terrain easier. He would keep going as long as he could. He knew he was unwell, perhaps seriously, and that he would have to rest, and possibly not get going again. But that was unimportant. With the coming of light a new landscape was emerging. The pampas here was different from yesterday, and yet familiar. It rose and fell more softly than before, and was deeper of hue, lush and viridescent. It grew, spreading out all around him with the thinning of the mist; soon everything was touched softly golden with the coming sun.

A tree appeared, far in the distance, a single wide-limbed tree perched on its own little rise, like an island. It was an *ombú* tree, just like the one from his childhood, with its giant turned-up branches like an inverted umbrella. It would do, he decided then. Good enough. Journey's end. He would crawl beneath its protective arms this fine new day, lie down and surrender.

He dreamed of men on horses, galloping from the mist like ghosts. Of the smell of leather and corn-husk cigarettes, of rasping insects, muttering voices, and an impatient stamping of hooves. Then he dreamed he was flying, six feet above a carpet of green, borne upon a noble-headed beast with a mane that danced in the wind, a broad back and flanks of warm velvet. Then he dreamed of a timber house set amid tall trees alive with the raucous chattering of parakeets. Of a sudden stillness, hushed voices and a cool, high-ceilinged room smelling of peach blossom and wood resin. Then for a long time he was just floating, cast adrift on a raft of straw. Travelling the world, for centuries, in search of wide skies and green valleys, tumbling streams and boundless, cattle-filled plains. Drifting like a leaf on the breeze, searching for the place where he might one day settle and never have to leave.

When he awoke, however, he knew instantly that he was in the classroom of a furious, stick-wielding Irishman in a red wig. Flynn was there right now, standing, silhouetted against the window. Rigid with terror, Michael knew that at any second he would turn, catch them smiling at each other and launch into the attack. He struggled, fought to rise, but was helpless, his arms and legs like lead. And Flynn was turning now, his arm raised, ready to strike.

'Don't hit her!' he croaked, kicking feebly at his sheets.

'Hit who?' asked Gertrudis, opening the curtains.

270

She came to him, placing a tiny vase of blood-red verbena flowers at his bedside. 'Well. Are you awake now, or still ranting?' Her hand touched his brow. 'Hmm, better, perhaps. Now, drink this, it is an infusion of leaves from the *Anacahuita* bush. A little bitter, but excellent for the fever.'

'Great-aunt Gertrudis.' It was the room. The bedroom at Sombreado that Flynn had converted into a schoolroom. 'Am I really here? Is it you?'

The glimmer of a smile. 'Of course. Who do you think has been tending to you these past days? As if I didn't have enough to do, what with Father as well.'

'Don Adrián? He is here? He is ill?'

'Did they not tell you, Miguel?'

'Tell me what?'

'He is dying. From the inside. The cancer eats at his chest.'

'I must go to him.' Michael began struggling again, but quickly fell back, panting and giddy.

'Don't be so idiotic; you are not going anywhere. Neither is he, he has plenty of time yet, so be patient. Now then, I must leave, but will return a little later. When I do, I expect to find this infusion all gone.'

'Gertrudis, wait, I . . .'

'What? What is it?'

'I . . . I just wanted to say. I am very happy to see you.'

She hesitated, stooped, kissed him quickly on the brow. 'I, too, Miguel. We are all happy to see you. Now, rest.'

He passed the remainder of the day in a dream-filled haze. He slept, he awoke, Gertrudis came and went, bathed him, brought clean bedding, honey and water, a beef broth. Gradually, with each visit, he learned the details of his arrival. That passing gauchos had found him out at the *ombú*, at dawn, three days earlier. That they had no idea who the bedraggled youth in the torn city clothes was, but how, when they tried questioning him, he produced a blade from a sack, a short, silver-handled *cuchilla*, and before he passed out dead at their feet, kept shouting something about being a Rapoza.

'So they knew to bring you to Sombreado,' Gertrudis said briskly, tucking his sheets. She seemed exactly the Gertrudis of memory, her thin brown hair tightly fastened, as always, in a bun on the back of her head. She still wore old-fashioned clothes, a floor-length dress, tight at the waist, with a plain lace collar buttoned at her throat. As though time had stopped for her, decades earlier. Perhaps, he reflected, as she fussed around him, she was a little more communicative, a little less intimidating, than the stern and unsmiling Gertrudis of his childhood. Perhaps she had just found it hard to relate to him then. Or he to her.

'Anyway,' she scolded. 'Why on earth did you not warn us you were coming? We could have made arrangements to meet you.'

'It was, well, it was a hurried decision.'

'You did not discuss it with your mother? Or grand-mother?'

'No. Nobody knows I am here.'

Early in the evening he was roused once more from drowsiness by a soft tap on the door. His eyelids fluttered.

Francesca and Carles Luenga were standing at the foot of the bed. He, his thumbs hooked into his wide leather *cinto*, regarding him like an underweight bullock, she, her eyes wide with disbelief, bearing a cloth-covered bowl.

'Miguelito?' she whispered, fighting the tears. 'Look, I made you *dulce de leche*. It is your favourite.'

They stayed a while. It was a little awkward. There was so much to say, nobody knew quite where to begin. It didn't matter, he was just overjoyed to be with them once again. They had both aged, of course, were both diminished slightly from the tall, full-statured people of his memory. Thinner, too, their faces weather-etched from wind and sun, hard toil, too little rest and an existence eked from paucity.

'How is the estancia?' he pestered. He wanted to know everything. 'The horses, the Herefords? How are all the men?'

The Luengas exchanged glances. 'Sombreado goes on, Miguelito. Yet all things must change. There will be plenty of time to speak of these things. When you are stronger. For now perhaps you should rest.'

He sensed anguish behind the warmth of their gaze. 'Of course. And what of Antonio, and Maria? How are they, I long to see them.'

'And you shall, soon. Antonio lives in Melo. He has a family of his own, now. A fine wife and two small sons.'

'Does he manage his own herd of shorthorn? As he always planned?'

'No. But he has employment, in a packaging factory. The

hours are hard, but the pay is regular, and the work secure. That is the main thing.'

'And Maria?'

'She too is well. She lives on a large estancia north of Arbolito, owned by a wealthy Argentinian family.'

'Not here?'

'We must all work, Miguelito. She has a position in domestic service there.'

Later, after the Luengas had gone, Michael waited for Gertrudis to return.

'Why do Antonio and Maria not work here on the estancia, like their parents?' he asked, watching her tend the candle at his bedside.

Gertrudis hesitated. 'That is not for me to discuss.'

'Why not?'

'Because you must ask the Quemada family, back in Montevideo. My sister's husband, José-Luis, your grand-father. And his important politician sons. They manage the finances for this place.'

'Are the Quemadas in difficulty?'

'Difficulty?' Gertrudis allowed herself a wry smile. 'I think not.'

'But then why—'

'Not tonight, young man. For now you must rest.' She snapped the sheets straight at his chin, brushing his hair, almost without thinking, back from his brow with her fingers.

His eyes were closing. 'Would you be able stay, for a short while?'

'As you wish.' She sat, her hands neatly in her lap, her small face to the failing light at the window. Outside swallows sliced the sky above Sombreado, their shrill calls lancing the still night air. In the barns bats stirred, unfolding membranous wings, flitting silently out into the dusk to fish the rising tide of moths and insects. Smoke rose from the Luengas' chimney. Miles to the north a young woman, their daughter, rode slowly through the night towards her home.

Chapter 10

He was sitting propped in a chair on the porch, swaddled in blankets, a cushion at his neck, like a convalescent octogenarian, when he saw Maria approaching. Even at a kilometre, and across a decade of time, he knew it was her. He waited patiently, sparrows pecking unnoticed at biscuit crumbs at his feet. Unhurriedly, and with her back still straight after so many hours in the saddle, she rode up the track, through the gate and right to the foot of the steps.

'Hello. I heard you had the fever.'

'Yes, but it is over.'

'Good. I brought you some fruit.'

'That was very thoughtful.'

'How is your great-grandfather?'

'Quite comfortable, thank you. He is resting.'

'I must pay my respects to him. Also to your great-aunt,

and to my parents. Then see to the horse. Then perhaps we might talk.'

'I would like that very much.'

They passed the morning on the porch. The day was cloudless, if fresh; Michael felt the sunlight caressing his face like the touch of a warm hand. Between measured spells of polite conversation he dozed. Once or twice he awoke to find he was alone, immediately wondering, panic beating at his chest, whether her return had just been a dream. But soon she reappeared, bearing a plate of figs, or a jug of lemon water.

'You don't have to do this,' he protested. 'I am really much better.'

'Of course. Tell me, how is your mother?'

He found, reconsidering the matter anew, that a welcome space had grown up, a sense of detachment, between him and the subject of Aurora, indeed of everything connected with Montevideo. He thought back. His grandmother's house and family in Prado, his rooms, Willi Hochstetler, Atlantic Mercantile. Mr Martin. That final dinner with Millington-Drake. Then the dawn flight from his lodgings, the solitary march to Willi's house. Ransacking his drugged mother's bedroom for money while she lay, undressed and insensible, amid the wreckage of her bed. And her life. It had all happened. But not to him, he almost felt. To someone else.

He recounted a greatly abridged version of his month thus far in Uruguay. It was not his intention to mislead or omit, but as he spoke, conscious of Maria's deep brown eyes studying his, he found that speaking of these things was almost an irrelevance. An unwelcome distraction. Like the visits the Quemada family used to pay to Sombreado when they were children. Unusual and exciting in many ways, but unsettling to the natural rhythm of their lives – particularly hers. Always, once the visits were over, everyone breathed a sigh of relief.

It was also hard to concentrate. This he put down to fatigue and a residual muzziness in his head from the fever. But it was unquestionably also to do with Maria. The transformation in her was astonishing. His last memory of this, his unrelated twin sister, the picture of her he had carried with him these past ten years, was of a strong but gangly tomboy with whom he used to climb trees, or fail to beat in horse races, or wrestle with out at the *ombú*. Now before him sat a quiet young woman of great poise and beauty. Shining, raven-black hair swept back from a smooth forehead into a clasp at her neck. Her mouth was full and broad, her nose straighter, her eyes deep and wide, slightly upturned beneath thick eyebrows. It was still her, still Maria, with the dusting of freckles across her nose, the tiny scar on her chin from falling from a tree, and her head held, slightly cocked, like a bird's, when she listened. But the ungainliness was all gone, the awkwardness, the boyishness. Especially the boyishness. She was a young woman. With a young woman's body. There was no mistaking the tightness of the hips of her work breeches. Nor the swell of breasts beneath her blouse.

'You must be tired, Maria, riding all night like that.'

'It is nothing.' Her obstinacy was unchanged at least. 'I come most Sundays.'

'How long can you stay?'

'Only until this evening. I must return to the estancia by morning.'

'You should rest before you leave.'

'I will. Later.'

'Tell me about it. The estancia. Your work.'

'It is large, much larger, than Sombreado. The owner, Señor Peréz, and his wife are from Buenos Aires. They come and go, as owners do. The estancia breeds mainly short-horn cattle and special horses for polo. Their son, Alonso, manages matters for them.' Her eyes flickered. 'He is twenty-five. I keep house, cleaning, cooking and so on. Sunday is my day off. I visit my family then.'

'Do you like it there?'

She hesitated. 'I had to find work. There was none for me here.'

During the afternoon, at his request, she took him by the arm, helped him to his feet, then they made a slow tour of the garden and grounds together. Michael couldn't help noticing an air of neglect about the place. Fencing held together with baling twine, a collapsing roof in a shed they used to play in. Brambles knee-high in the untended peach orchard. There they paused for him to catch his breath.

'Do you remember how we used to lie here, watching the blossom fall and trying to imagine it was snow?' she said.

'Of course.' He puffed dizzily. 'I remember everything about this place.'

Sombreado had grown tired and sickly, he realised. Like him. But his strength was already returning, while Sombreado's ebbed away. What had happened? He must find out. They walked on, Maria's arm, her support, her very proximity, both familiar and strange. Comforting yet troubling.

Before they knew it, it was time for her to leave.

'For how long will you be here?' she asked, tightening the girth of her saddle.

'I am not sure. For as long as I can. Will you visit again next Sunday?'

'Would you like me to?'

'If it is not too much trouble.'

'It is no trouble.'

'Well. Until next Sunday, then.'

She mounted, the horse skipping in circles while she stretched fingers into faded leather gloves. 'I kept all your letters, you know,' she said, and cantered away.

He passed the week reading, resting, regaining his strength. Each morning he walked, short distances at first, a little further with each passing day. He made a full inspection of the estancia, jotting notes into a pocketbook as he went. So much needed doing; soon the notebook was filled. He spent time with the Luengas, Francesca especially; Carles was out on the plain, frequently overnight, single-handedly tending Sombreado's dwindling herd. In the evenings Michael would duck beneath the low doorway to sit with her in the old dirt-floored cottage of his infancy. Spotlessly clean, warm and homely as always, he realised now that it was nevertheless little more than a hovel, and his foster parents practically paupers.

'Do you not receive payment?' he asked her one night.

'We used to,' she said, fidgeting with embarrassment. 'But times are difficult, Miguelito, we are very fortunate still to have our house and some work. Many like us do not. And Antonio sends money, a little, when he can. Maria, too.'

He resolved to tackle Gertrudis on the subject, but it was soon obvious she was scarcely better off. The reason she appeared so old-fashioned to him, he realised, so unchanged from a decade or more earlier, was because she was still wearing exactly the same clothes as then. Her dresses were neatly pressed, but endlessly repaired, her collars frayed, her shoes clean but split.

'What on earth has happened?' he demanded one night. They had dined on thin mutton stew, last year's sweet potatoes, hard bread. She had filled his plate, he noted, yet allowed practically nothing for herself. 'I'm not hungry,' she'd said dismissively, when he objected. 'I have more than enough. You and Father need it.'

'Please tell me,' he persisted.

She shrugged. 'It is simple. Your grandfather, José-Luis, has no interest in this place. Nor have his sons. None of them has for years. Without investment and management, inevitably it has fallen into decline. Taking us with it.'

'But that's, it's, well, it's disgraceful. Don't they realise?'

'I doubt it. I doubt they ever give it a thought. They are important businessmen, and senior Colorado Party officials, of course. Colorados have always cared little for the plight of the people of the interior, Miguel, you know that.'

'Yes, but this is your brother-in-law. And your own sister. Florentina. Does she not care what happens to you? Or Tata, her own father?'

'Florentina and I are very different, you know. I expect she has little idea that things are as they are.'

'Then you must tell her!'

'No. I cannot. If she cares she will find out for herself. Also, she is my younger sister; there is an issue of pride, and other, historical, differences.'

'What historical differences.'

'They are not your concern.' She broke off, patting a napkin to her mouth, fussing with the plates. It was only then that the truth of her situation dawned on him. Two sisters, born into a respected but impecunious family high in the interior. One, the younger, prettier perhaps, attracts the attentions of a wealthy and important city businessman, marries him, moves to Montevideo. Lives well, raises two ambitious sons and a wayward daughter, puts her humble origins behind her. Meanwhile the other is left behind to take care of their farm and their elderly widowed father. Alone. With nothing.

'It's not good enough, Aunt Gertrudis. Something should be done.'

Again the dismissive shrug. 'I will not complain. Beg for their help? Never.'

'Of course. But someone else could.'

On the Friday, when Gertrudis was quite sure the risk of

infection from his fever was gone, Michael was permitted to visit his great-grandfather. 'Don't expect too much of him,' she cautioned.

'Tata?' He knocked cautiously. The old man was seated, stretched out upon a worn leather couch in his library, his pegleg discarded on the floor beside him amid mountains of newspapers, books and magazines.

'Who is that!' he scowled, fumbling for spectacles.

'It is me, Miguelito. I have brought hot water for your maté.'

'Miguelito? I know no Miguelito. Where is Gertrudis? Go away and leave me in peace.'

'But, Tata . . .' Michael hesitated.

'I said leave, boy! Or do I have to fetch my *canón*?'

'No. No, that won't be necessary.' He set down the flask and left the room. A little later he was back. This time he banged hard on the door, flinging it wide.

'Who in hell are you?' demanded the old man again.

Michael stood in the gaping doorway, hands on hips. He had dispensed with the remnants of his city clothes and was wearing simple gaucho garb borrowed from Carles. Boots, breeches, blouse, leather *cinto*, and a white *pañuelo* about his neck. 'I am Miguel Rapoza of Sombreado. Charrúa, Blanco, and great-grandson of Don Adrián Rapoza.'

'Are you indeed,' Tata blustered, regarding the tall, fair-haired youth before him. 'Then why the hell didn't you say so earlier. Do you still have the *cuchilla* I gave you?'

'Of course.' Michael reached behind him, pulling the little silver-handled blade from his belt. 'It goes where I go.'

'Pathetic! Much too small, a child's knife. We must do something about that. Particularly with the world going completely mad. Now come, boy, over here. Quickly! These damned newspapers, the print is too small, you must read to me of the Teutons and their insanity. Everything. My God, just let them try coming here with their blitz-krieg and see what greets them!'

Michael stayed an hour, reading aloud, drinking maté, discussing local politics and European war. Tata's mind seemed razor-sharp one moment, astute and coherent, but then would lapse into fanciful nonsense the next. He gabbled incessantly. Twice, in mid-flow, he broke down, doubling over on the couch, racked by uncontrollable coughing spasms. These convulsions went on for a minute or more, Tata gasping helplessly, a soiled handkerchief clutched to his mouth. When at last they subsided, he would gulp dark liquid from a phial, before flopping back on the couch. Michael, helpless, could only watch, and wait, newspaper in hand. He wished he could do more. Tata's ancient body had grown so thin and wasted, his fingers like bony claws. The skin of his weather-beaten face was deeply creased, and sallow like parchment, his once neatly trimmed beard lost amid a sea of stubble.

'What about the doctor, great-grandfather,' he asked gently after one attack. But Tata just shook his head. For minutes he lay there, eyes closed, panting for breath, as though unconscious. Then a rheumy eye popped open.

'Saravia gave me this house, you know. The Eagle himself, General Aparicio Saravia. For leadership and loyalty to the Blanco cause beyond example. Did you know that, boy?'

'No, great-grandfather, I did not.'

Soon, Sunday came around. Early morning found Michael, an unfamiliar knot of anticipation in his stomach, pacing the wooden boards of the porch, his eyes anxiously scanning the horizon. She arrived as before, trotting steadily up the track to the house. This time, however, seeing the dark rings of fatigue under her eyes, the stiffness of her body as she dismounted, he insisted she rest for a few hours.

'But I don't want to rest,' she protested. 'I came to spend time with you.'

'You are.' He led her into the big house, bade her lie on his bed in the old schoolroom. 'Remember this place?' he smiled, helping her with her boots.

'I remember your courage, how you held Flynn back with your knife. Heaven knows what would have happened if Don Adrián hadn't arrived.'

'I wanted to kill him. For hurting you.'

She lay down, hands clasped uneasily over her stomach. 'This feels strange. I don't think I should be here. Why don't I rest at my parents' cottage?'

'Because I say you need a proper bed, and you are our guest here. Now, I will return in an hour or two, then we can talk.'

'Can't we talk now? Just for a while. Please?'

He hesitated. 'I suppose. But only for a minute or two.'

'Yes, Señor,' she teased. 'Whatever you say.'

But within a minute or two she was asleep.

They ate a simple lunch together on the porch. In the afternoon they walked again, revisiting old haunts, recalling forgotten incidents and events, tentatively rediscovering a rapport they'd both feared lost for ever. After a while, their earlier awkwardness began to evaporate, silences became comfortable rather than cumbersome, misunderstandings grew fewer. Comprehension supplanted explanation.

'Tell me about England,' she asked at one point, leaning over the gate of the paddock. Ahead the green pampas stretched down and away before them, woolly fair-weather clouds drifting across the sky like grazing sheep. He wanted to, but Michael found he could not. England was just a name to her, a famous but meaningless dot on a melon-sized globe long ago. In any case, what would he tell her? About the apartment in Marylebone, that first desperate winter, the misery, the damp and the cold. His mother weeping on the stairs: 'I'm trying Michael, I am trying.' Or Holbrook House, perhaps. The loneliness, the taunting, the fights. The beatings. Running home, only to hear his parents' furious shouts through a door. Francis Habershon: 'Sometimes it is necessary to become what we are not.' Killer: 'Sorry, but your mother's gone.'

'It was cold, and rained a lot. Mostly I just wanted to come back here.'

She nodded, satisfied. It was good enough, he realised. For now. 'I knew you would. Sooner or later.'

'You did? How?'

'Because this is your home.'

They walked on in silence. It was as though neither of them wanted to be reminded of their other worlds. That subconsciously they were striving to recapture and retain something delicate and fragile, that might slip from their grasp and shatter if they allowed the outside to intrude.

Like her work, her other estancia. He'd already sensed it was something Maria didn't care to discuss. 'Do you have to return north tonight?' he asked. Shadows were lengthening, the visit's end drawing near. For a moment she said nothing, her eyes on the horizon.

'Yes.'

'Why?'

'Alonso, the owner's son. He made me promise to be back before morning.'

'That is unreasonable.'

She looked at him then, her brown eyes searching his. 'Life is unreasonable sometimes, Miguel. We both know that.'

He prepared food for her while she made ready, tucking bread and cheese into her saddlebag together with a canteen of fresh water.

'It is not right that he makes you travel so far, alone and at night,' he said as she mounted. 'Next Sunday I will accompany you some of the way.'

'There will be a next Sunday?'

He glanced up at her. But she was smiling.

Days passed into weeks. A pattern evolved. As soon as he was able, Michael began work at Sombreado. There were no hands left to work on the farm, save Carles. Even the faithful old *peón*, Alberto, had gone, leaving no one to mend gates, clear brambles or sweep stables. He would undertake these matters himself, he decided. Rising early, working until noon in the traditional manner, resting through the middle of the day and resuming work in the evening. Soon, paths were appearing where before bushes had barred the way. A broken weather vane swung free after years frozen on west. An old cart, with no mule to pull it, but a newly repaired axle, was proudly pushed, thick with dust, from a shed and back out into the light.

But Michael knew he was only scratching the surface. More serious maintenance was urgently needed. Quite apart from the outbuildings, the main house was in a parlous condition. The roof leaked, floorboards crumbled underfoot from the voracious onslaught of termites, once neat paintwork was long faded and peeled, windows were broken, the chimney cracked and the water cistern did not function. He made more lists, set up a workshop in one of the sheds, collecting everything together that he could find of possible use. It was a pitiful audit – tools enough, but no materials at all. No timber, nails, glass or wire. No bricks, cement or sand. No roof tiles or pipes. Not so much as a pot of usable paint.

That evening after supper, he visited Carles in his cottage. 'I want to make contact with tradesmen in the area. Can you put the word out, ask them to visit as soon as possible. There is much that we need, and that needs doing.'

'But Miguelito, they will not come. Many of them have still not been paid from work carried out years ago.'

'They must come, Papa Carles. We need them.'

'But what should I tell them?'

Michael thought for a moment, then came to a decision. 'Tell them this. Miguel Quemada, of the wealthy Montevideo Quemadas, has returned to Sombreado after, well, after years of travelling abroad. Tell them he intends to carry out restoration work on the estancia. Tell them he has the full support of his mother's family in Montevideo, and his father's in London for that matter, and that he will personally see that their accounts, old and new, are settled in full.'

Within days the first, a carpenter from Melo, arrived in a cart. At first he eyed Michael warily, but eventually, impressed by the earnest young man's lineage, exotic foreign demeanour and intriguing manner of speaking – not to mention his bludgeoning persistence, he agreed to begin work the following week. Others followed: before long a steady trickle of artisans and suppliers ebbed and flowed daily along the track, Gertrudis looking on in silence.

With work underway, money was suddenly the overriding priority. Late into the night Michael drafted meticulously crafted letters to his relations. They were long, humble epistles, tactfully illuminating the injustices of the situation, begging forgiveness for his presumption, and respectfully requesting support in his well-intentioned endeavours. Reading through them, however, he quickly concluded that the time for pleasantry and propriety had long since passed. The need was urgent and immediate. So he tore them up and fired off a salvo of telegrams instead. 'Situation at Sombreado dire, stop, send money immediately, stop, respectfully Michael.' He sent one to his grandparents in

Prado, another to Aurora and Willi, and a third, after only momentary hesitation, to Keith in London.

There was an anxious lull, a tense week of nothing but stretching nerves, hollow promises and increasingly belligerent tradesmen. Then one morning an ancient motor *camioneta* came sputtering up the drive. Michael saw it first, while balanced atop a ladder sawing dead branches from a poplar. Gertrudis appeared from the house, Francesca too, drying hands on her apron. Men stopped work. Michael watched from above. The van pulled up. It was laden with boxes of groceries and domestic supplies.

'What is all this?' Gertrudis demanded of the driver.

'Your usual delivery, Señora.'

'What usual delivery? There hasn't been such a thing for years.'

'An unfortunate misunderstanding, Señora. But your account has been settled, with interest and credit, and specific instructions forwarded to us to continue delivering fortnightly. As usual.'

'Instructions? From whom?'

'From a firm of accountants in Montevideo.'

One by one in the ensuing days, Sombreado's tradesmen and artisans reported similarly fortuitous developments.

'But who is doing all this?' Gertrudis fretted one night at supper.

'Those who should have been doing it all along,' Michael muttered, ticking off items on a check list. 'Aunt Gertrudis, don't you feel we should ask a better physician to visit Tata. Surely more could be done to relieve his discomfort?'

Gertrudis looked on. So much was happening, so quickly. Repairs to the house, a fully stocked larder, doctors coming out to visit. Michael had even been talking with her about a trip to Melo to buy her clothes. And with Carles about purchasing livestock – and not just poultry or a gelding for the wagon. Breeding bulls, criollo brood mares, those new Corriedale sheep. He'd even begun talking about motorised farm machinery.

The change in him was startling. It was as though he had suddenly discovered his life's purpose. As though escaping England, and then Montevideo, the nightmare march across the pampas, the days of delirium that followed, had all been part of a predetermined process. Like a metamorphosis. In the space of just a few weeks he was casting off an entire persona, like an ungainly gosling losing its down, emerging, strong and sleek, ready to take wing and fly continents. His personality too, that was changing. He was still Michael, still quiet, introspective, unfathomable. But there was an assuredness about him where before there had been uncertainty. Resolve was replacing hesitation. Confidence supplanting diffidence.

It was all highly unnerving, Gertrudis brooded. But also, she had to concede, rather thrilling, somewhere deep inside. Moreover, there were other, more physical manifestations of this metamorphosis. Catching sight of him, purely by chance, that afternoon, labouring shirtless in the yard, she couldn't help but notice how tanned his back was from the sun, and how sun-bleached his hair. How broad, too, his chest and shoulders were becoming. And the hardness of his stomach, the thickness of muscle on his arms. The sturdiness of his thighs.

Maria noticed these things too. Early each Sunday she came trotting up the drive, tired but smiling. Michael, kissing her dutifully on both cheeks, would help her dismount, prepare her breakfast, see to her horse and insist she rest. When she awoke he would be waiting, seated at the window of the bedroom, reading, writing notes or simply watching her. The rest of the day was theirs, walking, going for an excursion in the gig, resting on the porch. Always there was a tour, he proudly showing her the latest developments – a pair of criollo foals in the newly fenced paddock, a pen full of ducks, or freshly painted weatherboarding. She strolling quietly at his side, nodding and smiling, basking in the warmth of his enthusiasm, striving to quell the cauldron of emotions seething within her.

Early one Sunday afternoon in November she awoke from her rest to find the bedroom empty. Stepping from the sunlit schoolroom into the cool of the hall, she stopped. A vision of white was spread before her.

'Miguel?'

She must still be dreaming. A snow-white tablecloth covered the refectory table. Place settings, silver knives and forks, ornately patterned plates, crystal glasses, napkins, all carefully arranged upon it.

'Miguelito, what is this?' A fragment of remembered image came to her from long ago. A party thrown here by the Quemadas. Music, dancing, a feast on white linen, candles, tail coats and sumptuously flowing dresses. She and Michael peering, agog, through a window.

'I knew all these things were hidden away here some-where,' he said, positioning a vase of flowers. 'Wait here. I will be back in a moment.'

Six places had been laid. Her parents, rather awkwardly, were standing behind two of them. Gertrudis, poker-faced, at another.

'Mother?' Maria raised eyebrows at Francesca.

'Don't ask me,' Francesca whispered nervously.

'It is called Sunday lunch, evidently,' Gertrudis said. 'It is something that happens in England. On Sundays.'

'What happens?'

'Everyone has a meal, together, in the middle of the day. On a Sunday.'

'Everyone?'

'Yes, everyone!' Michael called from the library door. He was pushing Tata, glowering ferociously from the wicker seat of his new three-wheeled basket chair.

Michael propelled him to the head of the table. 'What the devil is the meaning of this!' The old man glared at his place setting. Everyone froze. Francesca, the colour visibly drain-ing from her cheeks, appeared as though she might faint. Gertrudis was shaking her head, lips tightly pressed. Carles looked on impassively. Maria held her breath.

'Tata?' Michael whispered.

A bony claw reached out, slowly picked up a knife, exam-ined it and replaced it, firmly, on the other side of the setting.

'There! That goes there! And I hope you've got some decent wine for these glasses; we're not having any of that French goat-swill.'

Afterwards, she and Michael rode out to the *ombú*. It was the first time they had ridden together since childhood. Inevitably they raced; inevitably she won.

'You've lost your touch!' she triumphed, flopping to the grass beside him. The afternoon was hot, her head swam from the exhilaration of the ride, and the warm rush of the wind in her hair. Summer was coming, the pampas turning from laurel-green to the colour of ripening corn, blushed purple with flower. Insects rasped, a short distance away a *mulita* armadillo busily scraped red earth from its burrow.

'Yes, well, you were always the better horseman.'

'True.'

He lowered himself, cross-legged, to the ground beside her. For a while they were quiet, the only sounds the rasp of cicadas, the rustling of wind through leaves, and the occasional snort and stamp of the horses. Soon their breathlessness subsided.

'Do you remember playing the Indian game here?' she said.

'Yes.'

'I had to pretend not to hear you creeping up on me.'

He nodded, thinking back. 'Imagine what it was really like to live here then. In the olden days of our forefathers.'

Maria rested her chin on her knees. 'Was it not like this? Pasture, cattle, horses?'

'No. There were no horses or cows in the time of the

Charrúa and Guaraní. They hunted on foot, for guanaco, or the rhea bird.'

He liked to speak of Uruguay's past, she had discovered, of its history. It seemed to be important to him. To settle him. Like a reassurance. She just loved the sound of his voice. 'No cows?' she encouraged. 'Where did they all come from?'

'The first European colonists brought them, in the sixteenth century. Jesuit missionaries mostly, some Spanish and Portuguese. Not all these people were greedy and murderous; many tried to settle peacefully on the pampas, working hard to establish themselves as the first *estancieros*. Some succeeded, staying for many generations. They married into the Indian races, raised the first mestizo families, all the while their cattle thrived and multiplied.'

'What happened?' she prompted, spellbound, their shoulders lightly touching. He was gazing out at the plain, his back propped against the broad trunk of the *ombú*, his fingers lightly brushing the grass. The neck of his shirt was open, a sheen of perspiration glistening like fine dew upon the smooth skin of his chest.

'Life was very hard. There were many incursions from invaders, outlaws, jealous landowners. Disease was widespread, bands of brigands pillaged and plundered, death from sickness or murder became a way of life. Soon many of these estancias fell into ruin and much of the region became wild and uninhabited once more. The abandoned cattle though, and the horses, roamed free across the fertile plains, turning feral, and multiplying by the million. Soon the pampas was carpeted with them.'

'And the people? Those who stayed?'

'They, too, became feral, living free and untamed on the pampas. These were the first true gauchos, the mixed descendants of the Indian and settler races. Our ancestors, Maria. They became a part of the land they lived upon. All they needed they had at their feet. They captured and tamed the crossbred horses, and made a simple living trading beef, hide and tallow from the millions of wild cattle wandering the plains. It was hard, but straightforward. Most of all they had their freedom.'

'Freedom.' Her head still buzzed from the excitement of their ride, the afternoon's heat, the unaccustomed headiness of wine. 'Miguelito,' she found herself saying. 'Miguelito, my brother . . .'

'Maria, I . . .' He was shifting on the grass beside her, hesitant suddenly. 'Maria. I feel I must speak to you frankly.'

'Of what?'

'Well. It is true, as you say, we are as brother and sister. Yet now that we are grown, I find that I no longer feel that way about you.'

'Oh,' she nodded, breath held. 'I see. What way do you feel about me?'

'As a man, for a woman. A beautiful woman. Not as a sister. Is that wrong?'

'I don't know. We are brother and sister only in our minds, of course, not our bodies. But . . .'

'Yes.' He rose quickly to his knees. 'And so much has happened since we were parted as children. So much has changed. Our lives are not the same.'

'Indeed they are not. There are complications now, Miguel.'

'I sense that. Of course, I understand you must have many admirers in the area. Suitors, even. Perhaps you have already formed attachments . . .'

'With the boys of the district? I have never seen my future with them.'

'But what of your employer. Señor Peréz. His son.'

'Alonso?' Her gaze flickered. 'He is weak, like a spoilt child. But, well, as I say, it is complicated. He may be weak, but he is also important, and his parents, they were generous, they gave me employment. There is a future, of a kind for me there with them. Him. You must understand, Miguel, things have changed since you left us. Steady work is so hard to come by. I am indebted. There are . . . demands. It is a difficult situation.'

'Are you in love with him?'

'I . . . No!' Flustered by his directness, her eyes broke away. 'Love has nothing to do with this! I had no choice. I needed work, needed to support myself, and my parents. That is all. You were not here. I had no choice. You don't understand.'

'Do you not have feelings for me, Maria?'

'Yes. No! I don't know! It is not as easy as that, Miguel, there are no simple yes-no answers any more. You vanish for ten years then appear out of nowhere and expect everything to be straightforward, and as you wish it to be. But life isn't like that. All is different now. You and I, it is impossible, can't you see that?'

She turned her back on him then, fighting tears. An awkward silence grew. It was getting late, the *ombú*'s giant shadow lengthening about them. Nearby, their horses dozed, stock-still in the settling air, neck to neck. Far to the west, a leisurely procession of cattle traversed the distant horizon beneath a sinking orb of gold. 'I should prepare to leave,' she whispered.

'Maria?' His hand touched her shoulder, turning her gently to him. 'Maria, forgive me, you are right. You had no choice. And it is true, I did expect simple answers, and everything to be as I wished. As I had dreamed. That was foolish. And wrong.'

'Yes, it was.'

'I'm sorry. I have ruined your day, ruined everything in fact.'

'A little.' She sniffed. 'Although, I thought your Sunday lunch was nice.'

'I'm glad.' He hesitated. 'But, Maria, there was one thing, just one simple answer, that I did find when I came back here.'

'What do you mean?'

'That first day. All those weeks ago, do you remember it?'

'What day?'

'The first day you rode up to the house, and I was waiting on the porch, wrapped in blankets like a feeble old man.'

'Oh. That day. What about it?'

He reached out, lightly brushing a tear from her cheek. Her eyes glistened, round with uncertainty. 'When I saw you sitting up there. So proud, so beautiful . . .'

'Yes?'

'I knew you were the reason I had come home.'

At the end of November Michael spent a fortnight out on the plain rounding up cattle with Carles. They hired two casual *troperos* to assist them, rode sixteen hours a day, camped in the open, and lived on handfuls of dried fruit, maté and jerked beef carved from a joint by *facón*. By day they herded, counted, roped and branded the white-faced Herefords. By night they slept out beneath the stars.

'How do we know they are all ours?' Michael asked one morning, jotting herd statistics into his notebook. One of the *troperos* knelt across a roped calf, the second, pumping bellows, fanned coals white beneath a glowing branding iron.

Carles looked on. 'We cannot know for sure. Some of Sombreado's boundaries are formed naturally by creeks and rivers but the rest is fenced. Or was. It has been a struggle to maintain it these past years, with no men and no money. I did what I could, but inevitably there were gaps.' He shrugged. 'We lost some, we gained some. It is the way of the plains.'

'It is also evident that we don't have many left to drive to auction. We must reinvest. Tell me, Carles, what is your view of these Holsteins we hear so much of?'

'Dairy cattle?' The two *troperos* exchanged shocked glances.

'Yes. I read that they are quite a success in the south. Merino sheep, too, from Australia. They are proving popular for their wool. Perhaps we should look into it.'

They passed one evening in an ancient gaucho bar, or *pulperia*, a dilapidated mud and thatch hut smelling of sweat, hand-rolled cigarillos and cane rum. The bar was dark and airless, thick with leather-faced men with watchful eyes who drank and smoked and argued, and fell silent and stopped their '*truco*' games the second the four of them entered.

'Rapoza,' Michael heard one of their *troperos* muttering, like a password. It was enough, the moment of tension quickly passing. In no time he was seated upon an upended crate, a glass of brown *caña* before him. The circle of onlookers seemed to be waiting, so he picked it up. '*Salud.*'

'*Salud!*' The raw spirit scorched his throat like acid. He gasped, spluttered. Knowing, manly chuckles were exchanged; someone nudged his back.

'You are the English one, no?' Another was refilling his glass.

'That's right. Well, half-English. Half-Uruguayan, too.'

'The better half!' More raucous laughter, another cry of *salud* and a second fiery draught hit his throat.

'The war,' someone else said. 'You English must win. Here in the interior, Uruguayans are *sympático* to England.' Murmurs of approval from around the room.

'Well, um, thank you,' he replied, raising his glass once more.

'Yes, but in Montevideo there is much support for the German cause; you must be very careful there.'

'Oh?'

'He is right. There are spies running everywhere!'

'Ah. I'll be sure to bear it in mind.'

Another man was elbowing his way to the fore. 'Your great English battleship, *Royal Oak*, in London, blown to Hades. Poum! Everybody dead. Very bad.'

'What? What did you say?'

'It is true, I tell you! I read it in the newspaper. Just last week. A German submarine creeps up the Rio Thames in the dead of night, steals like a fox right into the great British Navy harbour called Scapa, and then torpedoes the English battleship *Royal Oak* where it sits at anchor. Eight hundred men killed in an instant!'

It wasn't possible. *Royal Oak*. He'd seen pictures of it at the Coronation review in '36. Massive, a floating fortress of steel, indestructible. The man had to be mistaken. Or the newspaper. But something about his account rang chillingly true. Something terrible must have happened. A British ship, hundreds dead. And London? His father. Donald. It wasn't a false war any more, he realised, a phoney war. It was really happening.

That night, his head filled, and reeling from *caña*, he lay awake on his spread poncho, staring up at the bottomless swirl of stars turning slowly overhead. He was eighteen. Back in England, tens of thousands of boys his age, his contemporaries, people he'd been at Westminster with, were exchanging school suits for khaki, joining regiments, being selected for pilot training, or walking up gangplanks to board warships. To fight. Possibly to die. They'd talked about it endlessly in the sixth form common room those final months together. If the balloon goes up, they said, one after another, I'm in. Straightaway. No nonsense. I'm for the

Army. Me, I'm going to fly Hurricanes. No, it's the Navy life for me. And what about you, Villiers? Care to compromise your high and mighty pacifist principles to fight for your country? But killing is wrong, he'd pleaded. War is a failure of reason. There must be a diplomatic solution to this, common sense must prevail. The words rang in his head; he'd sounded just like his father, doggedly refusing to confront trouble head-on. So you *are* a lefty then, Villiers, they'd taunted. A Marxist conchie objector. A fifth columnist. Or are you just a coward? Running away across the world.

The next morning, a Saturday, they began the long drive back to Sombreado, the herd ambling peacefully before them. Michael rode alone all day, pensive and withdrawn. Carles and the others, in any case occupied with strays and stragglers, left him in peace. 'Too much *caña*,' one of the *troperos* diagnosed sagely. But towards nightfall Carles cantered up beside him.

'Troubles, Miguelito?' he asked directly.

Michael stirred, as though from dreaming. 'Carles, no, it is nothing. I am sorry. I have not been of much use to you today.'

'We have it in hand. These two are capable and diligent workers.'

'Yes. It would make sense to be able to offer them something more permanent in the way of employment. Perhaps we should look into it.'

'Why not.' Carles lit up a cigarette. 'You will leave us again soon, no?'

'Why do you say that?'

'The problems of the world, of Europe, your home in England. These are not our problems, but I sense you believe they are yours.'

'I'm afraid, Papa Carles. I want to stay here, live with you. With all of you.'

'I know.'

'And I, I have strong feelings for your daughter.'

'I know that too. Francesca and I have discussed the matter. It is something pleasing to us.'

'It is?'

'Yes. In any case it is good that you two are close. We were concerned for her, something is not right to do with her work situation.'

'What do you mean?'

'I'm not sure, she doesn't say; perhaps it is nothing, perhaps it is for you to ask. Listen, Miguelito, soon we must make camp for the night. At this rate we will not arrive back at Sombreado until noon tomorrow. We three can manage the herd; you ride ahead, be there to meet her as usual in the morning.'

'Papa Carles, I . . .'

'It is all right. Go. With my blessing.'

He rode through the hours of darkness, following the moonlit paths and streams at the trot, the North Star at his back, until a little before dawn the motionless silhouette of the *ombú* appeared in the distance, marooned like a giant sailing ship upon its little humped island. From there it was half an hour, at the gallop, to the house in the trees.

She was already there, sitting on the front steps, waiting. Without a word they embraced, clinging tightly to one another in the melting dawn mist. 'Miguelito,' she whispered fearfully. But he hushed her, his finger to her lips. Then he led her through the sleeping house to the school-room. There, slowly, touching and caressing, they undressed each other in the semidarkness, folded their limbs together, and sank back on to his bed.

But the following Sunday she did not come. He waited, anxiously pacing the boards of the porch. He took Tata's field telescope, climbing to the swaying tops of the tallest poplar to peer, far out to the distant horizon. He saddled up, galloping out a way along the track, then back again in case she had arrived by a different route. But by mid-morning it was clear something had gone wrong.

'Something has gone wrong,' he said to Gertrudis, hurriedly collecting a bag of clothes and provisions together. Francesca looked on anxiously. 'I am going out to find her.'

'Perhaps she just decided not to come this week. Perhaps she has a cold.'

'No. She would come, I know she would.'

'What if she has fallen somewhere, on the road. Injured herself, perhaps? What if she has been attacked? Or assaulted? What then?' Francesca was close to panic.

'Calm yourself,' Gertrudis soothed. 'Miguel will find her. And when the men have fetched Carles back from the river, they too can help with the search. Miguel, do you not think you should wait until they get back?'

'No. They will be two, three hours, at best. I must go now. They can catch up.'

But they wouldn't catch up. He left a few minutes later, immediately kicking his horse into a flat-out gallop. She wasn't lying at the roadside, thrown from her saddle or way-laid by assailants. She was too clever for that, and too good a horsewoman. Something else had happened, he'd sensed it as soon as he'd woken. She hadn't even set out. He was sure of it.

The day was one of blistering heat and motionless air. Glassy mirages shimmered on the dirt road ahead of him. Limp, dissipating scraps of cloud hung, pegged to an azure sky, like rags on a line. *Hornero* birds sought shade in their fence-post mud houses, snakes slithered from his path into the moist warmth of the ditches. Little else moved, the road deserted of people or vehicles. Only the rush of wind, the fleeting rasp of insects and the startled whirr of pampas par-tridge came to him above the ceaseless ringing of hooves. He rode as fast as the horse could carry him, without pausing for rest or water. By noon the animal was spent, flanks heav-ing, eyes rolling in its head, its neck a frothing sweat. Nearing Arbolito he slowed, searching, until he came to a small estancia set back from the road. He galloped to the door, dismounted, pounding furiously. A man came, news-paper in hand, dressed for Sunday.

'Rapoza,' Michael gasped. 'Of Sombreado. Please, horse.'

'Ah, yes. The English one. Come, we have spare.'

There was no question, no discussion, no explanation. His name was his pass, his word his bond. It was the way of the country, the dying tradition of the roaming gaucho. Your horse tired, you swapped it for another. Twice more during the afternoon he stopped, knocked and exchanged, each time without question. 'Your undertaking is clearly of great necessity to you, my friend,' one *estanciero* commented, leading a fresh animal from his stable. 'I wish you Godspeed and a happy outcome.'

He arrived at dusk. He became lost, had to stop and ask for directions. 'Peréz? Estancia Peréz, can you help me?' At last he was cantering up a tree-lined drive towards a large white-painted hacienda.

A maid came to the door. It wasn't Maria. 'Wait here, I will fetch the master.'

He waited, in an ornate marble-floored hall of gilt furniture, crystal chandeliers, a sweeping oak staircase. The thunder of hooves still rang in his ears. Sweat, gritty with dust, covered his face and clung to his back. Apart from snatched gulps of water, and a peach pressed on him by one of the estanciero's wives, he had consumed nothing all day.

A man arrived, early twenties, dressed in a silk shirt and riding jodhpurs. He had neatly groomed black hair, was clean-shaven, looked freshly bathed. He carried a riding crop. 'Yes?' he said, dark eyebrows raised expectantly.

Michael caught a waft of cologne. Suddenly he was unsure what to say. 'You are Señor Alonso Peréz?'

'Indeed.'

'Maria. Maria Luenga. She lives here.'

'Yes, she does.'

'May I see her?'

306

'Impossible. She is working.' He was snapping the riding crop against his boot.

'I thought today was her day off.'

'She forfeited it. Through disobedience and insolence. Now, I'm sorry, I have business to attend to, ah, Señor . . . ?'

'Quemada. Miguel Quemada.'

The snapping paused. 'Quemada? No connection with the Montevideo Quemadas, by chance? My father is friends with Enriqué, the Colorado lawyer?'

'Enriqué is my mother's brother.'

'Really?' The man eyed Michael doubtfully. 'Well, be sure to pass on the best regards of the Peréz family when you see him. Now, if there's nothing else—'

'She's leaving.'

'Excuse me?'

'Maria. I've come to ask her to leave with me. Now.'

Peréz scoffed. 'Let me assure you, she will do no such thing!'

Headlights had appeared at the end of the drive. Michael ignored them. 'Well, we shall just have to see. Will you call her, please?'

'No, I will not, but I will call a manservant and have you evicted this . . .' Perez moved forward as though to brush past him, the riding crop raised to his shoulder.

'Stay there!' Michael's *cuchilla* was drawn from his belt before Peréz had taken a step. At the same moment Maria appeared on the stair.

'Miguel!'

'Maria!' Michael kept the blade pointing at Peréz.

Outside the motor car was pulling up. 'Please, it's all right, don't be alarmed!'

'But Miguelito, my God, what is happening, what are you doing here?'

'I'm, I'm here to ask you, to come with me. To be with me. For ever.'

'This is a criminal outrage, Quemada! I shall have you arrested. Have you any idea who you are dealing with? My father's family has enormous influence . . .'

'There are no simple yes-no answers, you said, Maria, do you remember? Under the *ombú*. Nothing is straightforward any more . . .' Car doors slammed and seconds later a fist was thumping the front door. Michael glanced at it in alarm, his blade still at Peréz's throat. 'But, but this is straightforward, Maria! You are the reason I came back to Uruguay, the reason I am here now, the reason for everything. I want us to be together, as we were always meant to be. Come with me, please!'

'My God, Quemada, be assured, you will pay for this.'

'But, Miguelito, I . . .' Maria began to descend.

Peréz's arm shot out, 'You stay there!' She stopped. But before anyone could move, or speak further, the front door opened and two men entered wearing suits and trilby hats. 'Michael Villiers?' one of them enquired politely, in English.

'What?' Michael looked from them to Peréz. 'What is it? I am Villiers.'

'What the devil is the meaning of this intrusion!'

'Ah. At last.' The men ignored Peréz, apparently

308

oblivious of the stand off. 'Mr Luenga of Sombreado said we might find you here. You're to come with us.'

They looked familiar. The embassy? Atlantic Mercantile? 'Come? Where?'

'To Montevideo.'

Michael glanced at Maria. Her cheeks were in her hands. 'Why?'

'We will brief you on the way, but you must come now.'

He hesitated. His *cuchilla* was still drawn, Peréz enraged, before it. Maria watched fearfully from the stair. He would not leave her. Not now.

'No. I'm not moving until you tell me what this is about.'

'It's about an old friend of yours, Michael,' the second man said. Michael recognised him now. One of Mr Martin's men. From upstairs.

'What old friend?'

'Hans Langsdorff, captain of the German pocket battle-ship *Graf Spee*.'

Chapter 11

It took precisely ten minutes to establish that a fourteen-foot rowing boat powered by four men with oars was not going to outrun a two hundred-foot submarine. We paddled off gamely enough, us rowers peering back through the curtains of drizzle behind, Michael facing forward at the tiller. At first it looked as though Harrison's ploy might actually work. No conning tower burst up from the depths, no loud-hailer shouts or warning shots came winging our way. It scarcely seemed possible.

'Are we giving the so-and-so the slip, Sub?' he asked hopefully.

'I'm not sure, Will. It depends how good a lookout he's been keeping.'

Ridiculous though it was, it was immensely heartening just to be doing something. Lolling about in a boat going

310

nowhere is a demoralising business. I remember *Daisy* breaking down once; we had to stop engines so Chief Balcombe could fix a broken fuel line. Five hours we sat there, dead in the water, the waves lopping against *Daisy*'s sides. You never saw so many long faces in your life. But the minute repairs were completed, the engine telegraph rung ready, and forward momentum regained, both ship and crew were magically revived.

We, similarly. The exercise re-energised us, restoring circulation, thawing our bones, stretching numb limbs. We began to row faster. Soon we were going at it like men possessed. Sniggering broke out. I think it was to do with the sudden release of tension. Even Frank Tuker got into the spirit.

'The dozy sods!' he tittered. 'We've caught them with their pants down. Come on, lads, put your backs into it.'

'I am putting my back into it! Anyway, why are we whispering?'

'How the hell should I know? Keep pulling; if we can put a mile between us in this clag, he'll never find us again!'

He was right, although overlooking one small disadvantage of the thick weather. In any case it was academic. Within minutes, with fatigue quickly catching up with us, the mood became less jovial, more dogged. Villiers kept us rowing, asked us to speed up, then slow down, steering us in different directions, his gaze fixed on a point off to one side.

'No go, Sub?' I puffed.

'Afraid not. He's off the starboard beam somewhere.'

311

We looked, I saw nothing, but then the aptly named eagle-eyes Giddings spotted it. A pencil-thin length of drain-pipe, three hundred yards away, poking about four feet above the waves.

'Attack periscope bearing green six-oh, sir!' he sang out, exactly as trained.

'Yes, thanks, Albert, I see it now.'

'Bastards!' Tuker gasped. We all flopped, wheezing, over our oars. I found my head was spinning like a top.

'Thank you, everyone,' Michael said. 'That was useful.'

'Useful!? We flog our guts out and the lieutenant finds it useful!'

'Tuker . . .' I panted. The man was really starting to get on my nerves.

'It's all right, Stephen. It might have appeared a pointless waste of effort. But in fact it has told us something important. He can be positioned.'

'He can be what?'

'Positioned. No matter what course we steered, he stayed about three hundred yards off our starboard beam. Without fail.'

'And what bloody use is that when it's at home?'

'Seaman Tuker, if you don't belay your insubordinate bloody whining right now, I'm putting you on defaulters!'

'Don't you come the lah-de-dah Mister bloody Midshipman with me, Tomlin! I couldn't give a tinker's cuss if—'

'Frank, for God's sake stow it!' Harrison punched him on the shoulder. 'Carping won't get us anywhere.'

'What do you think he's up to, Michael?' I asked. Villiers was still staring in the direction of the periscope.

'I don't know. It could be that he's got some kind of mechanical problem that's preventing him from keeping up with the convoy. Or perhaps he's just at the end of his patrol. Low on fuel and ammunition, looking for one last go at something before heading for home.'

'Sub?' Giddings enquired. 'Sir? I've been thinking. We can't hardly see the submarine at only a couple of hundred yards in this clag, right?'

'That's right, Albert.' Giddings had now worked out the one small disadvantage of the thick weather.

'And we damn near gave him the slip, even though he's right on top of us.'

'Yes, we did.'

'So, the point is, if we can't hardly see each other at a few hundred yards, what hope have we ever got of being spotted by a rescue ship?'

The autumn of '42 blew into winter with a howl. Had we but known it, or had the time or energy to care, history would later record two dismal statistics marking this, the lowest point in the Battle of the Atlantic. Firstly, some of the worst weather in living memory, and secondly, truly awful Allied shipping losses.

Seven hundred thousand tons went to the bottom in October alone. November was even worse. It wasn't as though we weren't making headway against the U-boats, indeed some thirty-odd were sunk that autumn. But it wasn't nearly enough. Time after time we limped into port like chastened sheepdogs, our flocks decimated. One convoy in particular, ONS 154B – a slow homeward-bound one – sticks in the memory. We set off from Nova Scotia with forty-five ships. Almost immediately we ran into an easterly gale that stopped us in our tracks for days, so bad that some of the more heavily laden merchantmen had to turn back for Halifax. The rest of us plugged on, bashing into monstrous, foam-streaked seas that stove in steel plating, tore iron stanchions from the deck and washed away masts, radomes and aerials like so much flotsam. *Lily* lost her four-inch gun, all half-ton of it, ripped from its mountings and swept clean away one foul night without anyone even noticing. Eventually it was decided to route us to the south to try and escape the worst of the weather. But that also took us deep into the gap, hundreds of miles out of range of any possible air cover. Within hours, a U-boat wolf pack, later estimated at a dozen submarines, had homed in. A running battle ensued that went on for three days and three nights without a break. The crew of *Daisy* and the other escorts, in other words, stayed at action stations, in weather defying description, for a straight seventy-two hours. When at last, stupefied with exhaustion, we finally shambled into Liverpool, twenty ships, almost half the convoy, were gone. As one of *Daisy*'s able seamen put it, 'All this *and* twelve and sixpence a day.'

Patently, it could not go on. Stung by the appalling losses, Churchill himself intervened, setting up a special anti-U-boat warfare committee and installing, with characteristic cunning, a hard-nosed ex-submariner called Horton to head up Western Approaches Command. 'Stop the rot and quick' was Horton's brief, more or less. Never was the hiring of a poacher-turned-gamekeeper more timely. Indefatigable, aggressive, ruthless, Admiral Sir Max Horton was just the right man for the job. In the First War he'd torpedoed a German cruiser then sailed home with the skull and cross-bones flying from his flagstaff. He knew how to think like a U-boat commander, understood the importance of coordi-nating resources and, staying one jump ahead, was contemptuous of failure, expected utter commitment and total compliance in equal measure, and drove everyone like galley slaves.

Training was the first priority. Escort commanders and their officers were detached from their ships and sent off on rigorous anti-submarine training courses at the Western Approaches Tactical School in Liverpool. There they were interrogated on their experiences, drilled remorselessly on all the latest tactical developments, and shut into special curtained-off booths to play 'the game'. This involved car-rying out attack after attack on imaginary U-boats around little toy convoys laid out on the floor. It sounds almost childishly unsophisticated, but woe betide anyone who didn't treat it with deadly earnestness or, worse still, mis-managed a situation. Gradually performances improved, more effective anti-submarine tactics evolved, attack pro-cedures and manoeuvres became standardised, and a coordinated unity of thought and purpose emerged.

Another priority of Churchill's committee was to do

something about the numbers of new U-boats being delivered, so Air Marshal 'Bomber' Harris was persuaded to mount raids against Germany's shipyards and also the submarine maintenance pens in western France. The Coastal Command boys, too, were given more effective aerial depth charges and began to get better at tracking and attacking submarines from the air. Also, vitally, although it would be at least six months more before the gap would be closed, a few genuinely long-range patrol aircraft at last began to come on line.

Then there was all the hush-hush stuff. The top secret things we didn't hear about. The 'special intelligence'. From the very outbreak of hostilities, both sides had been working flat out to crack the enemy's radio traffic. The Germans scored first with their 'B-Dienst' system, which, despite the Admiralty's best efforts, meant that Karl Dönitz often knew of a convoy's composition, sailing date and route almost as soon as we did. This gave him a huge advantage in the positioning and deployment of his U-boat force. But he too had to send and receive this information to his submarines by radio, so the German boffins devised a fiendishly complicated cipher machine called 'enigma' to encode and decode the messages. To try and crack enigma, the British put some of the country's best brains to work in a motley collection of huts in Bletchley Park, but it wasn't until May 1941, when the destroyer *Bulldog* managed to capture an enigma machine from a sinking U-110, that they really broke through. It was a cat-and-mouse business, however. We had the code cracked for a while, then the Germans added more knobs and wheels and we lost it again, some-times for months, before we broke back. We at the coalface were unaware of it at the time, but throughout that awful autumn and winter of '42, enigma was almost completely blacked out, indecipherable in other words, which might explain why they always seemed to know where to find us, but we rarely had any idea where to look for them.

Apart from these ongoing secret struggles, Max Horton's brisk new broom, renewed offensives by bomber and Coastal Command, and all the rest of it, there was one more front-line factor for Churchill's committee to deal with in this endless war of attrition. After three years in the job it was becoming clear that our antiquated destroyers and trusty little Flower class corvettes were no longer ade-quate for the task asked of them. Simply too small and too slow, they badly needed updating, or, better yet, replacing. Horton pushed hard, Churchill concurred and before long plans for sleek new twin-screw River and Castle class escorts were approved and put in hand.

But approving and putting in hand is one thing. Getting them built and delivered into service quite another. In the meantime, *Daisy* and her rust-and-rivets cohorts, punch-drunk, storm-tossed, ragged and out of date, like bare-fist brawlers at a boxing match, were put once more unto the breach. At the beginning of November, after a week's wel-come respite among the ramshackle houses, sloping streets and cosy wharfside pubs of Londonderry, we received orders to join a fast outward convoy bound for St John's, Newfoundland. At dusk the same day, oiled, watered and victualled to the gunwales, we slipped our mooring, wound our way between the sinuous, magically quiet banks of the River Foyle with its grassy slopes and overhanging trees, pushed our nose once more into the broad waters of the lough, passed Carrowkeel, Moville and then finally the very end of land itself, at low, craggy, Malin Head, and on out into the Atlantic.

'What the hell's all this gubbins on my foredeck, Sub?' Walter Deeds demanded a week or so later. Shipboard life always quickly returned to normal. We were westbound, halfway across, heading into the gap. A fresh southeaster shoved ranks of grey rollers up from behind, lifting *Daisy*'s stern, breaking along her sides with a hiss.

'It's called hedgehog, sir,' Martin Brown announced proudly. 'It's that new forward-throwing mortar system the boffins dreamed up.'

'Ye gods. It looks like a trolley-load of oversized stick grenades. How does it work?'

'Well sir, twenty-four mortar bombs, sir, each one carrying thirty-two pounds of Torpex. You fire them off forwards, sir, ahead of the ship, in a pattern, just as you are running up on the target. They arm themselves at preset depths and go off upon contact with the target.'

'Thirty-two pounds! What good's that? You might as well throw mud pies at the bastards. Have you tried it out yet?'

'No, sir. Just about ready now. I think.'

'Right. Well, get on with it.'

A trolley-load of stick grenades it might look like to

Captain Deeds, but to me and the ratings standing next to the contraption it looked like a very nasty hole in the boat indeed if anything went wrong. There was a certain amount of edging away and hiding behind windlasses as Martin donned flash hood and tin helmet, and positioned himself, a little nervously, at the controls. Up on the bridge, Strang and the lookouts watched with interest.

'Ready to fire hedgehog, sir!'

'Yes, yes, for pity's sake get on with it.'

Martin pressed the tit, we all ducked, there was an impressive crump and twenty-four mortar bombs streaked off skywards, like fireworks at a display, splashing into the sea fifty yards ahead of *Daisy*.

We waited. 'What happens now?' Deeds asked.

'They explode, sir.'

We waited a little longer. 'When do they explode, Sub?'

Martin looked uncomfortable. 'Well, um, after you've remembered to take off the safety clips, I suppose, sir.'

That night rattlers, another integral component of shipboard routine, went off at ten. *Hornbeam* had picked up a contact. Minutes later the first torpedoes were hitting home. Quickly, but without fuss or panic, *Daisy* swung into action, exactly as she had dozens, scores, of times before. By the time I reached the bridge the night sky was alight with starshells and chandelier flares. Towards the front of the convoy a familiar angry flicker where a stricken tanker burned. Deeds and Villiers were at the front of the bridge, conferring quietly, while about them the ship sprang to readiness.

.

'Signal from *Vehement*, sir. Four U-boats presently estimated in area.'

'Acknowledge, please, Yeoman. Helm, port-twenty.'

'Port-twenty, Coxswain now at the wheel, sir.'

'Thank you, Coxswain.' Another flash, this one much closer, then a third, an armaments ship just half a mile away, a few seconds later the dull boom of an explosion rolling like thunder across the waves towards us.

'That's our sector! Fire starshells, engine room ahead full, helm midships. Tomlin?'

'Sir!'

'Crow's-nest, Mid, quick. Off to starboard, you might spot something.'

I leaped for the ladder but the bridge wing lookout beat me to it.

'U-boat sir!' his voice rang piercingly shrill, almost girl-like.

'Where away, lad?'

'Fine on the starboard bow, sir, one mile!'

I stopped in my tracks, unsure what to do next. In that instant everything had changed. We had acquired a target, could actually see it, were already turning in towards it. The crow's nest was superfluous. Deeds had it covered though; he had everything covered. He was magnificent. Without taking his eyes from the tiny smear of the U-boat's wake, his arm beckoned me back on to the bridge, as though he knew this might be my only chance to see the enemy with my own eyes. Then he just went into action, calmly, seamlessly, as though activated by a switch. Standing there, four

320

square, balancing his body instinctively against the tilting of his ship, moving as one with it, bending to voice-pipes, dictating signals, issuing orders, assessing, calculating, controlling. The organic nerve centre of his lumbering steel machine. In command, in other words. Doing exactly what he had been put there to do.

'Engine room, this is bridge. Chief, are you there?'

'Bridge, yes, Captain, this is Chief Balcombe.'

'Pull out all the stops, now, Arthur, everything you've got. There's a target on the surface up ahead.'

'Right you are, sir.'

'Bridge, Asdic.'

'Yes, sir, we'll be ready to pick him up the moment he's under.'

'Thank you, Number One, won't be long, now. Helm starboard-ten. Radio, get a signal off. *Daisy* to *Vehement*, have enemy contact visual on surface, am engaging. Woolley, how's that four-inch of yours?'

'Just coming on to bear now, sir, ready to shoot in a second.'

'Hold your fire for now, Sub, I'm going to try and ram him.'

A few glances were exchanged at this piece of news. A dived U-boat under electric motors has a top speed of only about eight knots or so. But running flat out on the surface, as this one was, they were capable of seventeen. *Daisy*, with the best will in the world, might just struggle up to fifteen. Bolder U-boat captains knew this and some, like this one evidently, chose to exploit this speed advantage by making a run for it on the surface after an attack. We'd never catch him in a straight-line race, but *Daisy*, her bows now lifting spiritedly to the seas, was approaching this one obliquely, curving round in a perfect arc to cut her off.

But it was going to be very close-run thing. Soon I could see the U-boat clearly through the binoculars, a slender black hull in the white 'V' of its wake, very small, it seemed, but fast, pushing through the waves rather than over them, the spray flying from its conning tower. A minute more and a figure could be made out on its bridge, staring back at us, watching us, calculating, like us.

'He's got some nerve, I'll say that,' Deeds murmured, eyeing his adversary back through the lenses. If we did actually manage to overrun and ram him, the U-boat was dead, no question. But we might not be quite quick enough. Dick Woolley's four-inch gun was already within range. I could see him staring up at us from the bandstand, his arms spread in exasperation, desperate to open fire. But if we did start shooting, the U-boat would dive immediately, and any chance of a ramming would be gone. Then we'd be into the familiar grind of an Asdic pursuit, box searches, depth-charge patterns, hours of guesswork, more box searches and all the rest of it.

As our courses converged I saw, as did Deeds, that we weren't quite going to make it. Suddenly we were just a quarter of a mile away from him, but he was practically stern on now, and starting to pull away. Deeds didn't hesitate.

'Shoot, Woolley!'

At the same instant, behind us, an enormous flash lit the sky. The U-boat's victim, the armaments ship, had vanished, exploding in a single monstrous ball of fire. Seconds later a hot shockwave shook the bridge, followed by the sky-splitting thundercrack of the explosion. For a second *Daisy* and the U-boat were lit, as though by flash-bulb, frozen in motion, like a tableau at a pageant. Then the flash died and darkness engulfed us once more. The U-boat captain had beaten us, was pulling away, but, alarmed by the sheer might of the explosion perhaps, or the spectacle of our charging bows in that dazzling instant of light, he panicked. Blinking myopically in the sudden darkness, I searched ahead with the glasses until I found him. The conning tower was already empty, the slender hull tilting downwards. As I watched, the four-inch barked once more below us; a second later a gout of spray burst alongside the vanishing submarine.

'Keep shooting, Woolley! Asdic! Strang, he's going down now, stay on him; my guess is he'll break to starboard and then go deep. Brown! Depth-charge rails, stand by for a quick pattern, shallow depth, we'll be passing right over him any moment!'

So it began. Like so many others before it, and yet unlike any other. Within the first few minutes Deeds signalled *Vehement* for back-up. Two escorts hunting a quarry together were infinitely more effective than one. But *Hornbeam* and *Fuchsia* were already chasing a contact of their own, and that just left *Lily* to guard the flock. 'Unable detach assistance at this time,' *Vehement* replied. 'Hold on as long as possible, will send help when can. Good hunting.'

Three hours later we were still hunting, and still on our own. We were also by now twenty-five miles astern of the convoy, heading away from it, in fact. Our quarry, temporarily lost to us, scuttling about somewhere in the depths far below like a rat down a coal mine.

'What exactly does "as long as possible" mean, Sub?' I asked Villiers quietly.

'Knowing Walter Deeds as we do, Mid, I expect it means just that. He won't give up unless ordered to.'

He was right. Dawn saw us sixty miles behind and into the fourth box search of the night. After an initial flurry of activity, including a brief period of excitement when one attack yielded an oil slick, later attributed to a leaking freighter, the trail had gone stone cold. Scurrying about in circles trying to reacquire the target quickly proved fruitless; the only way to proceed was to divide the map up into areas, or boxes, and search them one by one, using the Asdic to sweep for possible contacts. It was a protracted, laborious, fuel-consuming process, and, for all we knew, a complete waste of time. I spent much of the night helping Michael in the chart room. Drawing up the boxes, calculating headings, times and distances for each leg, and passing this information to Deeds on the bridge and Strang down in his smoky Asdic hut.

'It's an odd business this, Mid,' Deeds said at around eight, leaning over the bridge rail with a mug of kye. He'd been there all night, and he'd been there three years, but he might just as well have been discussing the cricket. In the flat morning light his face was deeply weather-etched, his grey eyes alert, but sunken, rimmed with fatigue. 'I know he's down there, sitting it out. And he knows I'm up here, waiting for him to make a move.'

'Yes, sir.'

'He's too slow to escape submerged, y'see. The moment he tries, we pick him up on Asdic. If he keeps nice and still, however, and quiet, we lose him again.'

'Yes, sir. I see. If he doesn't move he can't get away. But it's also much harder for us to find him.'

'Precisely. So, at the end of the day, it all boils down to time, and nerve. Because neither of us can afford to stay here and we both know it. He can't remain submerged for ever; he has to come up for air and to charge his batteries. Similarly, we can't hang about square-searching the ocean indefinitely. Apart from the cost in fuel, we've a job to do back with the convoy. So the question is, which one of us will give up first?'

Not Walter M. Deeds RNR was my bet. We fell into contemplative silence, he hunched over the rail, me sipping my cocoa and watching the incessant rolling ocean. In just months it had become my entire world, together with the ping of the Asdic repeater, the whistle of wind through the signals mast and the surge of waves along *Daisy*'s hull. Life outside these things had lost all meaning.

'I suppose there is always the chance we've lost him, sir.'

'Always, Mid. But I don't believe it. Not this time.'

The tantalising waft of frying food came to us suddenly, borne from the galley vent by the wind. A watch was changing, men appearing on deck, relieving others now heading below for breakfast. U-boat or no, shipboard life went on. Deeds, too, was making for the companionway steps. 'I'm popping below to see the Chief for a few minutes, Mid. His lads were getting a bit jumpy, what with the din from all the depth charges. Think you can manage things up here? Villiers is there in the chart room if you need him. Any problems, you know what to do.'

'I, well, yes, thank you sir, I'll do my best.'

'Good lad. You have the bridge.' He turned to go, then stopped. 'I believe I shall see it out here, you see, Stephen,' he said, just like that, and was gone. It wasn't until much later that I realised what he meant.

My command lasted ten minutes. It was the proudest ten minutes of my life. I was actually in charge, *Daisy* mine. My duty might have been to do absolutely nothing, but I had been given the chance to do it. Earned the chance to do it. Most of all, more importantly than anything, Deeds felt he could trust me to do it.

I made the most of it. Hands clasped behind my back, I paced back and forth a bit, mainly for the benefit of the lookouts, just like Hornblower on the poop deck. I leaned proprietarily over the rail, so the four-inch crew could see me. I waved to Strang having a smoke outside the Asdic hut. I squinted out along the compass, sighting on a seagull. I studied the sky in a meaningful way.

I was just on the point of summoning the courage to call 'starboard-ten' into the wheelhouse voice-pipe, in order to dog-leg around an imagined obstacle in the sea ahead, when all hell broke loose.

'Bridge, Asdic, we've got a contact! Sector red three-oh, more than two thousand yards, it's turning to port.'

Just for a split second I thought I was dreaming, or that it was a practical joke. But it was no joke, this was really it, and it had to go right. When you get a contact at extreme range like that, the initial procedure is always the same. You turn straight towards it and bang on full speed. That's all. I'd watched it happen so many times before, I didn't stop to think.

'Sound rattlers! Helm port-twenty, engine room ring full ahead, captain to the bridge!'

Seconds later and my glorious command was over. Alarms went off, feet stampeded along decks, *Daisy* turned, heeling on to her new heading. Strang darted back inside the Asdic hut, Michael arrived on the bridge, closely followed by Deeds.

'Well done, Mid, you found the slippery so-and-so!'

Not true – we all knew that – but the thump of hands on my back certainly made it feel like it. Within minutes we were running in for the first attack. This time Strang held him, locked solid in the Asdic cone, the echoing 'ping-go' of the repeater on the bridge getting steadily shorter and louder as the range closed. Beside him there in the hut was a pair of buttons. When the range got down to a couple of hundred yards or so, the echo would become instantaneous. This is called Asdic blind time. The Asdic officer hits the buttons and a specially programmed clock takes over, timing the last seconds before release of the depth charges. Four catapults fire one charge each, sideways, out from the waist of the ship. Sloping racks at the stern roll as many more as you like out over the back. A pattern might consist of as few as four, or as many as fourteen charges. A few seconds after hitting the sea they reach their preset depths and begin to go off, exploding with a muffled clang that shakes the entire ship. The sea astern jumps and bursts skywards. Then you wait for the spray to settle, turning back towards the target to try and reacquire it with the Asdic. If you can't, it might be because it is now a shattered wreck, falling in pieces to the sea bed. Equally it might simply be creeping away to fight another day. Either way, you begin the whole procedure again, until you are sure.

This went on all morning. With two or more escorts in the hunt, the task would have been greatly simplified. One holds the target locked in an Asdic cone, guiding the others to an exact position over the top of it. But working on our own meant much higher degrees of uncertainty, and greater opportunities for the U-boat to elude us. Time after time we ran in, dropped, waited, carried out lost contact procedure, searched, found him, began all over again. Deeds' technique was to save ammunition by keeping as close to the target as possible, staying at speed after each pass, turning hard on our heels, and keeping our patterns tight. Even so, our depth-charge stocks were soon dwindling, and, racing about flat out like that hour after hour, so were our fuel reserves. Not only that; with every passing hour, the convoy drew another twelve miles further away from us.

'Clever bastard this!' Deeds shouted to us from out on

the bridge wing, scouring the sea astern with his binoculars. 'He knows we're on our own up here. He also knows from the noise of our propeller that we're just a piddling corvette. And he has a pretty damn good idea therefore that we're running short of fuel, depth charges or both.' He lowered his glasses, still gazing aft. 'In fact, I say he knows far too bloody much!'

'Bridge, radio, sir. Signal from *Vehement*.'

'Yes, read it!'

'*Vehement* to *Daisy*. Estimate you are now more than a hundred and fifty miles astern of convoy, advise break off and rejoin.'

'Advise?' I muttered to Michael. Divining the true meaning of orders from escort commander was like trying to break 'enigma' sometimes.

'He's leaving it to the skipper,' Michael replied. 'He won't order him to break off from a confirmed enemy contact until he has to.'

'Yes, but on the other hand, he knows that if we don't give up and set off after them soon, we'll never catch up.'

'Precisely, and he wouldn't be very happy about that. So what would you do if it was your decision, Stephen?'

'Break off and rejoin the convoy.'

'Yes, so would most people. But what do you think he'll do?' He nodded towards Deeds, standing out there on the bridge wing, in his duffel coat and boots, his hair waving in the wind, his revolver hanging round his neck, shaking his head at the empty ocean astern.

'Stay here and slug it out until the last possible moment.'

By mid-afternoon we had all but run out of depth charges. We had also been in pursuit of our quarry, on and off, for seventeen straight hours. Nerves were becoming a little frayed. Then, after one pass just like all the others, there was a lull, an inexplicable forty-minute hiatus when no trace of the target could be found. We waited. It was as baffling as it was frustrating. Also, something had begun to niggle. I went down to the Asdic hut to see Strang.

Bad idea.

'Hello, Number One,' I called from the doorway.

'What.' A grunt from the foetid gloom within.

'I wonder, do you have a moment?'

'No, I don't. What do you want.'

'Oh, nothing. Well, actually, you see, I've been thinking, as it were. The thing is, you know how, after we make each pass, we seem to lose him . . .'

'Yes, thank you, Mister Tomlin, I am aware of that.'

'Yes. But then we reacquire him again. Sometimes off to port, sometimes starboard, sometimes way astern. All over the place, really.'

'Is this going to take much longer?'

'No, well, you see I just wondered, if we were to check back through all the plots of all the attacks we made, then draw little diagrams showing where he turned up again, relative to us, that is. Well I just thought, perhaps, what if there might be a pattern? Of some sort. As it were. What do you think?'

'What do I think?' His face appeared suddenly in the doorway. 'I think you should mind your own business. I think you should get back to the bridge, do your job, and leave me alone to do mine. I also think you should concentrate a little more on your duties and a little less on drawing little pictures, or scribbling your infernal bloody memoirs for that matter. Finally, I think you should be addressing me as "sir", or "lieutenant", not as "number one". That's what I think. Do I make myself clear?'

I stood there, blinking idiotically. Strang, framed in the doorway of that stinking little hole, spittle on his chin, his eyes wild and bloodshot, his cigarette trembling in his fingers. I told myself that it wasn't personal, that he didn't mean it, that he was just all in. But still it stung.

Back on the bridge Deeds, too, appeared to be nearing the end. 'Why not get below for a bit, Captain,' Michael was pleading with him. 'Just half an hour or so. I'll call you the moment anything happens. I promise.'

But Deeds was beyond rest. 'We're not going to get him,' he kept saying, pacing to and fro. One hand was inside his duffel coat, sort of rubbing his chest. An untouched plate of sandwiches stood nearby. 'Not this way, some other way, perhaps, but not like this, not any more . . .'

A boiler-suited engine room artificer appeared on the bridge, clutching an oily scrap of paper. 'From Chief Balcombe, sir. The fuel figures, sir, like you asked.'

Deeds read the paper, balled it, tossed it overboard. 'Bridge, depth charges.'

'Depth charges here, sir.'

'What have we got left, Sub?'

'Just the four, sir. One either side, two on the rails.'

He straightened, very slowly from the voice-pipe, his back to us, head hunched. We waited, *Daisy* clambered cheerfully up on to a crest, then dropped down the other side, pea-green seas, white with sparkling foam, bursting from her bows. He turned to us then, a resigned smile on his lips.

'That's that, then, lads. We're calling it off. Number Two, get a course plotted to rejoin the convoy; get Mr Tomlin here to work it out. Yeoman, get a signal off to escort commander please, lad. *Daisy* to *Vehement*, abandoning target sixteen-thirty hours at position . . .'

'Bridge Asdic, contact! Echo bearing red three-oh!'

'Asdic, Number One, are you quite bloody sure about this?'

'Yes, sir, good firm echo, moving slightly left to right, range eighteen-hundred and closing, depth about two-hundred feet.'

'Jesus, is he playing with us or what?'

'Don't know, sir. But there is something else.'

'What's that.'

'I have it on good authority that, as we pass overhead, he'll turn sharply to starboard and dive to about four hundred.'

'And how the hell d'you know that, Alan?'

'Ask the Midshipman.'

In the end it was nothing but a huge, hollow anticlimax. *Daisy* ran in exactly as she had always run in. Her four remaining depth charges splashed into the sea just like the scores of others before them. The only difference was they were dropped in a tight cluster and all set to go off at the same depth, and at the same instant. They did, the sea erupting in its usual spectacular fashion. Down in the engine room the stokers cursed us anew for the din, up top binoculars were trained aft, searching through the drifting curtains of spray. The circle of white water where the charges had gone off spread slowly outwards, like a ripple on a pond, the churning water within it gradually growing smooth and still. Exactly as it always did. But then it happened. A black, bubbling gout of oil and air broke surface. Nothing more. We watched, mesmerised, as it settled into a flat spreading stain. Then the hydrophone operator in the Asdic hut reported the sounds of collapsing bulkheads coming from the depths. A moment later there was a dull, resonating boom from far below, more air and more oil broke surface, this time with a few wretched pieces of debris, fruit boxes, empty lifebelts, a mattress. We waited, wanting more. A surrender flag on a stick, perhaps. A glimpse of smashed hull briefly breaking surface. A lifebuoy with a U-number on it, as a souvenir. Bodies. But there were none. It was gone, they were dead, and that was that.

There used to be this tradition, in Navy days of old, called piping through the fleet. If a ship distinguished itself in some way, such as in battle, it would be invited to sail up and down past all the other ships in its squadron, or whatever, and they'd all cheer like mad, fire cannons of salute, send signals of congratulation whizzing up and down their yardarms, by and large making one hell of a fuss of it. Sadly, the tradition has died out somewhat since the glory days of sail, but I had heard recently of one corvette, *Verbena* it might have been, being feted through a convoy for shooting down a dive bomber. Of course it wasn't quite the same thing; a convoy is made up of merchant ships, many of them foreign, which don't tend to do things quite tiddly, as we say in the Royal Navy. Nevertheless, *Verbena* had a wonderful time steaming up and down the columns, getting waved at and cheered by everyone, except the Greeks, who hadn't a clue what was going on, and generally basking in the glory of the moment.

Secretly, I was rather looking forward to a similar reception when we rejoined our convoy. Fantasising about it, in fact. But it was not to be. Because we never did rejoin it. We ran out of fuel instead.

From the moment we turned *Daisy*'s stern to that oil-black circle of sea and set off westward once more, we knew it was going to be a near thing. The convoy was a fast one, by now just four days out from Newfoundland and steaming at eleven or twelve knots. To catch it would have required us to run at full speed for thirty hours or more. With fuel reserves already low, it seemed a tall order. After a surprisingly subdued meal in the wardroom, a few hours rest in our bunks, a wash and a change of clothes, the navigating officers set to work, endlessly recalculating speed versus distance, versus fuel remaining, versus a different speed, and so on. I also spent a fair amount of time running up and down to the engine room, checking sightglasses and dipping tanks, trying to estimate to the nearest drop just how much usable fuel oil remained.

Not much was the answer. By the second morning it was clear we could never keep full speed up and make it to St John's, so Deeds ordered us to slow right down, and fantasies of being piped through the fleet went out of the porthole. By the third morning some very evil looking exhaust indeed was issuing from *Daisy*'s funnel. 'What the hell are you burning down there, Chief?' Deeds demanded down the voice-pipe. 'We're making more smoke than a Bridlington chip shop.' Sludge mostly, came the unamused reply. We slowed down some more.

By the final dawn, with the easterly wind still blowing over the stern, as it had been all week, we were watching out anxiously for the Newfoundland coastline with handkerchiefs over our mouths.

'I've got the stokers emptying a hundred gallons of Admiralty compound into number four tank right now,' Chief Balcombe reported to us. 'I'm mixing that with about twenty gallons of paint oil, some thinners, all the gunnery oil and a couple of drums of that mineral oil from the galley.'

'Very good,' Deeds said, wiping his eye. 'Will it get us there, d'you think?'

'God knows, but they'll be able to smell us coming, that's for sure.'

We eventually crept into St John's at dusk that afternoon with the engine turning on little more than hot fumes and willpower. We even had sails up – Dick Woolley's idea – two canvas awnings rigged to the mast using baulking timber for a yard. God knows what it must have looked like, but I suppose it helped pull us along.

'Do you require assistance?' *Vehement*'s signal lamp blinked from the gathering gloom. They were all there, our escort group, *Vehement*, *Fuchsia*, *Hornbeam* and *Lily*, lying quietly at anchor among the ferries and trawlers of Fisherman's Creek, duty done, their convoy handed over to an American escort. Behind the four grey ships, the wooden houses of St John's crowded the rocky shore, hemmed in by steep, snow-dusted cliffs. Gannets wheeled high overhead. Music from a radiogram drifted across the water; we could smell drying kelp and smoking fish.

Deeds lit up a cigarette. 'Reply: "Only if you know how to gybe a corvette."'

'Sorry, can't help,' *Vehement* answered. Then another signal came, from *Fuchsia*'s bridge this time: 'Did anything interesting happen on your cruise?'

'Not much,' our Aldis lamp clattered in reply. 'Saw two Arctic terns.'

Then it happened, just as we were coming abeam, just as Dick Woolley and his boys were busy trying to gather in his sails, as the anchor party at the bows was preparing to let go. A flash of light from the muzzle of *Hornbeam*'s four-inch gun, a puff of smoke and, a moment later, a single, rolling boom. Then *Fuchsia*, another single round fired from her four-inch. Then *Lily* and finally *Vehement*. Four simple salutes echoing around the bay like thunder. It meant more than any piping through any fleet could ever mean. At the same time, their four Aldis lamps started flashing, simultaneously, almost in perfect synchrony, although God knows how they organised it. Our poor signalman was having a fit trying to write it all down. But there was no need, we could all read it, it was the same message from all four.

'*D-A-I-S-Y, D-A-I-S-Y, give me your answer do. I'm half crazy all for the love of you . . .*'

There was one hell of a party, as I recall, although little of it sticks in the memory, unsurprisingly. Just odd remembered images. Huge pink gins in *Vehement*'s wardroom to kick off with. Dick Woolley and Martin Brown doing some dreadful Flanagan and Allan routine in front of a bemused escort commander. Deeds guffawing with glee, however, slapping the table and bellowing, 'Brown and Woolley! Just like a pair of Hebridean sheep!' Rowing back to *Daisy* to find two petty officers on the foredeck, drunk but absolutely serious, dancing a real hornpipe to the music of a stoker with a fiddle. Everyone stopped to watch; it made the hairs stand up on the back of your neck. The yeoman of signals presenting Deeds with a ship's pennant. Snow-white, piped with blue, an immaculately stitched daisy in the centre of it. Villiers, dressed in his gaucho garb in the moonlight, bloody great *facón* and all, shinning to the top of the signals mast and tying it to the masthead. Cries of 'Stand by to repel boarders!', followed by a fearsome muddle of a brawl as one of *Lily*'s whalers tried to sneak alongside. Chief Balcombe, worn to exhaustion after days trying to keep *Daisy*'s propeller turning, fast asleep on a Carley float, a bottle of rum someone had labelled 'spare fuel' tucked under his arm.

Alan Strang. The only sober man aboard. One of the most extraordinary things of all. He'd volunteered, virtually insisted. Somebody has to keep an eye on you lot, he'd pointed out. So why not me? Watching silently from the bridge, just the red glow from his cigarettes showing, while all about him the entire ship's company went mad for a few hours.

It was to be the first and only time.

'Cracking bash though, wasn't it, Mid?' Harrison said, huddled into his corner of the whaler. 'Didn't somebody fall overboard?'

'A stoker from red watch. Coxswain had to fish him out using boathooks.'

'That's right. Threatened to have him up before the skipper for leaving the ship without a pass.'

'I would liked to've been there for that.' Albert Giddings' head was hunched deep into his shoulders, pimpled cheeks nipped blue with cold. 'I didn't hardly have a chance to get to know anybody on *Daisy*, this being my first trip and that.'

Tuker, silent for a while, was shaking his head. 'And you're much the better off for it, boy, take it from me. Leastways this way you haven't just lost all your best mates in the world.'

We pondered the point for a while. Ten seconds or half an hour, it made no difference, time had long since ceased to have meaning. 'Yes, that's true enough,' Harrison said eventually. 'But I still wouldn't change it. None of it. I'm proud of what we did on *Daisy*, bashing back and forth in all weathers. Protecting the convoys, hunting down that U-boat. Proud to have known my mates too, served with them. Even now they're all gone. I wouldn't have it any other way.'

It seemed to have grown very much colder, an all-pervading, will-sapping cold that chilled us to the core. It was difficult even to summon the energy to talk. Surrender to it and sleep, that's all any of us wanted to do. Every so often one of us would, or would begin to, but then some-one, usually Michael, would drag him back with a comment, or question, or story. For surrendering, giving in, would have been easy enough. But it would have been a betrayal, a waste. As Alan Strang had put it on the night of the party, 'the whole point of it all would be lost'.

'I'm sorry, Mid,' he'd said, straightaway. I'd gone up on to the bridge, specifically to see him. We had some unfinished business to attend to, and in my inebriated state I felt we should have it out. Man to man. But he instantly took the wind out of my sails. 'I'm sorry I bit your head off like that. It was inexcusable. And nothing personal, believe me.'

'Well. That's quite all right,' I replied magnanimously. 'Sir.'

'Number One is fine, Mid.' He managed a grin.

'You see,' he went on, 'we all have our own private ways of getting through this insanity. I believe you may know what mine is.'

'I believe so, Number One.'

'Yours, I think, is to write it all down.'

'Yes, I suppose it is.'

'That's good. And make sure you do. All of it, start to finish. Otherwise, if nobody knows, then what was the whole point of it all?'

Odd comment, I thought, at the time. Less so, now.

I raised my head, turning stiffly to look over the whaler's gunwale. The sleety drizzle had stopped for the moment, the cloud lifting a fraction. Perhaps it was a little brighter. My watch had long given up the fight against the salt water, but it must have been the middle of the afternoon. There were just a few hours of daylight left, after that only endless hours of freezing darkness, when the seductive lure of oblivion becomes more private, more personal. Less resistible.

Giddings was talking. Mumbling. 'I 'ad this little dog once. When I was nine. Scratcher, his name was. I loved him to bits, then one day he got run down by a grocery van. I told my Mum I wished I'd never had him, because then it wouldn't have hurt so much when he got killed. She said yes, but you had 'im and loved 'im and that's a special thing, and it's what you'll remember when the pain of his going dies down.'

'Did it die down, Albert?' I asked, watching Michael. He was staring at the horizon, engulfed in thought.

'Yes. But I still miss 'im.'

'We're all misfits, you see, Stephen.' Strang had gone on, his face ghostly white on the moonlit bridge. 'We shouldn't be doing this, any of us. Deeds, well, he's bloody retired. He should be tucked up by the fire at home. He's got a heart condition, did you know? Hardly anybody does, certainly not the Navy. He's a forty-nine-year-old reservist with a bad heart. So what the hell is he doing out here? Brown, Woolley, they're just office clerks. Insurance brokers and accountants. They weren't meant to be charging around the North Atlantic killing Germans.'

'Me?' I asked, emboldened by the gin. 'You? Villiers?'

Strang snorted. 'You, Stephen, are running away from your name, and the fear of failing to live up to it. I'm an alcoholic with shot nerves. As for Villiers. Well . . . Michael . . .'

He hesitated, unsure whether to go on. A drink or two inside him and I believe he might have. As it was, he just said this: 'Michael has the least reason of any of us to be here, yet, perversely, he is the glue that holds us together. Being here, right in the thick of it, yet not participating, is his way of dealing with it.'

'Not participating? What do you mean?' I asked. But it was all he said.

Chapter 12

'I'm sorry, Michael, for dragging you back here like this. I trust you are well rested after your holiday,' Millington-Drake said, sipping tea from a bone-china cup. They were in his office at the British legation headquarters on Plaza Matriz. Its corridors seemed much busier than Michael remembered, full of new faces, most of whom he didn't recognise, many in uniform, all of them in a hurry. But then so much had changed, so completely, in so little time. It was Tuesday 12 December. Two days since he had been picked up from the Peréz estancia near Melo, over two months since he had escaped Montevideo, a lifetime since leaving England.

'It wasn't a holiday; it is where I live.'

'Of course, I beg your pardon. Your family there. They are well?'

'As well as possible, thank you. How did you know where to find me?'

'My dear chap,' Millington-Drake chuckled. 'It is our job to know where our people are. It wasn't difficult, you'd said many times it was where you wanted to go.'

'Then, if you knew where I was, why didn't you bring me back sooner?'

'Ah, yes, well, that was me, I suppose. We were going to. Mr Martin, whose real name is Rex Miller by the way, wanted you hauled back here the very next day. Not best pleased, he was, when you disappeared, as you can imagine. But things were reasonably quiet, on the German legation side, at that time. In any case, I felt we had already asked quite a lot of you, and you could probably do with the break. Spend some time out there in the open air, have a rest, gain a fresh perspective on things. I find a change of scenery often helps straighten the mind, don't you?'

'Sir, I'm not going to be a spy any more.'

'No? So how are you going to help your country in its hour of crisis?'

'Uruguay is my country. It is neutral, as am I.'

'Yes, but it is not quite as simple as that, is it? You also hold British nationality, your father and brother are British. You are, perhaps I should remind you, eligible for call-up to the British armed services.' Millington-Drake watched him over the rim of his teacup. Two months and the boy was scarcely recognisable. For a start he was no longer a boy, no longer the diffident, hesitant youth he had known in September. Apart from this new-found assertiveness, physically too he was completely changed. Before him, broad, tanned, his hands toughened, face weathered, sat a man. A strong-willed one at that.

'I don't believe fighting wars solves the world's ills,' Michael was saying. 'I believe the best way to stop this war is for the major neutral regions of the world, such as Russia, the United States, Asia, and South America, to exert diplomatic pressure on the Germans to withdraw from Poland, then set up and oversee multilateral talks aimed at bringing about peaceful solutions to the territorial disputes.'

'Ah, yes, your beloved Russia. Marx, communism, peace and comradeship for everyone, and all the rest of it. That would be the same "neutral" Russia that just signed a pact with Nazi Germany, would it? Oh, and then last week attacked Finland, by the way. An independent, defenceless, non-communist country.'

'What?' Michael was visibly shaken. 'What did you say?'

'Yes, it was shock to us, too. Nor, Michael, I must tell you, is this just about Poland any more. A very great deal has happened since you left us.' He rose to his feet, walking, teacup in hand, to the window. A great deal, evidently, had happened to Michael, too. There had been a young woman, the driver had reported. A pretty young thing, name of Luenga. And a dispute with some Argentinian youth called Peréz. Personnel was running checks on them that very minute. Michael wanted to bring the girl to Montevideo. As his fiancée. Absolutely not, the driver had rightly insisted. There was an awkward standoff, Michael, knife in hand, stubbornly refusing to budge. In the end the driver had agreed to take her with them as far as her parents' house. It was cruel, Millington-Drake knew, what they were doing to these young people. Cruel too, so ruthlessly to demolish a young man's cherished beliefs like this. In other circumstances he would have loved to spend time explaining matters to Michael, discussing finer points, debating issues. But things had changed; there was no more time for finer points.

'This is highly confidential, Michael, but you must trust me that it is also true. Germany will invade both Norway and Denmark within the next few weeks. They are small, poorly armed countries, and will quickly fall. As are Belgium and Holland, which will follow soon thereafter. Once they are gone, France will be attacked, probably not later than April.'

'But, but, it's incredible. Something must be done.'

'Yes, but by whom, Michael? England will be next. If all goes according to Germany's plans, she will be in their hands by the summer.'

'How can you possibly know all this?'

'I can't tell you that, you must just trust me that the information is definite. The Germans are meticulous in their planning, they write everything down. That can be a weakness.' He went on more lightly. 'Intelligence, you know, is not just about eavesdropping on cocktail-party tittle-tattle. It is vital, respected work, and a fine career for a bright young man with a gift for it.'

'I'm not doing it any more.'

'So you have already said, yet you also say something

must be done. I'm sorry, Michael, but it is no use your being naive about this. Proposing that Germany simply pull out of Poland is absurd. As for your suggestion of other, so-called neutral regions of the world intervening, Russia, I think you'll agree now, is certainly not neutral. Asia is a smouldering powder keg of internal belligerences. The United States, thank God, is tacitly supportive of the Allies. South America? Some countries here sympathise with the Allies, many are openly pro-German. Most sit on the touch-line waiting to see who takes the upper hand, and only a very few, like Uruguay, genuinely try to maintain neutrality. No, Michael, as a diplomat it pains me to concede this, but the truth is, diplomatic efforts to negotiate a peace in this war, by neutrals, or by anyone, have failed to make the slightest difference.' He turned from the window. 'Do you know why?'

Michael, ashen, was shaking his head.

'Because diplomacy relies upon common sense and reason. But common sense is useless against fanaticism, and you can't reason with despots. I applaud your ideals, Michael, really I do, but they are completely unrealistic. Like it or not, it is time for the world, and everyone in it, including you, to take sides.'

He walked, head reeling, from Millington-Drake's office and down to the street. Stepping into bright sunshine, his senses were immediately assaulted. Montevideo, after the tranquil freshness of Sombreado, was like a pressure cooker, overboiling with people and thick with midsummer heat. He began walking, pushing slowly through the currents of passers-by towards his lodgings, his ears assailed by shouting street vendors and grinding traffic, the smell of sweating crowds, motor car fumes and rotting refuse in his lungs.

It was all to do with ships, Millington-Drake had gone on to explain, after things had calmed down a bit. Ships. Our merchant ships and their warships. Submarines, too, possibly. Nobody knew for certain, and that was the problem. What was known, he said, was that the Germans were operating a raiding force in the area. Like pirates on the high seas. This force comprised at least one, maybe two, or even three warships, possibly submarines, too, plus support vessels supplying them with fuel and stores. Or so it was presumed; again nobody really knew. But they did know that this force was wreaking havoc. At least nine British merchant ships had been sunk in an area covering the entire South Atlantic and even round the Cape into the Indian Ocean. Yet apart from garbled distress messages and confused sighting reports, no firm information about the make-up or location of this force existed anywhere. It materialised, as though from nowhere; it struck, then it vanished.

But it had something to do with Hans Langsdorff. The man Michael had seen from *Runswick Bay*. The man in the immaculate white uniform smiling from the bridge of his ship, *Graf Spee*, while it was disguised as another. That much was known, Millington-Drake said. What was also known was that the head of the German legation himself had once mentioned Langsdorff's name in Michael's presence. He might do so again. So, find out, Millington-Drake had urged, find out anything you can. Do this for us, just see this one thing through, and we will ask no more spying of you. That's a promise.

He lay on the bed in his room, untouched since he'd crept from it that misty dawn so long ago. He thought of Maria. I am coming back, he'd assured her, tightly holding her hands in the moonlight outside Sombreado, just two days earlier. He'd kissed her and promised. I will write as soon as I get to Montevideo. The instant I find out what this is all about. Then I will come back and we shall live here together. No war, no Alonso Peréz, just us, Sombreado and that is all. Yet the paper lay waiting, blank on his table. What could he say? Lies? It is nothing, my dearest. A week or two's unfinished business here at my desk with Atlantic Mercantile. Or the truth? British Intelligence wants me to use my mother's connections to find out about German warship activity. Moreover, although I hate this work, and hate everything to do with this war, recently I have been feeling increasingly uneasy about my non-involvement in it, and about being away from England at such a time.

Unable to rest, he rose from his bed, went to the balcony, a tightening knot of anxiety in his stomach. An orange sun was setting over the harbour, the sky streaked pink with feathery wisps of cirrus. It is worse, Maria, much worse even than that. Sides, Michael, Millington-Drake had said over and again. It is time to choose sides. Tell us about your job, the Germans used to say. At Willi's parties. Dalldorf, the red-faced information officer, his arm draped around Michael's shoulder. Atlantic Mercantile, isn't it? And what do you do there? Merchant ships is what he did there. Ships and their cargoes, sailing dates, destinations. Really, Michael? How interesting. You must tell me more . . .

I thought everything was so clear in my head, Maria, so simple. I thought that if I buried myself in rebuilding Sombreado, in making a new life for us there, that the war could never touch us. That my life in England, and here, Atlantic Mercantile, the British, the Germans, everything, would just go away. But it hasn't gone away, Maria, and it won't. Not unless I make it.

Early in the afternoon of the next day he returned to his old offices in the Palacio Salvo. His desk at Atlantic Mercantile was exactly as he had left it, his former colleagues nodding a cursory greeting, as though he'd been away an afternoon. He nodded back, sat down, telephoned upstairs and asked to speak to 'Mr Martin'. Rex Miller, as he now knew him to be, head of British Intelligence in Montevideo.

'What do you want?' Miller asked frostily. 'I'm very busy.'

'I'm sorry, sir, I'll try and be brief.' He took a deep breath. 'One of the main reasons I left Montevideo had to do with your not being honest with me.'

'About what?'

'About your name, for a start. About what you did. And about what it was you were asking me to do. It was never fully explained and I resented that.'

'Fair enough. Anything else?'

'Somebody followed me here this afternoon. From my lodgings. A man.'

'Did you recognise him? Was he from the German legation?'

'No sir, I believe he is local. I think he may have been hired by an Argentinian family called Peréz. He's waiting in a bar across the street.'

'Right. Leave it with me. Anything else?'

'Well, sir, when I was here before, it is possible I gave the Germans, inadvertently, information about some of our shipping movements.'

'I doubt it. What you handled down there was mostly out of date or fictitious.'

'Fictitious?'

'Yes. Made up. We had to be careful. Anything else?'

Michael sighed. 'Possibly, sir, one more thing. From my conversations with the Germans, and from things I overheard, it was always my impression that Langsdorff, or whoever it was, was acting alone, and not part of a bigger force.'

'Why do you suppose this now, and why did you not report it then?'

'I did, sir, but as I say it was only an impression. If the subject came up, which was very rarely, references were always made in the singular. 'It' and 'he', never 'them' or 'they'. I may be wrong, but that's the way it came across, one ship and one man. And if I hadn't made that point clear at the time, I thought I should do so now.'

There was a heavy pause on the line. In the silence he heard the faintest rumble of thunder far out over the Atlantic. He glanced to the window, but the sky was clear, flawlessly blue.

'We know,' Miller said at last.

'You know? But yesterday, Mr Millington-Drake said . . .'

'That was yesterday, today things have changed. But you were right to tell me, Villiers, and I appreciate your being frank.' The voice hesitated, as though still undecided, then went on. 'You heard that thunder just now?'

'Yes, I did.'

'It isn't thunder. At around dawn this morning the German pocket battleship *Graf Spee*, under the command of Hans Langsdorff, was spotted by three British cruisers searching for it about two hundred miles east of here. A little to our surprise, perhaps, Langsdorff turned and immediately engaged all three of them. Fighting has been continuing, on and off, all day. The thunder you hear is their gunfire. The four ships are currently about fifty miles away, and closing the Uruguayan coast.'

'My God. What will happen?'

'It's three against one. We'll blow him to kingdom come.' The voice paused again. 'So, you've come to a decision, then?'

'Yes, sir. I suppose I have.'

'What made you?'

'I am against oppression, sir, that's all. People should be allowed to live their lives as they choose.'

He hung up the telephone, tried to concentrate on his work. But it was impossible; throughout the afternoon and evening rumours flew back and forth like leaves in the wind. Gunfire rumbled in the distance, then stopped, for hours. It was over, somebody reported, bursting through the door.

The German is sunk! It was on the wireless. No, no, it was one of the British ships, someone else contradicted. Names began to filter through. *Ajax* was one of the cruisers, it was reported. *Achilles* another, *Exeter* the third. Fast, powerful, with eight-inch guns that could fling a two hundred and fifty pound shell twenty miles. *Graf Spee* was stopped, he heard later still, Pulverised to a wreck, her propulsion system destroyed. But then – no, she was underway again, it was *Exeter* that had been crippled and forced to break off. Now there were just two left in pursuit, boxing the German in, forcing him, every hour, a little closer to the shore.

He gave up pretending to work. In any case there seemed little point now that he knew his job was complete fiction. He found notepaper. Dearest Maria, he tried yet again, while all around the gossip spread like fire. They had just been seen, the three remaining ships, so the latest news went. From the lighthouse up the coast at Punta del Este. Twenty miles off, still firing the occasional salvo at each other. Dearest Maria. Please know, firstly, that I love you more than anything in the world. But the life I thought I had left behind in Montevideo has returned to haunt me. Now I must stay here and fulfil my obligations, and consider my responsibilities to my father and brother, and my duty to England which is in grave peril. I believed that the war had nothing to do with me, that it was something of little consequence, taking place thousands of miles away. But I was wrong, everyone in the world is affected. As I write these words it is raging just a few miles from our shores, I have been listening to its thunder throughout the day..

'Hello, angel. Are you writing to me?'

'Mother!'

Aurora, her eyes misty behind a haze of net veil beneath a pillbox hat, stood before his desk. She was wearing one of her closely tailored Hollywood suits, with cream gloves and matching handbag. 'Mother, what a wonderful surprise.' He rose, kissed her on both cheeks through the veil. She smelled of cigarettes and expensive scent. 'How did you know I was here?'

'I have my spies!' She winked mischievously, then immediately her face creased into a frown. 'You didn't come to see me,' she pouted. 'That wasn't nice.'

'I, I was going to, Mother. Really. But I've only been back a day or so, and everything has been so busy, especially what with today's events. Did you hear?'

'Of course! It's all over the evening newspapers, and the wireless. Isn't it exciting? Shall we go to Figaro's? That new bar down on the *rambla*. Everyone's going there, thousands and thousands. They say the final battle will be played out before our very eyes!'

He hesitated; she was right, everyone was going there, or somewhere, for suddenly the entire office was deserted. He folded Maria's letter into his pocket, and led her to the elevators.

The *rambla* was packed, the evening warm and festive. He checked repeatedly, but there was no sign of the man who had followed him earlier. People strolled, arm in arm, along the sandy waterfront, or sat on the beach, or crowded into seaside bars and cafés decorated with paper chains and

Christmas lights. Everywhere there was gossip and specu-lation, an air of excited anticipation. 'What fun!' Aurora cried, elbowing her way into a bar. 'Figaro! It is me! Have you a table, at the front here? And champagne! Two glasses.'

'How is Willi?' Michael asked dutifully, an hour or so later. They were half way into the second bottle. Night had fallen, with it a calming of the mood. Crowds still wan-dered the *rambla*, but, despite endless rumours, little more had been seen or heard of the three fighting ships. Aurora had in any case long since lost interest, endlessly recounting the details of her life since Michael's departure. Of his early morning visit to steal her money, his ten-week absence from her life, of Sombreado, the war, even of the wellbeing of her dying grandfather, she made no mention at all.

'Willi is on splendid form! Anxious to see you, of course. You must come round for dinner. That reminds me, there is a big reception planned for this Friday evening. At the German legation on Plaza Zabala. You simply must come.'

'Ah, I, well, Mother, I'm not so sure that's such a good—'

'Angel, but you must! Willi would never forgive me. Everyone will be there, all your old friends.' She nudged him conspiratorially. 'Herr Langmann's daughters will be there, you know. I've told them all about you and they are most anxious to be introduced. Just think, angel, if you were to become romantically involved with the German ambas-sador's daughter!'

'I can't, mother.'

'But you must, it would be very rude not to.'

'I mean, I cannot become involved with someone. I already am.'

'What? But why didn't you tell me, angel! Who? Who is it?' Her pillbox hat lay on the table between them, together with a silver cigarette case and two shot glasses of some clear liqueur she'd taken with the champagne. As beautiful, as voluble and as excitable as ever though she was, he'd nevertheless been unable to ignore an air of desperation about her. The way her eyes roved ceaselessly through the crowds, as though searching for someone. The way she was quite unable to sit still, or concentrate on one subject for more than a few seconds. The way she drank, and smoked, non-stop, and with a kind of purposeful intent.

'I'm in love with Maria, Mother. I mean to make her my wife.'

'Maria? Maria who?' An expectant half-smile was pasted to her lips.

'Maria Luenga, of course. Who else?'

She laughed. She held his eyes for a fraction of a second, mouth open in astonishment, then simply collapsed, rocking back and forth on her chair, slapping the table, spilling her drink. 'Maria! That is so wonderful! Maria, Maria!' Heads turned at other tables, bemused, keen to share the joke. Michael smiled back politely, waiting.

'Mother, please.'

Still she laughed, pulling a lace handkerchief from her bag to dab at her eyes, swallowing champagne, spluttering, convulsed, uncontrollable. Slowly the spasm passed, the laughter subsiding into fitful giggles. She reached for the cigarette case, still sighing. 'Angel, that is so wonderful.'

'I am serious.'

'No you're not.'

'I am.'

The amusement vanished from her face. 'No, Michael, you are not. She is the penniless daughter of a common servant family. I won't hear of such a thing.'

'You won't?'

'No, in fact I forbid it.'

Now it was Michael's turn to laugh. 'You forbid it! Mother, have you forgotten? You gave me into the care of this common servant family when I was a baby. You left me with them for eight years!'

'That was for your health! Your chest, it was weak, the cholera, the doctors—'

'No! It was because I was an inconvenience to you. Always was. Indeed, I still am! You don't want me, except as a plaything, someone to amuse you and show off at parties. You never wanted me. You never wanted any of us!'

'Michael!'

But he was already stumbling for the door.

Later, he walked, alone, west along the *rambla* towards the Ciudad Vieja, the immigrant quarter, and his lodgings. It was around midnight, he was a little drunk. The crowds had thinned but still many hundreds wandered the waterfront, enjoying the balmy night air, the expectation, the waiting and wondering. Do you know what's happening? Have you seen anything? What's the news? I hear they all went aground on the Banco Inglés. No, they are licking their wounds somewhere off Maldonado.

At the bottom of the *rambla*, where the river entrance curves into the harbour, he came to the Escollera Sarandí, the southern breakwater, an untidy jumble of boulders and concrete blocks stretching like a callused finger nearly a kilometre into the sea. A narrow cement path ran atop it, thickly lined as always with drifters and tramps, the homeless, the curious, or simply the restless, taking the air, talking quietly, sharing a maté, hunched in sleep or lucklessly dangling fishing lines into the muddy waters. He turned on to it, began slowly picking his way among them towards the distant harbour entrance light. Nearing the end, he stopped, turning to look back across the bay. A kilometre away the city sparkled at the water's edge like a handful of spilt jewels. All around it the harbour glowed in the moonlight; beyond, high on the mount that rose behind the city, a lighthouse blinked. '*Monte-vide-eu!*' Magellan's lookout had cried centuries earlier, from the top of his swaying mast, the very first foreign eyes to behold the land. See the hill!

Around him, people were pointing. A murmur of anxious surprise rippled through them. 'My God!' somebody exclaimed. 'My God, what is that?'

A shadow, huge and dark, was creeping slowly through the water towards the breakwater, bathed in hazy moonlight. It was a ship, a vast warship with long, pointing turrets and a foretop reaching high into the sky. Engines could be heard, low, throbbing diesels. Then a klaxon sounded, and a bell, orders drifting over the water from a loudspeaker, in German. Michael pushed forward, past astonished onlookers to the edge of the breakwater, scrambled up on to one of the huge boulders to see. He saw. It was him. It was Langsdorff, it was *Graf*, he'd know it anywhere, even in moonlight. The triple eleven-inch turrets, the Arado seaplane, the Imperial Navy flag fluttering from her mast. She was so close, as close as she had been from *Runswick Bay*. He felt he could almost reach out and touch her. He smelt diesel fumes, cordite, scorched steel. She had struggled and fought, been hit, burned; he could make out a rent in her bows, damage to the superstructure. He watched, together with the others, in hushed awe, as she began to turn. He was bringing her in, his huge ship. Langsdorff. Damaged, in secret, in darkness, without a pilot. Conning her quietly past the breakwater and into their harbour.

At seven the next morning there was a briefing in Rex Miller's office. Michael recognised Captain McCall, together with a number of other naval officers, Atlantic Mercantile personnel, and legation staff from the offices in Plaza Matriz. There were also several men in suits and hats whom he didn't recognise, some of them quite elderly. Miller had pinned a large map of the harbour on to a wall, *Graf Spee*'s position, at anchor in the inner harbour, outlined in black.

'Surveillance, gentlemen, as close as we can, and around the clock. That is the first priority,' Miller began, tapping the map with a ruler. 'Now, obviously we were never expecting anything quite like this, so our somewhat limited resources are going to be stretched pretty thin. We are very grateful to Mr Daniel here; he and his colleagues from the Retired Expatriate Seafarers Association are going to mount observation posts in the old customs house here, the rowing club here, and the immigrants reception building over here. We're also going to try and get observers aboard Allied merchant ships anchored in the harbour. Information will be collected and brought back to the command post in my office, using teams of runners made up of these young chaps here . . .' He gestured around at Michael and some others.

'What sort of information are we after?' one of the retired seafarers asked.

Henry McCall stepped forward. 'Anything and everything. Especially movements of personnel or equipment on and off the ship. Any sign of activity, such as repair work, loading of fuel, stores or ammunition. Comings and goings of her captain and officers, and, of course, any hint at all that she might be preparing to get underway. We also need as accurate a picture as possible of the damage she has sustained – particularly to her weaponry, range-finding and propulsion systems.'

'What's the plan?' another asked.

'The plan is to get her kicked out as soon as possible. Today if we can. This is a neutral port; we can't do a thing while she stays here. *Achilles* and *Ajax* are stationed twelve miles away at the mouth of the Plate, waiting to finish her off the moment she crosses outside territorial waters. The German legation has appealed to the Uruguayan government, claiming she is unseaworthy, and that under the terms of the Hague Convention she should be allowed to stay and make repairs. We say that's hogwash and that she's seaworthy now. Millington-Drake is mounting the diplomatic counter offensive, lodging a formal protest with the Uruguayan Foreign Minister as we speak. Any more questions?'

There were a few, then the meeting closed, the various groups dispersing. Miller gestured for Michael to stay behind.

'How close are you to the Germans these days, Villiers?'

'I don't know, sir, I've rather lost touch since I left Montevideo.'

'That might be to our advantage. On the other hand, if they do suspect you're working for us . . .'

'They might use it as a means to feed back false information?'

'They might use it as a means to take you behind a wall and shoot you, Villiers. Be under no illusions, this thing is turning very ugly. Otto Langmann and his Nazi Party chums from BA are rushing about Plaza Zabala like scalded cats. Word is that Hitler himself is hopping mad, thinks Langsdorff should have slugged it out to the end, even if he had nothing left to fight with. In truth, we haven't a clue what they're going to do, so a fly on their legation wall would be unbelievably useful to us right now. But liable to get swatted, if you get my meaning. You should be aware of that.'

'Yes, sir.'

'Do you think they'll let you near the place?'

'Possibly, sir.' He hesitated. 'But, may I ask, sir. About the man who was following me yesterday . . .'

Miller smiled drily. 'We believe in taking care of our own, Villiers. You won't have any more bother from young Mr Peréz or his thugs.'

'Thank you, sir. And my relatives in Cerro Largo?'

'None of you. Now, are you going to help us with the legation or not?'

'I have a sort of invitation there tomorrow evening.'

'Good. Go. Anything you can learn will be valuable. But be careful.' Miller checked his watch, sweeping notes and drawings into a briefcase. 'Meantime, get down to the harbour and lend a hand with the observers. See if you can't sneak a close look at the brute. Go dockside if you can; there's *Graf* sailors waiting to ferry people back and forth. Suppliers, contractors and so on. You might pick up some gossip.'

Michael sent a quick note to Aurora accepting her summons to the German reception, then hurried down to the harbour. There were indeed a great many people coming and going. Thousands it seemed. But little chance of getting on to the docks; security was tight, a fully armed Uruguayan guard barring the gates. Crowds thronged the *rambla* and surrounding streets, searching for vantage points. Many took to the roofs and balconies of nearby buildings. He forced his way back to the breakwater he'd stood upon the previous night, but a policeman stopped him on the threshold. Off-limits, he said. Too many people fighting to get on. It's madness, he added, photographers, reporters, newsreel crews arriving by the bus-load. Everyone wants to get close. There was even some American journalist setting up a live radio broadcast, CBS and BBC relaying it around the globe. The whole world, he said, a little proudly, was turning its attention on to Montevideo.

In the end, he had to double back through the narrow streets of the commercial quarter, all the way round to the north corner of the harbour, more than a mile up the bay. Here, away from any excitement, away from the crowds, there were no locked gates, no security guards or policemen. He ducked under a wire fence, threading his way carefully through the warrens of sheds and warehouses back towards the inner harbour. It took nearly an hour, but finally he drew near. A rusted tugboat, listing and derelict, was moored to a quay at the western corner. Double-checking he was unobserved, he sprinted across and slipped aboard.

Before him, through the cracked glass panes of the tug's wheelhouse, barely three-hundred metres away, *Graf Spee* lay at anchor. She had been at sea a very long time, he saw immediately. Months, probably, without respite, the immaculate paintwork he remembered so well from *Runswick Bay* now rust-streaked and fading. Weed and barnacles trailed at her waterline. Recently added camouflage on her superstructure, a painted-on bow wave, and the remains of false gun turrets evidenced her many changes in identity. In the glare of full sunlight, the extent of visible battle damage was now plain. A shell had punched through her hull, leaving an eight-foot rent in the port bow, another had pierced her on the waterline. Her upper superstructure, bridge and funnel were pocked with holes from shell splinters. The forward gun turret drooped drunkenly. Michael reached into his pocket for paper and pencil. As he jotted, a motor launch detached itself from the dockside and sped towards her, figures in white clustered at the stern. Officers, possibly Langsdorff himself, were returning aboard. He noted the time, wedged himself into a corner of his spider-infested wheelhouse, and settled down to wait.

At dusk he crept away, returning circuitously to the Palacio Salvo offices. Miller was not there but one of McCall's men, Johnston, took his notes.

'Any developments?' Michael enquired.

'A load of British merchant seamen prisoners was released from her earlier. Apparently Langsdorff used to get everyone off the ships before he sank them. Decent of him. As for repairs, the Germans have officially requested two weeks to make *Graf* safe for sea. We're still pushing hard for her to be evicted now. The Uruguayans sent a team of inspectors aboard to assess damage; rumour is she'll get seventy-two hours.'

'And then?'

'She must leave, if not she'll be interned here for the duration of the war. Something German High Command won't allow in a month of Sundays.'

Johnston instructed him to be back at his tugboat vantage point by midnight. 'Until then, get something to eat, and put your head down. Busy day tomorrow.'

But food and sleep were the last things on his mind. An hour after leaving Johnston, he was knocking on the door of the Quemadas' house in Prado.

'Miguel?' His grandfather, José-Luis, newspaper in hand,

opened the door to him. 'My God, is it you?' Nearing seventy, retired, but still an influential government figure, José-Luis seemed to have shrunk in the ten years since last they had met. Always slight of stature, he was now at least a foot shorter than Michael, and stooped, his once lustrous side whiskers thin and grey. Spectacles clutched to his nose, he peered up at his grandson in disbelief. 'My God, look at the size of you. Have you heard about the battleship?'

'Of course, grandfather. But with your permission, I am here to ask about my mother and father.'

They ate in the big dining room together. Or rather Michael ate while José-Luis and Florentina looked on. Out of politeness, he waited until the plates were cleared before broaching the subject again. In the meantime he told them what little he could of *Graf Spee*. They talked also of the progress of the war. Of the difficulties of maintaining neutrality. And of Sombreado.

'I wanted to thank you,' he said. 'For responding so quickly to my telegram. The one asking for money. It was very generous.'

Florentina looked away. 'We had no idea Gertrudis had allowed the situation to become so bad.'

'She misses you, I believe, grandmother.'

'Nonsense,' Florentina blustered. 'In any case, it is not us you should be thanking for the money, but your mother.'

'Mother?'

'Yes. Well, perhaps more accurately, her "gentleman friend", Herr Hochstetler. He made all the arrangements, we merely agreed to the terms.'

'Willi? But that is unbelievable. Why would he want to do such a thing?'

'You must ask him yourself; we have no discussions with him.'

'Because he is German?'

'No. Because he is in sin with our daughter.'

Gradually he gleaned some of what he wanted to know. Florentina did most of the talking, José-Luis, lips compressed, nodding in sad agreement. Aurora had always been a troublesome daughter, it transpired, overactive and unruly from childhood. At puberty it got worse. Moody, given to tantrums, she allowed herself to be pursued by any number of suitors, most of them unbefitting, and developed a hunger for expensive living and party society. It was a great worry to them, and a disappointment. They didn't understand it, but blamed themselves.

Michael watched and listened, mildly surprised at his own dispassion. As though he was conducting an interview about a vague acquaintance.

'Why do you think she became like that?' he asked.

They didn't know, didn't understand. She was very intelligent at school, more gifted in many ways than her brothers. But, well, it was true perhaps, they concentrated too much on their sons' educations, their careers, their lives, perhaps paying too little attention to the needs of their little sister.

'You know, Miguel,' Florentina went on. 'The moods. All the men, the endless parties and champagne, and the rest. I do not believe these things brought her contentment. The only time she was ever truly content was at Sombreado, when she was much younger. She loved it there. It freed her from the urges that drove her in the city. She could be the carefree young girl she once was.'

'But when she visited me there, with my father, she couldn't wait to leave.'

'That was much later. She was already changed by then. Already lost.'

Lost was a word they used repeatedly. They liked him, by the way, they said. Keith. Genuinely. José-Luis especially, believing his sensible English manner would be a calming influence on Aurora. They were happy to approve the marriage, too, even if it turned out Keith wasn't quite the man of means they had assumed. There were difficulties from the start, they knew that, well aware how hard Aurora found it to give up her wild ways. But when she announced she was pregnant again, and going to live with her family in London, they were happy, believing at last she had assumed her responsibilities as mother and wife.

'And when she returned here?'

'Unpardonable.' Florentina began to rise. 'There is no excuse for it. Since then we have had little contact with one another.'

'She tried her best in London.'

'No. She abandoned her family to become mistress to a married man.'

'Willi is married?'

'Of course. He has a wife and children in Germany. He goes there twice a year to visit them, then returns here to his life of debauchery and sin.'

When the interview was over Florentina led him, alone, to the hall. At the doorway, he tried one final time.

'You say that what she did was unpardonable. But perhaps that is all she craves. Your pardon.'

'No, Miguel. She craves what she is and there is no saving her.'

'I believe she is very unhappy.'

'Unhappy? What has her happiness to do with anything! And how can you defend her after all she has done to you? She is married to your father yet sleeps with another woman's husband. She spends money as though the world is ending. She becomes drunk in public, flaunts herself, and is utterly without dignity, decency or honour. She is nothing but a shameless and profligate harlot who thinks only of her own wants and addictions, and will stop at nothing to satisfy them.'

'Addictions?' A cold shiver touched his spine. The bruises, the coin-sized bruises on her thighs. 'Grandmother, surely . . .'

'Miguel, she is alcoholic. And a morphine addict. For years, now. Did you not realise? Three or four times a week she visits her quack physician in the Ciudad Vieja. We know, because once we had her followed. She goes to his filthy room, lifts her skirts, and allows him to see and touch her in return for injections of morphine. Your mother, Miguel. This is the woman she has become.'

He awoke from restless dreaming at around dawn. Cursing himself for his feebleness, he raised his head to the wheel-house window. But she was still there, *Graf*, exactly as she had been all night, huge, motionless, bathed in floodlight. He breathed out, stretching cramped limbs, grinding sleep from his eyes, shaking the grogginess from his head. Outside, first light tinged the sky over the city rose-pink; tendrils of mist hovered above the bay. Rats frolicked on the tugboat's rotting decks.

They had been working on her all night. The salvage teams, shipwrights and engineers, hurriedly shipped over from pro-German Buenos Aires when the intractably neutral Uruguayans declined their help. Barges, tugs and lighters surrounded her, like lackeys about a dowager duchess. A rough steel patch was being riveted over the hole in her bows, another team on a scaffolding worked high on the funnel, others repaired damage to decks and fittings. Fourteen days, Langsdorff had asked for, to repair his ship. He had less than three. Eight o'clock Sunday evening was the deadline. Leave by then, President Baldomir's ruling decreed. Go out and face your pursuers – now incidentally reinforced by a third cruiser – or face internment, dishonour and disgrace.

Michael scanned the ship. Something else had happened while he'd slept. An area of deck had been cleared of workmen and debris. Right beneath the three giant pointing fingers of the aft eleven-inch turret. Stanchions and railings had been erected around the swept area. In two corners, standing to attention, but with their heads bowed, two uniformed sailors kept watch. It was a guard of honour. Behind them upon the scrubbed deck, lay row upon row of flag-draped coffins.

Graf's dead were brought ashore later in the morning. Michael followed them, passing behind the suddenly subdued crowds lining the pavements. Escorted by their officers and three hundred of their shipmates, the melancholy cortège of thirty-seven coffins wound its way along Avenida 18 de Julio, turned left on to Bulevar General Artigas, and on, up through the city to the Cementerio del Norte. There the sailors stood to attention beside their fallen comrades while two German pastors conducted the funeral rites. Uruguayan government officials were present, and a mounted guard. *Graf*'s released British merchant seamen laid a wreath, as did the German expatriate community, which turned out in force. Michael recognised several, including Willi Hochstetler, his head respectfully bowed beneath cloud-blown skies. Of his mother there was no sign.

In the centre of it all stood Langsdorff. In his white tropical uniform, as Michael had first seen him, but with ceremonial medals, white gloves and sword. And unsmiling, this time. Throughout the service he remained still and erect, the dignified focal figure of authority. Yet there was no disguising the fatigue in his eyes, the aura of isolation, and his anguish at the duty he was now performing.

At the end, when the pastors were finished, Otto Langmann, head of the German legation, made a jarringly patriotic speech. Langsdorff, by contrast, spoke only a few quiet words in praise of his men, then stepped forward to scatter soil upon every casket, the crowd looking on in spellbound silence. At last it was over. He returned to his place. Orders were barked, rifles lifted to the skies, shots rang out. Then it happened. Langmann, the two pastors, the German officials, civilian expatriates, all of them, snapped out their arms, hands outstretched, in the Nazi salute. But in the centre of them all, a figure in white came slowly to attention, his gloved fingers to the peak of his uniform hat, in the traditional salute of his ancient Navy. Breaths were indrawn, a shocked murmur rippled through the assembly. A sentence was passed.

'How was the funeral?' Rex Miller asked later, back at the office.

'Moving,' Michael replied. 'Interesting, too. I get the impression Captain Langsdorff may be in trouble.'

'You bet he is. I heard about the salute; it'll be all over the papers by this evening. Berlin won't like it one little bit. Not only that, it turns out he was contravening orders when he engaged our cruisers in the first place.' Miller was riffling through his desk for papers. 'Bit of a puzzle, our Captain Langsdorff. Now then, are you still on for the German legation tonight?'

'Yes, sir.'

'Good, because there's been a complete change of plan. Their Lordships at the Admiralty, in their infinite wisdom, have now decided they want us to keep *Graf* bottled up here in harbour, so they can get more ships lined up outside. As if three wasn't enough. Millington-Drake's having a total fit. He's just spent forty-eight hours persuading the Uruguayans to throw *Graf* out. Now he's got to start persuading them to keep her in. It's an utter lash-up, and we still have no idea what Langsdorff's plans are. Is he staying in, or is he going to try and break out? Anything you can glean would be an enormous help. Got that?'

'Yes, sir.'

'Right. But for God's sake be careful. Act normally, watch your back, and if things start looking tricky, get the hell out.'

Things looked tricky from the beginning. He passed the afternoon at his lodgings, trying to rest. But rest was impossible. At eight he rose, washed and shaved, changed into his best suit and made the short walk to Plaza Zabala. He had to wait thirty agonising minutes on the pavement under the suspicious gaze of the legation doorman before Willi and Aurora finally pulled up in a cab. Aurora was in dark satin, Willi wore an evening suit with black armband.

'Michael, it is so very good to see you again!' Willi said, pumping his hand. Michael embraced his mother, but her response was stiff, her eyes averted. The doorman, his gaze still on Michael, ushered them in.

'I have to say, I'm not sure whether this is a wake or a celebration,' Willi went on. They followed guests across a marble-floored lobby towards a wide staircase. 'This *Spee* business is causing enormous difficulties for everyone. Some people say it is completely inappropriate to be holding this reception; others say it is vital to demonstrate the solidarity of the German people here.'

'What do you think?' Michael glanced back. Aurora trailed in their wake.

'Disaster. The whole blasted business is a disaster. Berlin is extremely angry, consequently everyone here is nervous.

It is damaging diplomatic relations with the authorities in the region, and doing incalculable harm to the interests of the German business community. I think it's all a bloody disgrace; Langsdorff's off his head, and I've a good mind to tell him so.'

'He's coming tonight?' They were approaching a large, elegantly panelled room crowded with guests. Many, it seemed to Michael's heightened senses, turned to observe their arrival. Waiters bearing trays stood, sentinel-like, at the doors.

'Of course. He and his senior officers. How could they not? It would look very bad. Ah, Reiner! Reiner, my dear chap. How wonderful to see you again! Tell me, how is your lovely wife? You remember young Michael, here, of course . . .'

He circulated, he mingled, he renewed acquaintances, he was polite and charming, even to the German ambassador's daughters who blushed and giggled throughout. But apart from them, nobody seemed very interested in his presence. Slowly he allowed himself to relax, a little. He learned quickly that the subject of *Graf Spee* was completely off-limits. Nobody mentioned it at all, at least not within hearing. Not even, when to the accompaniment of polite applause from the guests, Langsdorff and his officers arrived. Michael watched and applauded too. Within minutes they had been absorbed into the crowd, little islands of white amid the drifting dark currents.

Later he began searching the room for Aurora; she had seemed so unnaturally subdued earlier. Then a hand touched his shoulder. 'Michael?' He jumped, turned. It was Dalldorf, legation information officer, controller of propaganda, keeper of the party faith, most dangerous man in the building. 'Michael, good heavens, we haven't seen you here in months! Where have you been hiding yourself?' Always tell the truth, Miller had briefed him, right at the beginning. When engaged in small talk, keep it as accurate as you can for as long as you can. They will ask questions they already know the answers to. To sniff you out.

Michael forced himself to smile. 'Herr Dalldorf, how nice to see you once again. I have been away. I went to stay with relatives of my mother's, working on their estancia in Cerro Largo.'

'Oh, yes, you have mentioned it before. But what of your employers, at Mercantile Atlantic? Did they not mind so lengthy a leave of absence?'

He knew. He knew exactly where he had been, and for how long. Michael's throat, his whole mouth were suddenly parched. 'My job was always of a temporary nature, Herr Dalldorf, and to be honest, rather dull, I'm afraid. I am a country person at heart. My ambition is to have a land-holding of my own.'

'Really? After the war, perhaps.' Dalldorf had rested a hand on Michael's back, was steering him, gently but firmly through the guests towards the rear of the room. Michael felt panic rising like brush fire. He could barely think.

'As soon as possible, Herr Dalldorf. The war is unfortunate, but it is not my war. I believe strongly in Uruguay's neutrality, and therefore, as a Uruguayan, my own.'

They had reached the far corner of the room. A door was set into the wood panelling there. A man in a suit stood guard, hands clasped, before it. Beyond it, Michael sensed, lay oblivion. Dalldorf had stopped smiling.

'Let us be completely frank with one another, Michael. There is no such thing as Uruguay's neutrality, nor anyone's. Here in so-called neutral Montevideo, for example, sympathies are clearly with the British, a fact that has become ever more evident these past few days. That is dishonest. I believe it is time people stopped hiding behind masks of neutrality and declared their loyalties openly. Don't you?'

Sides, Michael, Millington-Drake had said, over and over. It is time for everyone to take sides. Even you. His cheeks were flushed, his collar stiffly tight suddenly at his throat. He glimpsed the distant faces of the guests beyond Dalldorf's shoulder: unseeing, oblivious, idiotic, like penned sheep. 'Herr Dalldorf, it is my earnest hope that a peace can be found from this war. But I genuinely seek no personal involvement in it.'

'As you say.' Dalldorf regarded him closely. 'Why are you here, Michael?'

'I was invited as a guest of Herr Hochstetler's.'

'Dear Willi. And you were at the funeral of our gallant fallen sailors today?'

Don't lie. Not unless you have to. 'Yes, sir. I have acquaintances among the German community here. I attended out of respect. I hope it was appropriate.'

'Quite appropriate.' Suddenly Dalldorf's hand was on Michael's shoulder. 'Today. But not tomorrow. We must all take great care now, Michael, to ensure our words and actions cannot be misinterpreted.' The fingers dug, hard, like talons. 'So, after today, it will no longer be appropriate that we see you here. Or anywhere. Ever. Do you understand me?'

Michael nodded blankly. 'As you wish, Herr Dalldorf.'

Still the hand gripped. Harder, painfully tight. Then with a final shake it released him. 'Good! Tonight, however, you must stay, enjoy the party. I insist. Sadly I must leave you, there are pressing matters to attend to. But please convey my regards to your mother, and be sure to pass my respects to your grandfather, Señor José-Luis Quemada, when next you see him.' He turned, the door opened, then he stopped. 'Oh, and please also pass Señora Quemada my condolences at the sad death of her father.'

With that he was gone, the door closing quietly behind him. Michael, stupified, could only stand and gape. The man at the door sniffed, began paring his nails. Michael turned, forced himself towards the bleating throng, the waiting herd, until it closed about him and he was merging with it once more. He began searching it, hunting among the pasted-on smiles and forced laughter. A glass appeared in his hand, he emptied it, then another, a third. Stunned, disorientated, still he searched. At last he found her, sitting alone upon a window seat.

'Mother! Tata. What has happened?'

'Michael, please, we have to talk.'

'But Tata. Tell me.'

'He is gone, my angel.'

'But, it cannot be. When?'

'Two nights ago. A message came today from Gertrudis. I am so sorry, I know how much this must sadden you. Michael, please, there are things we must discuss . . .'

He pushed through the throng once more to the entrance, stumbled blindly past staring waiters to the stairs, and down to the marble hall. Glass doors led through to a courtyard garden, it was quiet there, the night warm, the garden scented. A little fountain splashed, bougainvillea bloomed along neatly tended beds. He found a seat, slumped on to it, face buried. Irreplaceable. It was all he could think of, all he could comprehend. Tata the irreplaceable, last of the great gauchos, his idol, his anchor, his saviour, his guide. Gone.

'Troubles, my friend?'

It was Langsdorff. Even before he had pulled his face from his hands he knew it. He was half-turned, his back to Michael, studying the fountain, one hand tucked protectively into his uniform jacket. Hit by a shrapnel splinter, he'd overheard at the funeral. During the battle. The range-finding equipment had been knocked out by British gunfire. So Langsdorff had climbed to the foretop, alone and unprotected, to direct *Graf*'s shots himself. Splinters from an exploding shell had hit him in the shoulder and arm. But he'd refused to show it in public, refused to carry it in a sling.

'I . . .' Michael floundered '. . . I just learned that someone dear to me has died, sir. From my family. Someone I loved and admired very much.'

376

'I'm very sorry,' Langsdorff said. 'I know what that feels like. Today I lost thirty-seven people I loved and admired very much.'

'I, forgive me, sir. My problems. They are nothing, compared . . .'

'That is not what I meant, young man, please do not apologise. On board a ship, you see, they are all your family. It is a wonderful thing, that sense of kinship. The Navy is unique in this respect. But if you lose one, or lose a hundred, the pain is the same. Like losing fathers, brothers, sons. Today I lost sons.'

'Yes, sir.'

Water splashed at the fountain. Peels of laughter, the clink of glasses, spilled from upstairs windows.

'And you?'

'My great-grandfather, sir. A very great influence from my earliest childhood.'

'He died at peace, then, I trust. Not at war, like mine.'

'He was very old sir, it is true, and sick. But proud of his warrior heritage.'

'He sounds like a remarkable old gentleman. A Uruguayan?'

'Yes, sir. His name was Don Adrián Rapoza.'

'And yours?'

'Villiers, sir. Michael Villiers. I was born in this country, of a Uruguayan mother. And an English father.'

'I see.' Michael waited, breath held. But Langsdorff seemed unmoved.

'You know, I read that when the first European invaders

arrived in this country, there was no name for it. So for generations it appeared on maps simply as The Profitless Land, because there was no gold and no silver. And yet people came and settled here. They did so for what they could raise with their hands from the soil, not for the riches they might plunder from beneath it. There is more profit in that than in all the gold and silver in the world, no? A life with honour, a people worth defending.'

'My great-grandfather felt that most strongly, sir.'

'I am sure. Because perhaps he knew, in the end, war is about people. Not borders, or territories, or even entire continents. It is about the people who make their homes in these places.'

Langsdorff's back was still to him. 'Will you serve in this conflict, Michael?'

'I, I believe so, sir. I have been thinking of joining the Navy.'

'There is no finer way to serve. It was the Navy that taught me about decency and honour. And a little time yet remains for a man to conduct himself in war with honour. Like your great-grandfather.' He turned to Michael one final time. 'I will leave here, as they ask, and do so in peace with this country. You may tell them that.'

At noon the next day, Saturday, Rex Miller debriefed him. It was a short meeting. Michael explained that he'd learned little from the other guests at the party, as no one had wanted to discuss *Graf*. 'She's an embarrassment to them; my impression is they wish she'd never come, and the sooner she leaves the better. Langsdorff and his officers were made welcome, but only because it would have looked bad to the outside world if they were not.'

'Indeed,' Miller grunted. 'Odd though, they must all know she's had it the moment she's out of neutral waters. It's almost as if they've washed their hands of her. What else?'

'Dalldorf told me in no uncertain terms that I was never to be seen anywhere near the place again.'

'No surprise there. I think it's time you made plans to leave Montevideo, Michael. And soon. Dalldorf's not one to mince his words. Anything else?'

Michael held his gaze. 'I'm afraid not, sir. I left a little early, after I learned from my mother that my great-grandfather had died. It was something of a shock.'

He passed the afternoon on a final six-hour watch in the wheelhouse of his tugboat, now one of the observers' prime positions. A stool had been brought to sit on, paper and pencils, flasks of water. A pair of field glasses hung from a hook. The air smelled strongly of tobacco, the floor littered with cigarette ends. Watching, his chin resting on his arms, as the object of the world's attention swung quietly at anchor, he felt mildly resentful that this, his personal command post, his private place of vigil, had been so violated. Aboard *Graf* there was a marked scaling down of activity. Either the repair work was nearing completion, which seemed impossible after just two days, or it was being called off. Cancelled. As though trying to save her now was a waste of effort. He thought again of Langsdorff and their talk in the courtyard garden. Why had he declined to tell Miller of it? Because it was private, that was why. Not secret, but private. Because, at the end of the day, telling Miller about it would make no difference, to anything. Langsdorff now had less than twenty-four hours to leave with his ship. He was a man of honour. Even knowing the fate that awaited him, he'd keep his word.

At nine he was relieved by one of the runners from Palacio Salvo.

'It's utter mayhem out there!' the youth reported breathlessly, disgorging bags of food on to the floor. 'The whole city's camped out along the harbourfront, you can't hardly move. Music, dancing, lights, bunting, the lot. They've even set up a public address system to keep everyone up to date. There's stalls selling ice-creams, balloons, *Graf Spee* souvenirs, everything. Look, I bought this little periscope thing, for seeing over people's heads. I tell you, it's the world's biggest party!'

'Like the ones they used to hold at public executions.'

'What's that? Oh, yes, rather! By the way, talking of executions, *Renown*'s racing down from Rio to join the three cruisers waiting outside. *Ark Royal*, too, if she can make it. It's going to be one hell of a fight!'

'You think so.' He handed the youth his notes and field glasses, climbed back up to the dock and walked slowly back to his rooms to begin packing.

Aurora was waiting for him. Sitting on the edge of his bed.

'I hope you don't mind, angel, I asked the *portero* to let me in.'

'No, Mother,' Michael sighed. 'I don't mind. But I am very tired. Could this not wait until tomorrow?'

'Of course.' She began to rise. 'It was thoughtless of me, what with Tata, and Maria, and all that must be on your mind.'

Something about her manner stopped him. 'Mother. What is it?'

'Nothing. I wanted to apologise, that's all.'

'For Maria? The other night at the bar?'

'That, yes, in part. I had no right to speak to you as I did. Indeed, I have no right to speak harshly to you about anything.' She looked haggard, suddenly, in the fading light. Gaunt, prematurely aged. She was ordinarily dressed, too, he realised, her face pale and unmade, her thick hair brushed back into a simple clasp at her neck. There was a tremor in her voice he'd not noticed before. A quietness. A sobriety.

'Mother. Please, sit down. What is this about?'

He gave her water. For a while she said nothing, sipping, watching the birds at the balcony, listening to the restless murmur of the crowds below.

'Do you remember,' she began. 'In London. That first winter, before Donald was born?'

'I remember.'

'There was a period, just a few days perhaps, when the fog rolled away, the sun came out and the frost sparkled on the windows like sugar icing. It was still very cold, so cold that sometimes you and I would put all our clothes on, climb into bed, and huddle together in our overcoats for warmth. Down in the street, you took my hand and told me to take small steps, for fear of slipping. The pond froze over in the park, you were entranced at the ducks walking on it. We jumped on frozen puddles. Our noses turned red and our eyes watered. Yet, although it was cold, just for those few days the sky was clear and of the deepest blue I ever saw. Completely different from our skies here. And the afternoon sun hung in the sky like a golden orb, touching everything with the softest yellow. It was quite magical.'

'Yes.'

'You were so brave that winter it made my heart cry out.'

He stayed up late, writing his letters, tidying his belongings, making ready. Then, before dawn, he prepared simple provisions, unlocked his door and descended to the street. Striding quickly through the fading darkness, he headed away from the crowds, out of the old city and north around the bay. The ancient fort, on the hill at Cerro, stood high above the western shore, four kilometres across from the harbour. It took him two hours to walk to it. Circling the whole bay, first along the *rambla*, past the Italian amphitheatre, the railway station, the waterfront petrol refinery at La Teja. Then down on to the stony shore itself, among the driftwood and seaweed, abandoned hulks and decaying jetties. At last, just as the sun was rising over the city behind him, he reached Cerro and began the climb up the rough scrub hillside to the fort.

The scene from the top was all-encompassing. The fort had been skilfully positioned to provide commanding views of the bay, the city, the harbour, the estuary, and on, far out into the ocean beyond. He could see everything, yet was detached from it. A lone observer, like a hovering bird. It was what he wanted. He propped his back against the fort's rough wall and settled down to wait.

Little happened. In the harbour all appeared quiet. To the south, distant smoke betrayed the positions of the three cruisers patrolling the horizon. Apart from these, the climbing of the sun, the circling buzz of aeroplanes and the effortless glide of a hawk traversing the hillside below him, nothing moved.

'There is something that I have to tell you, angel,' Aurora had said the previous night. She'd sat on the edge of his bed, the water glass trembling in her hands, head lowered like a chastened child. 'It is about your father.' Michael had waited. Knowing, somehow, yet not wanting to know. 'Your real father.'

Willi Hochstetler and she, well, they were very close, she said. For some time before she met Keith. Very close. 'I was young, and impetuous, and foolish. And careless . . .'

Around noon he ate a little, folded his jacket under his head, and slept, waking in the afternoon to the indistinct echo of loudspeaker commentary drifting around the bay. The day had grown hot, a sultry heat haze shimmering low over the city. A distant anticipatory murmur rose from ever-thickening crowds now thronging the harbourfront like ants. Beneath him, the glassy brown water of the harbour lay motionless, dotted with anchored ships, tugs and tenders scurrying between them like clockwork toys. *Graf Spee* remained, unmoving in the inner harbour. But there was activity aboard. Awnings had been rigged. A barge had been positioned alongside, on the side away from the dock. Unseen by the multitude on the shore, tiny figures in white, scores, hundreds of them, were descending into it. They were getting off. They were leaving.

He, too.

'What will you do?' Aurora had asked.

'Return to Sombreado. There is nothing more for me here. I want to attend to Tata's funeral, spend time with Maria, and see to the house.'

'Will you stay long?'

'As long as possible. There is much to be done before leaving. Financial arrangements to be finalised, building works to put in hand, livestock to attend to. It is a new beginning for Sombreado, mother.' He hesitated. 'You could come too.'

'Perhaps I could.' She smiled. 'And then?'

'I would like to learn something about medicine. Study it. Also, there is this.' He unfolded a newspaper clipping, handing it to her. 'It is called the RNVR. Mr Millington-Drake told me about it.' The clipping was from a month-old copy of the London *Times*. 'Young men wanted to join Royal Navy Volunteer Reserve,' it said. 'Previous boating experience preferred but not essential.'

'The Royal Navy? Michael, is this really possible?'

'It won't be easy, and will no doubt take months to organise, possibly longer. But I can begin the application process from here, through Mr Millington-Drake, and Father, back in London.'

'No, I mean, is this possible, now that you know who you really are?'

'Knowing that my biological father is German doesn't change who I am, Mother. It complicates matters, yes, but it doesn't alter the way I feel. I am half-English, that is what I feel. I don't believe in war yet I feel I must somehow help. Perhaps in this Volunteer Reserve, and with medical training, perhaps this is how.'

Aurora stared at the clipping. 'I can't believe how calmly you're taking it.'

'Probably, deep down, I suspected something like it. Willi has always tried to be more than just a friend to me. Like an uncle. Lifting me to his shoulders when I was little. Outings in his car. Cards and birthday presents sent over to England. He took an interest in me, always tried to make me feel included. Even lately, sorting out the funding business for Sombreado. He didn't have to do that.'

Something was happening. The tugs and tenders had gone from *Graf*. Everyone must be off, he realised. But not everyone. The sound of her klaxon drifted across the harbour. Smoke curled from her funnel, her great anchor rose, clanking, from the sea bed. A few minutes later, exactly as the sun touched the horizon, her ensign broke out on her main mast and she began to move.

Slowly she inched forwards, turning, carefully manoeuvring around within the tight confines of the inner harbour. Without assistance, without tugs or pilots. Exactly as she had arrived. Michael realised the crowd had fallen quiet; even the tinny blare of loudspeakers had ceased. Three-quarters of a million people watched in silent awe, millions more listening around the world as, at the very instant a brilliant sunset was streaking the sky with jets of gold and pink and violet-green, *Graf Spee* cleared the breakwater and steamed slowly out into the channel.

Unable to watch, unable to turn away, he waited for the end. Barely four miles out and still in plain view, *Graf* turned suddenly to starboard, as though making a feint for Buenos Aires and safety. But it was no feint. She slowed, then stopped, her anchor chain rattling into the sea one last time. The ensign was lowered from her mast, a launch drew up alongside, paused, then pulled away again.

The first detonation erupted from deep within her like a volcano. Other explosions quickly followed. Flames and debris flew high into the air, pursued by a towering black smoke column that climbed and spread out high above her like a smothering blanket. Rings of white water widened from her as with each successive explosion the great ship heaved and twisted in the shallow waters. Then at last the incendiary charges went off and she was quickly engulfed, end to end, in flames, hiding her final self-immolation from view.

It was exactly eight o'clock on the evening of Sunday 17 December 1939.

Chapter 13

Martin Brown told me what happened when Michael joined *Daisy* fourteen months later. I'd already learned how Walter Deeds had been pushing for another first lieutenant to replace the ailing Alan Strang. What he got was Villiers, a sub with as little experience as Brown and Woolley put together. Understandably, he was less than pleased. Worse was to follow.

About three days into their first convoy together Michael asked to speak to Deeds in the wardroom. Martin just happened to be returning from his cabin, the way one is, and overheard their conversation. It went something like this:

Villiers: It's about the duty roster, sir.

Deeds: What about it?

Villiers: I would prefer not to be put in charge of the four-inch gun, sir.

Deeds: Oh? Well, I suppose I could put you aft on the depth-charge rails.

Villiers: I would prefer not to be put on depth charges, either, sir.

Deeds: Why, in heaven's name?

Villiers: It's hard to explain, sir. I'll gladly take on any duty on the ship you ask. But not those. Not guns or depth charges.

Deeds: For God's sake man, I'm not running a Girl Guides picnic here you know! You'll do as you're blasted well ordered.

Villiers: Yes, sir. And I will do anything you ask, sir. But I cannot do that.

Not exactly word for word, but that was the general gist of it. Deeds, by everyone's account, was completely unapproachable for the next week, incandescent with rage, not just at Michael, but at everyone – particularly the powers-that-be for sending him this lunatic. Michael was left high and dry, dutyless, his name struck from the roster altogether. Deeds' sole instruction to him was to stay out of the way until they returned to 'Derry, when he would be kicked off.

But, before that could happen, they all had to spend five weeks in the close confines of a small ship together. That intimate on-board sense of family Langsdorff spoke of is spot on. Sending someone to Coventry on a warship is very difficult. In a Flower class corvette, quite impossible. In any case, Michael was such an oddly likable cove, it wasn't long before the other officers, motivated partly by curiosity no doubt, began to talk to him. And take to him. Eventually the skipper too weakened. For all his bluster, Walter Deeds was not a malicious man. Far from it; he'd already stuck it out with Strang, and spent the best part of a year training up Brown and Woolley. I think he genuinely needed to understand Michael and the curious set of principles by which he chose to live his life. They began to talk.

What Deeds learned was that, in Michael Villiers, not only had he been handed a first-class officer, but the key to making *Daisy* work. Like the vital final missing cog in the machine. His expertise at the navigating table was flawless, he was a meticulous and dependable officer of the watch, and he was a born organiser and administrator, happy to help out with the mountains of paperwork ship's captains are burdened with. The crew liked him. A good listener, blessed with that gift for defusing a situation long before it ever blew up into an issue, he was uncomplicated and honest in his dealings with them. In return, they trusted him, and in placing their trust in him placed it in all the officers. They, too, responded with newfound confidence. In just a few weeks the disparate tangle of threads that made up *Daisy*'s human complement began magically to knit together. Deeds saw this, and even if he didn't fully understand it, was astute enough to recognise that Michael, in some way, was partly responsible.

There was one more thing he recognised. Michael had studied medicine as part of his training. Indeed, he was forever being sent off on top-up courses when *Daisy* was in port. Deeds suddenly had a ship's medical officer who not only knew what he was doing, but in whom he could confide over his heart condition. Angina, so I am told, is not a disease but the symptom of one, such as a defective heart valve or hardened arteries. Acute, debilitating pain spasms and breathlessness that attack from nowhere, angina can be triggered by stress, excitement, physical exertion or nothing at all. But when it does strike it is agonising and incapacitating. Deeds should not have been at sea with it. Later in the war, he wouldn't have been, for eventually nearly all ships were assigned fully qualified MOs – real doctors, in other words, drafted in as ship's officers, rather than the other way round. At the first attack Deeds would have been sent ashore for tests and that would have been that. Michael, I know, would have liked to have seen the skipper properly treated, given the choice. But he wasn't given the choice, and being a crew member first and medic second, accepted his captain's right to decide for himself. Thus the two men came to an understanding. A pact. Michael was spared guns and depth charges, if he kept his trap shut about Deeds' angina.

As for the rest of the wardroom, the issue of Michael's non-shooting status was perplexing to everyone at first. What the hell's the difference? Strang and the others would argue. Who cares who actually pulls the trigger or presses the buzzer? In the end everyone on the ship is involved in trying to attack and kill the enemy. You're right, Michael would smile infuriatingly. Often that was all he would say. Or he might go on to explain how he saw *Daisy*'s main role as being about defending and protecting. About saving lives, not taking them. It was those aspects of her job, he felt, wherein lay his duty.

It was a fine dividing line, he was the first to admit. And

he certainly wouldn't have got away with it in the real Navy. Even as a 'temporary gent' in the RNVR it was an untenable position, which is probably why he kept it to himself until assigned to a ship. Nor could he ever expect promotion from such a standpoint. But that didn't matter: Michael wasn't motivated by promotion, he hadn't joined for a career. Put simply, treading his fine line, like a high-wire artist, allowed him to balance his deeply held beliefs with his equal need to serve. That's all. It was good enough. Pretty soon life aboard settled down, the weeks turned into months, and with *Daisy* at last running like a Swiss watch – we even started winning at intership cricket – everyone quickly grew to accept it.

Nearly everyone. As a Johnny-come-lately to the wardroom, I too found this paradox intriguing when Martin told me of it. I had a go at Michael the night of the party, in St John's. After we sank the U-boat. Then again I probably had a go at everyone that night.

'Is it killing people *per se,* Sub?' I demanded, with gin-fuelled directness. 'Or is it simply killing Germans?'

Michael considered. Our relationship, after seven months closeted together, of sharing the same few square feet of cabin, the same watches, the same highs and lows, everything that comprised existence aboard *Daisy*, was much closer than that of just shipmates. He was my friend. Yet often I felt I hardly knew him at all. 'Both, Stephen,' he said. 'I believe as a matter of principle it is wrong to kill people. I have a particular personal difficulty, however, with the killing of Germans.'

'Because . . .'

'Because by birth, strictly speaking, I am German.'

'Ah.' Oddly, it didn't seem nearly as momentous an admission as you might think. But then I was drunk, and busy attempting to frame the next, crucial question.

'Are there no situations, therefore, that you can imagine, when you might just, conceivably, envisage yourself killing someone?'

Again he pondered. Perhaps recalling a small boy holding a mad Irishman at bay at the point of his *cuchilla*. Or Alonso Peréz. Protecting those closest to him, in other words. His family. 'Possibly,' he conceded. 'But not very easily.'

We steamed home from St John's in triumph two days after the party. Hung over, but in triumph. The group collected a fast inbound convoy off the Grand Banks, we bashed through some fairly wretched weather crossing the gap, lost four ships out of fifty to U-boats, sank none in return, and put into Liverpool twelve days later for a boiler clean, several rounds of congratulatory drinks from Max Horton's staff, and some well-earned leave. It had been an ordinary, almost routine crossing, by the curious standards of the day. But unknown to us, the last happy one *Daisy* would ever make.

The skipper went home, for the first time in months. It was a mistake. Gladys Deeds – she of the spidery handwriting – took one look at her exhausted wreck of a husband, put him straight to bed and called the family doctor. Despite Walter's protestations, an unstoppable chain of events was set in motion that would result in his summons before an Admiralty medical board the next time we were in port.

The board's findings – that his seagoing days were over – were inevitable. But typically slow. Had they arrived a little sooner, before *Daisy*'s final patrol in December, Walter Deeds' life might have been saved.

I, too, went on leave, a rather happier homecoming than his. Striding up the drive, my notebooks and diaries, which for some inexplicable reason I'd decided to take off *Daisy*, tucked safely in my bag, I noted a welcome absence of earlier foreboding. The house was full and gay. Apart from my mother and sisters, by chance both my father, by now a fully fledged commander, and my grandfather, the retired rear admiral, were also there. It was not the ordeal I had once feared so greatly. They were both undemanding, respectful of my need to spend time alone and to talk only of so much and no more. They understood it, simply because they had both experienced it, something I had never appreciated before. There was now a common connection between us. Of course there was also a certain amount of lantern swinging, too. Once the ladies had left us after dinner of an evening, the three famous sailors, sitting around the fire swirling brandies, tongues would loosen, anecdotes, stories, confessions, emerge. Emotions, even. I finally spoke of the hollowness I felt following the sinking of the U-boat. Both nodded, my grandfather, the consummate warrior, confessing he'd felt the same watching a German cruiser going down in the First War. There is little joy to be had, my father added, in watching the death of a ship and her crew, even if they are the enemy. Late another night he said something else unexpected:

'I probably pushed you too hard, you know, Steve. When you were younger. Family tradition is a terrible burden sometimes. When all this war nonsense is over, if you decide you want to come out of the Service, and lead some other life, you know I won't stop you.'

I recognised then, with his own father sitting, slightly aghast across the room, that he too understood the misery of unfulfilled expectation.

Leave over, I returned to *Daisy* the afternoon we were due to sail. Most of the officers and crew were already back aboard. Including Deeds, feet up in the wardroom. 'Don't ask,' he growled from behind his newspaper, when I enquired after his leave.

Michael was aboard, showing his father and brother around. I had heard about them, many times of course, but never met them. Keith Villiers, fifty, rake-thin, diffident, smiling politely yet utterly bemused by it all. Young Donald, twelve or thirteen, dark and stout, irrepressible, charging hither and thither, mad with excitement. 'She's so huge!' he kept shouting, while us old lags exchanged amused glances. After the tour, Michael brought them into the wardroom for tea. We all pulled ourselves up a bit, even Strang. Deeds especially made them welcome. 'I can do Morse code, sir!' Donald told him proudly. 'Good for you, lad, try some of Mrs Woolley's ginger cake.' It was an oddly touching scene, the three Villiers men squashed together up at the end of the table. I sensed much more than simple affection. Keith, the man Michael chose to call father, yet who was completely unrelated to him. And the effervescent half-brother nine years

394

his junior. They weren't his, really, in many ways. Weren't his people, his responsibility. Yet he had made them his, and thus his reason for being in this war. The strength of the bond between them was evident to us all.

The two of them, Keith and Donald, watched, standing on the quay beneath leaden November skies, as we sailed. Night was falling, a blustery wind blew cat's-paws across the greasy water of the dock. Just as we were passing through the dock gate, they both waved.

'Yeoman,' Deeds said suddenly. 'Aldis lamp. Those two standing there on the quay. Send this. Slowly, mind you. Send: 'Goodbye from *Daisy*.''

That night, with *Daisy* bouncing north through the short seas of the Irish Sea, I settled down to sort through the mail sack, dumped on board by the harbour-master's office shortly before we'd sailed. For me there was a telegram from my father. He wished me a safe passage, the first such communication of its sort I'd ever received from him. I still have it. Among the stacks of other letters was another telegram, this one for Michael. It was a week old, post-marked from Montevideo.

He was lying on his bunk, resting before going on watch at midnight, when I gave it to him. He read it, read it again, then folded it back into its envelope. 'I'm sorry about this, Stephen,' he said. 'But when we get to Nova Scotia, I'm going to have to leave the ship.'

Late in the afternoon, just an hour or so before the onset of night, the clouds over *Daisy*'s lifeboat began at last to lift, and break, solidifying from a featureless grey pall into discernable shapes and shades. As they did so the visibility returned, the sea taking on a pewter-like hue, while heaped cumulus shower clouds emerged from low on the horizon like mist-shrouded hills. There was no sun, as such, but shafts of silver-grey pierced the overcast far to the west.

Not that we noticed. Snow-covered, sodden, chilled to the marrow, the effort of staying awake, and therefore alive, was hourly growing more burdensome. Blackness beckoned in ever-more seductive welcome. In those latitudes, in January, night lasts for more than sixteen hours, temperatures can plummet to ten or more degrees below freezing, lower still once you factor in wind chill. We were in an unprotected open boat, wet through and inadequately clothed. We had already spent half of one night and all of one day in such conditions and barely made it through. Now, with the second night in prospect, despair, or more properly, indifference, was setting in with a vengeance.

Only Giddings seemed unwilling to let go. Young Albert Giddings, whose terrified screams had drawn us all together in the first place.

'Sub? Sub! Shouldn't we be playing another game, sir? Or having another one of them discussions, or something? Sir! Wake up! Tell us about *Graf Spee* and all that again, please. Sir?' On and on he went. 'Here, Frank! Harrison, look over there! I can see something. Over there, look, for God's sakes! Here, Mid, what's that? No, look, really. Over there!'

Slowly, we'd shift cramped, feelingless limbs, turn cracked eyes to the horizon, and look, as bidden. But always it was nothing. A piece of driftwood perhaps, a wandering seabird, a shadow on the waves. Nothing. Recrimination would follow:

'How many bloody times do I 'ave to tell you, Giddings, there is nothing there! Now for Christ's sake put a bloody sock in it and leave us in peace!'

'It *was* something! It was, I'm sure of it. Look again, do!'

'I'm warning you, Giddings—'

'Leave him alone, why can't you?' Harrison croaked. 'You've been going on at him all day.'

'Oh, 'ark, the leading signalman speaks! And who the hell rattled your cage all of a sudden?'

'Christ, but you're a whining bastard, Tuker. No wonder everyone on blue watch hated the bloody sight of you.'

'Why, you snivelling little shit, 'ow dare you speak to me like that—'

'Did they?' I couldn't resist joining in. I hated him pretty much too. In any case, perhaps we all knew, except Giddings, that we were just playing out the hand, making a few final token throws of the dice, before we gave it up for good. 'Did they really all hate you, Frank?'

'No, they bloody did not! I was extremely popular, among the older hands 'specially. You ask any of them, Wally Stitt, Ernie Dixon, any of 'em!'

'How can we, you idiot, they're all dead.'

'We have to warn them!' Villiers said, suddenly.

'What? Warn who?'

'The escort, we have to warn them.' They were the first words he'd spoken in ages. Hugging himself, deathly pale, the top of his *boina* and shoulders of his leather jerkin frosted white with snow. 'If *Vehement* has sent one back to look for us, we cannot just sit here and allow her to be blown up like *Daisy*. We can't allow it. We have to find a way to warn her.'

There was a pause. Tuker caught my eye. For the first time all day our thoughts were in accord. Michael was becoming delirious.

''Ow d'you think we ought to go about doing that, then, Sub?' Frank asked gently, as though humouring a confused pensioner.

'I don't know, I don't know.'

'Do you really think someone's coming?' Giddings asked, ever hopeful.

'I, I don't know that, either. I've been trying to think. But it's so cold.' He struggled into a more upright position. 'But if they are, we have to do something to warn them off. We, we've only got about an hour. After that it'll be dark and it won't matter any more because they'll never find us. We must think of something. Try and warm up a bit. Mid? Stephen? What have we got left to eat?'

'Plenty.' I began crawling painfully forward. 'I'll look in the bow locker.'

'Good. See what else is in there we might use to make a warning.'

'There's the flares, sir,' Harrison said. 'And I've still got the signalling lamp.'

'Yes, yes, that's good, but how do we use them without the U-boat seeing?'

With fingers like sodden cardboard, I fumbled at the

catches on the bow locker. I, too, had been pondering that point, on and off. The U-boat captain had it well planned. He was waiting, somewhere in the vicinity, just below the surface at periscope depth. Too shallow for good Asdic contact, yet too deep for radar. Practically undetectable, in other words, which is exactly what he wanted. The moment we started firing off flares or flashing lamps, he'd know we'd spotted a rescue ship. The ship, meanwhile, would assume we were just trying to attract its attention. All the U-boat had to do was sit tight, wait until she was a few hundred yards off, then let go at point-blank range. He couldn't miss.

'What about a noise? Fog horn or something?' Tuker suggested.

'Yes, but we don't have a blooming fog horn, do we, Frank.'

'It was only an idea, Harrison, you tosspot!'

'No, wait, Frank, it's a very good one!' Villiers fumbled at his life vest. 'The whistles! On the lifebelts. They'd only work over short distances, of course, but the U-boat wouldn't hear them, not at all.'

'See!' Tuker crowed.

'Not much in here, Sub.' I called, head in locker. Apart from the food and water rations, of which there were plenty, the locker held an assortment of odds and ends. Lengths of rope, fishing lines and hooks, a canvas sea anchor and warp, the flares, a signalling mirror – useful in broad daylight and on a sunny day, perhaps. First Aid kit, compass, binoculars . . .

'But, sir,' Giddings was saying, 'what if we do manage to warn off the rescue ship? I mean, what'll happen? Won't they just turn round and leave us?'

Of course they would. That was the whole idea. But at least they'd be saved. I'd assumed we'd all worked that out. But Giddings evidently had not. To my surprise it was Frank Tuker who set the boy's mind at rest.

'No, lad, don't be daft! They stand off, see, call up reinforcements, then come in and blow the bugger to hell. Then before you know it, we're all tucked up snug in some nice fuggy mess with a fag and a tot, you'll see.'

There was a box. At the bottom of all the ropes and junk in the locker. A rectangular wooden box, like an oversized cutlery chest, neatly made with reinforced brass corners and a hinged lid secured with a hasp and padlock.

'Sub,' I called. 'I think I might have found something.'

Michael left *Daisy* the moment we docked at Halifax, Nova Scotia. Ten days after I'd handed him the telegram from Montevideo. It was to do with his mother, was all he had explained. She was ill. The telegram had come from someone called Hochstetler.

Deeds, curiously, was more upset than angry. To all intents and purposes Michael was deserting. As captain, Deeds had every legal right to summon the coxswain and two armed men, arrest Michael and cart him back to England under lock and key. But he didn't, and that had to do with the mechanics of their relationship. Yet he was hurt, their parting more like the reluctant separating of a father from his son. A cheerless farewell took place around the wardroom table. We were all in there, when Michael came in, kitbag in hand.

'Will you be coming back?' Deeds asked simply.

'I don't know, sir.'

'How will you travel?' Strang asked.

'Scheduled air services through the United States. Then, I believe the US Army Air Force operate military transport aircraft down as far as Natal in Brazil. Trains run from there through to Montevideo.'

'Got enough money, old thing?' Dick Woolley, ever the accountant.

'Yes, thank you, Dick.'

'I will have to report this, Michael,' Deeds said. 'You do know that.'

'Yes, I do, sir.'

We shook his hand, all of us, rather solemnly, and watched him walk up the gangplank and out of our lives. It felt like losing a brother.

He left Nova Scotia in the icy depths of winter, arriving late one evening nine days later in a Montevideo gripped by a midsummer heat wave. He checked into a hotel in Pocitos then went straight to Willi Hochstetler's house.

'Oh, Señor Miguel!' the maid, Hortensia, greeted him anxiously. 'Quickly, she is in the hospital.'

Willi was there, hunched on to a chair at the end of a large ward, mopping perspiration from his brow. The ward was clean, but stiflingly hot, heavy with the stench of disinfectant, and crawling with flies. Visibly relieved to see him, Willi rose, tightly clasping Michael's hand.

'Thank God you came! She's been asking for you for days.'

'What happened?'

'It is her blood. It became infected. Several weeks ago. The doctors tried, there was some early success, we thought she was recovering, but then the fever took hold. Now she is very weak.'

'How long?'

'They don't know. A day or two, not more.'

Michael sat, gently taking her limp hand in his. Aurora stirred, eyes fluttering, then sank once more into unconsciousness. She was barely recognisable, her arms thin and emaciated, the sunken skin of her cheeks ghostly pale. 'That it should come to this, Mama,' he murmured, lightly brushing her hair back with his fingers.

They stayed together, Michael, his two parents, through the night. Outside, the air hung humid and unmoving. Bats fluttered at the casement. Familiar restless city sounds drifted to the window. Aurora's breathing grew deeper. Between silences, he and Willi talked a little, of the past, of the paths their lives had led, of what might have been.

'I failed you both!' Willi wept, inconsolably, at one point. 'I loved her, with all my heart, Michael. And you, too, in my way I loved you. I should have been honourable, been honest, with you, with everyone. I wanted to, wanted to make a worthy home, an honest family for you both. But I am weak, I know that. I had not the courage.'

'It is not all your fault, Willi.'

'Yes it is! It is all my fault. Your father, he was the honourable one, the courageous one. We were friends. I betrayed that friendship. Did you know, I tried to tell him, tell your father, Michael? After they were married, after you were born, still just a baby. I tried to tell him that this was all my fault, my responsibility. But I failed, even in that!'

'He knew, Willi. He told me quite recently. I think perhaps he guessed long ago. But for him, you know, it made no difference. He made a commitment, and stood by it. That is the way he is.'

'He is a good, good man. I betrayed him.'

Silence, save for the sighs and laboured breathing of other patients, fell for a while. Later Aurora stirred again, struggling, incoherent with terror, briefly to consciousness. They calmed her, gave her water, bathed her brow; gradually she quietened, sinking once more on to her sweat-drenched pillow. Across the ward someone groaned in agony.

'We can't let it end here,' Michael said, fanning flies from her face. 'I won't. Hospitals always frightened her. Have her family visited?'

'Yes. Her mother several times. I feel they are reconciled.'

'Good. Then we must act quickly.'

'You want to move her to their house in Prado?'

'No. We must get her to Sombreado. Right away. It is what she would want. Can you arrange transportation?'

'Michael, it is too late for that.'

'Perhaps, but we must try.'

They left at dawn, Michael carrying his mother's wasted body down to a motor ambulance in the street, Willi's Mercedes parked behind. Michael rode with Aurora, watching through the window, her hand in his, as the grey city landscape slowly gave way to ramshackle wooden *barrios*, then trees and fields, then finally the summer-baked pampas. They made good progress: with luck they would arrive before nightfall. 'It used to take three days to reach Sombreado when I was a girl,' Aurora would tell him proudly, like a teacher. 'Today, with motor transport, proper dirt roads and good weather, the journey can be accomplished in one. Uruguay is a model of twentieth-century modernity.' It was one of her favourite sayings.

She died as they were crossing into Cerro Largo. Gazing through the open window at an increasingly familiar landscape of rolling green, the smell of warm grass and red earth on the wind, he felt a tightening of her hand in his. He looked down. Her eyes were open. She was smiling. He knelt beside her on the rocking floor of the ambulance.

'Sombreado?' she mouthed, her brown eyes girl-like suddenly, wide with expectation.

'Yes, Mother. Sombreado.'

She pulled him closer then, until their cheeks touched, and her lips brushed his ear. 'Angel,' she whispered. 'Angel.'

They buried her in the peach orchard, close to where Tata had been laid to rest beside his wife, Matilde. A Quemada contingent drove up from Montevideo for the simple ceremony: José-Luis, Florentina, Aurora's brothers and their wives. These last did not stay long, their embarrassment and discomfort polluting the clear scented air of the orchard. Michael shared their relief when they left early the following morning. Willi followed later in the day, broken, bewildered. Michael walked him to his Mercedes, accepting his awkward embrace in silence. With Aurora's death, he realised, there was nothing more for them to say.

Only Florentina stayed, evidently with a longer visit in mind. Michael helped Carles carry a bulky trunk into her old childhood bedroom. Beside her sister's. By the evening calm had returned, Sombreado was theirs once again. They ate, everyone together, at the long dining table. The sisters Florentina and Gertrudis, Carles and Francesca Luenga, and Michael and Maria, their fingers tightly entwined beneath the table. The mood was reflective, contemplative. Quiet. But not grieving. Afterwards, Maria took his arm and led him down through grassy paddocks of criollo yearlings and new Holstein heifers.

'They are doing well?'

'Very well. The milk is unusually sweet and the yield encouraging.'

'What of the Herefords? The main herd, out on the plain?'

'The herd thrives, Miguelito, do not worry, all goes well.' She hesitated. 'How long do you have?'

'All my life. I want us to be married. Right away.'

'Yes, I too.'

They kissed. The warmth of her embrace, the softness of her lips, was as it had always been. Yet already he ached for its loss. He broke away.

'What is it, Miguelito?'

'It has been so long. This war, it is interminable. What if it just goes on?'

'Then we shall wait, and we shall be together when it is over.'

'You have that strength?'

'I waited for ten years, once, remember?' she teased. 'One or two more is nothing. And you?'

'I don't know. Sometimes it is as if it will never end, as though it is my destiny to be a part of it for ever.'

She had never seen him like this before. So drained, so full of doubt. She kissed him again, harder this time, her fingers gripping his back, her breath hot on his mouth, willing him with her strength. 'You are Charrúa, remember. And a Rapoza. Your spirit travelled here across the world with the first great wanderers. Your ancestors settled and prospered here in fear of no man, and as free as the wind. You are strong and I am with you, as I have always been, since we were brought together as babies. Tonight we will lie together, tomorrow we will arrange to become man and wife, and in a few short months we will be together for ever. Do you understand this?'

He allowed himself a week, just enough time to arrange a civil marriage ceremony at the *ayuntamiento* in Melo. It was a tiny affair, just the Luengas, Gertrudis and Florentina in attendance. Afterwards they all returned to Sombreado in the new Ford automobile Florentina had bought. 'We cannot possibly manage an estancia efficiently without decent motorised transportation!' she protested, sounding exactly like Aurora. There was more. After a wedding lunch of ceviche, rolled beef *matambre* and Francesca's famous *dulce de lece*, Gertrudis produced a bottle of Tata's favourite *caña* rum.

'As you know,' she began, pouring the pale liquid into tiny glasses, 'Don Adrián, our father, bequeathed Sombreado to my sister Florentina and I. As you also know, I have no children. In the fullness of time, therefore, the estancia would have passed to Florentina's children, that is Aurora, and her two brothers. However, both Domingo and Enriqué indicated years ago they had no interest in assuming responsibility for this place, and were happy to relinquish it to their sister.

'Florentina and I are agreed it is right to inform you of this today, your wedding day, Miguel. Upon Aurora's sad passing, and in accordance with her authorised wishes, Sombreado is bequeathed to her sons, Michael George José-Luis Quemada Villiers, and Donald Adrian Villiers. There are no safer hands into which this place could pass.' She upended her glass, downed it in one, banging it on to the table with a satisfied gasp. 'Tell me, Miguel. Your brother, Donald. He is skilled on horseback?'

Michael and Maria parted for the final time two mornings later, riding out to the *ombú* tree to watch the dawn together.

'This is where we began,' he said, drawing her to him. The last stars still glowed dimly overhead. Dew glistened at their feet. Across the plain, mist patches melted into the air, like fleeing spirits.

'This is where we shall go on, Miguelito. And where we shall finish.'

'I will always love you, Maria.'

'And I you, always. Be sure to remember this should your resolve weaken.'

He returned to Montevideo and began making arrangements for his journey north. But there was one final matter to attend to before departing. Briefly, he paid his respects to Eugen Millington-Drake, Rex Miller and the others at the British legation. He and Millington-Drake, now Sir Eugen, newly knighted for his role in the *Graf Spee* drama, dined together at the ambassador's residence on Avenida Jorge Canning. Inevitably the talk was of the battle and its unforeseen denouement.

'By the way, what happened to *Graf*'s crew?' Michael asked towards the end of the evening. 'I watched them disembark during the Sunday, before *Graf* sailed. Then I heard they were ferried to Buenos Aires. But what happened to them then?'

'Interned in Argentina. There were more than a thousand of them, too. Initially, the ratings were confined in the immigrants' hostel in BA, with the officers under very loose house arrest in the naval arsenal. Basically they could come and go as they pleased, so not surprisingly many of them went. Some have already made it home to Germany and are back in the war. The rest, which is well over nine hundred, are interned here and there. Some are on the island of Martin Garcia, others in a camp in Florencio Varela, the remainder spread out over the country. They're comfortable enough; the Argentinians have no axe to grind with the German Navy.'

'Are there none left in BA?'

'Just one. So I believe. One of the engineering officers, Höpfner, I think his name is. He's been ill, getting medical treatment at the hospital there. He works part-time for the naval attaché at the German legation. Why do you ask?

Wouldn't be thinking of paying him a visit, would you, Michael?'

He took the morning ferry, passing en route the single black wreck-buoy marking the spot where *Graf*'s twisted remains lay, barely covered by the shallow waters of the Plate. Arriving in Buenos Aires in the afternoon, he took a cab through the busy streets to the huge Cementerio de la Chacarita, off Avenida Córdoba. There, after a little difficulty, he found the German section and finally the simple raised plinth with stone cross that he sought. With the third anniversary of the drama just days away, the grave was already heavily bedecked with flowers.

Höpfner was there, waiting at attention before the grave, a slight man in an ill-fitting suit, his hatless head lowered. Michael, too, wearing his sub-lieutenant's uniform, came to attention, and saluted.

'Thank you for coming, Commander,' he said to Höpfner, after a while.

The German's eyes were moist. 'Shall we walk, Herr Lieutenant. I do not like to come to this place.'

Langsdorff, Michael learned, had been the last man off *Graf* before she blew up. He had planned to stay aboard, go down with his ship, but his officers contrived to save his life, insisting it was his duty to see the crew to safety. Reluctantly, Langsdorff accompanied the tugs and barges laden with his men to Buenos Aires. Once there he appealed to the Argentine authorities to treat them with respect, and in accordance with convention, an assurance that was granted. As soon as this was confirmed and he'd satisfied himself his crew were properly fed and quartered, he made his final preparations. The next day he addressed them in the grounds of the immigrants' hostel. He thanked them for their loyalty, reassuring them that they had discharged their duty to ship and country with distinction, and that they were now in good hands.

That night he dined with his senior officers, by all accounts in good heart, retired late to his room, unfolded *Graf*'s naval ensign about him, and shot himself.

'It was not his fault and it should not have happened,' Höpfner said, shaking his head.

'No. A tragic end for a man of such integrity. Do you believe he felt honour-bound to take his life, Commander?'

'There was no more honourable man in the Navy. As for taking his life, he was driven to it. He served his leaders loyally and courageously, yet they condemned him for a coward.'

'For bringing *Graf* into Montevideo? For destroying her?'

'For not returning outside to fight the British ships. Yet this option was never open to him, and they knew it.'

'What do you mean?'

Höpfner regarded him then. They were seated on a bench not far from Langsdorff's grave. A fitful wind, warm and moist, blew leaves among the rows of headstones. 'Who are you, Herr Lieutenant? Why do you come here with your questions? I have answered all the questions. Many times. Yet still you come. British Intelligence, German Intelligence, American Intelligence, I am sick of it, I tell you, and will talk of it no more!'

Michael stood, brushing dust from his cap. 'I understand, Commander, and will not trouble you further. I came here in uniform not as a military representative, but out of respect for Captain Langsdorff. He was of great help and influence to me at a difficult time. He was also instrumental in my decision to join the Navy. I will always be grateful to him for that.'

'But you are in the British Navy.'

'Yes. It is a little complicated, but it makes no difference, he understood that. He said the Navy is like a family, and that there is no finer way to serve your country. I believe he is right.' He reached out, gripping Höpfner's hand. 'Thank you for your time, Commander; may I offer you a lift back to your legation?'

'Just one minute, Herr Lieutenant.'

Pennsylvania, USA
24/12/42

Dear Donald

I am writing this to you on a train, travelling north across America. Please excuse the rather shaky handwriting therefore.

By now you and Father will have received my telegram about Mother's passing. I am sorry to have brought you this sad news. Mama had been fighting illness for some time, indeed much of her life was about struggle, both within, and with those about her. I can only tell you that when she died she was at peace, knowing she was returning to the place she was happiest in her life. Now thankfully her struggles are over and she is at rest there.

You never knew her very well, Don, being so young when she left.

I'm not sure I knew her much better. She could be so funny, so full of life and laughter. Also, I am quite certain, she loved us both. I promise you that. But she was driven by forces outside her control, and in the end these forces overwhelmed her. I believe it was a kind of illness; perhaps one day doctors might be able to treat it.

Sombreado was naturally a little sad, and I was there for too short a time. But even so, it was wonderful to see the Luengas, Aunt Gertrudis, and all the new animals and exciting developments taking place. There are important developments affecting you, too. You will hear about them in due course. I think you'll be pleased.

Something else I hope will please you is the news that I am married to Maria Luenga. It was a little rushed, but something we had planned for a long time. Even though we were parted almost immediately, and must remain apart for some time to come, we felt strongly that we wanted to marry now. I am very proud and happy she is my wife. She says she is greatly looking forward to meeting her new brother-in-law, (that's you!) and hopes one day before long you will come to Uruguay. Perhaps when the war is over.

The war. It is interminable, Don. Sometimes I believe I cannot endure another day. I once asked Tata what it was like to fight in a war without limit. He said simply that freedom has no limits. Is this a just war? A right war? I don't know any more. It has passed beyond the bounds of right and justice, now it seems it is just about killing. We must make sure, <u>you</u> younger people must make sure, when it is finally over, that something like this never happens again.

I confess I feel old and weary. This train is full of young American airmen. Bomber crews, on their way to a place called Nebraska to complete their training. Then they will be sent to England to fly *raids over Germany. Their war is only just beginning, they are very young and full of eagerness. I feel like a tired old man in their presence!*

It is Christmas Eve. In a week it will be 1943. Let us hope it is the last year of war in our lifetimes. Have a very happy Christmas, Donald. My thoughts and best wishes are with you.

With love, Michael.

He read it through, sealed it into an envelope and wrote the address, bracing himself against the rocking of the train. Outside it was dark, rivulets of rain streaked back across the windows. An airman, a dark-haired American in officer's uniform, was sitting opposite, reading a book.

'Excuse me,' Michael asked. 'Excuse me, Lieutenant . . .'

The man looked up. 'Hooper. John Hooper. Can I help you?'

'I wonder, Lieutenant, I need to get this in the post, rather urgently, but I'm not sure I'm going to be able to, before rejoining my ship that is. I was wondering . . .'

'Would you like me to mail it for you? It'll be no trouble.'

'I'm afraid I don't have the postage.'

The man smiled. 'It's no problem. Don't worry, I'll see to it.' He took the letter, tucking it into his bag. 'You're English.'

'I, well, it's complicated, but, yes, blow it, I am English.'

'That uniform, excuse me, that's Navy, right? But those rings, on your sleeves, they're unusual. Is it submarines?'

'No, not submarines.' Michael fingered the undulating braid band. 'This signifies the Volunteer Reserve. They call it the Wavy Navy.'

'Wavy Navy, I like that.' Hooper, who had dark watchful eyes, smiled again. 'Your war. In the Navy. Forgive me for asking this. How is it?'

'It's getting very hard.'

'What's this bloody gubbins, then, Sub?' Deeds asked suspiciously.

'It's called a Holman's Projector, sir. An anti-aircraft device, sir.'

'It looks like a drainpipe with a bit of hose attached to it.'

'Yes, sir, well, I suppose that is what it is, more or less.' Dick Woolley fingered the contraption nervously, the rest of us looking on. It was an apt description. The pipe, about 6 feet long and 4 inches in diameter, was bolted to *Daisy*'s rail, pointing skywards. Its base was fitted into a compression chamber, fed by an air line. On the deck nearby lay a rectangular wooden box. And a bucket. Of potatoes.

'Woolley, please tell me this is some kind of practical joke.'

'No sir, not at all. It's the latest thing in anti-aircraft measures, sir, the boffins dreamed it up.' He produced what appeared to be an empty baked-bean tin. 'What happens, sir, is you charge the thing by feeding compressed air into the cylinder at the bottom. Then, you take a standard issue hand grenade, pull out the pin, put the grenade into this tin can here, drop it down the tube, and fire it into the air. At the diving enemy aircraft. At least that's what the handbook says. Sir.'

Deeds, squat and bulky in his duffel coat and lifebelt, his

revolver slung about his neck, turned to survey the endlessly rolling ocean. The convoy, lines of ships in every direction, ploughed faithfully along beside us, as always. We were returning to Halifax, completing our first patrol since Villiers had left us nearly four weeks earlier. One unspoken question was on all our minds. Would he be there in Nova Scotia to meet us?

Things had not gone well in his absence, although perhaps this was more to do with bad luck than anything else. Bad luck and fatigue. We seemed to be permanently at action stations. In two crossings our group had lost twelve ships without sinking a single U-boat. Other groups' losses were equally bad. Enigma was still blacked out, so we were woefully short of clues as to what the enemy was up to. Admiral Horton, under growing pressure from Churchill, was on the rampage, taking it out on everybody, especially his officers. Shake-ups were afoot. Martin Brown, we had just learned, was being promoted and sent to another escort group. Strang, too, to his obvious consternation, was also up for transfer. I was to be made up to sub-lieutenant in the New Year, although whether I would be staying with *Daisy* was unclear. Villiers, despite an appeal from Deeds for compassionate leniency, was in deep trouble for jumping ship, and the skipper himself, unknown to us all, had just failed his Admiralty board medical.

But if the mood in the officers' wardroom was sombre, below decks it was downright dangerous. At work, there was a general absence of care and attention to detail. A sure sign of poor morale. Mistakes were made, some potentially

415

serious. Crewmen turned up on duty late, or even not at all. The number of defaulters dragged up before the captain every Sunday trebled. Disputes, even fights, were rife. An ugly incident blew up involving a stoker and his watch leader. Knives were drawn before the two men were dragged from one another. The morning we sailed from Londonderry, three of *Daisy*'s crew failed to return after a night on the tiles and were now, as was Villiers, officially AWOL.

It was exhaustion, I believe, putting it simply. Bone-crushing, mind-numbing, will-sapping exhaustion. In short, we had been doing it for too long with too little respite. But there was no respite to be had, because there was no one to replace us. The never-ending conveyor belt that was North Atlantic convoys could not stop, even for a moment. It just rolled on and on. Or it broke, and broke Britain with it.

'Dick,' Deeds said finally, his voice heavy with resignation. 'Are you really telling me, in all seriousness, that Western Approaches Command has approved this ridiculous peashooter of a contraption as a genuine countermeasure against attacking aircraft?'

'Well, yes, sir. It seems they have. Would you like to see it working?'

'I don't know. Would I?'

'We've been trying it out, sir. It shoots them for miles.'

'Hand grenades?'

'Well, no, sir. Potatoes.'

'Potatoes.'

'Yes, sir. We thought we ought to try it with something

other than live grenades, first, sir. Just until we got the hang of it.'

'Very prudent. Do you not think, however, unless you're proposing to try and down a Stuka with a King Edward, that perhaps you should try it with the real thing?'

It was bad, but could have been very much worse. Woolley opened the wooden box lying on the deck. Inside nestled twelve hand grenades, each in its own little compartment, each carefully wrapped in grease paper, rather like Christmas tree baubles. Dick selected one, putting his finger through the ring. As one, the rest of us stepped back a pace. With a nod to the crewman rather nervously holding the baked-bean tin, Dick pulled the pin and dropped the grenade into it. The crewman hurriedly fumbled the container into the end of the pipe, it slid to the bottom with a satisfactory clunk and Woolley gave the word.

'Fire!'

'Not ready yet, sir!' came an anguished cry from the man at the compressor.

'What!'

'Pressure's not up yet, sir!'

'Well, fire it anyway for God's sake, there's a live grenade down there!'

There was a rather lacklustre 'pifft' sound, like air from a ruptured bicycle tyre. A moment later the baked-bean tin made a half-hearted appearance at the top of the tube, flopped out and clattered to the deck. Rooted to the spot, we watched in horror as the grenade tumbled from it and went rolling away along the scuppers.

'Cover!' Deeds bellowed, hurling himself to the deck. But we were already running. Then there was a monumental bang. I turned just in time to see the meat locker, a large steel box welded to the deck to store our fresh meat, flying overboard, joints of salt beef and strings of sausages trailing after it.

How no one was killed or seriously injured I'll never know. There were cuts and bruises, Woolley sprained a wrist diving for cover, and blood poured from a rating's cheek from a piece of flying metal. Apart from that, and the loss of all our fresh meat of course, we had escaped unscathed. The captain, however, was unamused.

'Never, ever, *ever*, in all my born days, have I witnessed such a useless, dangerous, ill-conceived bastard of a contraption aboard a ship!' he roared, shaking with fury. 'Sub-Lieutenant Woolley, you will dismantle that thing, right now, and throw it over the side. You will then lock and secure that box of grenades, as far as possible from anywhere it might do harm, until we return to 'Derry, when we will hand it in and file a report. I want those things off my ship, do you understand me?'

So Dick got them off the ship. He put them in the forward storage locker of the port whaler. Even as we opened the box, levering the lock with Villiers' *cuchilla*, I knew, we all knew, staring down at those eleven carefully wrapped bundles, that in that instant everything had changed.

Michael, too. He seemed suddenly relieved, as though a decision had been made for him, a difficult problem solved.

He was calm, focused. He took complete control, outlining in just a few minutes what it was we all had to do, and when, and how. Even when, right at the very last moment, with the daylight dwindling to dusk, the ever-razor-eyed Albert Giddings spotted the distant speck of a ship far away on the black horizon; even then he was ready, swiftly adjusting his plan to suit the changing circumstances.

Just wave. The U-boat commander had instructed. If you change your mind, if you want anything, just wave and we'll come. So we waved. And he came. In fact, with *Lily* still nothing more than a far-off smudge, we did better than wave. We signalled. The single letter 'U'. In three different ways. He'll think we're calling him, Michael said. He'll think we're calling 'U-boat'. 'U,' he said. Just keep signalling the letter 'U'. So we signalled. Will Harrison flashing it out steadily in Morse with the signal lamp, dit-dit-dah. Young Albert, standing precariously beside him, an oar in each hand, handkerchiefs tied to the ends. Raising and lowering them, his arms outstretched at forty-five degrees, the semaphore signal for 'U'. And me, blowing on the whistle of my lifebelt for all I was worth. Two short blasts, one long one. Two short blasts, one long one. U-U-U, until our ears rang with it. Frank waited at the oars, ready to pull us into position the instant the monster rose.

And it rose. We called it and it came, boiling from the depths just like before.

'Now, Frank!' Michael shouted. 'Come round, round more! We have to get closer, we have to position him between us and the ship.' U-U-U. Seawater spewed from the conning tower scuppers, the ocean stopped boiling, she was up, fully surfaced, black and glistening in the gathering dusk. Any minute the hatch would open, the heads would appear and the game would be over. But *Lily* was getting nearer. U-U-U, just keep flashing, Michael said, keep blowing, keep waving. Do anything to keep his attention.

The hatch was open, the heads appearing. 'What do you want?' the German's voice shouted over the loud-hailer. 'I can see you, what do you want?' Two men were running forward along the submarine's deck to the eighty-eight millimetre gun, exactly as before. Another appeared in the conning tower, struggling with something heavy. Was he bringing the machine-gun? 'What do you want?' the captain asked again, bemused by the madmen in the rowing boat. Closer, Frank, bring us in closer, Michael urged. And keep signalling, don't stop, not for anything. U-U-U. Forty yards, thirty-five. 'What do you want?' U-U-U. Twenty-five. A cricket pitch. Close enough.

Now.

Michael is standing, feet braced, at the stern of the whaler, his *boina* on his head, his *facón* at his belt. Around the neck of his leather jerkin hangs a white rope lanyard, the lanyard of the revolver he took from the floating body of his dead friend and captain. Almost in slow motion, he raises the weapon in both hands, aims and fires. A loud metallic 'ping' as the bullet strikes the conning tower. Surprise, shock from the faces there. 'Now, Stephen, now!'

I stop blowing the whistle. Giddings drops the oars, grabs the box, pulls the first pin and passes up. The grenade feels solid and heavy in my hand. But about right, about the same. The off-breaks, Stephen. Just like we practised. Over and over. Bowling rocks at a circle marked out in the sand. Or a rubber ball into a hoop on the grass. Take your time, pick your spot and bowl. Michael fires again, the second bullet finds a target, a seaman in the conning tower cries out and lurches sideways. I bowl, the first grenade splashes short. Giddings passes another, I bowl again, this one glances off the U-boat's hull, clattering harmlessly into the sea. Too low, I must aim higher. A third shot from Deeds' revolver, another ricocheting 'ping'. There's confusion now on the submarine, orders, angry shouting. The men on the deck gun are uncertain; it's not loaded, as Frank had guessed, they don't know what to do. But the conning tower machine-gun is loaded, two men are slotting it hurriedly into its mounting. Seconds left, now just seconds. Another grenade, this one goes long and wide. One, just one, into the conning tower, that's all it would take. Another shot from the revolver, Will Harrison is still at the signal lamp – U-U-U – Frank paddles the oars, keeping us positioned, steady, square-on. 'Come on, boys,' he urges. 'You can do it!'

Lily is coming, she's hull-up now, three miles away, and charging from the darkness. Any second, they'll see her. Another grenade presses into my palm. I turn more side-ways, stretch forward with my left arm, keep my right arm back and straight, then throw, this time higher, straighter. This one looks good but vanishes from sight altogether. Another shot from Michael. Another hit. One of the men on the eighty-eight. He reels back, trips, stumbles into the sea behind. The second man turns to help him, sees *Lily*, cries out in alarm. There's shouts too from the conning tower, arms pointing. Another grenade, one more revolver shot, then there's a thud. A single low, muffled thud from deep within the U-boat. Then the machine-gun opens up, tearing the ocean to shreds in front of us. I feel the whaler shudder as bullets smash home, then there's a bang and the world goes black.

Chapter 14

Devised during the last century before the days of radio, the international code of signals is a means of conveying simple messages between ships using single letters of the alphabet. Usually they are cautions of some kind: watch out I have a problem, or, I am engaged in something hazardous, or, I am about to do something unexpected. The letter 'A' for instance, means I have a diver down. 'O' means man overboard, 'S' means I'm going backwards, 'Y' my anchor is dragging, and so forth.

The signal letter 'U' means: you are standing into danger. Earlier in the war it was also used for a while in a three letter group, UUU, often in conjunction with SOS, to denote: 'I am under attack by U-boat.' Michael's gamble was that when our waiting submarine captain looked through his periscope and saw us signalling the letter 'U' at him, he would assume we were hailing him: 'U' for 'U-boat'. We were. For a crucial few minutes though, we were also warning the distant *Lily*.

It was enough. *Lily* got the message, spotting Harrison's light signal first and Giddings' oar-waving semaphore shortly thereafter. (They said my whistle blowing *was* heard but I suspect they were just being polite.) Typically, the signals didn't stop her approaching, quite the opposite. But it did give her that vital warning. Instead of slowing down, as she would to pick up survivors, she went to action stations and cracked on full speed, charging in for the attack.

By the time *Lily* struck the submarine, ramming it fully amidships, it was already foundering. Many of her crew were evacuating, scrambling up through the deck hatches to escape the fire and smoke spreading below. *Lily* ploughed right over her, like a lorry over a bicycle. Incredibly, the U-boat briefly survived the ramming, thrown over on to her beam ends, afloat but sinking, and, with her conning tower smashed, she lasted a minute or two more. In all, twenty-eight of her crew escaped into the sea before her nose sank, her stern lifting, finger-like, into the sky. She hung there for a few seconds, then dived for the bottom, and that was that.

Two of the nine hand grenades thrown had found targets. One, the last, became lodged in the conning tower somewhere before it went off, killing or injuring several of the bridge party and effectively pitching the whole boat into chaos. But not before another, earlier one, must have fallen right through the conning tower hatch and down into the U-boat's control room. That was the dull thud of an explosion we heard just before the machine-gun opened up. A hand grenade wouldn't be powerful enough to breach a U-boat's hull, but going off in a confined space like that would have caused serious damage and injury in the immediate vicinity. For several crucial minutes the U-boat was without control or command. With *Lily* charging up from the gathering gloom behind, its fate was sealed.

Why was she there? Why did a lone submarine hang back from the rest of the pack in the hope of sinking an escort, when you'd expect her to be trailing the convoy, biding her time before the nightly sinking spree began.

Various reasons. Michael's guess that she was at the end of her patrol was probably right. By '43, Admiral Dönitz was making it pretty clear that he did not expect his U-boats out on North Atlantic duty to come swanning back to base after three or four weeks, with well-stocked larders, fuel in the tanks and unfired torpedoes in the tubes. They were expected to stay out until the very last possible moment, and then some. Indeed, he was beginning to deploy specially modified supply submarines called 'milch cows' to refuel and rearm the wolf packs while still at sea. If he'd had his way they would never be in port.

A sign of his mounting concern. Another was his recent edict to crews that, for the first time in the conflict, the destroyers and corvettes comprising the convoy escorts were to be considered targets, not just the merchant ships. This was significant. Max Horton later recorded that this single tactical change was the first hint that Dönitz was getting worried. He was right to be. The tide, impossible though it seemed that dreadful winter, was in fact beginning to turn. There were to be no quick fixes, no sudden decisive developments; ours was a war of attrition and they grind exceeding slow. It would be months more before the statistics began to confirm it, but the Battle of the Atlantic was starting to swing our way, and ultimately, although many might argue there was no clear victor, the Allies would prevail.

A number of factors were responsible. That Christmas the cipher crackers at Bletchley Park finally broke enigma. Horton at last had vital up-to-the-hour information on the numbers, disposition and movements of the U-boat fleet. Secondly, the mid-Atlantic air gap was closing. By the following summer, long-range patrol aircraft armed with increasingly effective aerial depth charges roamed far and wide, notching up a growing tally of U-boats sunk. Next, the bigger, faster, more heavily armed Castle and River class escorts began slipping down the ways and into the fray. These, together with better radar, improved Asdic, VHF radio – not to mention greatly enhanced training – all meant that fighting off the U-boat menace became a much more exact business. Even the madcap boffins began to score some success, with devices like 'squid', a superior successor to 'hedgehog', coming on line. I, like Walter Deeds, still think Holman's Projector was the most useless idea since ashtrays for motorcycles. But then I suppose without it I wouldn't be here.

You can tell by the length of the beards, by the way, how long a U-boat has been out on patrol. The crews don't bother shaving – it's a waste of time and fresh water, so the thicker the beard, the longer the patrol. Some of the men hauled from the sea around *Lily* that New Year's Day looked positively biblical, by all accounts. Our U-boat had been out for months. Having expended the last of its fuel and ammunition the night before, she was preparing to head home in slow time when, with her captain mindful of Dönitz's edict perhaps, and maybe a single torpedo remaining, he decided to hang about *Daisy*'s whaler on the off chance. It very nearly worked.

Not that I knew much about it. Or cared. For me, the days and weeks that followed were about only darkness and pain. The months after that, anger, self-pity, despair and more pain. Now though, eleven years on, life is about acceptance, forgiveness, gratitude and new hope. And setting records straight.

I caught two bullets from the U-boat's machine-gun. One hit me in the midriff, tore through the liver and came out the other side. The other smashed into my lower spine. What's left of it is still there and always will be. I was paralysed from the waist down, instantly and permanently. Albert Giddings caught one in the thigh, Tuker and Harrison escaped unscathed.

Michael was killed, hit several times in the upper body. He was buried at sea a day later. My last image of him, of the whole story of my war really, is of him standing at the rear of the whaler in his gaucho garb, one booted foot up on the thwart, his fair hair blowing beneath his beret, calmly attacking a two-hundred-foot submarine with a revolver. He died, as had his great-grandfather's hero Saravia, leading an insane charge against an insurmountable enemy. But more importantly, he died with his convictions intact. He died for his friends and his family, finally taking up arms against an enemy to save them. He did what he had to do and what he thought to be right. And in the end, his courage, strength of personality, and the sheer effrontery of his actions, in true gaucho style, carried the day. Tata would have been proud of him.

Who was he? The question began to haunt me a couple of years ago, around the time of the queen's Coronation. It was a decade since my war had ended with the changing of my life. I had, consciously perhaps, drawn a veil over the whole matter, and, apart from the odd exchange of Christmas cards, maintained few old Navy contacts. But then the Flower Class Corvette Association tracked me down. Parades and march pasts were being organised as part of the Coronation celebrations, they said. They wanted me to join theirs, one of the Navy veteran ones. I was reluctant, but Joanna, my wife, wasn't having any backsliding. Don't be such a spoilsport, she scolded, it's the perfect excuse to buy a new hat. So, come the day, we Battle of Atlantic veterans, medals clanking at our breasts, assembled under Admiralty Arch, and marched, or in my case was wheeled by a gloriously behatted Joanna, down Whitehall for a special service of thanksgiving at Westminster Abbey.

It was during that service that I spotted Will Harrison. First-Lieutenant Will Harrison. Our eyes met, a discreet exchange of signals took place and afterwards we adjourned to a pub for a gin or three. He told me his news, listened to mine without pity; I found that dredging the whole business up again was not so terrible after all, and, suitably encouraged by Joanna, went home to begin writing it all down.

Thus began more than two years' work. The intention at the outset was simply to tell *Daisy*'s story. But the more I went through my old notebooks, the more letters I wrote and received, the more I tried to make sense of it all, the more Michael's presence loomed large and central. At first he was just yet another oddball member of *Daisy*'s crew, one of many, you might think, with some justification. But gradually his role took on increasing significance. As Alan Strang said, he was the glue that held us all together. Writing *Daisy*'s story, almost by definition, meant writing Michael's.

Within a few months, to Joanna's growing despair, piles of papers, documents and correspondence were spreading across the dining-room table. Much of it concerned Michael. Francis Habershon, the teacher at Holbrook House who had befriended him, wrote a long and helpfully frank letter about Michael's time there. He talked of a misfit, a wary, isolated boy of fierce but suppressed intellect who kept himself to himself, yet nevertheless commanded the cautious respect of his peers. Michael's housemaster at Westminster remembered him as 'a complete loner except on the cricket pitch'. Yet also as someone unafraid to speak out in support of what were often controversial views for the day.

Keith Villiers was a regular correspondent, furnishing much of the detail of Michael's early life in Uruguay, as well as the London period and the events leading to his return to Montevideo in '39. He also cleared up the matter of Michael's paternity. 'In October of 1920 I had to go to BA to help out with some royal visit,' he wrote, with admirable candour. 'While I was there, Aurora, who had earlier been seeing a lot of Willi Hochstetler, discovered she was pregnant by him. There was never any question of their marrying – in any case, she and I were involved by then. The scandal of unmarried motherhood in those days would have been disastrous to her and her whole family. She panicked, hatching a plan to seduce me and make me think the baby was mine. It worked, although deep down I may have suspected. It didn't matter, I was very much in love. Years later, towards the end of our time together, she told me the truth. It changed nothing. I have always been proud to call Michael my son. By the end, he and I had grown very close. I miss him terribly.'

Donald was his, he added, in case I might have any doubts. Aurora, he insisted, was neither promiscuous nor unfaithful by nature. She was a depressive, though, he acknowledged, her later slide into alcoholism and narcotic dependency a great sadness to him.

There were many other contributors. I am grateful to Sir Eugen Millington-Drake for sending me his recollections. The Battle of the River Plate, as it is now famously known, will go down in history as one of the last great set-piece warship confrontations of its kind the Royal Navy will probably ever see. The behind-the-scenes diplomatic battle in Montevideo was also unique, and crucial to the story's ultimate conclusion. Sir Eugen's role in that was pivotal; he is without doubt one of the world's leading experts on the story, which has grown to almost mythical proportions. Yet one central question remains that even he can't answer. The pundits, from naval strategists to armchair enthusiasts, argue it endlessly. Books on the battle analyse it. There are *Graf Spee* reunions, where attendees from both sides get together over dinner at the Dorchester to rehash it all with salt cellars and sugar bowls, much arguing and quaffing of claret. There's even talk of a film, due out some time next year. But despite all the books, films, reunion dinners and armchair experts, this central question remains unanswered. Why didn't Hans Langsdorff at least try and break *Graf* out to the open ocean and escape? Why did he sit there in Montevideo for four days when, early on at least, with only two British ships trying to guard a river-mouth fifty miles wide, he might have slipped through the net to safety. Why? I can tell you why.

He didn't have any fuel.

He didn't have any fuel, nor, more importantly, was he allowed to tell anyone. It's what Höpfner, the interned engineering officer in BA, told Michael.

Graf was powered by what in 1939 were revolutionary and therefore top-secret diesel engines. These engines ran on raw bunker fuel that had to go through a pressurised steam-cleaning plant before it could be burned in the cylinders. The steam-cleaning plant, much of the pipework for which was located in the vicinity of *Graf*'s unarmoured funnel, was crucially damaged during the battle. For obvious reasons, the damage report submitted by the Germans to the Uruguayan government makes only oblique reference to this, stating that the ship's bakery, supplied by the same steam plant, was out of action. But a non-functioning bakery was not enough to persuade the Uruguayans to let *Graf* stay in harbour the two weeks needed to fix the steam-plant. Langsdorff certainly passed this information back to Berlin, but, angry and unsympathetic, they had nothing constructive to propose. In effect they'd already washed their hands of him.

What nobody ever knew was that he had practically no clean fuel remaining in the tanks. Within a couple of hours of breaking out, therefore, *Graf* would have been drifting, engineless. Dead in the water.

Sombreado. One day we shall get there, Joanna and I. She's a nurse, by the way. I met her some months after the shooting, a devastatingly pretty nineteen-year-old; she used to mop me up as I lay sulking in my bed at the convalescent home. It was a difficult time, the worst was over medically, but the whole business of coming to terms with my disability was proving too much. I gave up, I'm ashamed to say, sank into a vat of despair and didn't care who I dragged down with me. It was especially trying for my family and those that had to take care of me, like Joanna. One bright sunny morning she marched into the room, threw back the curtains and announced that if I didn't snap out of it, she would refuse to be my girlfriend. A year later she was Mrs Tomlin. That was ten years ago, and today she's bossier than ever.

'We're going to this place,' she said, not long ago, picking up a photograph of Sombreado from the dining-room table. 'Where is it?' It might have been Surrey for all she knew. When she learned it was South America she just shrugged. 'Well, we're still going.' She's right.

Donald Villiers had given me the photograph. He's twenty-five, a Cambridge graduate with a cricket blue and a first in philosophy. Currently he is considering his options, as they say. Law is one, agriculture another, politics a third. The Foreign Office is not in the running, apparently, much to Keith's chagrin. He's also an expert in all matters Latin American, particularly vociferous in his condemnation of the way history – i.e. Europe – pillaged his mother's country over the centuries, and the deprivation and social unrest this has wrought.

He stopped in on us recently, following his second visit there. Uruguay, he reported, is as beautiful, its people as hospitable and charming as ever. But presently it is a country ill at ease with itself. Since the war, fiscal stagnation, corrupt state enterprise and an ageing population among other factors, has resulted in economic collapse and political instability. Relations with neighbours are also poor. Only last year Uruguay was forced to sever relations with Argentina after its dictator, Juan Perón, imposed sanctions because of Uruguay's policy of harbouring Argentina's political refugees. Meanwhile declining wool prices and curtailed meat exports exacerbate a failing economy and rising unemployment. Civil unrest is growing. The whole region is in upheaval. Worse, Donald predicts ominously, will surely come before things can get better.

But Sombreado continues. Thanks to Willi Hochstetler's shrewd business sense (he returned to his family in Germany in 1946), the endowments he set up at Michael's instigation will ensure that Sombreado, unlike so many other estancias, will survive. Times are hard, but then times have always been hard, Great-Aunt Gertrudis argues. It is the way of life on the pampas.

She is still there, Donald recounts, her sister Florentina, too. Both in their eighties, both driving each other mad, but united in their passion for the place and its continued existence. They live there, in a sort of comfortable sorority, with three other women. Francesca Luenga was widowed in 1950, Carles struck down without warning by viral pneumonia. Without hesitation the sisters took her in, securing her future with them, although, despite there being a live-in help, she still insists on doing the chores about the big house and living in her little cottage.

Maria Villiers, too, lives with them. Still only in her early thirties, in effect she runs the place, dealing with the finances, employing the farm hands, managing the livestock. Soon Sombreado will be hers. She is ready, with a keen business sense and the best nose for cattle in the trade, so local reputation has it. With so many estancias going under, she knows diversification is the key to survival. The Holstein cattle and Merino sheep that Michael introduced were the saving of the place, she says. She has further development ideas, including a scheme for foreigners to come and stay there on working holidays.

The fifth member of the sisterhood is her daughter, Isabella. Born the September after Michael died, she is now a strapping eleven-year-old, fair-haired and green-eyed according to proud Uncle Donald, just like her father, but with her mother's Guaraní earthiness and affinity for the plains. Each day she attends the local *escuela*, driven there, if she is unlucky, by one ageing great-aunt or the other. She is an accomplished sportswoman and an astute student, her English now stronger than her mother's. She rides a horse better than any, taught by Sombreado's head gaucho at the age of five, without saddle or reins, and with her hands on her head. When Donald told her I was writing a book about her father, she gave him a note for us, insisting we come and visit.

Our tickets are booked.

Appendix

Tomlin's history of Uruguay (unabridged). Or, how Tata came by Sombreado

Early artefacts suggest that the first inhabitants of the region – Michael's beloved Charrúa and Guaraní Indian fore-bears, arrived around four thousand years ago. They had the place to themselves until the Spanish appeared in 1516. The Charrúa kept fighting them off but the first permanent set-tlement of Spanish Jesuits had established itself on the banks of the Rio Negro by 1624. Then, around 1680, the Portuguese arrived, contesting 'ownership' of the region with the Spanish for the next century. Cattle and horses proliferated, the indigenous population declined, some Europeans mixed with Indians to form 'mestizos'. The origins of the first true gau-chos – wild, free, living off the land – date from this era.

By 1777 Spanish rule had been established, but in 1810 revolutionaries under José Artigas (same birthday as Michael) began a guerrilla campaign, overthrowing the Spanish from Montevideo in 1814 and proclaiming independence as the BOU which stands for Banda Oriental (east bank) of the Uruguay river. Capitalising on the fledgling nation's fragility, the Portuguese then moved back in, annexing BOU to Brazil in 1821. Four years later and with help from Argentina, insurgents fought back against Brazil who finally recognised Uruguay's independence in 1828.

The ROU (Republica Oriental del Uruguay), as it is today known, was organised in 1830. But its leaders soon fell out, forming two main factions, the Blancos and the Colorados, so named for the white and red colours of their scarves. (Today the two main political parties still bear those names.) As always, the politics are complicated, but the Colorados tended to be associated with the administrative power base in Montevideo, constantly seeking ways to rein in the influence of the strong and popularly supported Blanco *caudillos* (leaders) out in the interior. By 1836 civil war between these factions had broken out, continuing on and off until the turn of the twentieth century.

Aparicio Saravia was one member of a large family of gaucho *caudillismo* – the charismatic Blanco folk leaders. He and his many brothers lived on the northern prairie borderlands between Uruguay and Brazil. For about ten years before his death from a sniper's bullet in 1904, Aparicio, known to his ragtag army of gaucho followers as the Eagle, waged an on-off campaign of insurrection against the infinitely superior forces of oppression sent north by the government. One of his most loyal lieutenants was Adrián Rapoza (Tata), a *domadore*'s son from Melo.

On 19 March 1897, in the middle of one such campaign, Aparicio's beloved brother Antonio, known as Chiquito, launched a mounted charge against an advancing line of government troops. Known later as the Battle of Arbolito, it was a piece of military madness. Most of Chiquito's men were armed only with homemade lances, literally sheep-shearing blades lashed to the ends of poles. They were outnumbered three to one by a force of trained regulars hefting Mauser rifles and supported by Krupps-made artillery. The charge was doomed before it started; nevertheless Chiquito's men, their white scarves flying in the wind, didn't hesitate, spurring their horses into the gallop. Tata was among them.

Most were cut down before they made it halfway. Four made it as far as the enemy line, Chiquito included. But then he too was felled, his horse tripped by *boleadores*. He was shot, lanced and hacked to death by sabre. Worse might have followed; dismembered and desecrated bodies of enemy leaders had been displayed before, to set an example and add insult to the *caudillos*' sorrow. Indeed, a similar fate had earlier befallen another Saravia brother, to the eternal despair of the family.

But one lone figure emerged from the smoking aftermath of that charge. It was Tata, his face a mask of blood and tears, his arms bearing Chiquito's lifeless body. Nearing his own lines a stray bullet struck him in the knee. He staggered on, refusing to stop until Chiquito was safely among his own. A week later, ravaged by septicaemia, Tata's left leg was hacked off by a barber using a wood saw. It was the end of his campaigning, but the Eagle never forgot his devotion. Forming a small corner of Saravia land-holdings in Cerro Largo, Sombreado, located not far from the site of Tata's gallantry, was his.

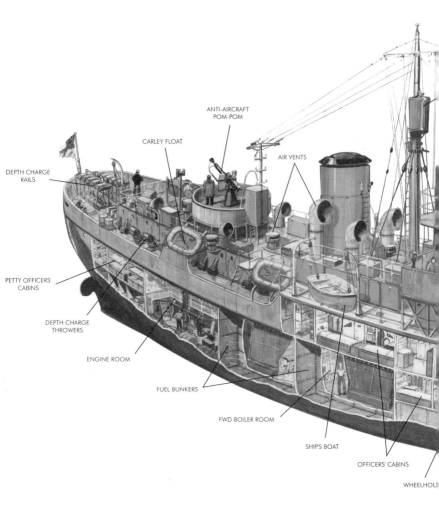

ANTI-AIRCRAFT
POM-POM

CARLEY FLOAT

AIR VENTS

DEPTH CHARGE
RAILS

PETTY OFFICERS'
CABINS

DEPTH CHARGE
THROWERS

ENGINE ROOM

FUEL BUNKERS

FWD BOILER ROOM

SHIP'S BOAT

OFFICERS' CABINS

WHEELHOU